Date: 4/17/19

LP FIC MOORE
Moore, Wayétu,
She would be king

SHE WOULD BE KING

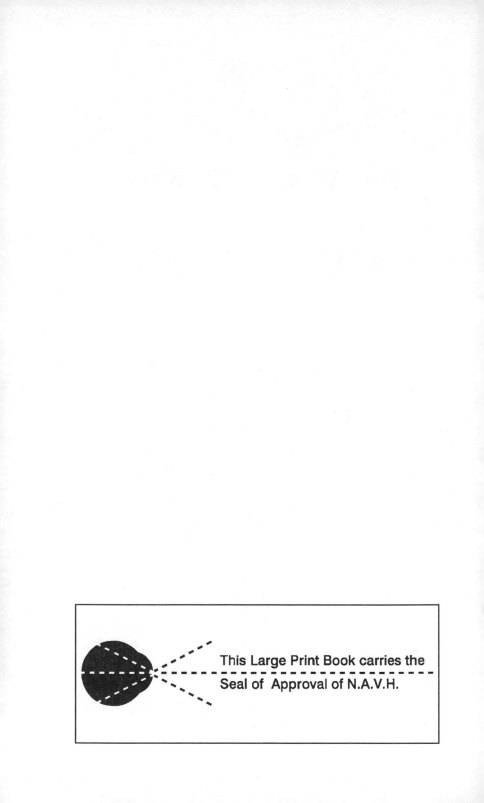

This Large Print Book carries the
Seal of Approval of N.A.V.H.

SHE WOULD BE KING

WAYÉTU MOORE

THORNDIKE PRESS
A part of Gale, a Cengage Company

Farmington Hills, Mich • San Francisco • New York • Waterville, Maine
Meriden, Conn • Mason, Ohio • Chicago

LIBRARY OF CONGRESS CIP DATA ON FILE.
CATALOGUING IN PUBLICATION FOR THIS BOOK
IS AVAILABLE FROM THE LIBRARY OF CONGRESS

ISBN-13: 978-1-4328-6217-6 (hardcover)

Published in 2019 by arrangement with Graywolf Press

Printed in the United States of America
1 2 3 4 5 6 7 23 22 21 20 19

To Gus & Mam

Princes shall come out of Egypt;
Africa shall soon stretch out her hands
unto God.
Psalm 68:31

CONTENTS

AUTHOR'S NOTE

When I was a child, my mother cautioned that I should always be kind to cats. She told me a story that took place in the West African village where my family and I hid during Liberia's civil war in 1990. She said: "In Lai, there was once an old woman who beat her cat to death. The cat resurrected and his ghost sat on her roof until her house fell down, killing her." Several years ago I attempted to write a short story about this woman and her notorious death. I did, and from that death, rather surprisingly, and thankfully, Gbessa was born.

{Gbessa is pronounced "Bessah"}

■ ■ ■ ■

BOOK ONE:
THE THREE

■ ■ ■ ■

GBESSA

If she wanted to continue, Gbessa first had to rid the road of a slow-moving snake. Greenish brown with golden eyes as difficult to gaze into as the sun, the snake's body was no different in color from the woods it had crawled from, and it seemed to Gbessa that the surrounding bushes were jealous of her departure, so they extended their toes to block her path. Orange dust stained the belly of the snake, which writhed as it hissed, and Gbessa pointed a five-foot stick in its direction. The snake was not afraid of her, or of the stick, and it raised its head and advanced.

The confrontation occurred several moonfalls after that searing hot day when she was banished from Lai for good. She had championed that path for weeks, stumbling over iron pebbles and timber branches departed from their roots, squeezed between sugarcane stalks, and still, refusing to look back.

Strands of her hair left her for the veils of clay grains that also traveled the long and pitiless road. Gbessa could not return. Safua was in the other direction, hand in hand with her rejection, and also those deaths. Gbessa lightly poked the belly of the excitable creature, and at once it lunged at her. She took a step back, only barely avoiding a bite on her shin.

I was there that day, drawn to her, just as I was drawn to those gifted others who were present the day the ships came.

"Take care, my darling," I whispered in Gbessa's ear. "Take care, my friend."

She glanced over her shoulder, as if she had heard me, or as if she hoped the movement was Safua, and the snake lunged again, this time biting her ankle before fleeing into the stalks at the other end of the road. Gbessa fell to the ground, yelling. She cried, and it was clear that her leg was in pain, but also her heart, because she held the tears captive, clenching her jaw closed through the sobs. She rubbed her ankle as if digging for bones, then squeezed the reddened skin where the snake had bitten, squeezed hard to relieve herself of the poison. Perhaps nothing would happen beyond the sting. Perhaps she would faint from the pain. But eventually, she would wake up. Gbessa rubbed her wound, but she knew then, as she knew always, that this poison would remain with her forever. She knew then, as she knew always, that she, like her love for Safua, would not, could not, die.

There were no Vai girls like Gbessa. The coastal village of Lai had seen only one woman as cursed — Ol' Ma Famatta — who they say is sitting in the corner of the moon after her hammock flung her there on her 193rd birthday. But even Ol' Ma Famatta's misfortune was nothing compared to that of Gbessa, whose curse was not only her inability to die, but also the way death mocked her.

Lai was hidden in the middle of forests when the Vai people found it. There was evidence of earlier townsmen there, as ends of stoneware and crushed diamonds were found scattered on hilltops in the unexpected company of domestic cats. But when the Vai people arrived from war-ravaged Arabia through the Mandingo inland in the early eighteenth century, they found no inhabitants and decided to occupy the province with their spirits.

On a plot of land one mile long and one half mile wide, they used smelted iron to build their village — a vast circle of houses constructed of palm wood from nearby trees, zinc roofs, and mud bricks to keep them cool during the dry season.

During the day the Ol' Pas sat together and drew lines and symbols in the dirt that represented how many moons it had been since the last rainfall, or the last eclipse or other wonders of the sky. They waited for the spirits to reveal themselves in nuances and uncover secrets of the land and its animals.

Among many things — like which Poro warrior would best lead upcoming defenses against local tribes so that the Vai army would return with cattle, harvest, and captives to help tend the village rice farms — the spirits also told the Ol' Pas to take care of the sensitive animals of the province — specifically, cats. The Ol' Pas then divulged to the villagers the news they gathered from the spirits.

Ol' Ma Nyanpoo never listened.

Before Gbessa was born, Ol' Ma Nyanpoo — old, bitter, widowed — was living only two houses down from Khati, Gbessa's pregnant mother. Ol' Ma Nyanpoo had a pudgy orange cat whom she beat regularly to numb her loneliness. The village elders warned Ol' Ma Nyanpoo of what the spirits had told them about beating cats, but she disregarded them — she was powerless to her pride, and she hoped she would make the spirits angry enough to reunite her with her deceased love.

When Kano, Cholly the fisherman's slave, knocked on Ol' Ma Nyanpoo's door to deliver to her the fish that her nets had caught, the pudgy cat stared hoggishly at the tin bucket. He hid behind the fire pit as Ol' Ma Nyanpoo closed the door in Kano's face and inspected the bucket for any sign of pilfering. When the cat's head peeked around the pit, she grabbed a fish from the bucket and waved it at him.

"You will not touch it!" she yelled, shaking the fish. Scales, saltwater, and blood flew, and the cat dodged Ol' Ma Nyanpoo's warning. That night when Kano finished his chore of cleaning fish for Cholly's wife, he blew the light from the last lantern away. The whistle his compressed lips made married the pungent smell of fish and journeyed through the village circle to Ol' Ma Nyanpoo's house, awakening the cat. The cat arose from the corner where he had been lying and probed the room. In the dark, his cold nose led a desperate search for Ol' Ma

Nyanpoo's bucket of fish.

Ol' Ma Nyanpoo's leg twitched and she snored expletives into the night. Alarmed, the cat positioned himself to run in the event that she leaped from her sleep to beat him with the redwood handle of the porch broom. But she remained in abysmal slumber in the murky room. The cat proceeded toward Ol' Ma Nyanpoo's fish, disregarding the likely retribution on the following day, when she would discover that her fish were gone. When he finally reached it, he lifted himself up to the rim of the bucket, careful not to scrape the edge with his nails. His eyes were large, his mouth ready, when a hard blow threw him across the room.

"I told you, enneh-so?" Ol' Ma Nyanpoo asked, lighting her lantern. The cat tried picking himself up, only to meet another hard slap to his head. He stretched his claws and hissed at the old woman. She struck his head once more and the cat shrieked, this time waking a neighbor, whose inquiring voice and lantern moved slowly toward the village circle.

The cat, determined to escape her fury, scurried over to the fire pit.

"Oh no!" Ol' Ma Nyanpoo said. "You'n going nowhere." She dragged him out from behind the fire pit by his tail. In the village circle, neighbors gathered outside of Ol' Ma Nyanpoo's door, baffled at what had made the old woman so angry that she had beat the poor cat in the middle of the night.

"I will teach you! You will feel it!" she said. The cat screeched, unable to escape the bitter widow. The neighbors' tongues became sour, their ears warm, disgusted at the Ol' Ma's audacity in offending the spirits. Cholly knocked on Ol' Ma Nyanpoo's door, but she ignored him and continued beating the cat.

"She will kill the thing," said Cholly's son, Safua, an already-handsome five-year-old boy with skin the color of a coconut shell and eyes that were always asking a serious question.

Inside, the cat lay in the corner as Ol' Ma Nyanpoo's stout figure and broom became blurry. Tired of seeing her, he let his eyes close, and his heart stop, and his mouth open.

A frozen Ol' Ma Nyanpoo stared down at his body. She had killed the last living thing whom she could call hers and was now absolutely alone. She walked to her door, out of breath. When she opened it her neighbors stood in the village circle holding lanterns that illuminated their overwrought faces. Cholly peeked into the house and noticed the dead cat lying against the wall.

"Ay-yah!" he said, astonished at Ol' Ma Nyanpoo's fearlessness. Upon seeing the dead animal, children scattered, returning to their houses. "The spirits coming for you," Safua said, the only remaining child in the circle.

"Bury it for me," Ol' Ma Nyanpoo said as Cholly looked inside of her house at the cat. He said nothing else to her and avoided looking her in the face; he called Kano to retrieve the cat, and Kano minced out of the village and into the woods, while a curious Safua followed, to bury the departed animal.

In the morning, Ol' Ma Nyanpoo's house fell down while she was still inside. She died immediately. When they dug up her remains from a pile of palm wood, straw, and debris, Ol' Ma Nyanpoo's fish were nowhere to be found. Ol' Pa Bondo, who woke up every morning to pray before the rooster crowed, who had slept through the night before and knew nothing of Ol' Ma Nyanpoo's wicked deed, said he saw the orange cat jump to the top of her house before it fell down.

"But the cat dead," Cholly said, refuting Bondo's claim.

When the elders heard of it they pronounced the day cursed, convinced that spirits had possessed the dead cat into coming back, avenging itself, and stealing the bucket of fish to quench his desire.

Because of the edict, on that day the drums outside of Khati's window were amply pounded. Her husband was already fishing at the lake, and she lay moaning in pain on a rectangular pallet woven with large palm leaves and stuffed with straw. Khati would have her baby soon, so in recent weeks her husband had risen before the rooster's song, and spent his hours at Lake Piso in hopes of catching enough fish to eat and trade in the village market. Neither Khati's father nor her father's father nor her husband or husband's father were talented enough fishermen to afford his household any slaves, so Khati had inherited nothing.

At the moment she opened her eyes and heard the beating of drums, Khati pushed her aching body upward from where she lay. She was a dark brown woman with a slender nose and arms, whose breasts and hips had fully developed only in the later months of her pregnancy. She knew by the rhythm of the drums that either someone had died or someone had been cursed, both of which posed a gloomy birth for her unborn child. Khati's stomach bent in distress. The gray of morning crawled from the opened window toward her sitting body, and exposed thin streams of sweat that descended her brown face and arms. Khati rubbed and patted her stomach, pleading for her unborn child to tarry just a little longer in her womb. She extended her hand to the floor from the pallet to drag herself to the window, but the uneven weight of her body made her baby's fingers and toes flex inside of her.

"No, no," Khati whispered to her extended belly. "Wait, small small."

She pressed her hand on the floor beside her bed and tried again, this time successfully dragging her aching body off the pallet and across the room to the window, where she rested her back against the wall. Khati grabbed the frame, hoisting her body until her eyes uncovered the baroque drummers outside.

Salt and dust stained the drummers' palms. The Ol' Pas marched around the drummers as their necks sank into robed shoulders. Khati knew what it would mean to have her baby at that moment, and she crossed her legs. Frightened that she would be seen, Khati collapsed to the ground, her body simultaneously hot and cold, her thin lappa imbued with sweat. She rubbed her stomach in great panic as her eyes canvassed the room for a solution to her disaster. Her pursuit ended with the door closest to the bush garden that led to the entry to the woods.

Before Khati could move, a liquid stream of blood and water toddled down her thighs, chased by a more abundant outpouring that left her lappa and the floor around her drenched. To keep from screaming, Khati clamped her bottom lip with her teeth until she could taste her own blood. She could not risk them hearing her, could not bear the delivery of a child on this day, when she would be forbidden ever to offer another to her village. Khati finally resolved that she would crawl as far as she could into the woods behind her house. The baby kicked, ready to approach the dim light in the opening.

"No, no," Khati said again, as the floor beneath her continued to dampen. Her legs quivered. She clutched her lappa and squeezed. It was no use. The child would come.

Khati dragged herself toward the door leading out to the woods. She used both of her hands and pulled her quavering body sideways. The child pushed. She squeezed her legs until her thighs ached from the resistance.

"Please, my child," Khati repeated. "Wait, small small."

The drummers pummeled away outside, and Khati pushed open her wooden back door and crawled toward a huddle of shrubs. She panted, drained, as she tried to stop the baby, first with an intermittent tapping of her stomach, then she reached one hand underneath her lappa to impede the liquid from where her child pushed its way out. When only several yards away from her house, at the end of a train of blood, with no more power to ignore the pain that pushed underneath her wet and sticky fingers, Khati fell onto her back against the waiting leaves. Unable to squeeze her slippery thighs together any longer, unable to constrain the willful head of her baby, Khati howled into the wind and sun.

The drumbeats ceased.

That was the day that Gbessa was born.

The elders declared that she was cursed.

In the dry season of 1831, there were no wars, and the fish and rice harvests were plenty. During the rainy seasons the children of the village sat with griots to learn the history of their people, as well as how to count and write, but in the dry season everyone older than five years worked. Vai boys went to Lake Piso to fish with their fathers, and Vai girls went to the rice farm.

The Ol' Mas sat together and spun cotton and goatskin into lappas for Vai women to cover themselves with, so that grain flies would not rest on their legs as they gathered rice on the farms. For their favorite Vai girls, those who would gift small portions of their harvest to the old women or send their slaves across the village to mind the pepper gardens surrounding their homes, the Ol' Mas soaked the goatskin in melted stone to change the colors to burgundy and sage. Although Khati was common, the Ol' Mas had once favored her for her meekness and the horizontal wrinkles across her neck, the latter a sign of great beauty among Vai people. The Ol' Mas never made Gbessa a lappa to cover herself with, and after Gbessa was born Khati no longer received burgundy cloths. Instead, Khati wrapped a wilted brown lappa made of rough pamkana cloth around her five-year-old daughter before taking her to the rice farm.

On the way to the farm, Khati and Gbessa passed through the village circle, where young children laughed wildly in a game of pebble throw.

"Gbessa the witch! Gbessa the fat cat witch!" the children sang as Gbessa passed them, several feet behind her mother. When she knew that she and her mother were passing Lake Piso, Gbessa searched past the breaks within the bushes in hopes that she would see her father. Gbessa's father, a fisherman whose reputation was destroyed by her birth, had never spoken to or seen her. He reasoned that since he would not receive any honor from his child, he could salvage what was left of his family's name by his hard work. He spent twenty-four hours a day at the lake fishing, cursing life under his breath, and nodding in and out of sleep.

"Come!" Khati called in front of Gbessa as she sensed her daughter stalling. When they reached the farm, Khati joined the women and instructed her daughter to sit on the outskirts of the field. Vai women, both wealthy and common, spent their mornings on the field closest to the village, collecting barely one sack of grain from the crops that grew on dry land, and gossiping among themselves, while their two dozen slave women and their daughters worked the outlying fields and swamps.

The women did not ask Gbessa to come into the field and chatter, unlike other young Vai girls who were invited to assist with farming and chores while eavesdropping on gossip about whose wolloh-and-rice dish was bitter. And since Gbessa was ignored by them, the sun took pleasure in having her all to itself, digging its impression into her pigment, making her skin the color of twilight. And since the sun did not have to share Gbessa with anyone or anything, her hair was also an object of its infatuation, and hung heavily down her back in a long and fiery red bush, further confirming the Vai ruling that she was cursed.

During Gbessa's eighth year, the rainy season was three months delayed. The Vai

32

women had gathered enough food for the coming months, but they worried they would not receive enough rain for the following harvest. Ma Eilsu, a clever woman who always had a single stem of straw wedged in the corner of her mouth, insisted the women take the matter to the elders. Together they ambled from the rice farm to the elders' lodge. Khati pulled Gbessa's hand behind the women when she noticed that the villagers had repudiated their daily chores and games, left the shade of the sloping coconut and mango trees, their weaving needles and animal skins.

In the lodge — a circular entrapment of coffee-tree trunks stacked atop one another — ten Ol' Pas lifted their heads from a bound silence as the women and their daughters approached them. The chatters of the villagers were abruptly silenced when the lead elder extended his hand into the air.

"Elder," Ma Groie, the leader of one of the lines, began upon notice of his nod. "Everybody want know what happen to the rain. We scared for the rice farm," she said. The women in the line hummed and sighed mutually.

"The girl come every day with Khati," Ma Eilsu, the leader of the other line, said, pointing to an unassuming Khati as she loitered with Gbessa in the back of the lodge. Afraid of the sudden charge, Khati squeezed her daughter's shoulders. The women pivoted toward Khati and joined in chorus with "yeh" and "the Ol' Ma right" against the small witch.

"Why not have her farm near the swampland, then?" Elder asked. "That's where most of the rice grows, enneh-so?"

"It'n matter if she farm near us or in swampland with the slaves them. You can't hide from spirits. They see her," Ma Eilsu argued.

The room commenced an unending vibration of agreement until Elder clapped his furrowed hands for the racket to stop. He sank his head and the room grew silent during his refrain.

"The girl getting too big," he finally said, nodding as his voice escaped him in sluggish and hoarse stanzas. "Closer to her dong-sakpa and childbearing years. It'n good thing for her to be in the fields."

"Yeh-oh. Yeh." The elders nodded in agreement.

"Take the girl home. Do not take her to the rice farm. She will not come back out until her dong-sakpa. You hear?" Elder told Khati.

Khati turned from the condemnatory faces of the lodge. She shuffled, with guilt, through the village circle back to her house. Gbessa nearly stumbled over her feet.

"What —"

"Sh, girl," Khati interrupted her daughter and looked forward. The crowd of nosy villagers in the circle parted as Khati and Gbessa passed.

"Ma —" Gbessa said as her head bobbed up and down beside her mother.

"Sh," Khati said and rushed inside, closing the door. Dazed, Khati stumbled toward a tall wooden pitcher and bowl that she kept near the pallet where they slept. Trembling, Khati tipped the pitcher and filled the bowl with water.

"Sh," Khati said, although Gbessa motioned with neither her body nor her lips. Khati stared at Gbessa until her vision eventually blurred and she could see nothing in the room. She extended the bowl toward her daughter, who slowly approached her on the floor, her hair more red than Khati had ever noticed.

Gbessa gulped and crossed her eyes toward the bottom of the bowl. She finished and when she lowered the drink from her lips, Khati's face was hidden in her palms and she wept into them until her fingers and arms were dripping wet.

It was a griot who told the village children of the woman in the lake, Mamy Wateh, whose bottom half was the body of a fish and who looked for people to drown so she would not be alone. She told them of the Gio people and their devils and how they danced day and night for one whole year to beckon rain to their village instead of walking to the neighboring village to ask for water.

"Ol' Ma Famatta was the first of them," the griot began one night, her voice as fine and cutting as barbed wire.

"The first of who, Ol' Ma?" Cholly's son, Safua, asked. He was nearly thirteen, dongsakpa, but he still sat behind the young Vai children and listened to the storyteller's tales every dry-season night.

"Sh, child," the griot said, pressing her finger to her lips.

"Ol' Ma Famatta was the first of the Vai witches," she said.

Lai was young then, the griot explained, as young as them, and Ol' Ma Famatta had walked through the desert with the first settlers of the old Lai. Her dog and four cats died before her and her husband and all the

36

Ol' Mas and Ol' Pas of the old Lai. She lived for 193 dry seasons. In the Ol' Ma's later years, Lai was stricken by wars and lengthy dry seasons. The elders, unsure of why their fortune had so quickly turned, were convinced that Ol' Ma Famatta's age was offensive to the spirits. When Ol' Ma Famatta heard through whispers that they were blaming Lai's fate on her, she bolted the doors of her house and refused to see any villagers. It seemed to everyone that she had decided to spend the rest of her days alone, pendulum swinging in an old hammock in the back of her house. The villagers knocked for weeks, but all they heard were Ol' Ma Famatta's grunts.

One day, a fisherman forced open her front door for the Ol' Pas. The men lumbered around the modest house in search of her, but Ol' Ma Famatta was not inside. When they reached her back porch, her old hammock was empty, and swung in rapid circles between its posts.

"The hammock threw her to the sky, enneh-so?" a small child interrupted.

"She stay too long. So the Ol' Pas say anybody who cursed will spend their dong-sakpa away from Lai in the forest," the storyteller said.

"I almost dong-sakpa," Safua said, remembering his age.

"You'n cursed," the griot responded.

"Ol' Ma, who go to the forest?" another child asked.

"Coco, the fisherman son with hands like frog," the griot said, stretching her fingers. The children huddled together.

"And Zolu, the small small girl born the day the sun go black," she said, pointing to the moon in the sky. Their eyes traveled upward toward the starry sky, where Ol' Ma Famatta sat looking down on them from the white hole in the middle.

"And Gbessa!" a child shouted.

The storyteller nodded and looked to Gbessa's house.

Gbessa peered through a peephole that had emerged from a crack on the wall behind the fire pit, as she did every time a griot appeared with a new tale, and a chill hummocked the unseen hairs of her skin.

"Gbessa the witch," Safua said lowly. The children squealed.

"Gbessa the witch! Gbessa the witch!" some sang as they ran.

They chased one another in a playful skirmish before finally retreating to their homes. Gbessa crawled to the bundle of straw next to Khati's pallet. She lay silently at first, before lightly tapping her mother's shoulder. Khati was startled, and her eyes shot open.

"Gbessa?!"

"Yeh, Ma," Gbessa answered.

"What wrong?"

"They will take me to the forest, Ma?" Gbessa asked.

A sigh broke Khati's hesitation, only to fall to more stillness.

"Sleep, child," Khati said. "Sleep."

On the following day, when her mother left to go to the rice farm, Gbessa wriggled to the peephole to look out the thin opening onto the village circle, where she hoped to find remnants of the storyteller's claim to her fate. When she pressed her eyes to the hole, she could see nothing.

She heard someone move on the other side. "Who there?" Gbessa asked, staggered by the prospective courtship. She crawled backward to regain her focus on the hole. "Who there?" Gbessa asked again, louder, and nearly choked with enthusiasm.

"Safua," said the boy on the other side.

They were blinded by the closeness of each other's eyes. Outside, other boyish voices called to Safua to hurry from the house before he was seen and punished.

"Go away. Go from here," Gbessa said,

surprising herself that she had found words despite the sudden heat that rushed to her skin and cheeks.

"Or what?" Safua asked, equally thrilled, amused by the daring witch. The developing muscles of his arms flexed and he waited to laugh, though his friends nervously giggled close by. "I'n scared of you. I'n scared of nothing," Safua said.

"You go from here," Gbessa said again after realizing from the laughter outside that he did not seek her as she sought him. She hissed at him. "I a curse. You hear them, yeh?" Gbessa crawled away from the hole. Safua caught a glimpse of her red hair against her haunting black face and gasped. He pressed his eye against the hole again.

"I will come back," he said. He waited for Gbessa to respond but she said nothing.

Safua's friends scrambled from Gbessa's house; they made bulbul calls into the air as the dust that jumped from their heels stained their backs. Heeding their warning, Safua ran.

He turned around and shouted, "Gbessa the witch, Gbessa the witch!" before catching his outbraved friends.

During the next few days, Gbessa's eyes were bound to the peephole. When the birds outside changed their song, her stomach dropped. When one of the children in the village circle laughed too loudly, she skipped a breath. Everything startled her: the rooster's wings, footsteps too close to the house from neighbors exchanging secrets, a mewling wind, and the shriek of the coconut tree when a machete reached its crown.

Every morning, Khati left Gbessa with no words before she rushed through a starlit dawn to the rice farm. Gbessa was forbidden to leave her mother's property, so Khati gave her daily chores to complete at home in her absence. First, Gbessa had to separate the rice grains, one by one, from the brown, scaly chaffs and lanky green stems on which they grew. On some days she stood two stems upright, facing each other, both drooping forward from the weight of their chaffs, and she pretended they were a father speaking gently to his daughter, two friends in conversation about the grebe bird's songs, and other musings that softened her sleep. "Papa, I want to go run in the rain," Gbessa whispered, moving one stem to the rhythm of her voice. "But the rain is hard, fine geh," she responded with a more authoritative voice as she moved the other stem. "Wait until the rain is softer. I will tell you when. Then you can go outside." The daughter would become upset and run away, falling onto the pallet and crying until her father came to console her. And he told her that she was beautiful and how much he missed her face, and he held her hand and went with her outside, protecting her tiny head from the hard and unforgiving rain.

After threshing the grain, Gbessa then separated the rice portions — some to eat, some to trade, and some to save for the rainy season. She saved most of the rice in a pamkana bag that was always half empty, then Khati traded a portion for the smallest fish and palm nuts, which Gbessa cooked daily with the remaining scant serving of rice, a meal that was enough to fill only a small child. She waited for Khati's return to eat, every day, though she was always so hungry that on a few occasions she resorted to chewing on the rice stems, her make-believe father, her only friends.

When she finished cooking, Gbessa crawled to the hole and peered through. There she saw that some families in Lai, like Safua's, ate throughout the day. These families had many people to send to the lake or farm, children and slaves alike. In the village market, when the warriors returned with tools or captives from newly acquired neighboring villages now part of the Vai kingdom, it was only families like Safua's that had enough fish, rice, or lappas to trade. During those battles, after a village was defeated, those who did not want to return to Lai with the warriors were killed; others who surrendered willingly came as captives and were traded as slaves to families like Safua's. Gbessa marveled at these families and their riches, their plenty children and food. Their houses had more than two openings, not just one door that faced the village circle and one that faced the woods. Some of their houses were two stories high. They had their fill of mangoes and oranges, of fish and plantains, cassava leaves and wolloh. They had many visitors — many villagers walked in and out of their plenty doors singing and drunk on palm wine. But common families, like Gbessa's, with few people in the household to farm and few to fish, ate once a day. It was only during wedding celebrations and after battles, which she also watched from inside because she and Khati were never invited, that both common and wellborn families ate and drank palm wine until Ol' Ma Famatta grew tired and left them to swallow the sunshine of other villages too far to imagine.

One afternoon, Gbessa watched the hole

so obsessively for signs of Safua's return that she burned both the rice and the potato leaves. It was her first time burning food since Khati had taught her how to cook, and she waited anxiously for her mother to return from the rice farm. She wondered if she would be beaten with a bush twig, as she had seen other mothers in the village beat their children when they did wrong. But that night when Khati returned and smelled the blackened greens that hugged the bottom of the pot, only briefly glancing toward the fire pit, she gave her daughter a plaintive look, full of weakness and pity, and she lay on the pallet with her back toward Gbessa, and she slept.

The following evening when Khati came home from the farm, Gbessa met her at the door with the fresh bowl of rice and greens. Instead of two wooden spoons, the bowl had one, and Gbessa offered it to her mother. Khati exchanged the bundle in her hand for the bowl in Gbessa's, and she sat next to the fire pit and ate. Gbessa watched as Khati barely chewed her meal before she desperately swallowed, breaking her rhythm only to release soft whimpers to accompany her tears.

It had been seven days since Safua's visit when, while preparing a pot of greens,

Gbessa heard a light scratching against the outside wall of her hut. She rushed to the hole, nearly falling headfirst into the crack.

"There who?" she asked, the words racing to meet the other side.

"There who? Whetin' you mean 'there who'?" Safua chuckled.

Gbessa lifted her tongue to respond, but nothing came out; her heartbeat just grew louder in her ears.

"That's what I will call you today, Gbessa the witch: 'ThereWho,' " he said, squinting through the hole to catch another glimpse of her.

"I a witch then why you come back?" she asked, seized by the same tinge of anger she had felt during his first visit.

"My friends them dare me, ThereWho," he said.

"Your friends them gut full," she replied and noticed that for a second, when he backed away from the wall to regain focus while wiping the sweat from his brow, he was smiling.

"You'n lie," he said.

In the distance she heard the laughter and taunts of boys blending into the collective din of antagonized chickens.

"What is your name?" Gbessa asked.

"Safua," he answered.

45

"Safua," she said. "Good meeting you."

"You, too, ThereWho," Safua said. His head moved vigorously on the other side of the wall, desperate to see her face again. "Tell me, how does it feel to be witch?" he asked.

"How does it feel to be stupid boy?" Gbessa asked without hesitation. Safua immediately laughed, and Gbessa touched her lips as they trembled with gladness.

"You are a rude witch, ThereWho," he said. "But I will spare your life when I am king."

"You? King?" Gbessa blushed.

"Yes. I will be the best Poro warrior when we return from initiation, so when I come back I will take a Sande, and I will be king," he said.

"What is initiation?" she asked. "And when?"

"Soon," Safua said. "Initiation what makes a warrior or queen. You'n know nothing, ThereWho."

Gbessa sat on the floor to rest her knees. She thought heavily on his answer, and felt, as always, excluded from the vibrant lives of those outside of her walls. Safua placed both hands against the house to assist with his focus, thrilled to notice her ungovernable hair, her slender shoulders and black skin.

"Hungry," Gbessa said finally.

"What?"

"You ask me how it feels to be witch. My stomach always hurting," she said.

"No food for the witch, heh?" Safua said. "Your Ma'n got help. Your father crazy man, you have no brothers and sisters, no slaves."

Gbessa hung her head in shame.

"I see your Ma farming. Some days she go into swamps, seh," Safua continued. Gbessa's thoughts of her mother wading in swamp water for ripe stems were interrupted by the sound of shouting outside. Safua's friends called out to him from the distance.

"Soon!" he yelled and ran away to rejoin them, five young boys of similar age and stature.

Gbessa pressed her face to the hole again, and in the distance she saw them patting Safua's shoulder and laughing, before they raced toward the lake. The farther he ran from her house, the more questions crowded the roof of her mouth.

He visited three days later, a stretch of time lengthened by the fact that as Gbessa searched through the peephole between her breaks in chores, she saw him once returning from the lake with a net of fish, and on another occasion he played in the village circle with friends; both times he looked toward her house to the corner where the two had met, and held his gaze in her direction until someone interrupted his trance.

"ThereWho. ThereWho," she heard one afternoon.

Gbessa knelt beside the peephole and pressed her face into the streaming light.

"ThereWho?" Safua asked.

"Yeh," Gbessa answered. "They will take me to the forest?" she asked, desperate to know before he departed again.

"Yeh. All witches go," Safua answered.

"Then what?"

"Then you die," Safua said. "You scared of death?" he asked a moment after.

"Should I be?" Gbessa asked, discouraged, and suddenly cold.

"I'n know. I'n know nobody who died and tell me I should be scared of it."

Safua shifted to the other side, waiting for more words to come.

"But don't be scared of forest," he said. "I will go to forest, too, for my passage into Poro." He struggled to see her face, twisting his eyes into various shapes. Gbessa remained quiet, made dumb by the terror of Safua's words.

"So I will die," she said, crying. "And what will you do? When you become Poro?"

Gbessa asked, wondering if Safua would visit her when death became her home. Distraught, she turned and leaned against the wall, gazing outward into the diminutive one-room house. She heard Safua shuffle outside, excitement building in his breathing.

"I will be the best warrior in Lai," he said. "I will defend the whole village, everybody, even witches like you, and I will conquer more villages for Vai people."

Before Safua could continue, Gbessa heard a struggle on the other side of the wall.

"Saffy! Move from there!" said a deep voice. Gbessa could hear the sound of slapping flesh and she looked out the peephole. Kano pulled Safua away from the house, across the village circle; he slapped the young boy's back again for good measure as they entered Safua's house.

That night when Khati returned from the farm, she had a fresh fish in her hand. Upon opening the door, she dropped the bundle of rice to the floor and stared at the medium-sized fish as its biting smell spread through the tiny room.

"It was on the porch," Khati whispered to herself. Gbessa could not tell if the tears in Khati's eyes were those that had made a home there long ago, and were as much a part of Khati's face as the infinitesimal moles atop her cheekbones, or if they were newer tears caused by the sight of the fish, which they hadn't eaten in two dry seasons. Khati squeezed the fish, and placed it in a wooden bowl near the fire pot. Before she looked toward the peephole, Gbessa waited for Khati to turn her face, and smiled.

Khati returned to the door to look across the village toward the giant circle of houses. There was nobody there to thank, and for a moment it looked as if Khati was facing Lake Piso in the direction of the husband who would never again come home.

That night as Kano's whistle blew the light from the last lantern away, and the whistle traveled throughout the village circle and entered the fissure of wood into Khati's hut, Gbessa awoke. She snailed toward the back door of her house. She considered what could happen if she was caught outside, but did not care, could not feel anything beyond the desire to run away. With every step, she watched Khati sleep, dreading an abrupt rising and the ultimate end of her escape. When Gbessa reached the back door her mother stretched between dreams. Gbessa remained still until Khati relaxed again and folded into a tight ball on her side. Gbessa opened the door and knelt outside as the drifting wind noticed and raced to meet her. She took in the night air and moonlight. The entry to the woods at the back of her house was only several feet away from her. But as the tree branches and bushes leaned toward her and atop one another, creating mazelike webs that were sure to obstruct her view, Gbessa looked up at the moon, where the old woman sat, a cheerful audience for her escape.

"Fa-ma-tta," Gbessa murmured toward the drooping gray outline hunkered in the corner of the moon, and she crawled into the woods. Leaves broke beneath her knees and palms, and Gbessa moved within the staid netting. She turned her head toward the night's frightening whispers and trembled, too afraid to go farther. Gbessa crawled to hide herself underneath a shrub. She sat up and folded her knees against her chest as the raucous noises enclosed her. Overwhelmed, she buried her head in her knees, exhausted and finally overcome by the misfortune of her life, and she cried.

A voice split her sorrow. "ThereWho? That you?"

"ThereWho?" she heard again. Although she was sure then that it was Safua, she was afraid to respond, since she was forbidden to leave the immediate vicinity of her house.

"What you do in the woods in the night? It'n good thing," he scolded.

"I'n know," Gbessa whispered. "I'n come before. I want to go from here," she said.

Safua laughed.

"Why you here?" she asked.

"I practicing sleeping in woods. For initiation."

"You'n get in enough trouble today? They will find you again and beat you," Gbessa said.

"No, that Kano our house slave. He say it a bad thing to go near your house but he'n tell my Pa. He good," Safua said. "And nobody see me leave. They'n coming find me here. They won't look behind your house."

"Because I a curse, yeh?" Gbessa whispered. She did not have to see him to know that he agreed with her. "I will die."

"Ah, your dong-sakpa coming soon, yeh? In five rainy seasons?" he asked, and the thought of it distressed him. "So you will run away?"

Gbessa fought tears in the darkness. "Yeh," she said.

"If you go you will make the spirits them vexed with Lai," Safua said after a brief

52

silence. "Don't leave."

"You a curse, you want go too," Gbessa said.

"They will find you after the rooster crow and they will punish your Ma," Safua replied.

Gbessa thought of Khati, whom she did not want to cause any more grief. "Yeh," she agreed finally. "I will go back. But I lost."

"Don't let them catch you. Good-bye," Safua said playfully.

"No," Gbessa pleaded, reaching out to grip the night before he left.

Safua laughed again. "I just joke with you. I will not leave you. I will protect you. You lost, I take you home."

Gbessa jumped as she felt a boyish hand on her frail arm.

"Why you help me? I a curse. You'n scared?" Gbessa asked him and anxiously sought his face.

"You'n different," he said finally. "You witch but you sound just like Vai girl."

Her heart raced.

"And I'n scared of nothing," Safua added. "I come to the woods plenty. I'n scared of nothing in the woods. I will be king one day and king'n scared."

"King Safua?" Gbessa asked softly,

pleased.

"Yeh. I leave soon. Come," he said, and crawled ahead of her through the murmurs of the woods and night. Gbessa followed his breathing with lowered shoulders, and with each advance she squeezed a handful of grass, letting the earth fold within her grasp. This time, instead of scraping her tender and unscathed skin, the ground beneath her was cleared of sticks and leaves, with only dust and mud to sink her limbs into. The moonlight met her at the edge of the woods, where Khati's house stood waiting.

"There. Go home," Safua said and left her as quickly as he had come. Gbessa silently thanked the brave boy, with hopeful eyes that pointed upward toward Ol' Ma Famatta, until her face disappeared, unrecognizable behind the transitioning night clouds.

On the early morning of her thirteenth birthday, Khati called Gbessa to the door, where a crowd of men gathered, waiting. Safua, who led the group of men, had been newly inducted into the Poro, the Vai society that recruited only the village's strongest and most promising boys. It had been five dry seasons since Gbessa had last seen Safua. Gbessa noticed he stood taller when he saw her. Did that mean that she was beautiful, then? Had her mismatching red hair and black skin settled down?

"Safua," Gbessa said faintly.

"You must come," Safua said.

"For what?" Khati asked, although she knew why.

"Dong-sakpa today. Enneh-so?" Safua continued addressing Gbessa. Gbessa nodded. It was her thirteenth birthday.

"You must come," he said again. Gbessa looked at Safua, but his eyes and shoulders were cold, his voice unfamiliar. Neighbors poked their heads out of windows and doors. She had emerged. This was the day.

"Dong-sakpa," an elder said approvingly.

"Gbessa the witch!" the children shouted.

As she walked with her captors along the footpath out of Lai, Gbessa's legs ached.

"Where you take me?" she shrieked.

Safua stopped walking and the men stopped with him. He turned and looked to where Gbessa stood waiting.

"You want, you can die now," he said, different from the young and inquisitive boy she remembered from their brief and secret meetings. She was overcome with grief, and she stared at the ground until the entry to a giant forest was before her. Layers of trees imposed on a grayish sky. In the intervals of leaves, yellow and plum-colored insects piloted through the heat amid the shouts of forest beasts and specters.

"Come," Safua said again, and this time he went ahead into the forest and left the collective of men behind him. Gbessa hurried to follow him, afraid to stay behind with the stone-faced warriors who waited. Safua tore rigid forest branches out of his way until his arms bore scratches and permanent marks of their passage.

"You were the one who look through the

hole that day," Gbessa said. She stopped and pulled her hair from a tree branch, where it had become tangled. "You change from then," she said.

"Come!" Safua yelled, noticing the sudden hesitation in her pace.

"I go to the hole another day and wait for you, but you'n come," Gbessa said after another long bout of silence. "And since that night, when you help me, I'n try to run away."

"Keep walking," Safua said, making sure the Poro collective was completely out of sight and could not hear him. He still saw a few in the brushes.

"What we doing here?"

Safua turned around and grabbed Gbessa's arm.

"You hurtin—"

"Then stop your mouth and walk!" he said and dropped her arm.

Gbessa rubbed the area where he had grabbed to soothe the ripe bruise, and followed him quietly.

"Here," Safua said, pointing to a hidden cave entry in the middle of the forest. Gbessa looked at the entry where he pointed. She shook her head.

"Go inside," Safua said, pointing to the entry.

Upon entering the cave, Gbessa saw two human skulls in a ray of sunlight. She sat down against the wall and waited for Safua, disrupting the stillness of the cave with tears. Unsure of whether he had snuck in through her sobs and sat waiting for her, and further angered that he would dare suspend her cruel existence, she called his name.

"Safua," Gbessa said. Her voice echoed. "Safua," she said again.

When he still did not answer, Gbessa left the cave and searched through the dense web of trees in the forest. Safua was gone.

She reentered and sat wondering what action to take. Nothing came to mind but an appeal for more tears, and she lay there as the sun, tired of looking for her, went down. "Fengbe, keh kamba beh. Fengbe, kemu beh." *We have nothing but we have God. We have nothing but we have each other.* She sang until her voice swallowed the moonlight and screeches of the forest, and she opened her eyes in the morning with a stain of tears on her face.

"Gbessa," she heard from outside. She thought the voice was a trick of her imagination, and closed her eyes again. Pain unsettled her stomach, and Gbessa wrapped her arms around her body in hopes that her hunger would flee.

"Gbessa!" she heard again. This time, she recognized that it was her mother's voice and rushed outside.

"Ma!" Gbessa shouted. She left the cave.

"No, Gbessa," Khati said, looking down and extending her hand. "Go back inside."

Gbessa obeyed her mother. She sat inside the entry and waited for Khati to join her, but instead, Khati placed a bucket in front of her daughter. It was the most food that Gbessa had seen at one time.

"What?" Gbessa asked.

"You must stay here," Khati said.

"For what?" Gbessa pleaded, unsettled at the thought of staying in the cave for one more night. "He'n kill me, I can run. Come with me, Ma."

"You knew it come, yeh?" Khati said with a hint of sympathy. She said this not as a mother would, but as a villager who did not know Gbessa at all, a villager who, like all of them, was complicit in her death.

"I come with food," Khati said and glanced behind her shoulder. "It not good thing, but Safua come to me in secret with food and say he will bring me. He was supposed to kill you but he favor you. He waiting on the road."

She remained silent and Gbessa nodded,

pleased at the sacrifice that her mother was making, the tradition that she was defying to feed her, and still deeply saddened that her sacrifice had limits.

"Thank you, Ma," Gbessa said. She wished Khati would hug her. Without a farewell, without an embrace, Khati left her daughter in the forest. Gbessa looked into the bucket at the ripe mangoes and cooked fish and rice. She wanted Khati instead.

"Ma!" Gbessa called after her, but Khati kept walking. "Ma!" Gbessa called again, this time creating an echo that disrupted the forest birds and made their sudden flight slap the leaves of the trees around her.

"Ma!" But her mother was now out of sight, also lost, in a deep wood.

And so Gbessa lived in the cave in the forest. Soon she ran out of the food in the bucket her mother had delivered. She scraped the leftover fish skin with her nails to ease her hunger. She shared her food with the forest animals, which at first were menacing but were eventually softened by her kindness. Gbessa then found plants, sugary leaves that she pounded before eating with a stone in a bowl she made of a broken skull. The forest creatures screeched if she touched a plant that was poisonous, and later left scraps of their raw meals at the entry to her cave, so she learned to trust them, to love them. But some weeks went by when Gbessa could find nothing to eat or drink at all. And those weeks grew into months, and she wondered when she would die of hunger, when her body would melt and her bones would commune with the many other skulls in that cave. Gbessa never melted, and although she felt the agonizing, irreconcilable pain of hunger, Gbessa did not die.

The animals of the forest did not seem to care about her immortality. They visited her daily, some eventually resting on her shoulder, some crawling around and over her growing curves as she lay. She became the forest's child; her curiosity, her otherness, her obscurity matched those of even the most different of the agile creatures of the wood. They cared for her as the sun did. And when loneliness exhausted her soul, when her echoes grew tired of keeping her company and she cried, the trees wept for her also, willowing back and forth during breezeless afternoons. The animals fed her as she thought mothers should feed their children, sheltered her as she expected fathers should protect their daughters. And when the sun peeked through the branches to find her, it was as she hoped lovers greeted their sweethearts. When it rained and the cave was full of animals with young who needed refuge far more than she, she sat underneath the unlocked sky until her entire body creased and folded from the charge of wetness.

To numb the pain during those years, Gbessa sang to herself, "Fengbe, keh kamba beh. Fengbe, kemu beh." The words ascended, joining the traveling wind, and sometimes it was as though someone were singing with her. "Fengbe, keh kamba beh. Fengbe, kemu beh."

It was during a dry-season morning when, after waking up, a sting prickled up and down her spine. Gbessa looked down at her body to see sated, round breasts hanging from her chest. As Gbessa's hands brushed the flesh of her chest, her stomach and heart collected warmth so new, so awakening that she desired to return to the village of her exile. She knew that she had been in the forest for a long time, because her bushy hair now hung to her knees. If their sending her there had been meant to kill her, they had failed, death had failed, and now she wished to go home. This time, rather than ignoring the desire to return, or distracting herself with the routines of the forest, she began to walk in the direction that she had come those many years before.

"I coming back," Gbessa said out loud, as she sensed the forest's sadness when she brushed past the trees.

"I coming back," she said again.

Later on that day, through a cloud of dust and heat, Gbessa traveled back to Lai on the road that the Poro had brought her along on her dong-sakpa.

In the distance, Safua played with his son in the village circle, slapping the small boy's head until he came at his father laughing, full of energy and enthusiasm. While playing, Safua was startled by a scream at the edge of the village.

"Go to your Ma," he instructed the boy. Safua headed toward the scream, as it escalated into a splitting chorus.

"That spirit there! That Gbessa the witch spirit there!" A woman pointed to the figure that approached them through the dust.

Safua squinted. He recognized her, as only he would, coming toward him wearing a wilted skirt of palm leaves. Gbessa had lived, but Safua had found a bride, a Sande, a queen.

"Stop!" Safua shouted as she approached him. She did not. "Stop!" he said again.

Gbessa walked right to him, met him on the edge of the circle. After searching his eyes, when she knew from the lines on his face that some years had passed since she had last seen him, she left him and headed to her old home. Nobody stopped her; nobody spoke after Safua's attempt.

When Gbessa entered her house, an old medicine man and woman sat in front of the fire pit chewing tobacco. Unlike the villagers, the couple was unmoved by her presence. Bells encircled their ankles and they chewed the tobacco with such gratification that she wanted some.

"Khati dead," the old woman said with ease, and bit another piece of tobacco. The sting of nostalgia was with Gbessa for only a moment; it quickly passed when she thought of the forest and how much of a mother it had been to her.

"Your Pa drown. Your Ma die after of crush heart. I try," the old woman said. "Long, long time," she continued, needing no inquiry or words to answer the questions that she knew Gbessa wanted to ask. "Stay here. You got spirit on you. You will not marry. Stay here."

Gbessa glanced outside, where the entire village peeked out of their houses, awaiting her reappearance.

"Five dry seasons pass you'n die," the old man said. "She the first, yeh?"

"Yeh. You'n die so they will not bother you. You spirit," the medicine woman said, trying to explain.

"You the first," the medicine man said. "If you'n die yet, you will not die."

"You bleed yet?" the old woman asked. Gbessa looked the woman in the eye, refusing to answer.

"No, you'n bleed. You will not bleed. You spirit. You will not die," she said. "But your Pa drown fishing," the old woman added. "Your Ma die after. Ol' Ma Kadyatu come look for her when she'n go farm. She was dead here. Crushed heart. Too lonely."

Gbessa went to where the couple sat and reached into the bowl of tobacco. She sat on the ground with them and chewed it until the sun went down.

That night, Gbessa could not sleep. She meditated on the words of the old man and woman. She had also wondered, many times while away, why she had not yet died, especially in those seasons when she had been tortured by her hunger.

The medicine man and woman slept with their eyes open, so Gbessa did not know when they had fallen asleep. She tried waking the woman up to tell her that she was

65

leaving. She called her, then she shook her, but the woman was crippled by slumber.

Gbessa left the house and village through the circle. Night flies followed her, rested on her arm as she walked.

"Fengbe, keh kamba beh. Fengbe, kemu beh," she hummed to them.

Gbessa continued until she passed the edge of the circle and headed out onto the main road. Winds blew, restless and enlivened by her acquaintance.

"There you are, my darling," I whispered into her ear. "There you are, my friend."

Gbessa passed through a brush of woods until she reached a mount of bushes that covered an opening, and pushed them out of her way. There was Lake Piso, displaying seventy reflections of a full moon, each ripple a different translation. Gbessa entered the lake and her hair floated behind her. The earth serenaded her, held the sum of her lived experience in its palm, and though she had left it, it still called her "daughter." She swam for hours and the water tickled her stomach and legs.

"Fa-ma-tta," she said, giggling at the moon. Gbessa thought of the cursed old woman who sat looking back at her, the only story that ever made her feel less unusual, more human.

"Fa-ma-tta," she said again, floating along. Poor old woman, she thought. What was Famatta's curse but the mastery of life? And now they shunned her for mastering death. Cursed the in-between.

Gbessa heard the shrub ruffle at the opening to the lake. Alarmed, she turned, but was so far into the water that she could not see. When she reached the shore, she heard the bush move again, and she followed the sound, but found no one near it.

"Meyahn!" she shouted. "Meyahn!" she shouted again, rupturing the night with her accusation. Whoever it was, was a coward, and she wanted them to know. Gbessa returned to the lake and sat on the shore as her breathing settled.

"Meyahn?" asked a voice, deep and incensed.

"Mm." She sighed, ignoring him. Safua fumed at her charge. Calling a Poro man a coward was punishable by death. Gbessa did not care.

"Stand," Safua said angrily.

When she stood and faced him, and his eyes caught hers, she recognized his bravery to be true. Gbessa suddenly felt drained of all energy. His eyes were brown. Gbessa at once wondered what color her eyes were, instantly conscious of everything around her.

"Meyahn?" he asked again, even more angrily than the first time. Gbessa knew he could not kill her, and did not care if he could. She nodded.

"Meyahn, go take your Ma to go feed you? Meyahn, go back when your Ma die to see you, all right? Meyahn, do that?" he asked.

She swallowed what felt like sharp stones.

"Poro do that? Enneh-so?" he continued. Gbessa's heart sank at his words. He had done what he had promised. He was king and indeed the head of the Poro, and now the most powerful man in the village. The darkness of her curse was powerful, but not as powerful as his title, his bravery. And still, whose bravery is not provoked by darkness? Was she that far removed?

He breathed as though a part of him wanted to slap her face, while the other part wanted to touch his mouth to her blackness, test it for consistency, try what he knew was more than just a spirit, whose flesh and blood stood before him more rife and sweet than they who refuted it. The two stood in the night, silent, never touching.

Just before morning, Safua turned away from Gbessa and returned to the village. Gbessa watched until he was out of sight, and then followed him until she reached the house where the old man and woman sat sleeping with their eyes wide open.

When they awoke, Gbessa watched them together; their synchronization made her hollow with loneliness. She reached inside for thoughts of the forest and animals, for remnants of the lake's icy chills, but none could come to her rescue. Outside the window, Safua was running around the village circle with his son, with no stain of the previous night, no lake, no extended stare.

"I'n dead," Gbessa said to the couple, who sat monotonously during their days, waiting for sick villagers to knock on their door.

"Hmm," the old woman answered, smiling.

"I living. I'n spirit," Gbessa persisted and stared out the window.

The couple laughed. "Mm-hmm," the old woman said, continuing to chew her tobacco.

"You living now. Now — you alive," she said.

Every night, when the medicine man and woman went to sleep, Gbessa went to the lake. Every night, Safua followed her and watched her through the bush. He had kept his childhood promise — that he would protect her, that she was no different. She trusted the sound of the waves, the illumination of night, before anything else. "Fengbe, keh kamba beh. Fengbe, kemu beh." Gbessa heard the voice coming from behind the bushes, in that deep certainty. She looked toward the bush, toward the siren. "Fengbe, keh kamba beh. Fengbe, kemu beh," Safua sang to her. She touched her mouth as his voice came to her on the backs of those night flies, resting on her shoulders, licking her skin. *We have nothing but we have God. We have nothing but we have each other,* she sang with him, trusting him, until morning came.

One day, as Gbessa readied herself to walk out of the house and to the lake, long after the medicine man and woman had stopped picking at their bowl of tobacco, their eyes closed.

Gbessa lost her breath. "Ma," she said. "Ma." She shook her. But the medicine man and woman, both at once, had departed to the moon and lake, to the forest and sand, gone, it seemed, like so many before them. "Ma," she continued, shaking her, hoping that the old woman's eyes would open. But the only thing that shook were her ankle bells. Gbessa sat on the pallet and waited for them to open their eyes. She sat during the night, and into the next morning. She sat as the wind knocked on her door. Gbessa remained still. They were gone.

In the middle of the night, Safua entered her house through the back door. His face fell as he noticed her gazing at the old couple, who he knew fell into an unperturbed sleep every night. A villager had once fallen ill during the night and writhed in pain until morning because no amount of yelling or shaking could wake the medicine people.

"They dead," Gbessa said. "They gone."

Safua looked at the couple and then back at Gbessa. He stood awhile, mulling over possible solutions, distracted by his purpose for visiting her in the first place. He picked up the old man and threw him over his shoulder. Gbessa ran to him and pulled his arm.

"No!" she said. "Put him down!" She shook at the thought of the kind old couple not receiving a proper burial.

Safua placed the old man back in his chair as the ankle bells chimed. Gbessa sank onto the pallet on the floor and Safua sat beside her.

"They go together?" Safua asked.

Gbessa nodded, and Safua looked as if he was in agreement with their deaths — two lovers sharing a life, working every day

71

toward also sharing one heart, and finally succeeding, would never die alone.

"They were old," Safua said. "It was time."

Gbessa continued staring at the couple in silence.

"You'n come to the water," he said finally.

"You will not follow me everywhere," she replied. "I'n yours to follow."

Safua did not have the words to plead, made weak by her disparaging claim.

"Your son. Your Sande," Gbessa continued. "You say you come to the forest. You'n come. I was there, yeh?"

"I was there. I hear you sing. I sing with you so you know I protect you."

"Protect me from what? You'n bring food."

"But you still live. How you still live?"

"You'n come for me. You think like them. I'n living. I a curse to you."

Safua looked at the old man and woman.

"I was there. I stop coming after they make me Poro head," he said.

Gbessa felt the tears rise in her stomach. "I will go back to the forest. The Ol' Ma and Ol' Pa dead. The people will say I kill them. I will go back," she said.

"And then — I will follow you," Safua said, his eyes also fixated on the old couple.

"No. I will leave then. I will go from Lai," she said.

"And still, I will follow you," he added.

"Then I will let them find me here with the Ol' Ma and Pa. They will kill me and I will go to the night, my sister. You will not find me in her," she said.

"And so every day I will go to Lake Piso and wait for you to come. And I will sit past the moon and wait for the rooster and Ol' Pa Bondo prayer. I will sing. I will follow you."

"Hmm. How you know I'n put spell on you? The medicine people say I a spirit. I a curse, yeh?" she asked.

Safua sat with her in silence. He seemed unsure of how to further extend his plea for the oil-black-skinned girl, his wind-darling-bride, his wilderness.

"I'n know," he finally answered. "I'n know."

Gbessa cried for the old man and woman, perhaps once a Poro king and witch, perhaps once a fisherman and the mother of a cursed child, perhaps once the forest.

And morning came.

Gbessa noticed that Safua was not there only when she heard banging on her door. She wanted to ignore the knock, but felt the old medicine woman, even in her passage, urging her to stand up and open it. When Gbessa opened the door, it was Safua's wife, the Sande. She held their son in her arms.

"Where the Ol' Ma?!" the Sande cried frantically. "Where the Ol' Ma?!" she yelled as her son moaned against her. Sweat covered his black face and chest and the young boy's eyes rolled back. He lay limp and shirtless in his mother's arms.

The Sande snapped at Gbessa, who struggled with her demands.

"The Ol' Ma! Please!" she yelled.

"They . . . they dead," Gbessa answered her.

The Sande screamed, losing all hope of her son's rejuvenation. The neighbors filed out of their houses; they ran to the Sande and held her as she danced with her son in her arms.

"She now come kill the medicine men. She now come kill them!" The Sande ran across the village circle back to her house. She pushed open the door and called for her husband.

"Safua! Safua!"

At the sight of his son, Safua took the boy out of the Sande's grip in panic. His mind left him; his spirit feared the worst. Safua ran with the young boy in his arms through the village circle toward the medicine man and woman.

Then he stopped as he remembered.

74

Gbessa walked out of her house, sur-rounded by the taunts of an angry and frightened village. "Gbessa the witch! Gbessa the witch!" children chanted loudly as she passed.

Safua stopped and looked down at his son. The elders and villagers watched him and waited for a verdict for the young Vai witch and what they suspected was a result of her sorcery. He had known he would have to choose one day, but he did not expect such a challenge to come so soon.

The wind blew whispers in Gbessa's ear as she stood facing the frightened Poro king, surrounded, it seemed, by everybody in Lai — surrounded, she knew, by the forest, and the road, and the lake, and the spirits, and the night, and the sun and the moon. The wind blew.

"There you are, my darling," I whispered in her ear. "There you are, my friend."

■ ■ ■ ■

JUNE DEY

■ ■ ■ ■

The elders say that where you find a suffering village, you will hear the wind give warning. The Emerson plantation was one of those. Always changing to something that is supposed to be better, always disappointing in its sameness, like a whipping stain that no amount of scrubbing can remedy. I lived at Emerson before. And that year, you would come outside to find the wind so deep in her feelings that she knocked over buckets full of water from the wash tables and stole clothes from the hanging lines before they hardened.

I was plain. Not tall, not short. Not pitch-black, not yellow. I was one of the more plain slaves on Emerson and when they used to call me by my name they would say, "Charlotte, go up to the kitchen house. One of them get sick and the Missus say they need help," and I walked up there so quickly I nearly fell forward, squeezing my skirt and careful when I arrived not to stutter when my tongue contorted with their language. "Yes'm, I know how," I hurried to say in that old language that no longer binds me. I did whatever was asked, as soon as it was asked, and the moment I set the last dish down I heard, "Charlotte, go on back now," and I would think while walking that they threw me around this way because I was so plain and no color to make a fuss over. But that was when they called me by my name, both my first and last — Charlotte Emerson. Emerson had been my last name since I was nine and any family or name before then was like the wind's spilled water or the dampened sheets missing from those endless lines.

For years I came and went, carefully, between the kitchen house and field. By the time I was thirty years old, when I worked in the kitchen house, which was not really a house but a cooking room extending from the main house, I worked with five others including two sisters, Henrietta and Darlene, the second being so beautiful that no man wanted the burden of keeping her safe.

Sometimes I would catch my reflection on the spoon's back and I did not think I looked much different from Nelsie, another kitchen slave who had not even reached twenty years. I would ask how I looked when I went to the kitchen house, as soon as I entered, except none of the other women answered, not even in passing, and the quiet after I spoke began to feel like its own person, a friend maybe, one I grew to expect and prepare for, the most dependable I had.

I knew that everybody was still quite vexed with me for the horrible thing that happened to Shan Emerson several years back, and for that reason, it seemed, they stopped speaking to me. Shan Emerson was a young daughter of some older neighbors of mine, my neighbors when I lived with seven other girls around my age, none older than twenty. Shan was so heavy, so much heavier than her pole-thin mother and father, that on several occasions while passing her shack, we would sneak a quick look inside to see what she was being fed. On some nights the girls I lived with had some too-long laughs, thinking that the only reason Shan was so fat was that her parents were stuffing her with all their rations in hopes that she would one day become a nurse to one of Master Emerson's grandchildren, a ritual that numbed the soreness we regularly felt from clearing land with our hoes and hands.

The horrible something happened on a

81

quiet morning — so quiet that I did not wake up to the door knocks or moving parts that filled the aisles of our quarters right before the sun rose. I had always been a deep sleeper but one of the girls usually woke me up before heading to the field. I knew I had slept for too long when, as I opened my eyes, I heard the song of some birds outside, weaving in and out of a lull so wonderful that I thought I was dreaming. The sun formed bright lines across the room through breaks in our shack's wood. The girls were all gone and I scrambled to pull my dress over my head.

Not even the nurses or unworking children could be found outside. Usually, all 116 shacks, each fifteen feet long and wide, lining three parallel roads, were perfectly unique. Some had planks nailed atop one another to cover holes and aging wood. A few had empty tin cups and broken sticks in front where children had gathered to play under the moonlight before they were ordered to bed. That morning all of the shacks looked the same, cold gray and closed against the sun. The clothing lines had all been rolled up and placed into the seamstress's shack, the chairs also, and even the circles that the children made with sticks in the dirt had been cleared away.

While I rushed toward the field, I heard the gallops of two horses in the distance. The voices of two men followed. I almost ran back but I was afraid they would be performing checks on the cabins and would find me in there and whip my back raw. As the voices got closer, I realized one was the overseer's, the cropmaster, Mr. Harris, a large man with teeth the color of corn and skin almost the color of his teeth. I stood there for a moment trying to figure out where to go, and, desperate, I hid in the narrow gap between two shacks.

Then I heard the whimper. I looked beside me and there was Shan, wedged deep into the small space. She looked up at me, a braided pigtail drooping over her eye, unable to keep her mouth closed from shaking.

"The governor here and my stomach went bad this morning," Shan said, and I was reminded when I heard the high pitch of her words of how young she was. Sounded not even ten years yet. I held my finger over my lips so she would remain quiet. Instead of heeding, a tear fell from Shan's eye and she ran from between the shacks toward the field, only to stand face-to-face with Mr. Harris and his associate.

"What you doing out here, girl?" Mr.

Harris shouted from his horse, startled.

"Sir," Shan almost yelled, surprised, "I's-sorry, Mr. Harris, sir. Please, sir," she said, squeezing her dress between her fingers, frightened to look up.

"Should be in the field," he said and climbed off the horse as his belly shook beneath his badly tucked shirt.

"Yessir. I'sorry, Mr. Harris. My stomach, sir, please, sir," she said, still looking down.

"Hands up against that shack there," Mr. Harris said.

Shan began to cry and plead, her girlish voice rising into the air.

Mr. Harris unwound the whip. His associate looked away as he struck Shan so hard she fell from the blow. Her screams split the day as the whip bit into her flesh once again, and a line of blood appeared on the back of her coarse linen dress. The screams kept coming, and so overcome with grief she was that she had fallen to her knees and stretched her hands out across the wall of the shack, as if hugging it, pleading to save her life. Unable to bear the sound of her screaming any longer, I ran to her.

"Mr. Harris, sir!" I said, and could barely believe I had run out and I was standing there until I looked down at my feet. And when Mr. Harris turned, his elbow knocked

84

me in the eye so hard I fell, hitting my head against a lonesome stone protruding from the ground. Both of their bodies — Mr. Harris's above me, and Shan's — became blurry, and I felt myself becoming tired, so tired that Shan's cries dimmed to a light buzz, like the chanting of a mosquito with a story to tell.

When I opened my eyes again it was night. I was huddled near the stone where I had hit my head. I touched the place on my head but there was barely a bruise remaining, only dried blood that I quickly rubbed away with the sleeve of my dress. They had left me there.

Shan's blood was scattered on the dust beside me. I was dizzy from the sight and smell, and I stumbled past the wash bucket tables. From inside the cabins, I could hear whispering, all kinds of chattering like something big had happened. But when I reached Shan's cabin, it was silent. I approached the door, but stopped just before knocking. I leaned forward, pressing my ear against the wood until through the dead air I heard the soft coaxing of a woman. The woman sounded like she was singing, but I realized she was praying.

"It ain't your fault, Shan," the woman muttered while Shan cried. I pressed in closer to hear and the door swung open. I nearly fell over. Shan Emerson's father stood there before me with a face so incensed that I could not immediately look at him. But as I raised my head to address the man, the door closed in my face, and I caught only a glimpse of Shan's mother and another woman tending to Shan's wounds.

"Sorry I ain't protect her." I could barely hear the words, but I tasted them so I knew I had let them go, and I returned to my shack at the end of the road.

From that day on, I noticed a distance between me and the others. Every morning was a long walk to the kitchen house or field as every eye I searched for, even the children's, avoided my passing. Punishment, especially the kind given by those who have nothing, can be a big and addictive thing. Cruel as it is, that small taste of power is juicy. It lasts long. I was never sure of what Shan had told them, but I suspected just knowing I was there hiding while the baby was getting whipped that way made their mouths sour at the sound of my name. Since it seemed everyone in the girl's cabin refused to speak to me, and the women I worked with had always mostly ignored me, and would make no room for my pallet in the kitchen house even if I could have convinced them to lend me a dress and silk apron as fine as theirs, I eventually moved into a condemned shack at the edge of the plantation, where I would live alone for the next forty years.

Something began to happen when folks avoided me in and out of those years. They ignored me for so long, they started to say things I knew they did not mean to say to more than one set of ears. But some things were said directly to me — mostly unkind things by Darlene. In the hallway entry to the kitchen house on my way in or out, she would find me sometimes and remind me that I was not beautiful. "You're a no-good woman," she would say. "God don't love you. Nobody love anybody as no-good as you." And in those moments I rushed past her, to my chores or back to the field. Otherwise, few things were said to me, or about me, at all.

I came to know so much about everyone. Everybody's business was a small part of my own. And like the silence that came after my words, I also came to depend on those accidental breaks in my routine when I heard things not meant for me to hear. Sometimes in the kitchen house Darlene and Henrietta would come to the pantry to share whispers and forget I was there dusting, or Edith would come sometimes with Darlene but not as much, and I learned all kinds of things that were happening on Emerson, big things, mostly about Master Emerson.

Some plantations in Virginia had already begun to farm wheat and cotton instead of tobacco, for instance, but not Master Emerson's. Cotton made the most money, since the white men from overseas were buying more and paying higher prices than they paid for tobacco. And wheat too. The men who told Master Emerson what was best for the plantation shared this many times, but each time he made a case for tobacco. Eventually Emerson became one of the last remaining tobacco farms in Virginia, and because tobacco was losing its popularity, the plantation started losing money and Edith had less and less money to go to town with. Then, instead of coming up with ways to make sure Emerson did not have to keep selling slaves, Master Emerson spent very little of his time on his plantation. He spent long months in New York and Georgia, where, I heard Edith say once, he took slave women to bed. This was something Darlene could not believe, and she left the pantry shortly after and accused Edith of not knowing anything at all.

During that time I also heard that when she had guests the Missus had a hell of a time making excuses for where Master Emerson had gone off to. She boasted that he had fallen off his horse and was being nursed back to health. Her friends let her share her lies, all of them; most knew just where Master Emerson was and pitied the Missus for the show she insisted on putting on. Then, when Master Emerson finally came home, the Missus was so scared that a quarrel would make him leave again that she never shared her disapproval more than once. Rather, she avoided him so she would not say or do anything that would cause him to disappear again. She put a lot of her time, and a lot of our time from the kitchen and house, into decorating the miles surrounding Emerson.

It was the most beautiful the plantation had ever looked — at least that's what Edith heard the guests say. The Missus had fenced the entire property with long gardens of exotic flowers and roses. Behind the mansion, the Missus built a ten-foot-high stone fountain in the middle of a one-hundred-yard stretch of land that separated her house from the tobacco field and slave quarters. She sold five slaves for that fountain and gave Mr. Harris some money so he would keep her secret from Master Emerson.

They never told me these things directly, but I came to know so much that I sometimes felt important. But nobody cared what I knew, not enough to ask. So on my walks home, I carried on full conversations with the winding cabin roads, the exploding stars, and the fireflies with glowing backs that folded in and out of my daydreams.

One night after I blew out my lantern and finally rested my head on the burlap sack, my door swung open. The wood shook against itself.

"Go on in there!" I heard. A pair of boots shuffled outside. In the darkness I jumped at the sound of slapping flesh. I heard a grunt and another meeting of flesh, this time harder.

"Go on in there!" a man's voice — which I recognized as Mr. Harris's — yelled. A harsh night breeze pulled the wooden door back toward its frame. More horses galloped toward the opening of my shack and I squeezed the sheet, leaning against the twilight's shadow as the bare wooden wall scratched my back. The approaching horses stopped in front of the shack. The mumbling of three or four men and their heavy footsteps reached the place where Mr. Harris beat the man. They dragged him toward the shack, while the man released several grunts after being kicked. They threw the lifeless body into my shack and chained the door. I sat still and afraid as the last gallop faded into the distance. I thought of crawling in the dark to find the body, but in the end I remained still. My hands trailed along my lap and thighs, the hard burlap sack, and the dusty ground on their way to the match and lantern on the floor. I placed the lantern in my lap and felt quickly for the opening; I struck the match and lit it.

As a dim light filled the yellow room, a man, a broken man, sat on the other end of the shack. He was surprised to see me, I could tell, though the blood from his wounds sat in the corners of his eyes. I wanted to know his face but could not make it out beneath the gashes and cuts, the forehead contusions, the twisted nose. But I saw his eyes. He was alive. I moved toward him, and without warning, he lifted his face to the ceiling of the shack, and he howled in the night, a muffled sound, as if he had no tongue, no breath, no food or bones, nothing in him but sadness and terror. So I remained still — afraid but relieved. He was alive. And I lay down and sought sleep.

When I opened my eyes the following

morning, the broken man stood at the door. The blood was still damp on his clothes and the shack smelled sweet. He shook the door and it did not open, just rattled on the other side. He turned around, periodically looking at me on the burlap sack, and the fear in his eyes from the previous night was clearer.

"How you?" I asked him.

When he was tired of fighting the door, which I suspected they had chained shut, he slowly limped to the other side of the shack, our prison, watching me carefully on his way there, and sat. His face was swollen and large welts had developed on the black skin of his chest and arms. Outside, a loud dash of horses approached the shack.

"They come back," I said.

I went to him and tried lifting him up. He stiffened, and that familiar terror returned to his eyes, and he held his hand up in what seemed like an effort to block me from touching him, but he was too weak to keep it up for long. He looked like he had become tired of everything, altogether, and he sat waiting for the wooden door to swing open, for death to finally take him. I ran for the small tin bucket beside the fire pot, and was thankful that I had remembered to fetch water on the previous night. I reached into the bucket of water and cupped a small amount in my palms.

"Drink," I told him, pressing my hands to his mouth. The water seeped through my fingers, so I tried again.

"Water. Drink," I said, this time splashing it on his face and tapping his cheek as he refused. "Please," I begged him. The man looked up at me, his eyes almost completely lost beneath the swelling, and I saw a small part of that fear fade from them. As the water found its way through my fingers and traveled down my arms, my hands remained at his lips.

He drank.

"There! More," I said, only to be interrupted by a chorus of chains and boots that walked straight to the man and lifted him off his feet. I remained kneeling at first, afraid to interfere, water and blood congregating in my palms.

"He ain't well!" I called out to the men. His captors continued on, ignoring my attempt. The broken man looked back at me over his shoulder while an iron chain was placed around his neck and fastened by one of Mr. Harris's patrols.

Passing men and women looked toward the shack and shook their heads. I watched until he had disappeared.

That morning I sped to the kitchen house. I was assigned to help in the house that week. Immediately to the right of the door there was a large window that overlooked the tobacco field in the distance. Darlene and Henrietta Emerson were at work, both cutting greens on a thin board on the middle counter. Henrietta's silhouette could fool anyone, at first glance, into thinking she was the overseer's wife. Henrietta was as pale as she, and had a thin, dangly frame and blond hair, tiny strings of which hung from a bonnet that she wore every day. Darlene was not so lucky. The only thin part of her was her waist, a feature that accentuated her distended backside and plump breasts whose nipples protruded out of a blouse or dress, no matter how thick. Instead of wrapping her hair in nets and bonnets like Henrietta, she wore it down her back in a wavy black braid that coiled atop her derriere like a resting snake.

I met the women at the counter and picked up a knife and a handful of greens to cut.

"They lock a man in my cabin last night," I said quietly to them, my knife shaking in my hand. "They came got him this morning and I don't know where he at," I whispered. "Looked for him a bit before I got here, but don't know where he at. Think he gone anyway."

"Where is my knife?" Darlene asked, searching about the countertop.

"I got it here," I said, annoyed that I'd been interrupted.

Darlene shook her head and walked away from me, rolling her eyes at me. "I tell you, you should have seen him," I said anyway. "Barely look like a man no more, just somebody soul that done bad things all they life, somebody soul that don't deserve no life no more or anything good, that's what he look like." Darlene shook her head again and I was so angry I almost cried, that even at that moment they could not help but continue to be cruel. The liquids on the stovetops steamed to a rapid boil. I went to pull Darlene's arm as the Missus came into the kitchen with her hands folded across her stomach. She looked toward the counter.

"You two girls come with me," she said. I hurried toward her but Darlene and Henrietta were faster and followed her out of the kitchen. I stopped, wiping my eyes, and I returned to the counter and continued cutting.

After leaving the house that evening I hurried past the fountain toward the slave quarters, the assembly of cracked shacks, to a cluster of young, barefoot children who chased one another around me. The deck of the quarters was occupied with nearly a hundred people — mostly women and children at that time of night. I went to the edge, to my old shack, which no one visited, no one wanted, and I opened the door, expecting what always waited for me: four walls, a bucket, a lantern, a burlap sack now stained with him.

But there he was.

There he was and I was instantly bewitched by feeling, struck by the creases, the bulges and veins of age. I felt old all over. Seeing him granted me a remarkable sobering of feeling, no matter how grim. The broken man sat against the wall, facing the door with his head in his hands and clothes now dried to a crust with blood. I crawled to him and held his face, a blend of relief, of confusion, and of the terror from his past day.

"You living?" I asked him. His face was still lost, but his eyes (or what I could make of them) slowly opened to me and remained there until deep into the night.

In the morning he was gone. I felt the emptiness, even from behind me. The burlap sack showed tiny spots of blood.

In the kitchen house later that morning, after Darlene caught up with me to recite those horrible things — that I was worthless and nobody to make a fuss over, lucky that I wasn't dead — I joined her and Henrietta at the counter.

"You heard of the Dey slave they brought here the other night?" Henrietta asked.

The women at the stoves nodded. One of them, plum-cheeked Nelsie, who barely ever left the house except when she was accompanied by Darlene or Henrietta, shook her head.

"What he do?" Nelsie asked.

"He tried kill his master, what I heard," Elizabeth, another kitchen maid who insisted on always wearing a hairnet low on her forehead, said from the stove.

"Y'all, don't get too talkative out here. This ain't the place for gossip," Edith said, turning around. She looked toward the pantry. Edith was the personal assistant to the Missus, but spent her mornings in the kitchen overseeing the preparation of breakfast. As old as Edith was, probably older than me, everybody talked about her, and everyone could still tell how beautiful she once was. Edith was a frail and orange-colored woman with almond-shaped brown eyes that sat in perfect symmetry above her nose and mouth. The women returned to their work, but I remained distracted.

"What he do?" I asked, and Edith waved her hand toward me as if I were a fly come to ruin her only meal.

"Had to have done something," Edith mumbled to herself over the stove.

"Say they kill his wife for a bad quarrel she had with her Missus. Wife was expecting his son. Apparently he was fighting everybody he saw when he found out. They say he went crazy so they sold him. You know Emerson ain't going to say no to a cheap slave, if he can afford it or not."

"Hmph," Edith grunted.

"I know him," I said. "Dey, this man you talk about, I know who he is; he the man I was talking about yesterday when I come tell you they nearly beat somebody dead outside my door. Come to find out his poor wife dead and gone probably wasn't wrong for fighting with that mistress anyway, just like he ain't wrong for wanting to fight for her or for wanting to take life from somebody else and give it to his wife and son."

That night I watched Dey eat the last of what he was able to hide in his trouser pockets from that day's meal. I watched him break the already-meager portion into tinier pieces and feed himself from the corners of his mouth, and he kept those desperate eyes on me. I watched him as the lantern light swathed his side, watched his shadow break and swallow.

Dey's face crept back, though he was still motionless and mute. It had been close to a month's time that he had been at Emerson, and every time he looked at me, I felt a pain in my lower back that changed the way I walked. One night, as we shared the small burlap sack, the door shook from the light force of a knock on the other side. Outside I heard the chain being slowly released and placed on the ground in front of the shack. The door squeaked as it gradually opened, revealing a circle of light from a lantern that shook within a woman's grasp.

"Dey," I heard. "Dey," the woman said again.

Dey stood up and walked to the door. I followed behind him.

"You in there?" the woman asked.

When Dey showed his face, the woman stepped back. It was Myrna — a young and handsome brown-faced girl who lived with some others in the shack closest to mine. In the lantern's glow the roundness of her face and eyes showed clearly in the night.

"I, I'sorry, Dey. I just noticed they forgot to fasten the lock here and want to bring you food while it's open," she whispered.

Dey looked at the girl in a stupor and down at the chains at the side of the shack. He looked past her as if he were about to run, but she held her finger close to her mouth and raced inside.

"Patrol not too far. I got some bread for you is all," Myrna said quickly.

The way she looked at him, the way she followed his eyes, made me feel something I'd never felt before; at once I felt that I, too, wanted to be addressed, wanted to be called by my name.

"We appreciate you caring and all," I said finally.

Myrna looked around the shack at the burlap sack and fire pot and attempted a smile as Dey stood and watched her.

"Here it go," she said, holding out to Dey a plate of bread covered by an old handkerchief. "Got to get back." Myrna blushed girlishly as she noticed Dey watching her face before his eyes trailed down to the slightly trembling plate. He took it from her.

"We all real sorry for what happened," she

said softly.

"Myrna, it's rude you come in here and not say hello," I said.

"Well then, good night to you," Myrna whispered. She noticed him gazing at the door. "I beg, stay here," she said. "Get well. Patrols them not too far tonight." She turned and walked to the door.

"Myrna!" I yelled. "Myrna, this my house!" I pleaded, running toward the door when Dey quickly held his hand out and grunted toward me.

Myrna, startled by the sound, turned around as Dey stood with his hand extended in the open night air. Her face fell with disappointment and fright, and she nodded toward Dey and closed the door. I stood shocked beyond the reach of Dey's still-extended hand. My face, more serious than I had showed him it could be, gradually fell as I hurried to the burlap sack to sit down. I was embarrassed and exposed. That he saw my rejection in this way, so soon, made me weep inside.

"My head," I said. "My head hurt real bad."

The headache numbed my anger.

"I ain't well," I whispered. The jealousy and confusion were more than I could bear. I closed my eyes.

Dey made his way to the burlap sack and sat, holding close to him the food Myrna had delivered. The lantern glinted and I held myself, the pain in my head relentless.

"Why she ain't say hello?" I asked. Dey reached over the burlap sack and touched my trembling body. His hand grazed the edges of my skin.

"My head," I was sure I said again before I fell asleep.

In the kitchen house the following day, it was hard to think of anything but him. Darlene had stopped me in the hallway and said those awful things to me again: that I was a cruel woman, destroyed and unloved by God. I worked throughout the day, avoiding her. When my head was not aching, in that loud and suffocating way that it had on the previous night, I thought of Myrna's face, Myrna's eyes avoiding mine while sparkling at Dey. And I thought of the way he had looked at me from over his shoulder that morning when they came to get him.

Outside of the kitchen house, a carriage approached from the fields. A patrol drove, his hands and skin marred with dirt. In the back of the carriage, three tall slave men sat with shovels, their heads and bodies swaying to the rhythm of the coach wheels. The women in the kitchen house rushed to the window. I followed and peeked over their shoulders. My heart sank when, among the passengers, I saw Dey, his head hanging low; he hugged his shovel.

"There he go," Nelsie said, looking at Dey.

"He mighty strong looking." Henrietta peered out the window. "Shame they beat him dumb. Hear he can't speak a word."

"Hmm." Darlene sighed. "What today is?"

"Look like they going to the cemetery this week," Edith said.

"Seem they ain't been in a while," Nelsie said.

"That's a good thing, I guess," Edith added. "Poor man already face so much death at his old place now he 'bout to learn all about ours."

"Look like they was real serious about not using wood for coffins no more," Henrietta said, shaking her head.

"Don't make no difference to me," Edith added. "Hell, when I die, bury me the way I came. Want to be ready to show God my scars and ask why." Their sighs agreed in the silence.

On the bed of the carriage, at the feet of Dey and the other two passengers, four bodies lay rolled in old sheets. Dey looked at me from the carriage and again my back ached. I caught my breath and returned to work.

This happened again the next day. The carriage pulled up and the women ran to the window to see who was on the cart, to count the bodies, and to take a look at Dey.

The following day was different.

The cemetery carriage pulled up to the house again, and I saw Dey sitting there in his silence and beauty, and I felt those sweet pains all over again. And while the women returned to work, whispering about visiting the cemetery that weekend with the Missus's permission to sing and leave flowers on the graves of the departed slaves, Dey waved his hand toward me, toward where I was standing. He beckoned me, and I was so surprised that I stopped thinking with a clear head. I felt cold. I snuck out of the kitchen house to follow the carriage as it continued down the main road. I followed carefully, hiding behind the crops in the event that one of the men looked up. Shortly after passing the kitchen house, the carriage turned at a narrow intersection, obstructed by weeds as tall as me. I waited until it turned before scurrying from the bush. I followed the sound of the rickety wheels; the carriage eventually halted in the woods beside a one-hundred-meter-long space that was partially cleared to bury men and women who had died on the Emerson plantation. The plots were tiny, too close together for any soul to rest in peace. Wooden posts jutted out from the ground, several feet apart, all listing the names and ages of the deceased.

Dey stepped down from the carriage. He pulled a cadaver from the coach and carried it to the edge of the yard. After laying it down, as Dey took hold of his shovel to begin digging, he noticed me hiding in the brush. He glanced at the others to see if I had been noticed. I had not. So again, he beckoned me.

When I was sure that no one was looking my way, I went to where Dey stood. As soon as I reached him, he grabbed my hand and led me through the cemetery. The pain in my head made me weak, but Dey squeezed my hand, so I continued with him across the yard, each step more urgent than the last.

We arrived at a small plot in the corner, neat and decorated with dead flowers, so dry and old that the petals had stuck together. He pointed to the wooden post — stared at it until I followed his eyes to read what so captured his attention.

It read: CHARLOTTE EMERSON, AGE 19.

A part of me wanted to laugh. What a cruel joke they were playing, and continued to play. But that tiny desire slowly withered. Before I could form the words to ask him, Dey pointed to my chest. His finger then pointed toward the wooden post, then back at me. I shook my head at him.

"What you doing?" a patrol shouted at Dey, placing his hand on his whip. "Get back with the others!"

Suddenly dizzy and nauseated, I held on to Dey to avoid falling. I squeezed my eyes closed and the day came back to me in rough layers, through the breaks of the drumming in my head. Shan Emerson's cries, the overseer's arm, and the collapse onto that sharp stone that had broken my fall.

"That what it is, ain't it?" I said, my mouth dry now, my mind racing as all of my interactions and my slipping memory circled me in revelation.

"That what it is. That's me there," I said over the grave.

Dey inspected my face closely. He heeded the patrol's warning and made his way back to the carriage quickly, and I followed. Dey returned to the cadaver he had unloaded from the carriage and resumed digging.

I saw his face and eyes droop, his bones almost shake beneath his brawny and muscular exterior. He looked as if even he did not know — could not answer why nobody ever mentioned the woman who lived in the shack at the edge of Emerson.

They could not see me. I lived my life beside them, beside all of them, and they could not see me. I worked by their side, late into the night, left my shack before the day broke and they still could not see me. Was I the only one who could not tell the difference between a life in bondage and death?

"Now you come make me old," I said to Dey. "Make me know things I ain't know much before. That what it is, though. I'm gone. I'm gone and can't nobody see me here but you."

I reached for Dey's hand and held it in mine, a touch that made my fingers itch and swell. He pulled it away and took some steps in the opposite direction. He was shaking. Sweating. He was afraid.

"No, don't fight me. There got to be a reason you was brought here. Reason you see me," I said, stepping toward him. "You see me, even if they don't."

Dey looked toward the patrol and wiped the sweat from his brow.

"I stay here with you. You hear? I stay with you."

He looked as if words enveloped his tongue but refused to come forth. His hands weakened.

"Yes?" I asked. And although his fear was evident, he looked toward me from the corner of his eyes, and he nodded. "Yes, Dey."

It felt good to me to say his name.

That night, when I was finally quiet, Dey held up the lantern beside the burlap sack as I lay down. He set it between us, so the light swayed against his jaw. Scars covered the round curves of his arms, his head pressed against his praying hands as he searched my eyes, in that musical way he did, and I was seen. He could see me. And I could see him. And finally, I knew. I knew who he was, deeply. I knew what he was thinking. I saw his memories race one another, mostly awful and hideous things, never resting. And I knew what he wanted — his wife and, mostly, his child. I lay facing him, fidgeting with my shaking fingers as the humidity from summer's end snuck in, thick with the darkness.

By the following May, my plain black hair was cast to weakened gray fibers that blew in the wind. He had made me old. Slopes and freckles had settled onto my face, around lines that I could feel deep in my bones at the slightest movement or gesture.

"You should know I'm having a child," I said one night. Dey turned on the burlap sack to face me. He had grown used to having me all to himself. He was, they perceived, out of his mind, forever muted by a broken heart.

"I know it because I feel it going on inside," I continued in that old language. "I been feeling it for some time now since spring come. And I suppose I think it's the child you lost. The child you always thinking of.

"I hope he ain't like you," I said after some time. "I pray for the fact he may be like me and can do something with himself 'stead of wandering around ole Emerson."

Dey remained silent.

"He may be strong like you but I sure hope he got some of me in him too. Maybe he can leave this place without nobody seeing him. I know I sure would have long been left if it wasn't for you."

Dey shook his head and I waited for a gesture, but when he remained silent, I continued.

"Know what you asking it can't be, but I tell you it is. Ain't never been with nobody my whole life but I know this you inside me." I waited again. "I see your thoughts sometimes and I see you want that baby back they take from you . . . and I want it for you so bad that I feel it growing inside me. I expect it ain't even mine I don't suppose it look nothing like me once I have it I think it ain't mine anyhow I think it look like you and your old wife like how it was supposed to look before they did what they did to you and her. You see? You come here and that's why they put you here thinking wasn't nothing or nobody in this shack but a old burlap sack and I was in here all along and we gone and made something good out of all the bad. Out of everything bad. That got to be the reason."

■ ■ ■ ■

June was born in August to humming locusts and a rising sun. My pain had little to do with labor, and was more because of the fact that my something good was forever leaving me to join the misfortune of our lives. From the soreness I knew that the baby was coming, and I gathered four buckets of water, two that I boiled and let sit over the fire pot. I borrowed sheets from the clothing line that afternoon and waddled into my small shack. Dey soaked one of the sheets in the boiling pot, and held me up as I floated in and out of consciousness. As the night approached morning, while my eyes were opened, the baby left my body and refuge forever.

My legs twitched and quivered as a humming squeal escalated loudly from my in-between. I suffered no pain. Dey cupped the baby's neck, wiping his small, pale body in the damp sheets. Dey cried and I looked at the boy and realized he did not look like either of us. I supposed I had been right, and he looked just like the wife Dey lost.

"I want to call him June," I said. "That's when I liked him the most inside of me, when I almost forgot everything else but him. Ain't no Emerson going behind his name, though, no it ain't. His name June Dey after his daddy name 'cause I ain't hold you inside of me for no Emerson." June did not cry as I rocked him. He closed his eyes and stayed close to my chest.

Dey kneeled in front of me, surrounded by bloodied sheets. Inside he fought to maintain a state of indifference. Strong, he was. Strong, and a good man. Yet even he was not strong enough to shatter what bound him — the suggestion that being good meant letting what you loved slip through your fingers to appease a man who questions your humanity. The suggestion that joy meant serving. The suggestion that, though misplaced, he was home. The suggestion that being good meant that he was to protect what was in this oppressor's interest, but allow his own flesh to meander about life until they were all an infinity of broken men. Strong then, yes. But not a good man. He would not be that.

I was proud of these thoughts of his. That heart of his. He wanted to breathe me in, if only for that moment. Silent he was and almost, almost happy — if he could only rightly have me, as men did women they loved, then, then he would promise to be good.

It was morning.

We were sleeping.

Dey shook me, and I looked toward the door. I held June Dey close. I was weak and could barely move. Dey gathered the sheets and placed them behind my body, and I could tell he was praying, hoping that his child was blessed with the same peculiar fate as I was. Dey stood at the door and waited.

As the men outside pulled the door open, he exited the shack before they had a chance to enter.

He passed Mr. Harris and the men, then looked back and waited for them to lead him to the field.

"Damnit, what's that smell, boy?" Mr. Harris asked. Dey looked down.

"You ain't shit in there, did you, boy? Damnit, couldn't hold it till morning?" He laughed. The other men, one with overalls, one in black pants and suspenders, joined him in laughing.

"Ain't think to dig a hole or something, boy? That's what you do, boy? Lie in your shit?"

Dey kept his gaze downward and waited

for them to pass him, praying that they kept walking and didn't look back.

"What you got to say?" Mr. Harris asked.

Day broke to June's crying.

Dey's eyes rose from the ground. Perhaps they would not hear it. Perhaps he was like his mother. Pray God, he was like his mother.

"What the hell is that?" Mr. Harris asked, looking toward the shack.

He went to it and pushed the door open. Inside lay a puddle of blood, blotted sheets, four or five buckets of water, and a newborn baby boy.

The men covered their noses. I cradled June Dey and felt them engulfing my boy with their eyes, examining him through furious lenses of greed.

"God help us," I whispered.

While one of the men grabbed the baby from where he lay, holding it up with only the loose grip of one hand, the others approached Dey and slapped him. He succumbed to the abuse until June Dey emerged from the shack, dangling from one arm in the morning mist like a loose tree branch almost departed from its trunk for the ground below. Dey lunged toward the baby, then was stopped suddenly by the strikes and punches of the other two men.

"Who the hell baby you got there?" they asked, kicking. "What the hell you done?"

I lifted myself from the burlap sack, heaving deliriously through the room and out the front door where a man stood shaking my baby, and two others — not far away — were taking turns pummeling the life out of Dey.

The man in front of me shook my baby boy, who had transitioned from crying to a stillness that sent tremors up and down my aching back. I slapped the man with the force of an army of enraged bats until his face became beet-reddish purple. The man waved his hands around his head. He dropped the baby, whom I caught screaming and held close to me near the door of the shack.

As they kicked and beat Dey, he covered his head with his arms. He saw the sunrise through the aperture, and in another corner of the sky a moon that had refused to leave that morning. *Sleep,* Ol' Ma Famatta coaxed. With resurgence, Dey stood up and threw the men off of his beaten body. When they all lay on the ground, Dey turned from them and made his way to me and our baby boy, knelt and stroked my gray hair with the marked and heavy palm of his hand, and covered us with his rugged body. I breathed into his chest.

"Boy finally gone mad!" Mr. Harris yelled upon the sight of Dey caressing the face of the small baby.

"We made something good," I said to him.

Before I finished my sentence, an explosion forced its way into Dey's back, crippling him as he fell to the ground beside me. In the short distance, smoke left the tiny mouth of a gun. Dey's eyes rolled to the back of his head and his body shook until stillness corrupted him. His spirit shattered into tiny parts that planted themselves into the ground.

I grabbed a handful of the dust beneath but could not find him.

"Dey!" I shook him as my long gray hair rested on his chest and lifeless arms.

"Dey, come back!"

Mr. Harris and the other men dusted themselves off and walked back toward the house and the coming morning. All the shacks that lined the parallel path to the house were closed, yet I heard families scramble and churn within them as the men passed. Some peeked through the wooden holes at the corners of their shacks. The trembling of others resonated where I sat, ruined and alone on the ground. I waited with Dey's corpse as the intensity and chaos of the August morning approached its peak. In a matter of minutes, a baby nurse ran to where I stroked Dey's damaged face. The maid lifted our baby boy out of my arms and dusted him off, before carrying him past the barn and the field, past the shacks and the clothing line into the mansion, where his new owners waited.

And again I was alone.

I waited for a moment in the aftermath, dust and blood beneath me, years and years behind me, my friend, my love, beside me. I could not watch him rot any more than he had in the mute and mystical dungeon of my company.

I stood up and dusted off my dress, my sticky face and hands. Limping, I walked past my shack, past the layered tobacco fields of Virginia. I walked past the picketed mansions, white and splendid in all of their glory from the road — hiding the stains of ruined lives behind the houses on tall wooden posts. I walked silently to the edge of the state until I reached the ocean. And the waters turned back. And I went with them, hoping I would reach the other side. I traveled through the ocean's mountains of liquid salt; passing corpses of the first and last; passing wild and mammoth beasts that followed me in the cold dark, sang to me when the silence of the ocean pushed hard into my ears.

I stepped onto the other side and staggered from the water, weeds dangling from my hair, skin pinched with time, shriveled and falling off my bones like fruit peels in impenitent heat. I rose on the other side and it was there that I melted away into a glorious zephyr.

"Come into the wind," a voice echoed in the air. A chorus of spirits, of ancestors, like me. A dimension of Charlottes. Those women, invisible for too long, became ubiquitous. I giggled and the palm branches on the coast blew toward the inland. I sighed and the sand rolled away from me in layers. I flew and the sky opened to release bountiful gray clouds of rain that washed the arms and the legs and the hair and the face and the suffering of my former, unjust life. On a beach on the coast of where I had arrived, not far away from the village of Lai, an old, stained dress lay embedded in the sand, a collar lightly raised only when cued by the wind. At the end of the dry season, when the dust blows from the west across the Atlantic, soaring in tiny parts to the distant coast, I meet all of those parts at the edge of the ocean. The dust comes and I lift it to meet me somewhere high in the air. I blend into it — into Him.

"There you are, my darling," I whisper in Dey's ear. "There you are, my friend."

It was in this way — after arriving on that coast and finding ubiquity, my gift — that I existed. In the wind, my spirit roamed the trees and hills, roamed the minds of my new world.

Several rainy seasons after I arrived, while flexing in and out of a forest of trees that never ended, I blew past a lonely girl who sat upon a branch. From where the girl sat, she enjoyed a checkered view of the forest's head and petted the crown of a bulbul while humming. Every time I returned to the forest, I saw the girl wandering alone, in and out of a cave almost completely hidden by shrubs.

"I can see you, my darling," I cried out as the girl wandered for years in complete isolation. "I am with you, my friend."

Gbessa's head rested on the wind and she giggled when it blew this way. "Fengbe, keh kamba beh," she sang. I followed Gbessa

121

when she left the forest at eighteen years old and returned to Lai. I eavesdropped on Gbessa and Safua's first stare by the lake; I followed Gbessa during the journey of her final exile that resulted in her fainting on a coastal beach.

For eight days after leaving Lai, banished from the Vai kingdom for the suspected killing of the medicine man and woman and the Poro prince, Safua's son, Gbessa walked down the road of the new world. Her hair hung tangled in a maze down her back, imploring her — as her feet, and back, and eyes, and breasts were — to stop. She did not. She could not. She was starved. Yet hunger was not her torturer but her friend. A snake spit poison into her blood. Yet death was but a tease. These things that suffered others cowered in her presence. She had lived, and still, she was living.

"Awake." I floated rapidly around Gbessa's fainted body. But my affection was lost on the unconscious girl.

So I went to find the king who had banished her. Safua. And it was through me that Safua was reminded of Gbessa: her smell, her voice, and even strands of her hair came toward him in sailing breezes.

One morning while the Sande kissed Safua's face in the dark, a draft of wind fell into his house through the front window. An upheaval of voices grew outside and Safua's shoulders tensed. He looked as though he thought it was Gbessa. I ran into Safua's door several times, so loudly that he made the Sande unmount him. I fell against his front door once more. I encircled his house and entered through the cracks and windows.

"Whetin' happening?" the Sande asked, panicked, as the wind charged around her lappa.

Safua rushed outside. There in the village circle were three men with wrinkled white faces. Safua noticed their heads first, and how they all wore oversize crowns. Their bodies were almost all covered, even their feet, and upon noticing this some villagers pointed and beckoned Safua as he bravely drew near to them. Other villagers hid in their houses. A few boys ran to the elders' lodge to summon them. The Poro warriors hurried to Safua's side with pointed spears carved of the finest palm wood.

The strange men had heavy loads, from what Safua could see — in addition to the cloths that covered everything but their necks, faces, and hands in the searing sun, assorted metal articles and ropes hung from their waists.

"Look there!" a warrior said to Safua as he pointed to the odd metal objects by each of their sides. One of the white men touched his metal article and five men behind Safua drew their weapons.

A parched hand squeezed Safua's shoulder, and from behind him, three elders gestured to calm the nervous warriors.

"We will welcome them," Elder said to Safua.

"They look like curse man there," a warrior shouted.

"They not ours to curse. They other tribe, ehn you see?" Elder asked the restless men and convinced them to lower their weapons.

When the visitors saw this they took their crowns from their heads and bowed toward the villagers.

"Ehn you see?" Elder asked confidently.

The men walked straight to Safua in teetering, uncertain steps, and the items at their waists clattered loudly.

"Hello. Greetings to you," one of the men said and the others joined him in showing their teeth. He bowed again. "We bring gifts."

The villagers mumbled probable translations of what the man had said.

"Gifts," he said again and motioned for the bag that his associate carried on his back. The associate pulled the bag over his shoulder and dropped it into the village circle. The warriors raised their weapons again at the sound it made.

Safua extended his hand and the Poro men lowered their spears.

"Gifts. Treasures. Useful treasures for your people," the leader of the men continued as he knelt down in front of the bag. He pointed to Safua. "Your people," he said, "will like these things."

Safua lunged forward and pulled the man to his feet by the collar of his shirt. The man's associates pulled the metal articles from their waists and the Poro instantly drew their spears.

"No, no," the strange man said to his associates. "Guns down. Not now."

The associates put their weapons back into the straps of their belts. Safua's breathing lapsed only a narrow inch from the man's face.

"Open the bag," Safua yelled and the man's skin looked as if it were burning. A Poro man approached the bag with his weapon. Two feet away from it, he thrust his spear into it. The warrior lifted the spear and prodded the bag again, confirming that nothing was alive inside.

"No food inside," the warrior said and

stepped away from the bag. Safua released the man's collar and he stumbled to the ground. His associates remained nervous and shifted where they stood. The white man held his hand up to his companions as he caught his breath. He smiled again at Safua. "Gifts," he said. He crawled toward the bag and gazed at Safua for mercy.

"Can I?" he asked, gesturing toward the bag. Safua folded his arms across his chest and waited. While he stood still, willing now to see what trinkets these strange visitors had brought with them, the man opened the bag and retrieved a square wooden object. Elaborate cylindrical patterns striped the back of the gift. The man offered it first to Safua, whose arms remained folded across his chest. He then held it out to another warrior, who grabbed it from him. When the warrior turned the object around, he yelped.

"Piso!" he shouted. "Lake Piso!" The Poro men surrounded the object and took turns holding it. Villagers who were watching the encounter from their windows pointed toward the crowd of warriors. Safua looked toward them but did not join them.

"A mirror," the white man said and slowly stood. "It is a mirror." He approached Safua again. "Pee-so. Is that what you call mirror? Pee-so?" he asked.

Again, Safua remained silent. I crashed against his chest. What hysterical ancestors, he thought. Strange visitors. Shiny trinkets. Gifts. And all he had hoped to see was her.

Two elders approached the leader of the men and placed their arms around him in welcome. The strangers followed the elders into the village circle, smiling but still noticeably shaken. The Vai women were told to prepare rice and chickens for them to eat. The warriors put away their weapons and the wind wept and wailed. One of the Poro men approached Safua and handed him the mirror they had been given.

"Like you holding Lake Piso," he said in bewilderment. "Your head in there."

Safua took the object from the warrior. The glimpse of his face — his tense jaw and fuming eyes, his skin and the hair upon his head, the hair around his mouth — made his body cold. His breath grew rapid, and before he could speak, he dropped the mirror to the ground, breaking it in half. The warrior went to pick it up and Safua stopped him.

"No," Safua said. "Leave it."

In the village circle the visitors humored Elder around a fire pot. Slowly, other villagers approached the strange men as Safua and the other Poro warriors looked on. I blew viciously, so strong that one of the hats flew from one of the strange men's heads and tumbled through the village circle. The children chased it until it landed beside Safua's bare feet.

"Take care, my darling," I whined in Safua's ear. "Take care, take care, take care."

"What's that?" Henrietta Emerson asked before looking out her window.

Darlene shrugged. "Somebody just came, or somebody just gone," she answered.

The women quickly dressed as their room door swung open.

"Get ready and go into the left parlor," Edith said, leaning half of her body into their room. On her way there, Darlene's heart plunged when she heard the voices that sailed to and from the wainscots of the elaborate parlor. Mr. Harris and one other field hand were in the room with Master Emerson and a squirming and apparently irked Mrs. Emerson, the Missus, on the cream parlor sofa. Mr. Emerson brushed the rim of the hat in his left hand with the pair of gloves in his right hand. He wore dark breeches that were tucked neatly into riding boots. Although gray hairs made a home on his blond and handsome face and head, that day's ensemble made him look as brave and ripe as he had thirty years before. He knew this, so even in his apparent irritation there were moments when he stood with his chest outright.

The Missus's face was naturally a pinkish color, but something had deepened the hue that day in her cheeks and around her eyes. She fidgeted with a lace-rimmed handkerchief in her lap. Their daughter, Carlotta, was visiting the plantation from Georgia, where she had just moved after a marriage to a cotton farmer.

"I suppose you hear the ruckus down there," the Missus said with a stern bottom lip. She finally let the handkerchief rest in her lap. She examined the women and took a closer look at Darlene.

"My goodness, girl, what have you been eating?" the Missus asked Darlene, as though her staring created an awkwardness that only an insult could remedy. Carlotta laughed.

"You should see the ones in Georgia, Mama; they're much bigger," Carlotta interrupted. She loved mentioning Georgia to people, and especially to her mother, since Carlotta, too, now had a mansion and slaves, a plantation and parlor to call her own.

"My slaves are helpful," Carlotta added proudly. "I picked up a useful crochet method from one of my kitchen maids that I'll have to teach Edith so she can make you a new dining mat set."

The Missus nodded, uninterested in her daughter's appreciation for her slaves. Edith came into the room cradling a small baby.

"You bathe him good?" the Missus asked.

"Yes'm."

"Good, because he's going to the kitchen house with the girls. I trust you ladies will continue just as though nothing had changed," the Missus said.

"Yes, well, Henrietta, we found this baby in that empty shack this morning," Mr. Emerson said, noticeably calmer than his wife. "Think he was stole in the night."

"Stole?!" Henrietta asked, shocked. "From who, Master?"

"I tell you, sir, there ain't no way he could've gotten out of that shack," Mr. Harris interrupted.

"Sure he found a way." Mr. Emerson nodded.

"It does seem unlikely," the Missus said under her breath.

"Besides, what would a grown nigger want with a baby?" Carlotta asked.

"It makes no difference now." Mr. Emerson wiped the sweat from his head with a handkerchief. "The girls will take care of the baby while we check the Edwards and Millicent places to see if anybody heard anything. He couldn't have gotten farther than those plantations."

"But —"

"These boys are becoming crafty," Mr. Emerson said before Mr. Harris had an opportunity to object. "You men have to think quicker. Hear me?"

"Yes, sir," Mr. Harris said.

"Doesn't matter anyhow, he's dead now," he reminded them disapprovingly. "He was a strong one, even sick, and they don't make them like him anymore."

"Yes, sir," Mr. Harris repeated.

"Henrietta —" Mr. Emerson looked toward the woman.

The Missus interrupted: "Edward, that's a horrible suggestion. The poor woman barely has meat enough to cover her bones; she can't care for a baby. That child would be much too heavy to carry around while she's working."

"You did say you wanted to keep the baby alive, Daddy," Carlotta added with a willing smile, amused that she had woken up to such a riddling and peculiar morning.

"Darlene will have to care for the child,"

the Missus volunteered. "She's built for it. He is not to be out of your sight, you understand, girl?"

They looked at Darlene and waited for her to answer. Her eyes and dignity sank into the parlor floor. She bit down hard on her teeth.

"You hear that, Darlene?" Mr. Emerson asked her.

If she had looked at Mr. Emerson, then Darlene would have, in that moment, killed him. Darlene looked up at the Missus.

"Yes'm," she said.

They were everybody's secret. They had met many times before in empty rooms, though on a few occasions he passed by the opening of the kitchen house and whisked a confident finger across the front of her blouse in the daylight. Darlene did not remember her first time with him, nor did it seem to matter since the day she realized that she desired his puce-colored lips to know her. He was gentle and most kind to her. He reminded her every day that she was beautiful, the most beautiful, and that if they had been born into a different world, she would be his wife. She missed hearing these fantasies when he went away. Her love for him tormented her; his promises and musty smell resurrected themselves every morning in her meditations.

It was in the night that he came to her, as if claiming a prize he was certain he had already won. It was in the darkness that he always came to her until she began to expect him, and on the nights when he traveled or remained downstairs, she knew that she wanted him again. It began with a conversation. The door silently swung open to her room one night and there he was. And he did not force himself onto her like what Edith shared had happened to her again and again before she and the Missus arrived at Emerson; he came to talk. He sat on her bed as she trembled under her sheets, and he asked her about herself. Where she was from and how she was liking Emerson. He was drunk, and she was young. He told her she was beautiful, so beautiful, and other things she had never heard anyone say, much less a white man. And the first time, he was gentler than Darlene had expected, as if he had convinced himself that it was truly mutual, and that she wanted him as much as he desired her. When he returned from his trips he sometimes brought her gifts — scarves that she would fold and tuck away underneath her bosom as she worked. This time his return would be bittersweet.

"Don't know how you can come in here tonight," Darlene said as the door opened and Master Emerson's face was revealed as it rose from the shadows. The moonlight pressed in through the curtain of her window, uncovering the wetness of her green eyes. Mr. Emerson sauntered to where she lay and took his hat off, swaying slowly, smelling of whiskey. "You been back nearly a week and this is the first you see fit to come check on me? When you been drinking?" Darlene asked, trying to hold back the girlish smile that gathered beneath her cheeks. He shook his head and coughed loudly until he collapsed onto her.

She lit the candlestick on her floor to find Mr. Emerson fallen back on her pallet. In his daze he let his head hang so that his cheek grazed the smooth surface of Darlene's soft and welcoming cotton sheets. It was then that he noticed Henrietta lying across the room, twenty feet away, where a dresser once stood. Henrietta lay facing the wall and breathed as though she were in abysmal slumber; however, Darlene knew that her sister was not only awake, but was aware of everything that was being said and done.

"What is she doing in here?" Mr. Emerson asked, propping himself up on his elbows.

"The Missus put her in here, two or so weeks now," Darlene said. "She know. I told you — she got to."

Mr. Emerson looked bothered for only a brief second; he then fell back down and let out a bass grunt that escalated to a low and bizarre laugh.

"It's funny to you?" Darlene asked, arrested by his drunken response. Before she could speak, Mr. Emerson lunged toward her and pinned her on her back. He kissed her aggressively, but in a way that was also considerate — a way that made her glad that he was there and had come to her.

"Your lips taste like whiskey," Darlene whispered into his mouth when he released her.

"You a drinker now?" he asked.

He remained close to her face and grinned while raising his hand to caress her temple. Darlene touched his head and the stiff and silky ancient fibers inched through her jittering fingers. She fidgeted underneath him to free her sore breasts from the pressure of his torso.

"I did miss you," Mr. Emerson said as his eyes crossed and he fell into another one of Darlene's bottomless kisses until she gently pushed him away. He came back toward her face, but she pushed more forcefully this time. Her stomach turned.

"Ed, I need to tell you something," she said.

"We'll talk after," he responded and came toward her delicate neck. While kissing her he reached down and slid his hand up her leg and thigh. The tips of her breasts hardened in his embrace. It was then that the words fumed inside her until the heat of her confession interrupted their kiss.

"I didn't do it," she said quickly, just as he lifted his head to take a breath from the kiss. "Ed, I didn't — I couldn't do it," she said again and his lips hardened and he searched her eyes for truth to her claim. As his face moved to process what Darlene had just said, Mr. Emerson sat up, stoic and harshly silent.

"I couldn't do it," Darlene said again. "It's just the day I went down there for it is the day Nathan died." She sat up in the bed, taken aback by his reaction. "You remember Nathan?" Darlene continued. "Nearly white he was with the blue eyes. Nathan?" She became worried but forced herself to continue to an audience of his muteness. "I just got to thinking I could say the baby was Nathan's is all. I couldn't imagine killing nothing that came from you and me," she blurted, correcting herself. "Nobody know and nobody got to know. I could raise the baby in here and let everybody know me and Nathan had something — when Riette and I made trips down for dress measurements. I was waiting until I started to show before I —"

"You were wrong," Mr. Emerson said, sobered. Darlene winced, immediately realizing how bitter her decision had made the man whom she considered her lover, who just as quickly as she exhaled shifted into the role of her owner, her master, her purchaser.

"Do you realize what you've done?" Mr. Emerson asked as he grabbed his hat from behind him and hurled it at Darlene. She raised her hands to cover her terror-stricken face and the hat roughly slapped her forearms before falling to the floor.

"Ed —"

"Don't!" he shouted with such conviction that the candlestick beside her shook.

"How far along are you?" he asked.

"Some time over four months already," Darlene stuttered through high-pitched whimpers.

"Do you have any idea how selfish — ?" Mr. Emerson said, standing up. He retrieved his hat from the floor and, overcome with fury, he raised his arm back as far as he could and struck Darlene with the hat several times until her hands, which she used to cover her head from the blows, swelled and reddened. She could not catch her breath from crying. When he decided he was finished, too exhausted and drunk to fully chastise this woman, who he was certain was a deeply selfish and stupid woman, he placed the hat back on his head and secured it. When he reached the door he looked back at Darlene, and although he wanted to destroy her in that moment for her carelessness, while at the same time hoping she did not notice his own self-chastisement for succumbing to his carnal temptations, he said with a straight face and shoulders: "You will get rid of it. They will come for you tomorrow."

Darlene hurled her body toward the door, where he stood, to beg at his feet.

"Please, it's too late! Ed, it's too late!" she cried. The instant he closed the door, Henrietta threw her sheets off of her body and sprang to where her sister knelt crying. Darlene leaped toward the door, but Henrietta pulled her back into a rhythmic embrace. Darlene fought and Henrietta pulled her again.

"Come now, sister," she cried. Henrietta stroked her sister's hair and held her until the sun came.

On the following night, after Darlene blew out her candle, she lay fully dressed in the dark and waited to be arrested by her fate. Her eyes were still swollen from the tears of the previous night. Across from Darlene, Henrietta sat upright on her pallet with her hands folded across her lap. She was fully dressed and even kept her shoes on from that day.

"Just go with them, you hear?" Henrietta whispered. "It'll be over soon as you know it."

When the door of their room swung open, a whelp escaped Henrietta's mouth. Darlene remained on her pallet as Mr. Harris entered, followed by two field hands who kept their fingers near the whips and guns at their waists. He stood at the door and looked at her, but remained silent. Henrietta, who wanted to avoid the wrath of Mr. Harris's impatience at all costs, went across the room to Darlene's pallet and lifted her up.

"Come, sister," she said in Darlene's ear. Darlene rested her head on Henrietta's shoulder, hastening her pace when she became cognizant of Mr. Harris's irritability.

"Girls have to walk faster than that," Mr. Harris said abruptly.

Outside, the moon lurked behind a few drifting clouds. The smell of tobacco was particularly ripe as they trailed across the field toward the slave cabins.

When they reached the rows of shacks, abrupt mumbling was heard behind the thin entrapments of wood, and just as quickly muted. They approached the last shack on the row to the far right, before approaching the condemned one, which was riddled with worms and termites, and Mr. Harris knocked twice before opening the door. Inside, two older female slaves waited for Darlene and Henrietta in a room with several burning candles, a tall wooden table that hosted shiny knives and other utensils, and two buckets of water that permeated the air with steam. Neither of the women had recognizable faces, and Darlene was instantly conscious of Henrietta's sudden apprehension, a realization that caused the uproaring cry that she had been holding in to bellow out of her as she draped herself over her sister's shoulder.

"Sh, sh, sister," Henrietta said, patting her back while her heart rapidly beat and she was sure her sister could hear it.

"Put her on the table," Mr. Harris said finally.

"No, I'll take her —" Henrietta tried reasoning with him, but the field hands rushed toward her and grabbed Darlene's now-flailing hands. Darlene struggled to remain in her sister's embrace but the men pulled her away and dragged her into the shack.

"Stay in there. Make sure it's done," Mr. Harris said, closing the door behind the men. He roughly pushed Henrietta away from the dwelling when she tried to enter.

"Sister," Henrietta sniveled, approaching the door again but afraid to touch it.

Darlene could not hear her sister or any other sound of the night over her own shrieks and yelling. She felt her own spirit falling out of her and hardening into a corpse that drifted to the shack's corner to witness the senseless mutilation. The realness — the vehement sensation of a sudden inhuman and endless separation from herself — is what kept her alive that night. That, and when her eyes could no longer bring forth tears and all she had were her screams, she could see through a thin crack in the roof of the cabin where the moon peeked in to where she lay on her back.

Sleep, Ol' Ma Famatta coaxed from the still moon. *Sleep.*

In the following weeks, Darlene could not remember the details of what had happened to her. Neither Henrietta's recollections, nor several rigorous searches in her mind to find a memory of the pain that would assist her in mourning for her stolen child, could bring it back to her when the sun raised her.

"What do you mean by that?" Henrietta asked, leaning over her sister.

"I don't know," Darlene said, and realized she didn't remember.

"Fine, sister," Henrietta said then, accepting Darlene's pretend absentmindedness as her sister's only way of coping. "That's fine."

Her only glimpses were on the few mid-nights sometime later when Mr. Emerson visited Darlene again; nights he was so drunk that he was certain he would not be haunted by her scent or body on the following day; nights when the only words he could physically afford to mumble were "Harris didn't hurt you, did he? That night?"

Then, with pride as big as though his orders had somehow saved her life, he murmured, "He better not have. Told him not to," and collapsed beside her, intoxicated, unchanging.

That night when voices died to owls and their songs, June Dey shifted in the roll of sheets beside Darlene's pallet. At first Darlene thought the movement in the baby's sheets was caused by insomnia-induced illusions, but after listening closely, she realized that the baby was not only fidgeting but wide awake.

Darlene felt a large presence around her, as if all of Emerson's copious fields of ghosts had summoned and were gathered at her feet. She lit a candle. The baby lay by her side, gawking with soft and moist eyes at the beautiful and tragically unloved woman.

"What's wrong?" Henrietta asked.

"Nothing, Riette. Just checking on the baby," Darlene whispered. She looked at June Dey, who gazed at her with eyes hundreds of years behind his tiny brown face.

"What's wrong with him?" Henrietta asked.

"Seem he keeping himself company here in the dark is all. Go back to sleep," Darlene said.

Henrietta did not require coaxing, and she lay down as quickly as she had risen. Darlene took June Dey from where he lay. His hands were balled into two fists that he held right below his chin. June Dey looked up at the woman with serious and godlike eyes and tightly pinched lips. He examined Darlene's angelic face, while inside of her the emperor of all emotions appeared in her fingers and forearms, her feet and knees, before rapidly growing into a feeling so cold and stiffening and particularly wonderful that before she knew it she was crying. Darlene held his fist and lifted it to her smile. She touched the softness of his hand to the softness of her closed lips, over and over again, until her kisses became rapid and her smile was elevated to the laughter that she held captive.

Wanting then to be as close to the baby as possible, and also to provide him with the fullness that just his stillness in her arms provided her, Darlene unbuttoned her nightgown and pulled her tan and plump breast from against her chest. She guided the end of the smooth appendage to June Dey's mouth until he grasped it and sucked, while finally and slowly closing his eyes. Her legs twitched.

"Ain't nothing in there for you anyhow," Darlene whispered to him. She was sorry for her emptiness and grateful that even after minutes passed, his mouth remained wrapped around her.

"They ain't give you a name, did they?" she asked as he continued to nurse with his eyes closed. "What's your name, child?" Darlene ran the back of her hand against June Dey's cheek. The light flickered and cracked on her nightstand.

"No answer?" Darlene giggled. "Too busy feeding on air. I ain't got nothing for you in there."

The baby continued to nurse.

"Moses. Moses is what I'll call you. You like that?" she asked.

"Moses," she said again. Darlene, now exhausted with happiness and pleasure, tried pulling the baby away from her nipple. His mouth remained tightly closed, so she grabbed her breast and attempted to pull it out of his mouth.

"Come now," she encouraged him. "No use in giving yourself gas. There's nothing —"

Before Darlene could finish her sentence, an off-white liquid escaped the corner of June Dey's mouth and streamed down his cheek.

"Oh my," she said. "Riette! Riette, wake up!"

Henrietta, alarmed at the beckoning, quickly sat up.

"What's wrong, sister?" she asked. She rushed to Darlene's side, startled to see her sister's naked breast in the baby's mouth.

"I'm nursing him and milk coming out. Milk coming out of me."

"What you doing nursing him? That can't be."

"I know, but look, sister." Darlene pulled her breast out of June Dey's mouth as he fed, and sure enough, milk surrounded the nipple and dripped down her skin and stomach.

"Oh my God. You ain't —"

"No, ain't no way." Her hands shook. Henrietta wiped some of the liquid off of Darlene's breast and pressed it to her tongue.

"Well, ain't that something," Henrietta said, not sure whether or not she was dreaming after the taste of bitterness filled her mouth. She did this once more: wiped the white liquid from her sister's skin and

148

tasted it. Henrietta shook her head in disbelief.

"Ain't that something," Henrietta said again.

"Riette, how can that be?" Darlene asked, stimulated by her coupled fear and enthusiasm.

"The body thinks on its own sometimes is all I imagine," Henrietta answered. "Don't worry. Just feed him." Henrietta rubbed her sister's back, while also confused and worried about Darlene's strange fortune.

Darlene led June Dey's mouth back to the milk.

"Who are you, young man?" Henrietta asked the baby, smiling curiously as she leaned in toward him. "Who sent you here?"

Not only did Master Emerson neglect to follow through on checking the surrounding plantations to inquire about the mysterious baby, but on the following day he set off on another trip to Georgia. Since he did not leave specific orders for Mr. Harris to attend to the matter, Mr. Harris chose not to address the embarrassing ordeal. June Dey stayed with Darlene and was allowed in the kitchen with the women, in a large pot lined with sheets.

The baby did not cry.

It was something that made Darlene love him more and spend all of her spare moments between her daily chores at his side or nursing him in hiding so that no one would suspect that she had been pregnant. Several weeks after June Dey's arrival, while Darlene worked in the kitchen house, the Missus entered with a doctor. They went toward June Dey and Darlene placed the knife on the counter and made her way toward him also.

"What are you doing? Go back to work," the Missus said when she noticed Darlene was following them.

"No, we need the girl," the doctor said. Darlene stood still.

"Well, come on!" the Missus demanded. Darlene met them in the parlor.

"This is the baby?" the doctor asked, raising him from the pot.

"Yes," the Missus answered quickly.

"I can tell you just by looking the baby has too much color to be hers," the doctor said.

"How can you be sure?" the Missus asked. The doctor picked June Dey up from the pot.

"Come here, girl," he said and held June Dey's face beside Darlene's.

"This baby doesn't share her features," he

said, putting June Dey back in the pot.

"You can never know. They're different than we are," the Missus insisted.

"Mulatto babies tend to have fair skin," the doctor protested.

"You can never know," the Missus said proudly, embarrassed.

When the doctor left the house, the Missus went back into the kitchen.

"Come here, girl," she said to Darlene. Darlene followed her again out of the kitchen house and into the parlor. The Missus sat down.

"Turn around," she said.

"Yes, Missus?" Darlene asked, stuttering at the strange and sudden request.

"Turn around," the Missus said again.

Darlene made a full rotation.

"You, girl, are a whore," the Missus said finally and exhaled deeply as if she had been waiting for some time since her husband's last departure to share her disdain for the beautiful slave. "I know that baby is yours, and I'm not sure what my husband had to do with helping you keep it, but I want you to know that God will one day punish you for your sins."

Darlene remained silent. She cared only about what would happen to the baby boy and who would nurse him if she were hurt

151

too badly.

"You and the rest of you nigger whores are the reason your people are cursed and always will be," the Missus continued.

Darlene kept her eyes on the woven carpet at her feet.

"You have no shame sleeping with married men, do you? No conscience?"

The Missus's voice cracked. She held her hand over her mouth and eventually, as Darlene stood with her eyes facing the ground below her, released a sound like a whimpering dog.

"Get out," the Missus said, as if finally succumbing to her sorrow.

On a normal day, following such a confrontation, Darlene would have found the closest mirror. There was one on the wall near the pantry, and another on the wall near the entry to the kitchen house. In that mirror she would have found her face, and she would have repeated the things that the Missus had said — that God did not love her, and could never love a woman as ugly and no-good as her. But then came this baby, this gift of a baby, this answer. That day, she passed the mirror and shuddered, but none of those words came forth. Instead, for the first time, she had something like a smile.

When June Dey turned five Mr. Emerson left again for an extended period, this time to Europe. He had been gone for only a few days when another doctor visited the house, doing the same things as the previous doctors, pressing June Dey's face beside Darlene's face, shaking his head toward the Missus in assurance that the young boy was not the love child of Master Emerson. When the Missus finally relented, the doctor left, and the Missus called Darlene back into the parlor for questioning. At times Darlene returned to the kitchen with a bruised face or torn dress. It was June Dey who saved Darlene from this abuse, so that even in her humiliation and sorrow she dwelled on the memory of his face. He woke up with her, ate with her, and slept with her on the pallet of the kitchen house attic floor. He became the dishwasher when he was six, and stood on a tall stool every day, looking out onto the tobacco field and past the plantation to a green and waiting world. June Dey knew, even in his childhood, of Darlene's beauty, since men who delivered fruit from the Emerson orchards would stutter and shake when they entered the kitchen and saw her. Once in a while men brought him an apple and made sure Darlene saw them give it to him. He inhabited her voice and laughter, and by the time he was ten he began to refuse the apples and even ignored the infrequent visitors, for fear that Darlene would begin to love another man more than she loved him.

One of the men once invited June Dey outside to collect an extra bag of apples to take inside for his mother. He paused at first and examined the man with suspicion.

"Go ahead, Moses," Darlene reassured him from the stove. "It's right outside."

June Dey followed the man out of the kitchen house through the back hallway. Near the tulip garden, the handles of a rusty wheelbarrow filled with apples were held by a pair of identical twins, boys a few years older than June Dey who were poorly kept. One of them had a husky body and a broad back; the other boy's body was lean with hunching shoulders. Their faces, however, were exactly the same size and shape. June Dey, who had not been socialized to interact with the other boys of the plantation, stopped when he noticed the twins.

"Come along," the man said as they approached the wheelbarrow.

The lean twin had either mud or dried

spit on the side of his face and June Dey winced at the sight of what looked like blood on the sleeve of the boy's old shirt.

"You scared, lil' girl?" the husky twin asked June Dey. His brother laughed and the boys carefully scanned June Dey from head to toe: his shoes and shirt and trousers, his hair and nose and clean brown face.

"You know if your Ma got room for two bags?" the man asked, totally occupied with how he could maximize his opportunity to please Darlene.

"No, sir," June Dey answered.

"Wait here, I go see," the man said, and ran to the back door of the kitchen house.

"Lil' girl, come here," the husky twin said once the man had disappeared. He left the wheelbarrow and took a few steps toward June Dey with clenched fists.

"You ain't hear?" The lean twin charged from behind before joining his brother to confront June Dey.

June Dey stepped back and shook his head.

"No?" the lean twin shouted so that only the three members of the prospective duel could hear. "No, you ain't hear or no, you too good to come here? White nigger what you is?"

June Dey thought to run quickly to his

155

mother but energy invaded his limbs in a way that made it impossible for him to retreat. He grew angry where he stood and, matching the shape of the husky boy's hands, he clenched his fists as well. The twins advanced toward him, realizing how much taller they were than him and were greatly empowered by it. June Dey remained calm despite the rage that filled him. It was not until the husky twin pushed June's head that he became surprised at the emotion that overtook him. June Dey grabbed the boy's fist and, without exerting any energy in his grip, the boy collapsed to the ground and squealed for mercy. His brother, obviously surprised at his twin's defeat, retaliated by quickly raising his fists to fight June Dey, who seized the lean twin's wrists and used them as handles to push the boy. June Dey threw him several feet away. The boy, in pain, massaged his wrists as he writhed on the ground. At the sight of the two defeated boys on the lawn, June Dey ran back into the kitchen house to Darlene, who was still being pestered by the older man.

"What's wrong?" Darlene asked him.

"Nothing, Mama," June Dey mumbled and joined Henrietta near the stove.

"Mighty hot today anyhow," the man said, laughing. "Well, I'll be going." He nodded toward Darlene and the other women once more. "You come with me to get the apples for your Ma?" the man asked June Dey, who shook his head before holding on to Henrietta's dress.

When the man reentered the kitchen with the two bags of apples, he looked over to where June Dey stood. He would have informed Darlene of the boy's odd deed and suggested a punishment, but as she smiled at him he did not want to risk upsetting her. So he kept it to himself, although from that day, whenever he visited the kitchen house he always looked toward June Dey as though the space where he stood was a difficult riddle or question that he greatly troubled himself to solve.

June Dey had been fifteen for several months when news arrived at the mansion that Master Emerson had fallen ill in Texas at the estate of one of his father's former clients. Convinced by his rising fever and chills that he was on his deathbed, Mr. Emerson wrote the letter home that finally ordered his property managers to purchase a neighboring one thousand acres. Since Mr. Emerson could not afford to purchase more labor (and had been financially incapable of purchasing for a long time), the remaining three hundred or so male slaves were to be separated by age and given field assignments accordingly. The older and stronger men would remain on the tobacco farm to tend the crop while the younger boys would begin working on the cotton farm, tearing out grass and weeds that would compete with the cotton crop for nutrients. Because of the shortage of help and the rate at which the crops would need to be cultivated to compete with neighboring planters and farms, boys as young as five and six were being called to the new land to help.

When Darlene heard of the recruitment of young male slaves for the new cotton farm, she worried that June Dey would be forced to leave the house, a prospect that made her burst into contained sobs several times during the day. When she did this, June Dey adopted the burden of her chores and finished in half the time they took Darlene. He then assumed the responsibilities of all of the other kitchen slaves and encouraged them to rest. She was too anxious on those few occasions, picking up what it sometimes took four grown and seasoned women to carry, to notice his speed, accuracy, and abnormal strength.

While it was obvious to most at that point that Mr. Emerson's neglect and infidelities had driven the Missus insane, she carried on in public as if she were healthy. When she felt like leaving her room or the parlor, the Missus wandered the mansion having mumbled conversations with herself. Even the way in which she walked had changed — no longer the dainty, short steps that she had trained her daughter so well in, but long and quick strides with her arms swinging high by her sides. When visiting, Carlotta dismissed her mother's behavior as caused by passing head colds and fevers. However, too overwhelmed to deal on her own with the bizarre turn of the Missus's behavior, Carlotta made a habit of creating excuses as to why she could not visit the Emerson plantation when requested, but would join her mother as soon as her father returned to town.

June Dey, tall and dark with sunken eyes and a sharp jawline, looked less and less like Darlene as he grew older. He was the best-kept male slave that the Missus had encountered, since Darlene had made an effort since his childhood to manner him and make him presentable enough for the house so that he would not get sent to the field. However, the Missus thoroughly enjoyed reminding him of his "miserable darkness" and "gorilla-like cheeks" while comparing his face to Darlene's. She would have sent him to live in the slave quarters as soon as he was able to walk, but seeing him move about the space while helping the women with chores, or the grace with which he served at her dinner parties, and later lifting crates and bags that were sometimes twice his size, she took odd pleasure in knowing there was a man, any man, in her close vicinity.

On an orange afternoon in spring when neither the wind nor the shouting of chastised slaves disquieted the plantation, the Missus entered the kitchen silently from the back door of the mansion. June Dey glanced over at Darlene, whom he could tell suffered greatly in moments like this — moments plagued by uncertainty.

"This house is mine. I want you out. Go outside now — all of you," the Missus said.

"Something wrong, Missus?" Edith asked after sucking back in the breath that had escaped her.

The Missus glanced at Edith but ignored the inquiry. At that moment Mr. Harris entered the kitchen house from behind the Missus with two field hands. He tried to hide his own anger and frustration, but was exposed after walking into the room when he did not, could not look at the Missus. Both of his dirt-stained hands were at his waist — one hand on his belt and one on the cowhide strapped tightly to his pants.

"Henrietta, Darlene, Nelsie; you all been sold to the Millicent place," he said, shaking his head in disapproval while still refusing to look at the Missus. "The rest of you go work on the new farm. The boy included.

They'll divide you into rooms when you get down there."

"Missus, who'll take care of you now?" Edith asked as she took a step toward her.

"Edith, get your things and go," she snapped.

"But Missus," Edith said and began to cry. "I was for you, Missus. I came with you. I take care of you and Carlotta. Take care of this house and kitchen for you."

The Missus turned her face from Edith toward the window, blushing and agitated. Edith had seen herself as the Missus's keeper since moving to the plantation with her, shortly after her marriage to Edward.

"Missus, you ain't well," Edith whimpered. "Let me stay in here and take care of you. I ain't got no business anywhere without you."

"Need as much help down there they can get," Mr. Harris interrupted, aware that reasoning with the irrational Mrs. Emerson at this point was no use.

Edith searched the Missus's eyes, the expression of which was diametrically opposed to the way the old woman had looked on the day of their arrival at the plantation, when she could not finish her cup of tea without gushing about her new husband. As Edith cried with grief, she saw that the Missus's eyes grew moist as well, and it was obvious to everyone who could see her, even in the betrayal, what rose up in the Missus's heart. Perhaps she had remembered the same day, the same moment, when she arrived with only Edith in tow. Perhaps she remembered the dizzying smell of tobacco leaves after exiting her carriage and the blue dress she burdened Edith to fasten tightly at the waist while they prepared for the trip.

"Just go," the Missus said, firmly convinced that total quiet and solitude would be her only salvation from her husband's idiocy and the financial blunders that would have the plantation bankrupt in a year's time. She sped through the kitchen toward the front parlor.

"Get your things," Mr. Harris said.

He then turned to leave the kitchen, and motioned to June Dey so he would follow him out and onto the new field. The women, all weeping now, scrambled to gather their belongings from the various rooms atop or surrounding the kitchen house. Darlene composed herself and took June Dey's shirt by the collar. Now at eye level, she looked directly into his face.

"Do what they say, you hear? I try to find you if they let me follow on errands, you hear?" she said and held his face between

163

her hands.

June Dey looked into the woman's face, and although he fully understood what her departure from Emerson that day meant, he was not worried for himself, but greatly stressed at how he would protect Darlene from so far away.

"Come along!" one of the field hands yelled impatiently from the hallway.

June Dey hugged Darlene and allowed her to cover his face with kisses. She then pushed him toward Henrietta, whom he also embraced and thanked in the silence for her kind spirit and comfort.

The Missus reentered the room and took deliberate steps toward Darlene. Darlene could feel the woman's anger and sorrow from where she stood; however, it was impossible for her to feel ashamed. She had dealt with the Missus's petty jealousies with grace, she thought, since the sin of her infidelity had been fully paid for on the night that her unborn child was stolen from her. This whole time she had borne the burden of all of Master Emerson's misdeeds, when what Master Emerson had done to her was because of his inability to face his wife with an illegitimate child. And that death, which she had lived with and somehow found the strength to lay to rest during the years she'd had with June Dey, now resurfaced and floated around her, raising the tiniest hairs on her neck, burning her cheeks and tongue.

"This is your fault," the Missus said to her with an unbreaking voice, though the tears continued coming. "You are a horrible woman and your sins will haunt you."

Darlene replayed in her mind the countless days she had stood before Mrs. Emerson. The memories that were shameful to Darlene — the nights she had cried over loving Mr. Emerson as she once did — emerged only in the presence of this miserable old woman.

So Darlene slapped the Missus as hard as she could across the face. Before Mrs. Emerson had a chance to respond further than raising her hand to rub her cheek, an incensed and heaving Darlene clenched a fistful of the Missus's hair with one hand while using the other to slap and scratch her face. The kitchen slaves rushed to break up the fight. Darlene's eyes became red with rage as June Dey grabbed her by the waist and pulled, only Mrs. Emerson's head was pulled along with her since Darlene would not let it go. The Missus screamed wildly, and it did not take long for Mr. Harris and his helpers to run back into the kitchen from outside.

"Take them all out to the cart," Mr. Harris yelled upon seeing the scuffle. "Tie them up."

Mr. Harris went to the Missus as the men rushed toward Darlene. When they finally managed to loosen her fingers from their grip on Mrs. Emerson's now-tussled and tangled hair, Mr. Harris slapped Darlene across her face. June Dey lunged toward him but was restrained by one of the helpers. June Dey realized then, after the man grabbed him from behind, that he could easily have escaped the hold, but out of pure surprise at what was happening and concern about what harm his actions would cause Darlene, he remained stiff in the helper's grasp as he was led to the cart. The Missus grunted as she straightened her hair and used her sleeve to wipe her bleeding face.

"Whip her to death!" she yelled as she followed Mr. Harris, spitting and kicking and still fighting Darlene while he carried her out. When the disorganized party reached the yard, a few helpers approached them, running from the tobacco field. Henrietta and Nelsie were thrown into the cart like logs of wood. Edith exited the house and stood with the few other kitchen maids, patiently waiting to be taken to the field and careful not to vex Mrs. Emerson or Mr. Harris any further. Mr. Harris used a rope inside the cart to tie Darlene's wrists; he then tied the end of the rope to a nail that protruded from the cart. Darlene, still incensed and insensible, pulled on the rope in hopes that it would loosen.

"Stop, sister," Henrietta warned from the corner of the cart as she held Nelsie. Darlene refused to acquiesce. Mr. Harris untied the cowhide whip from his waist.

"Whip her! Whip her to death!" the Missus shouted.

Mr. Harris released the whip onto Darlene's back. Darlene howled. It tore through her skin and blood stained her blouse. Every collision of the whip with her back awakened a new agony in her.

Seeing this from where he stood, restrained by two men, June Dey was transformed into an enraged brute in both his body and soul. Unable to contain himself any longer, June Dey pulled his arms away from the two men. When his hands were free, he punched one of the men so hard that the man's nose sprayed blood, and several teeth flew from his twisted mouth. He lifted the other man up into the air with ease and threw him some twenty feet away from them. Another man ran toward June

Dey, who, as he ran, lifted his leg and kicked the helper in the stomach, so hard that the man flew into the back of the cart and the afternoon echoed with his breaking bones as he fell to the ground. All astonished eyes shifted to June Dey's bulging muscles and tightly closed fists. Compelled and driven by his own strength, June Dey raised his fists to the other seven or so men who now surrounded him.

"Take out your hides!" Mr. Harris said, leaving Darlene and joining the other men around June Dey. While the two helpers closest to him untied their whips, June Dey crashed his iron fist into their jaws and noses. They stumbled and fell, covering their bleeding faces as they squirmed on the ground. A whip flew in his direction and June Dey caught it. He pulled the cowhide as the man holding the handle shuffled unwillingly toward him. He grabbed the whip with both hands and choked the man until his legs became weak and he hung in June Dey's grasp. June Dey then picked the man up and swung his body around so that his flailing legs kicked two others to the ground. The remaining men surrounded him and hesitated, afraid they would suffer the same fate as the mewling helpers spread across the lawn. June Dey's torn shirt hung from his back, exposing the veins that lined the skin of his muscular arms.

Mr. Harris shook his head in disbelief. Except for the men on the ground, everyone surrounding him had become quiet, including the Missus, who stared at June Dey in bewilderment. All of the overseer's helpers lay on the ground, confounded by the fifteen-year-old's strength. June Dey made his way to Darlene. She was on her knees in the cart with a sweaty face and bloodied back and looked at him adoringly as he approached her and untied the rope from her wrists. June Dey was unsure of what to do with her weak body. Before his thoughts could proceed any further, the cowhide whip flew into his back. The whip came again and crashed into him twice more. Then another whip joined in as Mr. Harris motioned to one of the helpers to assist him. It was not the fact that two men were whipping him that surprised him, nor the fact that the strikes caused him no pain — it was the look of shock on Mrs. Emerson's face and those of the kitchen maids on the lawn. "His back ain't scarring," Edith said, raising her hand to cover her mouth.

Mr. Harris and the helper continued to whip June Dey, although no blood escaped from his back. He did not even wince at the attack. June Dey turned around slowly as Mr. Harris now trembled in his presence. The whips fell onto June Dey's chest now, but as on his back, his skin did not break. Instead, each time he was struck his strength grew. Each time they whipped him, he became more infuriated and they sensed it in him. While beating him, the helper with the other whip looked down at his trousers as his bladder weakened and poured onto his clothes and shoes. Embarrassed and pale with trepidation, he lifted his gun from his belt. The maids screamed at the sight of the gun and the helper immediately fired it. The bullet soared toward June Dey and Darlene. It flew toward his chest. They expected that it would kill him on impact, expected that this would be his end and the boy would go from them as mysteriously as he had come.

But the bullet, as if repelled by his skin, fell to the ground. The slight puncture where the bullet would have made its permanent hole quickly healed in their sight, and the helper dropped the gun and ran away from them like a bullied child. The Missus, thoroughly flabbergasted and driven further into her insanity, fainted where she stood. Edith rushed to her and fanned her face, also unsure whether what she had just witnessed was real.

Wasting no time, June Dey took Darlene from the cart and cradled her weak body in his arms.

"Run!" Henrietta shouted as she noticed other men, white and black alike, approaching from the field. "Run, Moses!" she cried.

June Dey heeded Henrietta's warning with regret that he had to leave.

"Save her!" Henrietta yelled at him.

Darlene wrapped her arms around his neck and rested her head on his shoulder.

"Go, baby," she whispered to him.

"Go now! Go!" Henrietta shouted. The number of men who came toward him grew in the distance. June Dey remembered the stories Darlene once told him of the boys who killed giants, defeated lions for their people; the story of his namesake, who led slaves through water with mere words; the story of the man who found himself in the stomach of a beast, and still survived and fulfilled his destiny; the story of Dey the slave, who came and went from Emerson without ever saying a word, but left his legacy on all of their lips — the possibility of rebellion and true freedom in all their hearts. All were mere men. All were powerless but died with raised fists.

June Dey ran.

He ran around the side of the mansion on

171

the road where the horse cart had come and sped toward the main entrance of the plantation. He heard many men behind him, on foot and on horses. He was unsure how far he would or could go. Darlene whimpered in his arms as he ran, encouraging his passage with the slow rhythm of her breath. Bullets sounded behind them as recovered helpers chased him, while others ran in the other direction to spread the story of what they had just seen. The ground shook beneath him and a sudden blast of wind assembled on the road around him, following and running alongside the dangerously strong boy.

"Go now, my darling," I wailed. "Run with me, my son."

Enlivened by the unexpected reinforcement of the earth around him, his legs shifted rapidly in the direction of the sun. June Dey ran with great intent as the bullets, as the first had, bounced off of his skin and fell to the ground below him. They flew around him, breaking the afternoon like deafening cannonballs in the apogee of battle. He neither understood this strange power nor was sure that it was something he even wanted. He had never seen horror such as that which had been painted on the faces of those he had just run from. And throughout his sprint from the Emerson plantation, it was his awareness of this strength, and his lack of imagination about what he would do with it or where it would lead him, that made him suddenly conscious of Darlene as her grip around his neck relaxed. He was running too quickly to stop and the wind would not have let him if he'd tried. The bullets behind him had become fewer and fewer the farther he ran. He refused to halt the movement of his legs. Instead, he listened closely for Darlene's breathing and her soft whimpers. He squeezed her body for a response, but none came.

"Ma." June Dey exhaled. Nothing came from Darlene.

"Ma," he said again as he ran. Again nothing. Her hand suddenly fell from around his neck. Darlene's head followed and her neck and torso hung in his arms. June Dey felt liquid accumulate in his palms and finally looked down at Darlene. Blood covered her lifeless face. This was his mother. This was his poetic love, whose fallen shadow broke his spirit as he sprinted with the wind. She was gone. Darlene swayed lightly in the spring air, still beautiful even after the bullets that could not penetrate June Dey had burrowed into her skin. Everything that had just happened, everything he felt in that moment, in the dimming light of the escaping sun, was the very thing, the only thing he wanted to protect her from. Conviction gripped his heart as he escaped down the road with no end in sight. He was not afraid. After all, if he was not dreaming, if it had all been real, then fear was no challenge; man was no fair opponent.

His head throbbed. He closed his eyes and saw Darlene's face and body again. Blood flowed from her open wounds and into the river. It was with great difficulty that he finally let her go, released her to the roving tide and watched as she disappeared downstream. Sure that Mr. Harris would find dozens of other patrols to come find him, June Dey climbed a tree and hid between a web of branches that afternoon to give himself time to devise a plan. He looked down at his chest and there were no scars left by the bullets that had attempted to rupture his skin. June Dey reached his hand behind his shoulder to feel his back, and it was the same as the day before. No blood. Scarred by no whip. Soon it was dark, and he heard footsteps below him. They grew by the minute. Armies of patrols hunted him. June Dey could hear a pack of dogs not too far in the distance. At first he estimated the number at four or five, but quickly altered his estimation as the barks drew nearer, integrated with the beating hooves of horses. In the midst of the crunching leaves and the barking, he heard Mr. Harris's voice.

"Know you around here, boy," Mr. Harris shouted. A bird flew from a nearby branch and Mr. Harris shot in its direction, causing the other patrols to wince and cover their heads.

"Your whore mother with you too?" Mr. Harris continued.

June Dey's jaw tightened. He saw Mr. Harris from above, tiptoeing through the woods with an expression so foreign that June Dey squinted to make sure it was him: fear.

"That's right, your whore mother," Mr. Harris continued. The sound of the word in reference to Darlene hardened June's body. "You know everybody's had her, right? Bitch nearly trapped Master Emerson with her lies but we stopped it before she got too far. Took that baby right out. She was screaming today — it reminded me of that night."

Without another thought, June Dey jumped from the branch.

"Take care, my darling," I whispered.

As soon as his feet touched the ground, the dogs came toward him through the bushes, eyes red, and he smelled their hunger. Teeth, fiery eyes, and extended paws erupted from the twilight. June Dey grabbed a dog by its jaw and forced its mouth open with his bare hands. He flung the animal's body and grabbed another by its tail, breaking its back against a tree. Three were at his heels and legs — they bit and gnawed until June Dey kicked and pushed them, and the dogs yelped as they flew off him and into nearby bushes. He did this for nearly ten minutes, punching and kicking, throwing them into the midnight air until the remaining animals became afraid and ran from him.

The guns came next. This time he would remain still. Those woods were just as much his as anyone else's — his home, his protector, his mask in the night. He would stand against them. If death was his destiny then at least he could return to Darlene's side and protect her in the heavens.

The bullets piloted through the trees and bushes until they found his waiting body. They came toward him with vengeance and met his brown skin; however, as at Emerson those days before, the bullets fell to the ground after touching his skin. He had not been killed; he saw the shots fall from his skin like electric sparks with lightning shadows. The bullets came toward him. He had done nothing wrong and the bullets sought to touch his skin. Many of them came. All of them fell from him, unable to penetrate. Enlivened, June Dey screamed into the night. It echoed and echoed and echoed. His voice rang throughout the woods to the nearby farms and countryside. When the bullets stopped, the patrols peered through the darkness for the result of what they had done.

"He dead?" one asked as smoke rose from the mouth of his rifle. Another gasped at the sight of June Dey's still-standing body and heaving chest.

"Look!" he shouted, pointing toward the boy.

He was not dead. He had just been born.

■ ■ ■ ■

Norman Aragon

■ ■ ■ ■

When Callum Aragon landed on the coast of Jamaica, his assigned tour guides (Irish sailors who had settled along the coast and knew the island very well) pointed toward the mountains, where hills of trees mostly covered the little he could see of one of the remaining Maroon settlements in the distance. A popular British scholar, Callum had been sent to Jamaica to research and record the Maroons' historical revolts against their European masters through testimonies of those who inhabited the villages of Accompong Maroons — the single remaining collective of escaped Africans in Jamaica after the First and Second Maroon Wars. The guides showed him a house on stilts facing the beach that would be his, one with blue shutters and a wooden door, and asked him what he would need to get started.

Callum requested that his trunks of books

be put inside the house, and that someone go with him to the mountains immediately to begin his observation of a Maroon settlement.

"It's quite dangerous right now," an Irish sailor, whom the others called Ryan, said, wiping the dust from Callum's book trunk on his slops. Callum stared at the stain in disgust. Ryan was slim with dark and sunburned skin that was in sharp contrast to his blond hair and crystal-blue eyes. The sound of the waves against the eastern shoreline shouted through Callum's opened door. "Since the superintendent left there," Ryan added. Another sailor nodded in agreement, and pointed toward Callum's carriage and another trunk of books; a port slave, a young boy in his teenage years wearing linen shorts and a stained cloth wrapped tightly around his head to absorb sweat, ran to the carriage for the trunk.

Callum had heard about the recent departure of the Accompong Maroon superintendent, a British man who, like most men assigned to Maroon towns, was unprepared for what he had agreed to — the overseeing of a group of people who had rebelled against the necessity of having an overseer. The rumors on the ship suggested that after he illegally beat a Maroon child for trespassing on his designated property in their mountain town, they had terrorized him by leaving dead animals at his doorstep, burning his gardens, and sneaking into his home to fill his trunks of clothes with human excrement. The superintendent eventually left the island; his final task was to supervise the deportation of ungovernable Maroons to the British colony of Freetown in West Africa, and afterward he returned to Britain and swore never to set foot on Jamaican ground again. They had found no replacement for him.

"I believe the people have been given their freedom and land. What danger could come from such generosity?" Callum asked. He strolled through the two rooms of the quaint house — a main room containing a stove, bookshelves, and a desk and chair, and a small corner room with a bed and no door.

"They're in festival. Celebrating, sir," Ryan said.

"All of them? Aren't there dozens of settlements?" Callum asked.

"Yes, sir. All of them."

"And so we will join the ingrates," Callum said.

"No, sir," Ryan answered. "It'll be no good. They burn peppers to eat with their meat and it's unbearable to breathe in, sir."

"Peppers?" Callum asked. "Aren't they expecting us?"

The sailors glanced at one another briefly, and Callum looked from one face to another for his answer.

"One of the Accompong towns," another sailor said. "But it's no telling, sir. Talk about independence since the trade outlaw making everyone paranoid, sir. One day they welcome you and offer you a daughter and the next they run you off with a rifle."

"Oh dear," Callum said. He feigned a smile, to which the sailors responded with an equally unbelievable gesture of cordiality. "How many are there again?"

"No telling, sir," Ryan answered. "You know most were taken after the war to the British colony in West Africa. Ones who stayed, there's no way to keep track of. Nothing more to do up there but hunt and fuck, so babies are plenty, sir." He laughed heartily. The port slave returned with Callum's trunk, and just as soon as he set it down beside the desk, he hurried out of the room to wait outside.

"Well then," Callum said, noticeably uncomfortable. "I'd like to begin as soon as possible."

"How soon, sir?" Ryan asked.

"Today," Callum said.

184

Reluctantly, the lead sailor organized a caravan of three other seamen, who led Callum up the mountains toward the settlement. They were accompanied by two port slaves, young men who used machetes to clear a path through the thick bamboo and thorn-ridden shrubs of the forest that lay below the mountains. Callum Aragon fell and stumbled continually, but every time he stood back up, cursing loudly, he opened up a map as if it would actually assist him in navigating the vast forest. They traveled until a consistent thumping rhythm and synchronized moans finally buzzed in their ears.

"I say we stop here, sir," Ryan said, out of breath.

"Why would we stop here? I can't see a thing," Callum said.

"Mr. Aragon, you won't be able to see through the smoke, or breathe through the spices," he insisted, coughing. "Get some rest, and if you insist, we'll start again when the smell simmers down."

Callum folded the map into a square, half the size of his face, and headed farther into the mountains.

"Mr. Aragon, sir," the sailors protested, almost at once.

"No, no. I can go farther," Callum insisted.

Barely ten minutes away from the group, Callum coughed into his handkerchief from the storm of spices. Tears and an unmoving maze of forest trees blurred his vision. He took several more steps, but he trembled at the thought of what the woodland creatures would do to him if they discovered him alone, and so he returned to the sailors.

"When do you suggest we come back?" he asked them, sitting on a large tree stump to catch his breath.

"In two or three weeks," a sailor answered. "Take time and get adjusted. We'll return then."

Callum Aragon returned to his house on the beach and arranged his books while mumbling his regrets. At night he found that mosquitoes thrived in the ocean mist and humidity. The mosquitoes remained on one's skin after biting, and dug so far into his flesh that it took him a quarter of an hour to detach them from his body. He closed his bedroom window after pulling the fourth mosquito off his arm, and the house was then instantly thick with humidity, so Callum Aragon stripped to his bare pink bottom and lay on the floor to sleep.

Callum lingered around the house, reading and anxiously unpacking. The moon would replace the sun for two nights before Ryan returned, this time accompanied by a slave woman.

"What do you want?" Callum asked, still irritated by their previous endeavor on the mountain.

"Her name is Nanni, Mr. Aragon," Ryan said, pushing the girl toward Callum. "She's been living on the Williams plantation but she is a descendant of Accompong Maroons. Was captured during the Second War and never resettled. She can speak to them. The ones you're studying."

Callum raised his glasses to his face.

"You speak what? Ashanti?" he asked.

Nanni nodded. Various blackened and raised scars on her face and arms aged her. Nanni's hair was plaited into one short braid that barely reached the bottom of her neck. Callum lifted Nanni's arms from her sides and instructed her to spread her fingers apart. He gently kicked her bare feet with his shoes, at which she winced.

"How old were you during the war? When

you were taken to the plantation?" Callum asked.

"Thirteen year," Nanni said, gazing at her bare feet. She stole glances at Callum from the corners of her eyes, but remained reluctant to look up.

Callum gripped her chin and abruptly raised her face, revealing calm and childlike eyes filled with both curiosity and a fury she was unable to hide.

"I'll take her," he said.

"Mr. Aragon, I don't advise that you go up the mountain without one of us, sir," Ryan said.

"Sure," Callum said, pushing Nanni into his house.

Nanni stood beside the door with her fingers clasped at her waist as Callum sat down to write.

"Undress," he said. Callum raised his glasses to his face and waited. Nanni appeared anxious at his demand, but undressed as quickly as it seemed she could. Shaking, she stood naked before Callum, and looked out the window behind him at the ocean.

"Turn around," Callum said.

Nanni did as he demanded and made a full rotation. When she faced him again, he looked down at his paper.

"Your back," he said. "Why so many scars?" She was slow to answer. "What caused such punishment? Were they given to you by the Maroons or on the plantation?"

"Both do it. I try many time go mountain," she answered dutifully. "One time, other Maroon, them find me and beat me before them take me back to plantation. Then when I back Master beat me again hard. Scar stay."

"Other Maroons? They did not recognize you?" Callum asked, writing.

"Not Accompong. Them other Maroon. Take me back for money." Nanni looked down at her bare feet again, as if still searching for words to explain the betrayal.

Callum nodded, pleased, it seemed, to hear that the Maroons in the mountains were upholding their end of the treaty. Callum stood up and Nanni winced, taking a step back. The pace of her breathing increased, and she looked at him now, in the eye, awaiting what she'd accepted as routine, but Callum retrieved a pitcher of water from the counter and returned to his table, refilling his glass, and continued working. Her breathing settled, and Nanni watched him work, standing for close to one hour as Callum wrote in his journal, and raised his head for long spells as she met his gaze. Every time he looked up at her, it appeared as though curiosity was eclipsing her fear little by little.

Her chin and raised shoulders, her lean limbs and dark skin: everything about her made Callum's thoughts climb onto one another as they navigated his desire. His research had, for decades, kept him away from his barren wife for extended periods of time. He dealt with his urges through the comforts of night women. But Nanni seemed different to him. Calm, unafraid of him, yet so aware of her powerlessness that she was manipulated by it. After several hours of writing and an inability to concentrate, Callum placed his pen down and wiped on his trousers the leftover ink that puddled at the tips of his fingers. Finally, he rose and walked to her, blocking her view of the ocean. Callum cupped Nanni's neck, aggressively kissing her lips. His kiss pinched her, but she did not make a sound. Rather, his cheek grew damp with what he assumed were her tears.

Let me in, let me in, let me in. Although it did not come from his mouth.

For two days following Nanni's arrival, Callum Aragon kept her in his house. A port slave delivered fried fish and bread in the early afternoon, which Callum grabbed from the boy. He closed the door in his face to resume working. He documented Nanni's movements, gave her scraps from his dinner, and recorded how she consumed her food. He ordered two clean linen dresses for her and as she put the first on, he noted how she dressed: *with determined quickness.* And later, how she bathed: *also with determined quickness.* How she ate: *she is ambitiously gluttonous.* How she laughed: *rarely, once maybe, though I missed what struck her humor.* How she spent her days: *in childlike reverie toward the ocean. She is infatuated, it seems, and breaks her gaze for nothing.*

During the night, Callum Aragon turned in his sleep from the heat that surrounded him. He chose to sweat profusely instead of being bitten by mosquitoes that wandered into the house through its two windows. One night Nanni went to the bedroom window from the floor where she slept and opened it. When she returned to the bed, Callum slapped her. "No!" Callum said, as if reprimanding a young child. Nanni whimpered and rubbed her cheek. "Mosquitoes," he said, walking back to the window and closing it.

As soon as he lay back on the bed, Nanni returned to the window and opened it. When she returned to lie down, he slapped her again.

"Go close it!" he said. Nanni remained still. Callum Aragon, once again, left the bed and reclosed the window. "Stubborn bitch," he murmured on his way back.

When he lay in bed, Nanni stood up again. This time, instead of to the window, she walked out the front door. Callum followed her, alarmed.

"Where do you think you're going?!" he yelled. "Nanni?"

Nanni wandered around the front of his house under the moonlight. She uprooted a plant and in the dark Callum recognized the bright color of the marigolds. Nanni passed him and reached the window, tore a hanging string from her dress to tie the stems of the marigolds together, then tied them to a nail that stuck out from the window's frame. She retrieved a book of matches from his shelf, struck one to light the edges of the marigold stems, and blew out the fire from the dissipating stick. "Them don't like smell," she said, walking back to the floor beside the bed where she slept. She lay down.

"If you repeat that behavior, you will be

thoroughly flogged," Callum said before falling asleep. The next day he added to his list of observations: *industrious, though she lacks reasoning and simple obedience training.*

For three weeks, Callum wrote mostly during the day, asking Nanni questions and quickly recording her accounts. At night he pulled Nanni into his bed, squeezing and scratching her buttocks as he forcefully entered her. Finally, the sailors prepared for another trip up the mountains with Callum Aragon. They arrived early one morning and led Callum Aragon and Nanni as far as they could into the mountain before stopping.

"We don't plan on traveling as close to them as the last visit, Mr. Aragon," a sailor said. "This is at your risk. They negotiate, but as you know they can't be trusted, sir. We stay away from them, they stay away from us. We will take you as far as Hunt's Point, and the girl will guide you the rest of the way if you wish to continue."

"The girl? And if she does not comply? What if I am put in danger?" Callum asked.

The sailor handed him a shotgun in a stained white cloth. Callum looked at the gun with suspicion.

"A gun?" he asked.

"Yes, Mr. Aragon. Just in case."

"They have guns, too, yes?" Callum asked as a wave of chills made his knees shake underneath his trousers.

"Some of the villages. Yes, sir. Just be careful and you won't have to use it. It's a precaution, sir. Don't give a reason for them to be suspicious and they won't harm you."

When they reached Hunt's Point, Mr. Aragon petitioned for the sailors to stay with him longer.

"Too risky, Mr. Aragon," they all agreed.

"My plan was to use her to translate. I won't present her to them alone."

"We suggest you don't present her to them at all," one said. "Not this first time. Maroons aren't the same as they once were, sir. Doesn't matter if you go to them with money. It depends on the day you visit, or nothing at all. Funny like that."

"No, this group is not so bad," another added in an effort to defuse Callum's tension. "I've never been too close to them, but the old superintendent . . ." His voice trailed off as he noticed the change in Callum Aragon's expression at the mention of the man whom those in the village had successfully driven away.

Nanni stood behind them as Callum pleaded a useless cause. She gazed at her feet, and appeared to be concealing a smile.

Eventually, the sailors left them and began their climb down the mountain. An exasperated Callum grabbed Nanni by her shoulders.

"If I am put in danger and I live through it, I will find you and kill you," he said. "Do you understand?"

Nanni watched his face as his forehead and cheeks grew moist from the humidity. Callum noticed an expression he had not up until then seen on her face; her eyes glistened, and without acknowledging his threat, she continued up the mountain. He followed.

At around the same point where the sailors had stopped with him on previous trips, Callum knelt behind the bush with Nanni, carefully studying the colony of runaways. He then stood, as if he was going to approach them, but shuddered when he saw the rifles some wore across their shoulders. Despite how suspicious his hiding would look to the Maroons, he decided against approaching, to heed the warning of the sailors and keep Nanni to himself during the initial observation. "I suppose we will just remain here," he said, nervously peering through the leaves and hoping she understood that where they sat was as far as they would go. He caught Nanni looking at

195

his gun. She turned as soon as he caught her

"I will need you to watch carefully and interpret any gestures. Do you understand?" he asked her. "Tell me exactly what you perceive they're doing."

A group of children ran around the colony of shanties, and several women sat in a circle weaving nets of coconut leaves. Nanni straightened her back. It had been some time since she had entered the mountains, and the energy and spirit of the plants and animals around her made the minuscule bumps on the backs of her hands and knees rise. Nanni stood up and opened the gates of forest leaves.

"Where are you going?" Callum asked suddenly and felt his belt for the gun.

Nanni did not stop. Afraid to stand alone, he followed, placing his hand on the gun the sailor had given him. He pulled the gun from the buckle, shaking feverishly. He pointed it at her back.

"Stop or I will shoot," he said, but she did not, and he did not.

Nanni and Callum moved through the forest until they heard a rush of water. Nanni sped up. When she lifted the last branch, they stood facing a heavy waterfall that tumbled from a high cliff. The water fell into a clear, blue-green lake that glistened under the sun as though diamonds surfed its waves.

"My God," Callum said. At the top of the waterfall, three bluebirds assembled on a stick that hung loosely from the woods' edge. The water had such clarity that as Callum looked down he could name eight different kinds of fish by the color and size of their scales. The gun grew limp in his hand, until he eventually placed it back onto the belt.

"What is this place?" Callum asked.

Nanni sank into the lake. Callum searched below the waves for her moving body but saw nothing. He waited a moment for Nanni to surface, but she did not. Callum stood up, diffident.

"Nanni," he called, pacing the water's edge as he struggled to keep from falling.

He raised his glasses to his nose and tried again to make sure that his eyes were not tricking him, that the transparency of the lake would show her swimming underneath.

"Nanni," Callum said again.

He saw nothing. Only the fish. She had vanished.

The birds that congregated on the stick above the waterfall fluttered away together. Shortly after, three followed them. When

Callum looked up, four more flew away from the hills.

Callum rushed through the woods, spitting out leaves and stray bugs that entered his mouth as tree branches slapped his face. Unable to stop, he stumbled into an empty circle of dirt in the middle of towering trees. The birds' loudness grew to a screech, as through the forest Callum noticed two sets of eyes staring angrily at him and at the gun in his hand.

"No," he said, falling to the ground, noticing their black bodies.

He turned only to find one more set of eyes peeking from behind the trees.

"Obroni!" one yelled. *White man.*

"No, no. You see, you agreed to a conversation. I'm from Great Britain," he said. "I'm Callum Aragon. I came to observe."

One by one they drew closer to him. Callum folded himself and covered his head with his hands. He did not know what to expect — if he would be hoisted up and carried to the Maroon chief to be questioned about his spying, or if a man-made weapon would tear through his skin. Instead, he felt a warm body around his. Callum opened his eyes to see Nanni hovering over him.

"You remember this," Nanni said above him. "Say it." She was breathing heavily, smiling underneath her words.

"What-wh—" Callum stuttered.

"Say it or I leave you here and them kill you."

"I will remember this," he repeated.

The Maroons shouted into the wilderness. The settler was gone. Disappeared. While the Maroons wandered around the space Callum had occupied and searched the surrounding bushes, Nanni and Callum crept out of the circle, unseen, and down the blue mountain.

As Callum Aragon headed to the dock, he opened and closed his eyes several times for confirmation that this day had been real. It was either a dream or he was going crazy, and Callum grew faint at the plausibility of the latter. How could a group of drunk and uneducated Irishmen explain what had just happened? he thought. Callum pondered the excuses they would give for the fact that he had been seconds away from an attack before Nanni had saved him — before they had disappeared and she left him at the end of the forest: They're animals, niggers; we told you not to go; the Maroons are no longer British business; you were surely imagining this; we will go kill the girl. Sir. He stopped at that and returned to his house from a tortured walk along the coast, where the sand almost swallowed him.

Inside, Nanni sat at the table with an opened book. She saw him and closed it.

"Please." His tongue fought his words. "I have no experience with witchcraft. I only want — only want to return home."

She watched as he became bathed in sweat.

"I only want to return home," he said again, surprised that she had come back. He blushed through his terror.

"Not witch," Nanni said stoically. "It not Obeah. It my gift."

Overcome by his own panic and uncertainty, Callum ran to the bookcase and retrieved the gun. He pointed it at Nanni, though his quivering hand nearly dropped the weapon.

"Do it again," he demanded. "Voodoo. Obeah. Vanish," he stuttered. "Do it. It happened, yes? We vanished. Then we flew. I am not mad."

Nanni took a step backward.

"Don't move!" Callum shouted. The sweat now overwhelmed his face. He resisted the loss of balance.

"Cannot," Nanni answered him. "Cannot use here."

"You lie."

"No, no lie. Only in mountain. Or near others," she said.

"Other who?" Callum continued, his eyes unfixed. "There are others? Where is your family?" The implications compelled him.

"No family," she murmured.

"Then other who?" Callum took a step forward, though he was still noticeably disturbed.

"Others with spirit. With gift," she said.

"Sit down," Callum demanded. Nanni took a seat.

"You practice your . . . your gifts together? You and these others?" he asked. He could barely breathe through his growing excitement.

"No. In secret," Nanni said.

"On the plantation? Where are they?"

"One man. He Maroon too." She looked at her fingers resting on the table. Her expression fell when she said this. "He like me. Them take him to plantation from mountain after Maroon war and we stay there. Can't go back to mountain."

"And he vanished also?" Callum asked quickly.

"No. When I near him burn crop when him touch. And when I near he I —"

"Disappear," Callum finished.

"We try escape back to mountain one

night. I think I can make we go, think I use gift before them find us but I too tired and we too far from mountain. Them find us and hang him," Nanni said without encouragement. "They kill me, too, but sailor them come looking for plantation Maroon. Them bring me here."

Exasperated with intrigue, Callum finally placed the gun on the table. He was nearly out of breath. Nanni remained still, watching him. What news, what news, what news, what discovery, he thought. This advancement of species — and for it to exist among Africans. Mere Africans. He experienced everything and nothing at once — the most successful, the most accomplished he had ever felt was at that moment. And not knowing what else to do with this victory of reports, he cried.

"Why are you here?" Beads of sweat descended his neck. "You had your freedom today and you chose to — why did you, why are you back here?"

Nanni folded her hands in front of her.

"I have child," she said, herself in awe of the words. "Your child."

By this Callum was sobered. He had used her for only a few weeks since she was brought to him and what miracle — what fortune. Her calm face rested against the sun. His head ached from thoughts — cruel thoughts and intellectual thoughts and nostalgic thoughts and suicidal thoughts. She would have his child.

"Your books," she continued. "Teach me."

"*Teach* you?" he asked, bewildered. Tutoring any woman, much less a slave, was to him a waste of time.

"About Africa," she said. "Maroon them there. Freetown."

"How do you know that?" Callum asked.

"Woman on plantation tell me she hear from overseer they send some Maroon them on ship. Sailors them take them after war. Sailors go and I go too. Me and child. No raise in mountains. Obroni come again."

Callum picked up the book that was on the middle of the table, between the two of them. A child. A hybrid.

"You know of Africa?" he asked.

"I know," Nanni said. "But no way to go."

"You are serious?" he asked.

"You say remember I stay and no leave you. I save your life," she said. "Teach me, then you send me and child on sailor ship."

July 1, 1823

I have discovered a scientific phenomenon that I am afraid must shift the course of my original research. I am in utter awe of such acquisition and today was made immediately conscious of my own imperfections. I am currently studying a peculiar Maroon who was captured during an invasion; she is female and she is with child. She claims that she and others have extraordinary supernatural gifts and I have witnessed such talents for myself. It does not appear to be the tropic voodoo of which many have heard and some fatally encountered, but something much more fantastic. The Maroon can, within the blue mountains, vanish from eyesight. The Maroon insists that she is the only one alive of her people with such a gift and will abandon her native relatives for an assumed liberated existence in Africa. The Maroon and her child will travel with me back to Great Britain for further study.

Sincerely,
Callum Aragon

They named him Norman.

By the time Norman Aragon was two years old, he joined his mother in the morning as she fished and in the afternoon as she tended the land around Callum Aragon's home. He clung to Nanni near the stove in the evening as she prepared Callum's meals. While together, they were never allowed out of Callum's sight; Callum's obsession with his research was made more and more clear by the increasing closeness with which he walked beside Nanni. On the occasions when he visited town, he locked Nanni and Norman inside the house and asked a sailor to stand guard.

Nanni took joy and pride in nursing Norman, and simply by existing he made her smile each night on the floor beneath Callum's bed. However, once a month Nanni could be seen around Callum's yard chewing on angelica and parsley leaves until she reeked of them for days. Shortly after, Nanni would have her cycle, and seemed relieved when it came.

Norman Aragon was a curious boy, more brilliant, Callum noticed, than he himself had ever been even through his adolescent years. Rather than sitting still for Nanni to pull back his curly, light-brown hair with string, he preferred exploring the land around the house. He remembered words, memorized stories just as soon as they were told, and took great pleasure in visiting the ocean with his father and reciting the scientific names of fish.

Norman was reading when he was four,

and knew his way up and down the island and the shore by the time he was five. Callum allowed them to walk on the beach every morning as he observed them closely from behind. Callum Aragon studied Norman as he studied Nanni. He stretched the little boy's legs apart and measured his inseam once a week; he opened his son's mouth and ran his fingers along the insides of his cheeks just as frequently. He recorded his mannerisms.

"Why you do that?" Norman asked him in a developing accent that matched his mother's, through pink lips and pale skin that matched his father's.

"No questions, Norman," Callum would respond.

They visited the Maroon village once every couple of months. For the first encounter, Callum was able to eventually persuade two sailors to accompany him and Nanni. They left Norman in the house with a plantation nurse. Nanni was careful of which path to take up the mountain, and upon their arrival she went directly to a house that sloped downward from the shifting floor of the mountain. Outside, a dozen children surrounded two women, all of them performing a variety of tasks, from cleaning fish to completing high-stakes games of chase around the yard.

"Hello, Cuffie," Nanni had said as soon as a tall man emerged from the first of two houses filled with wives and young children. "Akwaaba," Cuffie said. He was holding a cup, which he handed to one of the women. Cuffie wore trousers and an oversize linen shirt that hung from his shoulders. He looked strong, and by the way he walked, it was clear that he was respected throughout the village. Shock covered his face when he noticed Nanni, her skin absorbing all of the sun, radiant despite her many scars. But behind that shock, there was a softness, perhaps a story. She was able to negotiate infrequent visits to the village for Callum's research — something he insisted he needed to contextualize the work he was undertaking with her and Norman. Callum had to agree to bring food or money for every observation, or else he would not be welcomed. They never stayed too long — mostly he just sat on a rock near some cultivated land farthest from the cluster of houses on three rows of hills, watching and writing ardently, as two or three sailors looked askance. On a few occasions, in Ashanti, Cuffie would ask her why she would not stay — a request she simply answered with the words "The child."

"I know him when I young," Nanni admitted to Callum later that day when he inquired about Cuffie. "Before war."

"Were you . . . lovers?" Callum asked.

"No," Nanni answered, too quickly for Callum to believe it was that simple. "War come," she said. "I go plantation. He stay mountain."

Callum Aragon — suspecting that, although Nanni was determined to get to Africa, she could not absolutely be trusted to remain loyal once she entered the mountains — had refused to let Nanni take Norman to the mountains alone. Instead the boy almost never left his father's sight, his father, whose hankering eyes became wide at the thought of how a discovery of such grand scientific fortune would be received in Great Britain.

Nanni noticed the infinitesimal shifts in Callum's gaze when he looked at their son, changes that eventually culminated in one that made her squeeze Norman tightly throughout the night as they slept. Callum sent for books from back home, which would arrive a few times a year in massive trunks that required several port slaves to deliver them to his house. In the weeks following the arrival of Callum's new materials, he barely ate, and Nanni became used to the sound of pages turning against the faint hum and flicker of the lantern's blaze, deep into the night.

He took their measurements once a week on Sundays, and one Sunday Nanni was in the garden picking peppers with Norman. Callum kept the door open so he could always see and hear them in the yard, and he periodically left his papers at his desk to walk to the front door to check on them. He had lowered his head only for a second to write something down, and when he raised it, he did not see Norman in the yard.

"Where is Norman?" Callum asked, rushing to the door.

Nanni looked over her shoulder, where she was sure she had just heard Norman pulling out weeds, to see that the boy was nowhere to be found. She leaped up in panic, and Callum rushed to the garden.

"Norman!" Nanni screamed.

"My God. Norman!" Callum shouted. He pushed Nanni out of his way to head to the beach. Nanni fell on the dirt, but quickly stood up again. She circled the house as Callum's calls for their son echoed in the afternoon. In the back of the house, the stiff branches of a shrub moved. Nanni ran to it and found Norman sitting at the foot of the shrub, drawing in the dirt. Nanni grabbed him by the shoulders so tightly that he yelled.

"How you? You run here?" she asked, grasping for the possibility that he also had a gift. A terrified Norman nodded, his curls brushing his forehead, and Nanni noticed a set of tiny footprints in the dust leading from the front yard to the shrub. Her hopes dashed, she held his jaw with her right hand and squeezed until he cried.

"Never do again, you hear?" she said with stern and unmoving eyes. "You no Obroni to move free. They kill you. You black." She trembled but did not release her hold. "You hear?!" she shouted and Norman nodded, still crying.

Callum approached her from behind and pulled Norman from Nanni's grasp.

"What are you doing? It's your fault he wandered!" he said, roughly pushing Nanni to the ground. She covered her head and looked away from him, but he did not strike her. Callum was also shaking, and he took Norman by the hand and led him into the house. Norman looked over his shoulder at his mother, and did not turn his head until he was out of sight. Nanni heard the door close and returned to the garden. She heard Callum navigating his mountain of papers inside. She heard his measuring tape and the closing of drawers, his mumbling as Norman finally quieted. Nanni expected that Callum would soon open the door so she could enter and prepare dinner, but that night, he did not.

She waited on the front steps throughout the night, as an army of mosquitoes left their mark on her body. Nanni cried under the moon, and would have run through the darkness to rest her head on the waiting arms of the mountain, but she thought of Norman, of the extent of tests and observations Callum would subject him to if she left him alone. So she stayed, humming to coax her pain, to beckon the morning, sleeping beside the marigolds, and in the brief moment when sleep did come, she had two dreams.

At first she dreamed of Freetown and its free men. She walked toward this place, this people, this thing she could barely imagine, wanting to touch it. They were neither moving nor speaking. They all looked like Maroons, except they wore clothes like the Master's clothes. "Why you got them skirts them on?" Nanni asked. The Maroons sat together around what looked like a master's table, unmoving, like a portrait. Her body was warmed by the memory of her time on the mountain, her childhood yam farm, her

211

friends, and then it grew cold at the memory of her time on the plantation, the breaking glass, the whips, the belts, the blood. This portrait reminded her of both. Nanni extended her hand toward them, toward this freedom, but before she could touch the hems of their sleeves, she was back on the mountain.

In the second she dreamed in blue, and in that color was Cuffie's face, not as it had been when last she saw him on the mountain with Callum and the sailors, but when they were young, during the war. Cuffie was not much older than Nanni, though his towering height and the demand with which he carried it made him look years her senior. The war was four months old and every day they heard gunfire and shouting farther down the mountain. The British soldiers were many, and Maroon men were not returning to the crown of the blue mountains as they once had. Cuffie came back one night and told her of what was happening farther down the mountain — Maroon men were chasing the Brits away in large numbers because the Brits did not know how to survive in the mountains, but still many were being dragged out of the mountains and to the plantations. Rather than hiding with the other girls, Nanni grabbed a knife to fight by Cuffie's side, that boy with whom she shared her gift freely, whom, before the war started, she had let hold her hand. In the dream she and Cuffie went as far as they had managed to during the war — just below the mountain. They killed everything that did not look like freedom. A faceless one, monstrous and much taller than Cuffie, chased him, and Nanni was able to vanish and destroy it, and it shattered into hundreds of parts and escaped into the sun. But she had gone too far outside of the mountain. Cuffie yelled for her, but it was too late. Soldiers grabbed her by the arms, and though she tried, she was unable to unearth her gift.

In that same dream, the color blue rained down on her arms, each melting drop more painful than the last, each second of penetrating heat less forgiving. She was on a sugar plantation and so tired that had it not been for the faceless men and their ropes and their metal, she would have fainted. She wondered if Cuffie would believe her if she were to tell him how hard she was forced to work, and what they did to her on days she was too tired to continue. To remain awake during those days, she walked in place; right leg and then left, the cries of others a most cruel song to which she moved. In the dream, Nanni looked down at her feet and they faded in and out of sight. Nanni turned onto her side and there was a boy, her friend, with a mouth full of words she could not hear, because the blueness and heat were loud, and all she wanted to do was rest. With his left hand he took hers. With his right hand he touched the sugarcane, and the fields erupted into flames before her eyes. The plantation melted to ashes; the dream felt real. So they ran. Nanni used her gift and they vanished. Ran toward the mountain, but she was too tired to endure. The heat pushed against her skin, and she was nearly out of breath from running. She panted and squeezed the boy's hand, but she knew she could not last.

So she awoke.

Callum stood above her as she lay on the porch. Startled, Nanni quickly stood, though the pain from the mosquito bites made her lose her balance. The bites covered her arms and legs — she felt them in her bones. Callum cleared his throat, and looked away from her wounds toward the beach.

"Make me and Norman porridge," Callum said and returned to the house.

Several times a month Callum visited the

mountains with Nanni and waited through the night. Sometimes it happened immediately. Sometimes it took a few determined minutes. Yet without fail, she would eventually disappear, her body nowhere to be found among the trees of the forest. Nanni would close her eyes and listen to the marriage of wind and water from a nearby stream, the rumored mountain boas in the distance as they glided on their bellies across deeply rooted trunks. Creek water cuckooing through isolated pebbles. And at once she was with her earth, and at once she became it.

What news, what news, what discovery. Callum Aragon would search his surroundings vigorously. *She was gone. It had happened again! What news!* He shouted with excitement, sweat poured from everywhere, his pupils swelled, his limbs were fluid, his contemplations were all, all corrupted.

"Nanni!" Callum shouted, laughing with barely half of his mind. "Nanni!" he shouted louder and with urgency.

And she returned to his picture.

"We go on ship soon, yah?" she asked, a motionless audience to Callum's hysteria.

He nodded and rushed to her, touching her arms and face to make sure she was fully there and that the astounding miracle had been real.

During Norman's tenth year, Callum informed Nanni that they would set sail midyear, and with finality, Nanni prepared herself for the journey. In the weeks before they departed, Callum grew more and more eager for the voyage, and on several occasions, Nanni found him murmuring to himself in the marigold garden.

"Where we going?" Norman asked his mother as she dressed him early that morning, when from their house they could hear the voices of the sailors collide in preparation for the trip.

"To Africa. Freetown. We be good there," Nanni said, raising her son's arms with shaking hands. She, too, was anxious. She had waited for this very voyage for years, to join the Maroons who had been captured and sent on a ship to Africa instead of to the hell of the inland plantation, and the reality of it made her heart rise and fall behind her skin.

"Africa," Norman said.

"To Africa. Africa like Mr. Aragon say. That where we from, you know. You play outside in Africa. Go run where you want. In open. You run and you never get tired running."

Norman held Nanni's hand and she hurried to the shore behind Callum Aragon, who nearly tripped over his feet as they approached. The sailors had already gathered his belongings and a few waved toward the unlikely family as they assembled with a few other expectant travelers from the inland. Trunks of cotton and clothes were also being shipped, along with sugar and other goods from the inland plantations.

"You had enough of the island, Mr. Aragon," a sailor said, smiling. He looked skeptically at Nanni and her mulatto son, then glanced toward the mountains as a rhythmic chant commenced alongside heavy drumming.

"Festival," Nanni whispered.

"Don't worry," the sailor said to Callum, attempting again to connect with the old man, whom they all feared the island had made senile. "You won't hear no drums in England." He laughed. Callum pulled Nanni's arm to board. Nanni stared at the sailor's lips and rotten teeth.

"To Africa, yah?" she asked, confused.

The sailor looked to Callum first, offended that this woman had addressed him to his face. Callum pulled Nanni again.

"Great Britain," the sailor answered and spit on the ground. The thumping in the mountains escalated and Nanni's heart pounded. Callum yanked her arm.

"Callum. We go to Africa, yah?" she asked again, defending herself against the sailor's biting words. Callum did not answer. He squeezed Nanni's arm and tugged at her to step onto the wooden plank of the ship. He looked assuredly toward the sailor as the wind surged into the ocean waves.

"Run away, my darling," I said, I shouted.

A distant morning sun buzzed and the lusty beating of the festival drums emerged onto the shore as Nanni finally understood the betrayal.

"No!" she yelled and pulled away from Callum in resistance. Nanni cried and kicked as Norman Aragon wriggled out of her grasp. He looked on as his mother fought Callum, endured his slaps and his stubborn hold on her frail body. The commotion drew attention from sailors and the few passengers who waited onboard the ship, as well as a number of final passengers on the shore. Her strength proved more than Callum Aragon could contain and with embarrassment he yelled at her to stop. Finally a sailor descended the plank from the deck with an unwound whip and, without hesitation, he flung it toward Nanni's legs. It lowered her to her knees as her tears surged. She scrambled to raise herself to her feet, though the blood was plenty. Through her peripheral vision she noticed Norman standing alone, crying while Callum and the sailors surrounded her.

"Go," she called out to him silently while wrestling with her captors.

Her eyes touched the mountains as the festival initiation continued with riotous drums and wailing. Norman Aragon's legs were stiff; fear kept him from leaving his mother. "Go!" she shouted, and Norman turned around and dashed through the sand toward the mountains. His tiny legs battled the rich grains and at once Callum Aragon and the collective of sailors dispersed. Nanni glanced at her legs with joy; they blended in and out of her sight. Her hands also, though quavering, alternated between the present and the invisible.

"Norman," Nanni said, crying. She stood in distress and focused on her son, whom Callum had caught and led back to the ship.

"Where's the girl?" a sailor asked, as he turned around. Nanni was not where they had left her.

"No, no," Callum said, and before he could protest further, Norman Aragon vanished from sight. The boy's hand dissipated in his grasp and a mass of yelps escaped from the deck of the ship.

"My God," a sailor said, desperately searching his surroundings for the woman and her child. "Black magic."

"Obeah!"

"Leave at once," another demanded of the ship's crew. The festival rhythm exacerbated their crisis and the crew shuffled to board the final passengers.

"We cannot. We cannot!" Callum Aragon protested and reached for the retreating sailors. "No. You do not understand. This is not voodoo. We cannot leave them here!"

The sailors ignored his appeal and retreated toward the ships.

Nanni held Norman Aragon on her hip as she ran. That his gift had manifested at such a time and saved their lives made her squeeze him against her body. The blood from her wounded legs stained the sand. She was determined to reach the mountains. Norman looked back at the serious melee of sailors and at his father, who chased the winds of the shore in vain for a glimpse of the escaping captives. The scrambling continued onboard the ship. Callum went to the edge of the plank, where a sailor stood, and he stole the gun from his waistband.

"What are you doing, sir?" the sailor asked, fear in his eyes. "Black magic, sir. Stay away." Callum pointed the gun toward the track of bloody sand in the distance and fired. "No, sir," the sailor said and reached for the weapon as Callum continued to shoot.

At the sound of the first bullet, Nanni's heartbeat soared. She dropped her shoulders but resumed her breathless pursuit of the blue mountains. Finally releasing himself from the sailor's strong hold, Callum ran toward the stain of blood and the mountains while shooting. Perhaps he could scare her into visibility. Perhaps he could kill one and take the other. Perhaps fate would not be so cruel as to expose the futility of a decade of research.

"Come back!" he screamed and fired the gun again and again.

After a despairing run, the moment she reappeared at the entry to the mountains, a bullet sank into her thigh. Nanni collapsed between the looming trees of the forest. She cried in pain, gasping for breath. Norman

Aragon rushed to his mother's side.

The lunatic cries of Callum Aragon were not far behind them. Nanni took Norman's hand and limped farther into the wooded area. The drums of festival raced through the mountains. Norman gazed upward at the blue mountain trees, reaching their arms outward to greet him, to hide him. Nanni stumbled over a fallen branch and hollered at the throbbing pain in her leg. Her skirt was almost completely covered in blood and the smell of it pervaded the dense forest. Norman Aragon attempted to pull his mother up by her arm but she protested.

"My leg," she said. "My leg." Nanni crawled over and rested her back against the closest tree. "Come here," she said to Norman. Norman went to Nanni and sat beside her. She hugged him and her tears touched the crown of his head.

"Think real hard for what you like most. You like to fish plenty, yah?" she asked. Norman nodded and his hopeful face made Nanni smile. "The people tell you the fish not yours, but they yours too. Think real hard on all the names of fish you like saying. And the mountains. The sand. That water. It yours, you hear me?" Norman nodded again and wiped his mother's face. He leaned against her and his mind went to the infant memory of their morning walks to the ocean. The drumbeats grew louder as Callum Aragon finally entered the mountains, a mumbling fool. He pointed the gun and fired straight ahead. Birds withdrew. Callum fired again to find that the gun had run out of bullets. Exasperated, he worked his way through the heat and drums.

"Nanni!" he shouted.

"Think on those things," Nanni whispered.

"Norman!"

"Think hard."

Underneath the shaking limbs of the blue mountain trees, Nanni held her son. The physical pain was not as great as the now-vanished hope of going to Africa. She wept as Callum approached in the distance. He shouted their names, fought his way through commingling bushes, and went right past them, coughing as he stumbled farther up the mountain, unable to see them. Nanni kissed Norman's head and felt an odd mixture of relief and desperation. She sat with Norman Aragon for some time while her body became weaker and her blood dampened the forest floor beneath them. Her son abided by her every breath.

A while after, from up the mountain, Callum Aragon's despondent screaming soared above the trees to the very tip of a Maroon settlement.

"Maroons find him?" Norman Aragon asked.

"Maybe. Yah," Nanni answered. "They find him."

"They kill him?" Norman asked, his voice softened.

Nanni looked over her shoulder toward the festival drums. Callum had entered the mountain screaming, with only a gun — no money or food to offer, and he was without her. Nanni hugged Norman, and with hesitation she nodded.

That night, from a distance, smoke rose from Callum Aragon's house on stilts. A blazing fire forced it to its knees. The wind carried the familiar smell of the room and shelves, and the sounds of cracking wood and the nearby ocean.

"You remember this," Nanni said to Norman while he lay beside her amid the chants of the forest that night. "Remember what happen. Remember you got spirit too. You got gift," she said again and yielded to the wind's footsteps. "Find your way up mountain. Up this way. Only this way so other Maroons them don't find you. Tell Cuffie you for me." The branches of the trees shook and swayed around them. "Make

your home in the mountain. In the forest.
They take care of you."

Norman nodded, though neither of them
could see each other's face in the night. Her
breathing eventually dissolved in his embrace.

The sailors burned down Callum's old home and condemned it with tales of island voodoo, and afterward they avoided the blue mountains. With each passing year, only a song would wander into the mountain forests, composed of the many legends born of Nanni's and Norman's disappearance on the shore.

Oh Callum was a lovestruck lad, came at
  dawn and left at noon
A friend of all, a gentle man, a scholar,
  friend, but gone too soon
What do you say became of him? Or th'
  mulatto lad he bore here too
Look to th' mountains, magic blue.
  Betrayed by th' love of a Maroon.
Betrayed by the love of a Maroon.

The day after Nanni's death, Norman Aragon wandered the mountains for many

hours, to the Maroon settlement to which
Nanni had given him directions, where a
village of Accompong Maroons took him in
after he revealed who his mother was. Cuffie
cared for him as his own. Norman and
Cuffie had buried Nanni with the help of
other Maroons, and planted marigolds
above the grave, flowers that carried the
odor of her weeping body. Norman hunted
with the Maroons and read from the many
books that Nanni had delivered to them
during her years with Callum, books, un-
read, that he found throughout the houses
of the mountain village. On very rare occasions, some one or two slaves would arrive
at the village from the inland plantations,
clothes muddy and tattered from their
escape, out of breath and desperate for
respite. On some of these days, the Maroons
would drag the escapees right back down
the mountain and return them to their plantations.

"Why they do that?" Norman asked,
distressed, the first time he witnessed this.

"We make agreement with the British
them," Cuffie told him. "We take no more
up the mountain." Cuffie looked away when
he said this, and Norman watched the path
that led out of the village until the Maroons
returned from the plantation, a bit richer

from the exchange. On other occasions — sometimes motivated by the state of the escapees when they arrived, sometimes by the money or jewels some slaves managed to steal and barter with Maroons in exchange for their freedom, sometimes by nothing at all — Cuffie and others would stop fellow Maroons from taking the slaves back down the mountain. Once or twice, he threatened the perpetrators with violence so obscene that Norman hid from the confrontation.

In the village, Norman spent most of his time alone. His reflection in the mountain lakes was different from the other children's; his skin and hair were closer to those of the sailors in the port than they were to the Maroons in the mountains. The older he got, the more quickly his hair grew, wild and unruly, with bountiful spiral curls that Norman cut with one of Cuffie's blades.

"Obroni!" is what Maroon children yelled toward him on the days he fought the other growing boys. One of Cuffie's sons, Solomon, picked on him the most.

"Your skin too white," Solomon told him one day. "And you got Obroni mouth. Obroni sound." He was the tallest among his peers, almost as tall as his father, and his requests were not usually met with dissent. "Too white to come," he continued. "Hogs them see you and run. Or other Maroon them. You stay here."

"I can hunt," Norman replied in Ashanti. Solomon did not respond to him; he turned away and headed down into the mountain forests with a few other boys. Norman ran behind them and Solomon stopped to push him so hard that he fell.

Norman had also tried to speak to a girl. Her name was Tai and she lived in the row of houses farthest up the mountain. Most of the houses looked the same — floorless cottages with shingle roofs — but Tai's was the highest, and every morning when Norman left Cuffie's house and prepared Cuffie's gun for the hunt, he looked up to see if Tai could be seen retrieving her family's shirts and trousers from the clothing lines. On the mornings she appeared, her dark skin and sharp features so dignified they caused a break in the morning fog, he felt enlivened, but also afraid, also like a man now, yet still like a boy clinging to his dying mother's last words.

At end of the journey that began at the first sight of her face, when he found courage enough to settle his spirit by speaking to her, he found her on the yam farm.

"Akwaaba, Tai," Norman said, afraid that

she would hear his anxious heart.

"Obroni," Tai said, without smiling, without looking up from tilling the ground with her slender fingers.

There were other girls around her, and when they heard this they laughed, and the sound of it paralyzed him. He had hoped to ask her if he could help her, if she would walk with him perhaps. But he left them there — Tai, who refused to acknowledge him, and her associates, still giggling as he walked away.

It was Nanni's dream of Freetown that numbed his loneliness. When he asked Cuffie about it, Cuffie sucked his teeth.

"Nanni know nothing about no Freetown," Cuffie said matter-of-factly. "She got spirit, she use gift for wrong thing. I got spirit like her I richer man. Africa gone. We here now."

Norman had been tapping his bare foot against the ground, and he stopped; his body stiffened when Cuffie said this.

"You think me don't know? Think your Ma the only one with spirit?" Cuffie asked. "Maroons get spirit plenty. Spirit what save we, bring us up mountain. But we here now no use for it, so it go. But it stay with some. Like your Ma. Like you."

■ ■ ■ ■

Loneliness while in the presence of others is a most cruel kind, and having grown tired of it in the Maroon village, when Norman was fourteen he built his own shack in the forest below the mountains where he could get a better view of the dock and shore. From his shack, Norman Aragon could see the ships and watched for four years as they left, each spring, for Africa. Inside his shack, against the wall and on a shelf was his inheritance: books, some on top of others, indiscriminate browns and reds, on the floor, atop a chair made of wood tied tightly together with string, and scattered across a small mattress in the corner.

He had learned from Nanni which plants to eat and which would kill him. He had learned which herbs to mix when he was not well — to cure fevers and stomach pains and to help him fall asleep. He remembered his mother's instruction of how to unearth the spirits in him, his gift, and used it on the few occasions when travelers or foreign huntsmen had braved the mountains. He knew that if he could unearth his gift again outside of the forest, he could sneak onto the ship and make his way to Africa. His fifteenth year was the first time he made an attempt, planning carefully since he knew another ship would soon leave the dock. But only a few dozen yards out of the forest, someone from the dock pointed his way, scaring him into retreating. An hour or so later, when one or two sailors entered the forest with guns, shaking with fear, they walked right past him, unable to see him.

He tried again when he was sixteen and seventeen, and each time those on the dock would eventually point his way, and every time he would retreat, sand and dust staining his bare back and torn trousers as he escaped.

Some mornings it was difficult for him to leave his home. He missed his mother. In those moments when Callum had asked Norman questions, the same questions he asked every day while pricking various parts of Norman's body with needles and thereafter quickly recording his tolerance, or lack thereof, to pain, it was Nanni who saved him. She would run out of the house wailing, disrupting Callum, who then usually called for sailors to retrieve her and flog her. And after being beaten or having to sleep outside, resting her body in the marigold garden to decrease the number of mosquitoes that feasted on her flesh, Nanni would eventually return to her work, or to Callum's table for questioning and observation. In idle moments Norman caught her staring out Callum's window toward the ocean.

"We go to Africa soon," she would whisper once she was allowed near Norman again, using the very last of her energy to spread her lips into a smile, one that looked as painful as the bites across her skin.

On a morning when Norman had managed to beat this sadness, he returned to his books. Within one of them, hidden behind a pile of others that Norman had not noticed before, was a folded piece of paper that hung out of its side. Norman pulled the sheet out of the book and opened it to discover a drawing signed by Callum. He had never seen Callum sketch before and he squeezed the page in his hands. There, in aged ink, was a drawing of what looked like a waterfall beyond an aperture of bushes and what looked like bougainvillea. Just beyond the bush, in front of the waterfall, was the outline of a woman. It was poorly sketched, but it was clear to Norman that Callum had attempted to draw Nanni. He stared at Callum's signature and noticed writing underneath, so small that he had to squint to read it. Norman pulled the paper closer, walking to his window to hold it under the light. In smeared ink, underneath Callum's name, were the words: the beginning.

Three Maroon men sat in the middle of a cluster of shanties. Near the ground, where they sat on shaved boulders, wearing old but neatly fitting shirts across their broad shoulders, were several machetes and a rifle. Outwardly, they resembled the men I once knew on Emerson. But there was something different about their spirits. The difference seemed more simple than that they were able to move as they pleased on that mountain, or were able to keep their right to their customs. Their spirits were alive. And most men I knew before, in that place, laid their spirits to rest the first time the cat-o'-nine-tails flew into their backs. And without a spirit, you cannot feel. You react, but the longer you exist in a world without your spirit, the less you feel. And feeling, no matter how low the emotion, is a gift. But in that place we stopped feeling when our spirits were killed. Laughter was a reaction. Tears were a reaction. Those screams were a reaction. But the source of them — the mother of joy, of sadness, or terror — was a ghost like me.

The Maroon men, alert, looked toward

235

the ruffling leaves as Norman approached, but continued their conversation as he neared. Several women sat against nearby trees weaving nets of coconut leaves. Norman glanced at them quickly, looking for Tai's face, and was grateful that she was not there, not present to exercise her power.

"And there we think he dead now," Cuffie said and stood from his boulder. "Akwaaba, Nommy," he greeted Norman.

"Akwaaba, Cuffie," Norman said.

"What'y need? They them hummock you house again?"

"No, no," Norman said. "Just want to ask you something."

"You still try go ship?" Cuffie asked. "Tell you no going now. Here home."

"Nanni said go," Norman said.

"Yah," Cuffie said and looked down the mountain in the direction Norman had come from. "What'y want know?"

"Nanni said she liked a lake up here," Norman said.

"Plenty lake. What you mean?" Cuffie asked.

Norman reached into a bag made of linen and retrieved the drawing. He handed it to Cuffie, and the other men around them leaned over to see it.

"Where do I find it?" Norman asked.

236

Cuffie stared at the picture, then glanced at Norman skeptically. He pointed beyond a tent in the distance, then resumed his conversation with the others.

"Thank you, Cuffie," Norman said. He hurried to the woods behind the tent that Cuffie had pointed out.

"When you serious you come live up here, help fight'n farm," Cuffie yelled after him.

As he approached the opening, he examined the sketch again. Norman passed the bougainvillea bushes and there it was, a waterfall so clear it appeared as if beads of crystals were diving into the mountain's open shell. Sunbeams glided across the face of the lake. Norman took off his shoes and placed his feet in the water, stiffening from its rigidity. But there he felt Nanni's presence in the chills. Her memory lingered on the scales of those fish he saw clearly surrounding his legs, kissing the sprouting hairs on his ankles. Every day he thought of the things Nanni had told him to envision. Norman closed his eyes and listened to the marriage of wind and water from a nearby stream. The feathered edges of those red-billed birds as they landed on the mountain trees, river water in the distance, the sound of falling leaves. And at once he could feel himself blending with earth, as well as his absence from it. He jumped into the water.

"Go now, Norman." He remembered Nanni's voice and heard it clearly, as the loudness of the lake pressed against his ears, as freely as the night she had left him. "Go now."

He was eighteen that year and the ship would be leaving soon. Norman, haunted by the words and promises of his mother, collected three trousers and the only other shirt he owned, as well as a map of Africa that he tore out of one of his books. He placed them in Callum's old leather satchel and lumbered to the edge of the forest. He meditated on his mother's words, each one committing the disappearing act he now wished he could emulate.

Rather than running toward the boulders as he had done in the past, to hide in hopes that the sailors would not see him, he went toward the ship steadily, his footprints neat in the sand. He considered those things Nanni told him — the chattering of the birds, the sound of the waves, the sand beneath his feet, the wind pressing hard against his skin.

"Go now," she had said. "Think hard on these things." Her voice, those many years later, still echoed. And Norman walked upright with the thoughts of the earth and those things he had lost his mother to. No sailor turned to point. No sailors saw him board the ship.

■ ■ ■ ■

MONROVIA

■ ■ ■ ■

In those days they called it Monrovia.

Monrovia was where they would meet.

Norman Aragon had climbed onto the ship completely unseen, and remained hidden under the quarterdeck for most of the two-month trip. He stole food from passengers and the crew to eat during the night. He vanished and toured the ship for what he could find, and retreated to a hiding place in the midst of the cargo. To distract himself from his hunger, he used the thin light from a crack in the ship to read and reread one of the three books he carried in his linen bag. I watched him through those openings; I spilled into his hiding places, turned the pages of his books. We did not have books on Emerson. That place where we lost our language, lost ourselves. They told us we had no history but darkness, so they kept the books away for fear we might understand the truth better, and thus find those lost selves. I watched Norman in the belly of that ship, eavesdropped on his conversations with those books he loved, and saw him draw nearer to the day that was to come, when the gifts of all three strangers would be needed.

Two weeks before the ship was scheduled to land in Freetown, Norman was so weak that he feared his gift would be affected. It became increasingly difficult for him to wait until night to retrieve food, and on several occasions during the day he glanced down at his hands to find that he was fading in and out of the light, his hands reappearing before him every few hours. Afraid that he was getting too exhausted from the voyage to make it to Freetown, his back aching from constantly sitting, his stomach empty and head throbbing from the ebb and flow of the ocean's waves, one evening Norman crept to the rations cabin.

He was searching through a straw bag for fruit or plantains when the ship rocked violently through a series of waves. Three large bags fell to the ground, and out of the bags yams and other vegetables tumbled to the floor of the cabin. Unable to maintain his gift, Norman emerged and fell, landing on his right arm. He scrambled to grab a yam, which he would have eaten raw, but at that moment two sailors opened the cabin door. They appeared shocked at the sight of Norman. Norman attempted to vanish once more, but his pain and weakness were too much.

"What you doing there?" a sailor yelled, though he didn't approach as the ship continued to sway. Norman's hair and beard had grown long during the trip, and though he tied his hair with a rope behind his back, the curls could be seen from the front.

"He's a mulatto lad, Johnny," the other sailor added.

Johnny looked closely at Norman, who was dressed like a Maroon and not an inland slave. The sailor looked visibly afraid, as if the possibility that he was looking at the escaped son of Callum Aragon, a boy they all thought was dead, had locked his knees. The story of the mulatto Maroon who had lived at the bottom of the mountain, the ghost son of a deceased scholar, was a popular one on the island shore. Too shocked to react, he pushed the other sailor toward Norman.

"Go ahead, Phillip," he said, trembling. "Grab him."

As if he had not made the connection that his friend had, Phillip rushed toward Norman, immediately punching him in the face and stomach. Norman tried to pick himself up, but his weakness would not allow him. Phillip hit him again, seizing him by the neck of his shirt, and pulled him out of the cabin.

"Where you taking him?" Johnny said.

"Throwing him over. Same's we do to other stowaways," he answered, taking giant steps down the hallway toward the quarter-deck stairway.

"No, no," Johnny said, pulling Phillip's arm. "He's from the mountain, sure of it. Look at him."

"So what?" Phillip asked him, confused.

"They're a dangerous lot. Practice witch-craft, don't you know? Haven't you heard . . ."

"Yes, I've heard," Phillip answered, visibly annoyed. "What you think's bound to happen if they find out up there we let a nigger board the ship and only now found him? We're in charge of the underdeck, what you think will happen?" Phillip continued to pull a powerless Norman down the hallway, but Johnny stopped him again.

"I heard stories about ships wrecking and tossing for days when they throw them over," he said.

"Rubbish."

"Swear it. Stories all of them, but still.

Maroons be careful with," he said.

Phillip looked down at Norman. "What do you suppose we do? I'm not reporting a blackie stowaway, that's for sure."

"Fine, then, we land at the American colony tomorrow, yes?"

"Monrovia," Phillip said.

"Yes," Johnnie said. "Tomorrow morning."

"Yes, Monrovia," Phillip said, loosening his grip on Norman's shirt.

"We'll tie him up tonight and leave him in Monrovia. Unload him with cargo," Johnnie said, encouraging his associate.

"No," Norman whispered. "No. Freetown," he struggled to say, so famished, so weakened from the beating that he could barely speak. "Freetown," Norman mumbled again, looking up at Phillip, who landed another punch in his face.

When Norman awoke, he lay in a dark room on a cold cement floor. He opened his eyes and noticed, near his head, a bowl of a liquid porridge underneath a cut of bread. A wooden pitcher of water had been placed right beside the bowl. Norman sat up quickly and devoured each cold and stale bite. He let out a prolonged breath after drinking the entire pitcher of water. It was

247

only then that he regained his will to concentrate, and noticed he was in a jail, his cell ten feet long and wide with a square, minuscule patch of dirt broken into the concrete where he could relieve himself. Norman winced at the pungent odor of the jailhouse. It was not the ocean he heard outside but rain, and with nothing to cover the window at the top of his cell wall, water spilled into the room.

"Akwaa . . . Hello," Norman said in English, quickly correcting himself from his Ashanti thoughts. He had been lying on a bare floor, his bag and books nowhere in sight. "Hello," he said again, this time a little louder. No one answered, and it did not seem to him like anyone else occupied the jail. Norman stood up with difficulty. He approached the jail wall and jumped, hoping to reach the window, but it was too high. Norman closed his eyes and tried to use his gift, but it was no use. He was still too weak. When he opened his eyes and found that he was still in the cell, Norman returned to the bars and shook them. There was an empty cell across from his. There were two more cells besides that one, on either side.

"Hello," he said again, in vain.

He was too weary to continue shaking the bars, so he sat back down, and with little ef-

248

fort he fell into a deep slumber.

The sunlight woke him the following morning. It leaked through the cell window, falling directly onto his face so that he squinted the moment he opened his eyes. His muscles were stiff from his lying on the bare floor throughout the night, so he sat up slowly and stretched them. A door opened at the end of the jailhouse hallway and Norman hurried to stand near the bars.

"Are you sure?" a voice asked, drawing closer to him.

"Yes, there will be more than enough room. It's only one man," another answered. Their footsteps approached. "He was caught stealing on a recent passage and sold to some port workers," he added. "They brought him here."

"Very well," the first said.

The men reached his cell and Norman stepped back, his face painted with astonishment that they were black. Both of the men were wearing full-length trousers and clean white shirts that sharply contrasted with their unblemished, unscarred, deep-brown skin. One of the men had gray hair and wore a vest and frock coat over his shirt, despite the penetrating heat of the jailhouse. Norman was at eye level with both of them, and was much younger in appearance; after overcoming his shock, he approached the gentlemen.

"Where did he come from?" the gray-haired man asked his associate.

"Jamaica," Norman answered, lowly, still weak from hunger. The men turned toward him sharply. "I want . . . I try to go to Freetown."

"Oh," the gray-haired man said, turning to his associate. "Well then. His English is somewhat proper."

"What crimes are you guilty of?" the associate asked, folding his arms across his chest. He examined Norman's tattered clothing.

"No crime," Norman said, speaking in the clearest English he could remember and muster, the only language he had been allowed to speak in Callum Aragon's home.

"I was told theft," the associate said, turning to the gray-haired man. "You stole aboard the passage?"

Norman stared at the men for a long time before nodding.

"They catch me stealing food," Norman said.

"They caught me," the associate corrected him.

"And was it a legal passage?" the gray-haired man interrupted. At this, Norman looked confused. "Did you pay for your voyage?" the man clarified.

"I was going to other Maroons in Freetown," Norman said.

"Very well, but did you pay for your voyage?" he asked again.

"No, but my mother was owed a debt. She was owed a voyage," Norman pleaded.

The men glanced at one another and back at Norman. The gray-haired one took a step toward the cell.

"You will be tried by a governor," he said. "It shall not be too extensive. Just state your case and if it is determined you are innocent, you will be released and can find work or make your way to Freetown. If you are found guilty you will be sent to the interior to contribute to the labor initiative. Do you understand?"

Norman nodded, though he hoped by then he could regain his energy and use his gift to flee.

"When the . . . when is the trial?" Norman asked.

"A few weeks' time, I'm sure," the associate said. Norman sighed in relief.

"In the meantime, you will stay here with the others."

"Others?"

"Two ships will arrive from America

251

within the week," the associate said. The men took a few steps past Norman's cell to view the other rooms in the jailhouse. They left him there holding the bars. Norman looked at his chafed hands. He closed his eyes and tried again to unearth his gift, but opened them to find that his hands were still visible.

"I am hungry," Norman called out.

"They'll bring your ration later today," the associate answered from down the hall.

Norman sat against the wall and listened to the now-echoing voices of the men in the dark and damp jailhouse.

"Let's hope there was no trouble on either voyage," the associate said. "Maintaining peace, or at least the semblance of it, is the first step in getting rid of them."

"You know it's going to take more than that to get those governors out," the gray-haired man said. "A free Negro colony. A free Negro colony and free Negros can't be trusted to govern it," he added disapprovingly, lowering his voice.

"Still, empty jails don't hurt our cause."

"Agreed."

The men approached Norman's cell. Norman remained seated on the floor but watched them carefully as they passed. He had never seen Negro men so well dressed or well spoken. Confusion unsettled his spirit, so Norman abruptly stood and called out to them.

"Wait," Norman said. "Where am I?" he asked.

The gray-haired man chuckled briefly and walked slowly to Norman's cell. Norman looked into the man's eyes, their cinnamon color identical to his.

"Monrovia," the man answered, with a smile he could not keep to himself.

A man entered the jailhouse twice a day to bring Norman food. The bread was hard, and the porridge was bitter, but Norman knew the only way out of the cell was through his gift, so he forced himself to swallow so that he could regain his energy. The man was not as well dressed as the previous jailhouse visitors. Although his trousers were also floor-length, his shirt did not fit him neatly, and was not tucked in. The man slid both the narrow bowl of porridge and the bread and the pitcher between Norman's bars, all the while staring at Norman's hair and clothes, always with a questioning look, as if he were also newly adjusting to his radical world. On the fourth day, Norman felt the weakness and starvation begin to fade. He paced his cell throughout the day for exercise. At the moment he expected his ration to be delivered, instead he heard a commotion outside the jailhouse. The doors swung open and the shouting echoed throughout the hallway and Norman's cell. He heard two cell doors open and close and footsteps descend the hallway to leave the jailhouse.

"Ain't shit," a man said from one cell. "They say we leave by tomorrow. Motherfuckers can't prove nothing."

"Shit, Damon," another said from a cell farther down the hallway. "You a motherfucker for this."

Damon spit and it sounded to Norman like he had collapsed on the prison floor. He sucked his teeth and the sound bounced off the prison walls.

"Swear I ain't touch her," Damon said. "Not the way they say."

Norman heard the other man spit.

"You got to believe me," Damon said.

"Don't matter no more. I ain't the one who got to believe you anyhow. It's them judges I gather," the other responded.

"Tomorrow then," Damon said, his voice more energetic than the other's.

"Oh, shut up then, Damon," the other man said and spit again.

The men gossiped through the night, at

moments shouting and cursing at one another, and in other instances they spoke carefully about what they would say to the governors the following day. Norman remained in the shadows and listened in silence. He learned that they were brothers, Damon and Sal, who had worked as tailors in Boston before they heard about the ships leaving for the free Negro colony in Africa. They had saved money, both earned and stolen (stolen, it seemed, by Damon), to pay for the voyage. Sal spoke the most, chastising his brother for his immaturity and warning him against speaking the following day during their trial. Another ship was to arrive in the afternoon, Sal reminded Damon, and they were to be tried first thing in the morning. Apparently, a young woman had accused Damon of touching her inappropriately, and while defending his brother from the accusation, Sal had been arrested as well, and they were taken to the prison as soon as they arrived at the colony.

Damon and Sal discussed all they had heard on the ship and Norman listened carefully. From the brothers, he learned that it was the dry season, and that in that year of 1845, a group called the American Colonization Society, to repatriate freed slaves from America, was exploring forty thousand square miles along the Atlantic. Damon spoke extensively about what he would do with his land. Monrovia lay along the coast — forty miles long and three miles wide — and was purchased by the ACS from some local tribes to use as a central city for the new settlers, the freed slaves. There were several organizations that had contributed to the American majority's interest in ridding the cities of free Negroes — from Maryland, Virginia, and Mississippi — but the American Colonization Society was the first and the largest. Sal had heard on the ship that the coastal land had a number of brick mansions with rubber farms that stretched for miles. In order to make money, the settlers sold the rubber and iron ore from their farms and mines to sailors and traveling merchants who roamed Africa's western coast.

The brothers spoke late into the night, while Norman wove in and out of sleep. The next morning, he awoke to more commotion outside the jailhouse. He noticed his porridge and water near the bars, and glanced at the window toward an early afternoon sun. Norman had slept much later than he had hoped, and wondered if the brothers were still in their cells, and if they had caused all the noise outside. He quickly swallowed cold and rigid mouthfuls of porridge and bread. The door of the jailhouse swung open and Norman expected the sailors to deliver prisoners from the morning ship, as they had delivered Damon and Sal the previous day. He drank the last of his water and looked toward the cell bars for those who would be delivered. Norman heard heavy breathing and the shuffling of boots.

"This way," someone shouted.

The commotion sounded like an intense effort to restrain someone. Norman approached the cell bars to take a look, and he saw a man's body thrust across the jailhouse hallway. The man, the same one who brought in his food ration every day, landed hard on the concrete and moaned in pain. Shouting now in what sounded like fear, the men in the entry continued the fracas. Another one was thrown across the hallway, landing next to the first man, who still writhed in pain. Norman pushed his face through the bars to see what was happening. There he saw a young man, who looked no older than he, whose muscles bulged underneath a stained shirt. The man looked to be fighting the jail keepers, all of them, alone. As Norman looked at the man's incredible strength, he squeezed the bars, only to discover that finally, his gift had returned. His hands faded before him. Norman gazed at the brawl and the young man looked up, looked him right in the eyes, and then Norman disappeared.

Norman Aragon traveled the coasts of Monrovia's Mesurado County during the day, and at night he found resting places in the forests and woods. He stole two shirts, a map, and a satchel from a nearby home, and he decided to roam the new land independently. Based on the map, he was making his way north toward Freetown, all the while seeing signs of how the settlers were expanding their mansions and farms from the coast to the inland territories, poking into the villages of indigenous groups.

In this place the day moved at a magician's pace. Every bend or creak of her neck came with armies of smells. The view from the highest peak revealed rows upon overlapping rows of forests and hills. The animals gossiped and were participants in quarrels and violent battles of tooth and claw in which all losers became acquainted with death.

In his second week in Monrovia, Norman wandered off a dirt road and into the forest to find a fruit tree from which he could eat. There he found a cluster of tamarind trees. Norman shimmied his way up a tree, his youthful muscles flexing underneath his skin, until he reached some branches where the shelled orange-brown fruit sprouted among thin green calyxes. He shook the branch until the bulk of the tamarinds had fallen from the tree. Norman then descended and gathered the tamarinds, only to find that the shells were empty. Norman trailed farther inland, suspicious and hungry. In the middle of the forest, a leaf the size of two adjoined hands lay atop a bush, holding a mass of tamarinds. He hurried to the bush and glanced at the fruit, but at once sensed that something was wrong. Norman examined his surroundings. He took several steps toward the bush and blended into the forest. In an instant Norman's body was thrust from the bush and the giant leaf and tamarinds scattered. Norman Aragon shouted as he landed. He had difficulty standing to his feet, and was unable to speak.

A young man with dark skin jumped out of the bush with raised fists, hardened eyes, and stains on his shirt that looked like blood. He did not resemble the natives who worked the rubber farms. He was rugged in appearance but still dressed like the settlers, and suddenly, Norman identified the familiarity of his face.

"You," he said, pointing. "It's you! From the jail?"

June Dey took a weighted step toward him.

"No trouble," Norman Aragon said as he held his back in pain.

June Dey looked confused, but he kept his fists up for protection.

"How you do that? Come up like that?" June Dey asked. Norman watched June Dey carefully; he raised his hands to block his face, and saw through the breaks in his fingers that June Dey was closely surveying his white skin, and his tall, curly hair.

"Don't want trouble," Norman said again, standing. "Just look for food."

"How I know that? How you do that?" June Dey asked.

"I did nothing," Norman lied and felt guilty for it. "And I got nothing. Just a small bag with some shirts. Nothing else. I was hungry and I stopped to eat," Norman said.

"I'm not stealing from you," June Dey said, to Norman's relief.

"You very strong," Norman said, examining June Dey from where he stood. "How did you manage to escape the jail? You fought all of them?"

June Dey did not respond.

"But you look hurt. You bleeding?" Norman asked.

"I'm doing all right," June Dey said. Norman took a step forward.

"Stay there!" June shouted.

Norman stopped. "I won't hurt you," he said, still cautious.

"Right, so keep your hands up," June said.

"Just seems like both of us travel alone. I can help find us food," Norman said.

"Still keep your hands up."

Carefully watching him, June Dey ran to retrieve the remaining tamarinds. He threw several toward Norman and devoured the rest.

"I . . . can fish," Norman offered after eating the tamarinds. "I plan to find water by the day's end for a proper meal. You should come eat."

June Dey cleared the ground of leaves to uncover stranded fruit and tore through the shells. "No water close to here," he murmured.

"I can find it. I know this — I know forests well."

"That's all right. Seem as though you

know some other tricks too," June Dey said and quickly stood. "Nearly scared me to death." He wiped his mouth.

"No cause," Norman said.

"Where about you from?" June Dey asked after finding that there was nothing edible left on the forest floor. "And how long you think it take us to find some water?"

"Jamaica," Norman answered. "And I estimate a few hours or so."

"Where that?" June Dey asked.

"The islands. In the Antilles," Norman answered but could tell by the motion of June's face that he did not know what was being referenced. "Below Florida," Norman continued.

"Florida," June Dey said, nodding. "A slave on the islands?"

"No. I was free," Norman said, swallowing hard, remembering that what he said was only partially true. "Don't mean much with color on your skin."

June Dey examined Norman Aragon. His skin was as pale as that of most of the settlers in Monrovia, but he was not properly dressed. Norman wore a pair of trousers torn at the knee, and a linen shirt with loose sleeves and several missing buttons.

"Where are you from?" Norman asked.

"Virginia," June Dey answered.

"How long have you been here?"

"Three weeks or so. This last week been hard, but I eat whatever I can find. You?"

"Same," Norman answered. "I landed not long before you."

"Yeah? What they put you in jail for?"

"Stealing food," Norman admitted, following a bout of silence. "On deck."

"Well. Look like neither of us going back there anytime soon," June said; he feigned a smile.

"I'm trying my luck at Freetown," Norman said. "It's Great Britain's territory and I hear Maroons are there from the islands. You should come." He looked closely at June's face, awaiting the rejection he had become accustomed to from the boys back on the mountain.

"All right then," June Dey said. He looked as if he wanted to ask Norman a question but instead said: "I'll take some fish. Took me two days to find these," June Dey said, returning his gaze to the empty tamarind shells on the ground. "What you been eating?" he asked.

"I fish. There are some plants you can eat also . . . other than the fruit. I'm still learning the land. Can you fish?"

"No," June Dey said.

"That's all right," Norman answered.

264

"Let's be on our way."

Norman turned his back to June Dey and started out of the forest.

"You swim?" Norman Aragon asked. "And my name is Norman. Norman Aragon." He held out his hand, realizing his teeth were showing through a widened smile.

"No," June Dey answered, shaking his hand. "My name Moses."

Norman nodded. "How did you bruise your back?" he asked.

"I got into a fight," June Dey answered.

Norman stopped walking. "Your wounds need tending? I know how to find an herb for wounds," he added.

"No. It ain't my blood," June Dey said.

Norman released a nervous sigh. "Okay," he said.

"Say, why you being so nice? Who sent you?" June Dey asked.

"Nobody. Happy to talk to somebody again, that's all. Ride was long," Norman said. He wanted to ask June about his strength, which he knew would be useful to him if they continued together, since the force with which June Dey had thrown Norman out of the bush had left him sore, and he tried to hide this soreness, anxious to make a friend out of him.

"Where were you headed to?" Norman

asked instead.

They stepped over a massive tree that had fallen.

"Didn't know. Hadn't thought about nothing. Just trying to survive."

"Yes, of course."

"You by yourself then? No Pa or Ma? Nobody come with you?" June asked.

"No, they both died when I was young. Ma was a slave on the island," he said. "You?"

"Same. Died some years back," June answered and shook off the painful memory. "You got people where you going?"

"Still don't know. Still trying to learn the coast but I think we can make it there in a few weeks' time if we keep north," Norman said.

"It sound good," June said. "I suppose that's what I'll be doing too."

They arrived on a beach in the amount of time that Norman Aragon had estimated. He held a sharp stick that he had retrieved from the forest, and as they proceeded up the coast he moved the stick along the sand and left a long trail behind them. Every half mile or so Norman went into the ocean and inspected the water for subtle cracks in the waves, signs that food was not far below the surface. The fish scattered, avoiding the sudden intrusion of Norman's legs into their home.

"I'll just fish here," Norman said.

June Dey collected sticks and other debris from the shore and placed them in a circle not far from where Norman was fishing. In the ocean Norman had his hands raised and surveyed the water for movement. Every minute or so after standing almost completely still in the water, he thrust his hands beneath the surface in hopes of pulling up food.

When June Dey had collected what he felt were enough sticks, he sat and screamed out to Norman Aragon: "Figure you know how to make fire too!" and chuckled. Norman continued to focus on the life beneath the waves, and finally caught three or so fish. He then made a fire to roast what he had caught, and June Dey worked quickly through the meal, leaving no flesh on the tender bones.

Norman's kindness seemed to disarm June Dey. With each bite, it was as if he would burst with stories of the times he had gone without food, or without speaking to anyone for months. Memories that looked to have returned and sat idly on his tongue.

"Thank you," June Dey said. Norman nodded. Norman had never had a friend his age, but almost instantly he knew that if one existed, June Dey would be it.

Norman left him near the pile of wood and hot ashes and headed toward a coconut tree in the distance. He returned with five coconuts that he cracked on a nearby rock. June Dey drank the water inside the coconut. His stomach became wide and he placed his hands on it, as he had seen Mr. Emerson and other men who enjoyed full stomachs do after meals.

They sat before the waning fire until the bottom of the sun kissed the ocean's surface.

"You arrived, my son," I said, circling June Dey as I whispered in his ear. "Rest, my darling." I kissed his face as I passed.

June Dey lay on his side in the sand. Night paralyzed him. He looked as though it was the first good day he could remember.

Before Monrovia, it had all occurred so quickly.

"You already missed the food for today," said an old man — dark, slender-faced, with new trousers, patting June Dey's shoulder. June Dey's eyes slowly opened to a sunset sail. His body had been covered with a sheet while he slept, and after being awoken by the man, he used one end of the sheet to wreath his face.

"Here. Take this," the man said, handing June Dey an apple that he sliced with a dull cutting knife. June sat up. He surveyed the brown faces on the ship, the dark blue ocean on all sides.

"We ain't there yet?" he asked.

"Got a long way to go till we reach Africa, boy."

"Africa?!" June asked with surprise. He thought the ship he had snuck onto would take him north to New York.

The other passengers looked toward June. Some smiled his way; some gaped at the stains on his shirt, remembered their pasts, and quickly turned from him.

"What Africa? This ain't the New York ship?" June asked.

"New York came and went. You was so tired you slept right through it," the man said. "Don't worry, they seen you and ain't wake you to ask for your ticket. Feeling sorry for you, I guess." The man's head was bald except for tiny gray hairs that coiled above his ears and in small patches across his face.

June leaned toward him.

"Where they at?" he whispered.

The man shook his head.

"Down below resting, or on the other side

of the deck. Somewhere 'round here finding something to do. Stop being so nervous." The man laughed. "Ain't seen so many free colored folks in they life watch." He bit a slice of his apple.

"Free?"

"Free." He leaned toward June Dey when he said this.

The man smiled and portions of the chewed apple peeked between his teeth.

"And you believe it? Free?"

"I think it's free as we gone be. Don't 'spect to find anything worse'n I already gone through."

The man nodded toward June Dey's bloody shirt. June looked down and remembered running his fist into a man's face. None of the blood was his.

There were so many questions he wanted to ask at once, but his weakness, and the uncertainty of how long it would take before someone discovered who he was and threw him off the ship, kept him quiet.

"How old you is?" the man asked him.

"Almost got twenty years," answered June.

"That's my boy age."

June nodded.

"He ain't dead. They sold him. Was in the field and swore he was out there. Get back my wife nearly passed out crying. Sold him right from under me. Can't take no more after that — we run away."

"You made it, huh?" June asked.

"Made it up to New York but my wife got sick; she ain't eat much. She ain't live much long after."

"Sorry."

"No need," the man continued. "Figure she with all the other family we done lost. Probably with my boy up there too," the man said.

The water crashed against the boat.

"You ever try find him?" June asked.

"What you think?"

June turned around and looked over the edge of the boat. He thought of his mother, Darlene.

"Always wonder what a place like New York was like."

"Ain't nothing," the old man said.

"You like it there for yourself, why you taking all the trouble to go to this here free colony?"

"What you think? Seem everybody I ever know ain't got time to do nothing. Someday you want time to do some things you never had time to do. That's all."

June Dey felt his stomach reach up and grab his throat.

"They can't be trusted," he whispered.

"Ain't trust them ever. Ain't starting now," he said to the old man.

"That's the way you see it, that's the way it's gone be. Don't make no difference now, though, since we already a few days out to sea. Be there soon's you know it."

"Tell me all you can about this place. This colony," June Dey said.

"They either finally got to feeling bad for what they done, or they got too many of us and want to send some back," the man said.

"Second one sound right. Nobody ask me if I want to go," he murmured.

"Better thank God you free, boy. Got many a people want be in your place." June Dey sensed that the man was offended and he nodded toward him. The man took a few deep breaths, settling his emotions, before he continued: "Man I work for in New York part of this church where folks took to buying slaves and setting 'em free. Ain't heard of nothing like it 'fore I went there so I ain't believe they was up to no good. Figure they likely take the slaves to they house for theyselves; thought they was them kind of folks. They ain't want nothing much, just ask to tell 'em stories of what we gone through while we was slaves. Somebody come write it all down and they end up teaching most us how to read and write f'ourselves.

272

"So I start helping them get together other men and women like myself that come up north to start working that think going back to Africa a good idea. Some of 'em ain't want no part of it. They figure it just another way of getting colored folks out the white folks' way in the north. Some colored folk say white folks don't want us working with them and all around them like we started to be, that's why they want us all back to Africa so bad. Plus, I tell 'em white folks in the free colony, too, making sure everything go right and they say, 'If it's free, why white folks got to be there?' "

"That's what I ask too," June Dey interrupted.

"Anyhow, I tell people, everybody I can. Seem most folks want to come folks been free they whole life. Folks been slaves want to stay till they hear everything good."

"I s'pose it is good if this ain't the first ship," June said.

"Boy. Boy . . . boy. . . . You dropped something, boy."

They arrived at Cape Mesurado on a Wednesday afternoon. "Boy!" the man shouted as June Dey walked ahead of him. Settlers waited onshore to direct the new travelers to waiting members of the new colony. "Boy!" the man called out as June Dey's steps became more and more rapid. He passed the waiting settlers. He sped by the American Colonization Society workers and sailors. "Boy, you dropped something!" the man shouted, gaining the attention of other settlers while June Dey ran as quickly as he could up the beach and away from the ship. I ran by his side; my baby, now a man with a gaze just like Dey's. My baby made his way back.

"There you are, my darling," I whispered in his ear.

The man opened the folded sheet of paper that had fallen from June Dey's pocket. Sketched on the page was a picture of June's face underneath the heading: WANTED: MOSES EMERSON: $100,000 REWARD. MURDERER, KIDNAPPER, THIEF, CANNIBAL, MUTILATOR, PRACTICER OF WITCHCRAFT.

"My God. That was him. That's the boy," he said and squeezed the sheet in his hands. It had been one month that he had entertained Moses Emerson the slave, unaware. Like many I had seen on the ship, he likely thought June Dey was a legend — the man whose skin never broke, who could defeat armies of patrols and their relentless bitches with his bare hands, and who had protected so many of their people as they journeyed north, a hero and the most wanted man in America.

"Take care, boy," the man murmured to himself and watched several sailors run after June Dey. Some stopped when they realized that it would be no use. The others would eventually capture him, but June Dey, although he was exhausted from the journey, had still managed to escape from the jail before he was even placed in a cell.

He was gone.

Norman Aragon awoke the following morning and found a corner near a peninsula of rocks to bathe. When he returned to the pile of wood and cold ashes and June Dey was still sleeping, he left again and explored the nearby woods. When he returned again and June Dey still lay on the sand, Norman circled June, who was now lying on his back. He knelt down beside him and lowered his ear to June Dey's nose. A flutter of sighs escaped him. Norman stood. He shook June Dey, but he did not wake up.

He tried again and June Dey remained on the sand. Norman sat beside June Dey and unbuttoned June's shirt, and as he'd suspected, a trail of red hives covered the boy's chest and upper arms.

"Poison," Norman said to himself.

He contemplated for a moment, then pulled June's body toward him. Norman placed a finger in June Dey's mouth and pushed it as far down as he could. June Dey's body jerked in his grasp. Norman pulled a wet finger out of the boy's mouth and June Dey vomited onto the shore. He lay weak in his puke as his body shuddered.

Norman quickly stood and returned to the forest, searching through the colorful plants and dried vines for a small herb that would detoxify his new friend. In the middle of the woods, there was a large cave with an opening that was partially covered by a berry bush. There, sprouting from a muddy wall, were tiny areca palms. Norman inspected the plant. In order for it to provide June Dey with the energy and nutrients he needed once he recovered, he would have to drink from the root of the plant, Norman thought. He feared that if he picked the plants and walked back to the beach to June, the roots would have dried in the sun by the time they got there. It was cooler in the cave, anyhow, and he knew that dehydration could only make June's state worse. He returned to the beach, where June lay just as he had left him, in a pool of vomit. He grabbed June's arms and dragged him from the beach and through the woods. In the small enclosure, he lay June against the muddy walls. Norman picked several plants, squeezed the stems, and fed June Dey.

Norman Aragon then exited the cave and went into the forest to find drinking water, a creek or lake from which to collect it. There, a long road spread before him between two palm trees.

"This way," I whispered in Norman's ear. He stopped and glanced at the woods around him, as though he had heard my voice, and I gently encouraged him off the road toward a diverging path.

After several miles, just as Norman Aragon was going to return to the main road, he heard a stream in the near distance. He pursued the sound. At the end of the path, a slender row of bush canes blocked the opening to the water. Norman pushed the canes out of the way and before him was a river of clear water that streamed inland. As Norman Aragon looked onto the river's shore, his eyes grew wide.

There, lying lifeless and striking, was a woman with oil-black skin and long red hair. Her hair was tangled with green leaves and she was almost naked; the cloth that hung from her torso was tattered and worn.

Norman wondered if the stories Nanni told him as a child of Mamy Wateh had been real, those stories of the Queen of Sea Atlantis and mermaids that had terrorized him in his sleep. He stood still, silent, gathering his thoughts, reasoning with himself. At last he stepped through the stalks and onto the shore. Standing a yard or so away from her, Norman cleared his throat.

"Hello," he said, shaking.

She did not respond.

"Hello?" he asked.

She moved her head toward him and he jumped. She then moved her head in the other direction and moaned. Norman took a deep breath and went closer to her, picking her up and throwing her body over his shoulder.

Her smell was strong; her hair scratched his skin. He was haunted and unsettled in the presence of the bedeviled carcass.

"But Africa need us," he murmured to himself as he carried her. "Remember your gift."

When Gbessa opened her eyes, it was Safua she hoped to see. She envisioned his pitiful eyes and remembered when he had sent her away. "You must leave," he had said. "You must leave and never come back." She thought of the previous night and his promise to follow her. He knew her thoughts and it was this understanding of what transpired that softened his eyes. At that moment she had hoped she would prove courageous enough to take his hand to run with her — to leave their village and escape with her to the forest forever — but she obeyed him like his child or his lover and walked away from Lai. His rejection was the last thing she remembered of him, yet he was the first thing she hoped to see once life crept back.

Gbessa examined the mark where the snake had bitten her. The pain had subsided. She was in a small cave with a dried vine tied to her wrist. The thick vine was tied to a stick that protruded from the wall of the cave. Gbessa's tongue tasted bitter, and she coughed from the bottom of her stomach. She noticed the areca palm on the ground beside her and spit on the floor. She was happy that she was able to see, since her last memory was a blind swim through moving water before fainting on the shore.

Gbessa examined the vine around her wrist. She played with it to free herself.

While she fidgeted, she heard a shifting in the corner of the cave. When Gbessa looked up, she saw a man with a bloody shirt who moved his head against the wall. He coughed and spit onto the cave floor, then rubbed his eyes with his hands. The man moved as if he was dizzy, intermittently drooping over to regain his balance. Gbessa moved at a quicker speed to relieve her wrists.

A man sat across the cave from her, and he looked as if he had had too much palm wine, dizzy and in the wilderness between dreams and morning. June Dey shouted as the sight of Gbessa struck him. His eyes trailed from her face as it obtruded from the black cave and to the clothes that hung loosely off her round breasts and hips, her dark thighs and legs. His breath was gone from him. He looked around the cave, perhaps for his friend, Gbessa thought, then June crawled across the cave toward Gbessa and tried to loosen the vine on her wrist. Gbessa kicked her legs out toward him in fear. He backed away from her.

"I will do it!" she yelled.

He did not understand.

"Trying to help you out," he said.

She did not understand his language either.

June Dey continued untying the string.

"Stop! I will do it!" Gbessa said, assaulting him with her eyes. She wanted to run.

June Dey followed the vine with his hand to where it was tied onto the stick that protruded from the cave wall. Desperate, he then grabbed the vine and pulled it outward. He looked different from anyone that Gbessa had ever seen. He pulled until the vine finally snapped.

"Good. Free," he said.

Gbessa held her hand up and the vine dangled from it. She immediately tore off from the hanging string and headed out of the cave. June Dey touched her arm.

"Where you going?" he asked.

She slapped his hand off of her and continued out.

"Wait, I only tried to help you," he asked again, this time holding her wrist.

At this, Gbessa flew at June Dey and grabbed his neck. Her advance made him lose his balance and he fell to the floor on his back.

With her hands around his neck, Gbessa squeezed. She sat on top of him and slapped him as hard as she could. June Dey regained his strength and they wrestled in the cave. As she slapped him, he tried to restrain her hands. He was able to grab both of her wrists for a moment and stop her violent advance, but as soon as she distracted him with a kick and her hands were free, Gbessa dug her fingers into his back and scratched downward. Gbessa's hands returned to her, without blood or loose skin and flesh. She gasped. June Dey remained still and stared into her face and Gbessa walked around his body, but saw that his back was neither scarred from her scratches nor bleeding.

"You curse too," she said to his face. "You curse." Gbessa touched his chest, where the last of the small hives trailed from his neck. She left the cave, and when she returned, she held a large seashell, the contents of which looked like green mud.

"Sit," she said, pointing to the cave floor. June Dey sat and she knelt in front of him.

Gbessa grabbed a handful of the contents of the shell and gently rubbed it on the hives. At first contact, June Dey could not restrain a sigh of relief at the cooling sensation. The mud sank into him. When Gbessa finished, she crawled to the opposite wall and sat facing him.

"You curse," she said again, though she understood that he spoke a different language. "I'n mean to hurt you. I thought you mean to hurt me," she said.

Gbessa was startled when Norman Aragon returned to the cave. He held two long sticks of roasted fish, and two large shells filled with water. Gbessa watched as Norman rushed to June Dey's side when he noticed the green color oozing from June Dey's chest.

"What is that?" Norman asked.

"I'm doing all right," June said. "She put something on there. Imagine it make the hives go away. What happened?"

"You ate poison, I think. I will have to teach you about tropical forests," he said and looked at Gbessa.

Gbessa sat against the wall near a pile of leaves. Norman Aragon stumbled to his feet, tripping and falling after looking into Gbessa's face. He blushed, quickly stood, and sat beside June Dey, and Gbessa's comfort diminished. She pulled her knees to her chest and fixed her body to stand up. June Dey stretched out his hand.

"He all right," he said, looking toward Norman Aragon.

Gbessa examined Norman, his white skin and foreign hair and eyes.

"You a curse," Gbessa said, pointing at Norman Aragon. "You a curse, yeh? Yeh?"

Norman did not understand. He appeared hesitant to approach her again, but he went over and knelt in front of her.

"I a curse too," she said as her eyes filled.

He told her hello in Ashanti, and Gbessa creased her eyebrows and curiously repeated him. Gbessa raised her hand to Norman Aragon's mouth as it moved. She touched his cheek and eyes and lightly pushed them with her fingertips. She then touched her own face and hair and smiled.

"She was trying to break free when I woke up," June Dey said, interrupting their clashing spirits. "She all right when she feel safe. She'll fight if she don't."

Norman Aragon nodded. "Well then," he said, exasperated. "We have food. Food. Fish," he said to Gbessa. "Food." He pointed to the fish. Gbessa looked at the meal and was even more impressed, more touched that these men had chosen to share their food with her.

"Others here too?" she asked, looking around the cave. She walked out to a waiting sun to see if more cursed wanderers were to be found. None were there and Gbessa returned to the cave where June Dey and Norman Aragon waited patiently, all eyes on her spellbound face.

As they dined quietly, with only the flicker of a small fire to accompany the chorus of their breathing, Gbessa looked around the cave in wonder. She had never seen a white man up close; she had only heard stories about them. Norman Aragon was not as Gbessa had imagined. He had no fangs or wings, no knife or stick. Just pale skin, tall hair, and a lap of fish and shells.

They were together now. It had begun. I dwelled in that hiding place with the three of them that night. However present the stronghold of loneliness had been on each of their lives, there lingered a hope that perhaps one day they would find others. In that moment, hope's shell melted, and it extended its limbs and breathed, became real. Became true. Alike spirits separated at great distances will always be bound to meet, even if only once; kindred souls will always collide; and strings of coincidences are never what they appear to be on the surface, but instead are the mask of God.

There was one footpath that led them to the hills from the woods where they slept. Norman followed behind Gbessa and June Dey, who took great care in clearing what he could of fallen branches and rocks for Gbessa to pass. Every time June Dey moved a branch or helped Gbessa over fallen trees, usually earning laughter or words in Gbessa's language that neither could understand, Norman stiffened.

"Thank you, yeh?" she said to June Dey kindly, but he could not know what she was saying. The road wound atop the hills between acre-long gardens of wildflowers and plants of untamed yellows, between swamps and grain farms that forced Gbessa to recall Lai and her childhood. "You doing all right?" Norman asked, sensing the hesitation in her step. Gbessa glanced at his mouth and continued. They stopped walking in the afternoon, and made a fire on land that had been cleared. Norman had picked several oranges when they passed the orange field. He had used a stick and struck each branch until his bag was full of them, periodically glancing at Gbessa to make sure she noticed. That night he shared the oranges with them in front of the fire. While they walked he also found a flower near a bush that grew wildly out of a cotton tree. He retrieved that from his bag as well, and handed it to Gbessa.

"For you," Norman said, and Gbessa took it from him and squeezed the stem.

A short while after, Gbessa left them to find a clearing where she could relieve herself, and June Dey, who had been quiet since witnessing Norman offering her the flower, finally asked:

"You like her then, huh?"

Norman guessed by June Dey's tone that he would try to pursue Gbessa as well. He shrugged, but the thought worried him. The light from the fire glowed against June Dey's body and face, a handsome face that caused Norman to feel as if he was shrinking just by looking at it.

"What you two gone talk about?" June Dey asked with a straight face, before bursting into laughter. He laughed so hard he held his stomach, and he reached over and patted Norman on the shoulder. Norman was surprised, elated, and eventually he joined June Dey, giggling, and also happy.

The next morning, the sun crept into the cave where they slept and awakened him out of his sleep later than usual. Outside of the cave, Norman heard what sounded like the rustling of leaves by local forest animals. As he stretched and prepared to begin his day, the movement outside escalated into the mad dash of dozens of footsteps trampling the dried leaves. The sound also awoke both June Dey and Gbessa. Norman held his finger over his lips to silence them before they could make a sound. He stood slowly and moved toward the exit from the cave. But by the time the sun hit his face and eyes, it was too late for Norman Aragon to run from it. Outside of the cave, a dozen or so men pointed rifles toward him. Upon the sight of their guns, Norman lifted his hands.

"Get from behind him!" one of the men said in French. *"Montrez vos visages!"*

"They're Frenchmen," Norman said under his breath. "Don't come out," Norman warned June Dey and Gbessa. Inside the cave, June Dey covered Gbessa's mouth with his hand. He peered through the opening as his muscles hardened underneath his skin.

"Vous êtes Américains?" one of the men asked, his gun waiting to fire at Norman.

Norman recognized the language as French, from a book he had read while on the mountain. He knew that France and England were occupying some colonies to the north, but he was unsure why they were exploring Monrovia's inland.

"Vous êtes Américains?!" the man asked again, this time taking a step closer to Norman Aragon.

A couple of the men had coils of rope attached to their belts. While still holding their guns, they reached for the ropes and began to uncoil them. Norman took one step toward the men.

"Y restez!" one of the men with the rope shouted.

Norman Aragon ran quickly into the forest, where his body completely disappeared in the trees. The Frenchmen, alarmed, looked frantically through the trees to find him — then back at one another in confusion.

"Le garçon!" they shouted. "He vanished!"

Before they could process what had happened, June Dey leaped from the cave toward them. The men quickly pulled the triggers beneath their trembling fingers, but the bullets flew toward June Dey and fell to the ground immediately after touching his skin. As some of the men took extra bullets from their pockets, shaking uncontrollably at the mystifying outcome that had met them, others ran. June Dey then advanced, pushing and fighting with fists that held the power of an army of one thousand men. They attempted to rival June Dey, but could not stand against the boy's strength and tenacity. Their bodies cracked under the weight of his fists. As June Dey fought, the ropes from the men's belts rose and tied their wrists and ankles as June Dey knocked them to the ground. Norman Aragon, after tying the ropes, appeared and finished the knots that held the Frenchmen captive. They shook in coupled shame and fear on the forest floor.

When it was finished, a dozen or so men lay on the ground with emptied rifles. June Dey stood and looked over at Norman. Gbessa hurried out of the cave and the three of them looked at one another, unsure of what to think of what had occurred, but just as equally enlivened by their collective power and possibilities. Gbessa ran from the mouth of the cave, jumping and clapping.

"Enh, you see?!" she shouted. "Curse do good. Curse do good!"

Shortly after exiting the forest, they heard a faint wailing. June Dey heard it first and thought it was a bird that had lost its way.

"You hear that?" he asked.

"More," Norman said. They ran inland, reentering the forest, and the wail grew into a chorus.

"You hear that?" June Dey asked again.

"Yes. Come!" Norman forged ahead.

In the distance, voices cried out and mingled with the heat of the afternoon. A thumping noise then met their ears and Gbessa stopped.

"Guns," Norman Aragon said.

"Let's go," June Dey said, advancing eagerly. Norman Aragon pulled him back.

"Be careful," Norman said. They hurried toward the noise. Motivated by the sound, June Dey ran ahead of them and entered the hills. Gbessa spotted a clearing in the woods and pointed to it. They knelt with their backs hunched and bodies lowered among the tall weeds and brushes. There was a hole in one of the bushes that barely fit all of their faces but allowed them to see beyond the woods and into a small village. They peered through the hole, and as they suspected, more men with rifles were revealed. Gbessa gasped. The Frenchmen poked their rifles at the villagers, who were tied together and seated in four long lines in the middle of the village circle. Their houses were engulfed in flames, as was a small rice field beyond the circle. A herd of goats ran freely about, scattering the land in avoidance of what they knew was the villagers' doom. The men were seated in one line, the women formed two lines, and the children were chained together and seated between the two sets of women.

The leader of the men's line, an old man with a pointed chin, the chief, looked up at the sun as it hid behind a stream of clouds.

The man looked to be praying in the Kru language. The Kru chief closed his eyes and leaned backward so his face was wholly fixed on the sun. The Frenchmen paced between the lines of chained Kru people. A few were in the distance in conversation. When the Kru chief opened his eyes, he gazed through the clearing and noticed June Dey's face. June Dey dropped his head. When he raised it again, the Kru chief gazed directly into his eyes.

"Come now, brother," the chief yelled in Kru.

Without warning, a shot resonated throughout the hills and the old man fell facedown onto the circle as blood flowed from his wounded head. The line of women collectively released a tortured cry that extended from the village circle into the woods. Norman Aragon looked into June Dey's eyes, then gazed through the clearing. He held his palm out toward Gbessa.

"Stay here," he said and pointed to the ground.

Norman then blended into the trees of the wood as his footsteps traveled the dust into the village circle.

June Dey was ready.

Gbessa looked through the clearing. As a Frenchman was reaching for his gun, Norman wrested it from his hands and threw it to the ground. The man bent down to pick up his gun and Norman kicked it. The man attempted to retrieve the gun once more, and when Norman did the same, causing the gun to appear as though it were gliding across the dust, the other Frenchmen shook with fear, vigilantly turning toward the forest. They pointed their guns toward the woods and sky, toward the villagers and their burning houses. Their guns were then pushed out of their hands and gathered in a pile near the field. Norman Aragon's footsteps appeared near the pile. June Dey took one giant leap out of the woods and into the circle where the villagers sat. He balled his hands into fists as the men surged toward him.

"*Le garçon!*" one of the men yelled. "*Le garçon!*"

June Dey ran toward the men with his iron fists. He came into their backs and sides with gathered fingers and a heaving chest. They attempted to fight back, but it proved a difficult task without their guns. Gbessa emerged and faced the chaos, untying the ropes from around the wrists and ankles of the villagers. A Frenchmen crept from behind Gbessa and grabbed hold of her neck, lifting her off the ground as she struggled to breathe. He then threw her down, continuing to choke her until he thought he had squeezed all of the life out of her body. When he believed he had killed her, the man turned to go, wiping his hands on his pants, but Gbessa sat up, choking. He turned around, bewildered, sure he had choked her to death. He returned to her, and before he could attempt to kill her again, June Dey seized the man's head by his hair and threw his body yards away onto a burning house. A Frenchman retrieved a knife from his boot and thrust it toward June Dey's arm. The blade made a sound against his unbreaking skin, the tip bending upon impact. June Dey eyes swelled, reddened; he pulled the knife from the man's hand and tossed it to the ground. The Frenchman fell, unable to steady his violently trembling limbs. His fellow Frenchmen looked on in amazement.

"Where are your fists?" June Dey asked, each step mightier than the last as he confronted the man. *Where are your fists?*

Norman Aragon finished untying the line of men, who leaped forward and joined June Dey to avenge their soil and the death of their dear chief.

The Frenchmen scattered toward the woods and hills. Norman Aragon untied the remaining villagers. June Dey nodded at Norman Aragon, and the villagers danced around him, and cried underneath the yellow sun.

"Where is the girl?" Norman Aragon asked June Dey, noticing that Gbessa was nowhere to be found.

"One of them tried to choke her. Thought she died but she sat right back up. Was lying right there," June Dey said. Norman glanced at the bush where he had told Gbessa to remain. He rushed to the outlying woods but Gbessa was not to be found.

"The girl!" Norman yelled at the villagers. June Dey ran from the circle toward the bush and Norman Aragon followed. She was gone. Norman Aragon heard the gallops of horses in the distance. They had lost her. At that moment another scream stirred the inner hills and the Kru villagers ran to find refuge and weapons.

"Another attack!" June Dey said, looking out into the distance.

"We got to get the girl!" Norman charged, but June Dey held him back.

"More need us," June Dey said. This was what Nanni had meant, Norman then thought. They were drawn back to this place, not for themselves, but to fight. June Dey pulled Norman's arm to follow him farther into the hills.

"She is like you," June Dey said. "Like us. Gifted. We will meet her again."

Norman saw the trace of Gbessa's face. He wanted to protect her, to know her, to follow her. She was gone, but June Dey was right and Norman knew it. This land and its marvelous power — this bewitching colony of free people — would reunite him with Gbessa the witch. This was not meant to be their last adventure.

Whatever happened, she would live. This is what she told herself after being dragged by her hair to the woods outside the village.

Gbessa screamed, but neither Norman Aragon nor June Dey heard her amid the chaos of the skirmish. She was fearful of what the men would do to her — their eyes reddened with hatred and an equal dose of fear. They panted heavily as they ran away. Her body was thrown over the back of a horse, behind one of the escaping slavers as he galloped away. The slaver did not have time to tie her up, so to make sure she was secured on the horse, he took hold of Gbessa's hair. The pain was great and Gbessa's head pounded as the strands of her hair were violently pulled with the reins. Her body bounced against the horse's back and Gbessa tried to fight with the man, struggling to free her hair so that she would fall off the horse and escape, but the slaver's grip was too strong, and she felt the pain at the ends of her toes. She would have called out for June Dey or Norman Aragon if she had known their names. She was no Sande, but surely women were not handled this way where this man was from, she thought.

She had never known her father and she had not been allowed to leave her house, so her village had not taught her how women were to be treated. But Safua had disrupted the rhythm of that cruelty with his voice, with her song. And the wanderers, June Dey and Norman Aragon — they had disrupted the rhythm of that cruelty with their actions. She hated that she was denied them all — stolen from them in broad daylight. Gbessa cried, still fighting to release the slaver's grip on her hair. There were three other slavers on horses, and the others followed far behind on foot. So great was the pain from the jerking of her head that eventually Gbessa passed out.

After some time, they arrived at a river where three large ships were docked. The two leading slavers climbed down from their horses to join an ongoing conversation on the shore with men who spoke with large gestures, arms flailing with each word. A few young boys rushed toward the horses, pulling their reins toward the ship. When Gbessa recovered, dizzy and with an unceasing headache, she saw the men yelling in the distance. She recognized some from the first confrontation outside of the cave and knew that they were all discussing what had happened between Norman Aragon and June Dey. One of the men charged toward the horse that Gbessa was mounted on — his body sideways, the sun against his back. The man pulled Gbessa's arm until her body fell from the horse. She was still weak, her body aggrieved and not yet recovered from all she had experienced in the preceding weeks. The slaver squeezed her cheeks, and she could barely make out the lines of his face through the tears that had settled at the rims of her eyes. Gbessa gripped his wrist and tried to push him, but the slaver slapped her face hard, and she lay heaving on the shore. The man yelled toward the shore and another slaver approached. He picked up Gbessa and she once again resisted, falling off his shoulder. He kicked her stomach and others shouted toward him from the ships. Unable to endure the pain, Gbessa fell out of consciousness yet again. She would not die. I will not die, she thought, as her eyes closed.

When she awoke she felt the splinter of jagged iron squeezing her wrists. The chains were heavy and connected her to a boat, stranded and partially buried in the sand. The river's water crashed against her. Gbessa tugged at the chains but they were fastened tightly to the boat, each jerk further chafing her skin. From afar, the slavers scrambled to prepare and board their ships, their words and motions desperate. The sun was bright and one of the men came toward her from the ships. She was too weak to continue trying to free herself, so Gbessa waited for him to come.

"I'n scared of you!" she yelled as he approached.

At twenty yards away, she could now see that he was carrying a blade that gleamed in the sun. "I'n scared of you!" Gbessa shouted. He reached her, looking down at her black and resilient body. Gbessa's eyes hardened. She spit at him, and further angered, the slaver stabbed her, digging the blade as far as he could into her chest and pulling it quickly out. Gbessa screamed and blood rushed outward to the river water below. The trader left as quickly as he had come, joining the others as they boarded their ships. Blood came from her breasts, from her organs, her heart. The pain stung her, crippled her. But I will not die, Gbessa thought, and it was as reassuring as it was terrorizing, so much so that again she lost herself, fainting in a pool of her own blood.

■ ■ ■ ■

BOOK TWO:
SHE WOULD
BE KING

■ ■ ■ ■

■ ■ ■ ■

THE SHIP

■ ■ ■ ■

When ships left those shores, I followed them. I heard people inside, though there was nothing I could do. No matter how strong I became, I could not turn the sea back. I saw black bodies jump from the decks and sink like stones into the ocean below. In the bottom of the deep, there is a city of stones where those ancestors linger. There were many ships that crossed, though one of them was different. And I followed that different ship to the Americas.

First, the large steamer arrived in Key West, Florida, battered by the long journey from an African coast, farther south than Monrovia. Inside, some hundreds of shaking black and naked bodies huddled together to keep themselves warm and guarded from whips.

"Take care, my darlings," I hummed. Although there was no sleeping there. No peace in the bellies of those vessels. The ship anchored in Key West in 1845, long after 1808, when slave trading had been outlawed in America. Shortly following the capture of the guilty slavers, the men in Washington held a summit to decide what would happen to the ship and the rescued Africans.

"Send the matter to Polk!" was the resolve. "To Polk!"

Polk, the new president, had many concerns of greater importance than this problem of Africans captured after slavery was outlawed. Annexing Texas, for instance, expanding the United States, taxes, Britain's hold on Oregon, and a barren wife. Southerners would always worry about the rights of their property, the sustenance of their wealth and their wives and daughters amid a more and more attractive and intimidating Negro male lot. Northerners also would worry that the free Negroes would distract from the natural progress of their cities and would remain suspicious that the rumors of barbarism and insanity among Negroes would prove true and one day endanger them, or, worse, would prove false, and the reformed Negroes would one day hold them accountable for past ills. Runaways. Property ownership. Slave education. Slave marriage. Fugitive slaves. Now Africa was added to the list.

Polk would have to justify his decision at every turn, especially a decision that included money from Congress and taxpayers for Negroes. He wanted little to do with the American Colonization Society and what he considered the self-righteous, vitriolic Quakers behind it. In fact, Polk believed they most certainly hated Negroes the most. To spend the money and time required to send them back would be as maniacally racist as the man who brands his slaves as cattle, as the patrol who hunts for the thrill of seeing black flesh burn, the bigot, the motherfucker.

If the ACS wanted them to have the land, then they would pay for it. No more government funding.

"Send them back," he finally agreed. "Settle them in Monrovia. And if other ships are found or captured, send them there also. Send them all back." The response was great: objections from the black free Negro population that refused to leave the United States, a disgruntled South that argued that Polk had indirectly criticized the ownership of slaves, a suspicious North that believed that Polk was acting in the best interest of the South and Southerners. *Send them back.*

The ship set sail for Africa on a clear blue

morning. Inside, some four hundred Africans headed back across the Atlantic after their freedom was granted and the American Colonization Society petitioned their return to the free colony. A grant paid for full meals and water, and the ACS made sure that they were provided with clothing and livable accommodations. The ship lost nearly one hundred Africans from illness before landing in Grand Bassa, eighty miles or so south of Monrovia. There the Africans were unloaded from the ship onto a beach of mingled dust and sand. The ACS decided that the Africans would be divided among the settlers to be civilized and Christianized, to work on farms and add to the overall economy and diversity of the free colony.

As the Africans crowded the dock and shore, they were organized in lines with their backs to the ocean under the close guidance of the sailors. While they sat on the shore, two men — explorers, it seemed — headed toward the dock. In the way they were dressed, they appeared to be sailors, but the obvious roughness of their hands proved that they worked the land and may have been farmers of the colony. From a distance one of the men carried what looked like a black sack over his shoulders. When they reached the shore they laid the black sack on the ground. The port workers approached them, and stepped back suddenly upon the realization that in the black sack was the body of a woman. It was Gbessa. Her hair hung so long down her body that it covered both her nipples and privates, as the loose and tattered sheets around her could no longer do. The Africans on the shore called out to her upon seeing her, leaning over one another's shoulders in curiosity.

"What is this?" a porter asked.

"Hello. I'm Timothy. This is my brother Elliot," one of the men said nervously, pointing to the other. The worker nodded.

"What do you have here?" he asked again.

"We're missionaries some counties north of here in the Grebo territory with the Bajan settlers."

"Mm-hmm." The porter nodded.

"The ACS has been monitoring the coast for illegal slavers and they found her chained up, bloody and unconscious on an abandoned boat."

"Hmm."

"They recovered her and asked that we bring her to the dock. Said you would know what to do with her," Timothy said.

"She still alive?" the porter asked and

nudged the woman's leg with his shoe.

"They said you would know what to do here. Can you take her?" Timothy asked.

"Sure. We'll take her," said the porter finally. "The governors are coming later today to divide these." He pointed toward the Africans. "The mayors will be here too."

He looked down at the black woman; her nipples were exposed now. Blood ran to his young face.

"This damned place," he murmured to himself and looked out onto the ocean.

In her sleep she chanted softly, "Gbessa the witch, Gbessa the witch," and at this I kissed her face.

The porter stepped away from her.

"She said something," the porter said.

"You should expect it," replied Timothy. "But she won't wake up. Even if you shake her."

"Gbessa the witch, Gbessa the witch," Gbessa chanted softly as the sun pressed against her eyes. *Sleep,* Ol' Ma Famatta coaxed from a daylight moon before Gbessa could open her eyes. *Sleep.*

Gbessa heard humming so close that the small hairs around and in her ears rose and moved with the sound. Then what smelled like potato greens and chicken seasoned with bitterleaf aroused her senses. Her face and body still stung from the memory of being slapped and kicked by the French army men when they stole her during the attack. Her wrists panged and itched from the shackles placed around them. When the Frenchmen ran away that day, they left her to die.

But Gbessa could not.

So for two weeks she lay chained to the boat, taunted by the salty waves of the ocean as they smashed into her captive body. She fainted from hunger and thirst. The wound from her stabbing healed. Gbessa was teased by the few memories she had made with Norman Aragon and June Dey. She thought of them and she opened her eyes.

In front of her, a girl, short, black, and petite, was pouring a bucket of water into a huge white basin on the floor. On each side of the basin were two small tables; one was bare, and the other had a dish of cocoa butter, a small and empty tin bowl, and hair ribbons that lay messily on top of it. Near the door there was a window hung with long sheets that rose toward the girl after being pushed by the breeze outside. Across from Gbessa there was a low bed, the same height as hers, neatly made, with a book that rested on the pillow. The girl's back was turned away from Gbessa toward the window. She wore her hair up in a high bun. Gbessa wondered why the mattress across from her was lifted off the ground with sticks of wood. She wondered why the window was boarded with transparent sheets. Gbessa tried sitting up on the bed, but a sharp pain down the middle of her back disrupted her attempt. She remembered the position in which her body had been tied to the ship, straining her back, and she fell backward and closed her eyes.

The girl nearly dropped the bucket upon realizing that Gbessa had moved. She set the bucket near the basin and went to the bed. She clutched a handkerchief and pressed it against Gbessa's forehead. It felt cool against Gbessa's skin and she was grateful. She opened her eyes.

The girl was startled and pulled her hand away from Gbessa's forehead. They stared at each other silently — Gbessa unable to move, the girl unable to speak.

"You slept a long time," the girl said finally. When Gbessa did not respond, she reached toward Gbessa's head and lightly pressed the cool handkerchief along the side of her face.

"My name is Maisy," she said.

Gbessa did not respond.

"My name," Maisy said slowly as she pressed her palm against her chest, "is Maisy."

Gbessa remained silent, not understanding what the girl was saying, but Gbessa recognized that she spoke the same language as Norman Aragon and June Dey, and all at once reacquainted with her loss, she turned her face away. Maisy held the handkerchief in her lap.

"You a Bassa girl?" she asked Gbessa in the Bassa language.

Gbessa did not understand.

"You a Vai girl?" she asked Gbessa in the Vai language.

Gbessa quickly turned toward Maisy.

"Yes? You Vai?" Maisy asked.

315

"Vai," Gbessa said and coughed. Her throat was dry. Maisy grinned. Gbessa attempted to sit up again but fell backward in pain.

"You must not try sitting. You not well," Maisy said in Vai. Gbessa's hands relaxed and she rested them near her sides. Gbessa was happy that Maisy spoke Vai and seemed kind. She wanted to stay near Maisy, and as Maisy spoke, Gbessa admired her face. Maisy laughed again, pleased that she could communicate with the woman.

Maisy returned to a table beside the basin to grab a cup that she filled with water. She hurried back to Gbessa and lifted the woman's head; she pressed the cup to her lips, tilting it until water streamed down Gbessa's face.

The coolness tempered Gbessa's warm skin, and the sheets that hung from the window rose higher and higher in her direction; she closed her eyes.

For the next few days Maisy was the first person Gbessa saw when she opened her eyes. She wiped Gbessa's body down with cool water, propped her head up and fed her, and forced teaspoons of crushed iron herb into her mouth so that she could regain her energy.

One day while Maisy was out of the room, Gbessa awakened from a dream, gasping for breath. It was not until she caught her breath that Gbessa realized she was sitting up without any pain or reluctance. She heard Maisy's footsteps outside of the door so she lay back down and closed her eyes. Maisy entered the room, and upon the sight of Gbessa's resting body, she lightly closed the door.

A few moments later, Gbessa sat up again and gazed around the room and out the window. She lifted the sheet from her body and ran her fingers against her dress, a dress similar to the gown Maisy wore to sleep. Gbessa stepped out of the bed and went to the door to leave the room, but it was locked. She went to the window and pushed it open, but in the distance — as the birds gossiped, and their melodious cries sailed to reach her window; in the distance, as my patterned gestures of affection met her, coaxing her still, "There you are, my darling, my friend" — an emotion moved within her to lay her back down. To rest. To wait. To stay.

On another day Gbessa lay in bed and Maisy swept the room while humming. Three women swung the door open, greeted Maisy, and went directly to where Gbessa slept. At first, they reminded Gbessa of Norman Aragon; they had his features, but unlike his ambiguous, pale skin, theirs was darker. The women wore tight blouses tucked into colorful skirts that brushed the floor as they walked, rescattering the dirt that Maisy had already swept into a small pile near the window. One of them wore a large white hat and she gripped a book to her stomach.

"Maisy, are you getting bigger?" the woman with the hat asked, approaching Maisy. She raised one of Maisy's hands from her side.

"I don't think so, Miss Ernestine," Maisy answered.

"You're a fine girl, Maisy. So beautiful you are," Miss Ernestine said.

Ernestine Hunter was the widow of a wealthy, free African American who had died during one of the first pilgrimages to Monrovia. She had used his money to build one of the largest coffee farms in the colony, and like the other settlers, she hired men and women from indigenous villages to work her land and care for her home.

Gbessa stared at the woman, who, like Maisy, wore a long skirt and a blouse that covered her arms. She glanced out the window for rain, as she had gotten used to doing when Maisy was getting dressed, confused as to why she was covering herself when the sun looked so ripe against the sky. These were a different kind of Sande, Gbessa thought, not quite right in the head. They spoke no African language she had ever heard and sounded almost like birds when they spoke. The fact that Maisy was able to speak to these birds in the same way she was able to speak to her made Gbessa at times believe that Maisy was a medicine woman or priestess — the most grand of all.

"Turn around let me look at you," Miss Ernestine said to Maisy. Gbessa watched as Maisy smiled uncomfortably. "It's a good thing, because you used to be dry," Miss Ernestine said, laughing. Dry was a word she'd picked up from indigenous workers she had hired. It was the word they used to call something small or skinny.

Miss Ernestine left Maisy and went to the bed to join the other two — Mrs. Johnson, and her daughter, Marlene.

"This is her?" Miss Ernestine asked as she moved closer to Gbessa, who leaned away from the women as they huddled around her bed. "She's awake!" Miss Ernestine said, turning toward the other two.

"Maisy, I didn't know she was awake,"

Mrs. Johnson, the woman of the house, said. Mrs. Johnson's husband owned one of the largest houses in Monrovia, not far from the ocean beach. He was one of the free settlers who led Liberia, a man who'd earned his wealth as a lawyer in America before making the long journey with his family. Among his passions was a burgeoning newspaper, which he used to publish subtle liberal campaigns against the presence of the ACS in Monrovia. His passions also included his wife, and his only child, Marlene.

"She is, Mrs. Johnson, but she still doesn't have all her energy," Maisy answered shyly. Gbessa looked quickly from Maisy's mouth to the women's, watched their gestures, but did not want the woman to touch her. None except her healer, Maisy. Not until she knew the others were human.

"How much longer do you think it'll be before she can begin to help you? The governor's ball is at the year's end. The work is too plenty for you to do on your own. If she's not well, we can always take in somebody else to help you. I don't want you to wear yourself out."

"She will be well by then," Maisy assured her.

"Where is it again, Mama?" Marlene

asked Mrs. Johnson.

"Marlene, don't sound so anxious," Miss Ernestine interrupted her. "You'll never marry, sounding as anxious as you do."

Mrs. Johnson laughed. "Let her be, Ernestine," she said. Miss Ernestine shrugged and turned to face Gbessa, at whom she could not help but stare.

"She is a beautiful girl," Marlene remarked. "Is that all her hair?" Marlene extended her hand toward Gbessa, but Gbessa moved away from the hand, while releasing a sound of disapproval.

"Yes," Maisy answered. "It's okay," she said to Gbessa, who was happy to hear Maisy speak in Vai again.

"How peculiar," Marlene said.

"I want house girls at the house but I want to make sure my sons remain Christian," Miss Ernestine said with a grin. By this, Maisy explained to Gbessa that night when recalling the conversation, Miss Ernestine meant that she took notice of the recent marriages between a few male settlers and indigenous women who worked on the farms. While only passably concerned that her son's children would be as dark as the indigenous men and women, she was mostly afraid of losing them, and she was known for going to unreasonable extremes to keep

321

them single.

"Yes, well, perhaps my lack of sons is my blessing," Mrs. Johnson replied.

"You sure she is not sick?" Miss Ernestine asked.

"The doctor said she is fine, but she'll have to get another physical when she is up," Maisy said.

"She is strange looking is my opinion. Where did all that hair come from?" Miss Ernestine asked. "And the color. You sure her people didn't practice witchcraft?"

"I don't think so," Marlene answered.

"She is Vai," Maisy interrupted.

"She speaks to you?" Mrs. Johnson asked.

"No, ma'am, but I tried speaking to her in different coastal languages and Vai is the only one she responded to."

"So peculiar," Miss Ernestine said, bewildered. "Do I have any Vai workers?" she asked Maisy.

"I do not think so, Miss Ernestine."

"You do not come to my house much anyway, Maisy. It offends me — after all, I am only one house over. Alice, you have to let her visit me and sew my curtains," she said to Mrs. Johnson. "Maisy is the only one who knows how to do it right." At this, Maisy smiled. "I will pay you more than she does," Miss Ernestine added, to which

Maisy giggled.

"Absolutely not." Mrs. Johnson laughed. "You will not send her back. I cannot imagine a household without my Maisy," She said, smiling toward her.

"Neither can I," Miss Ernestine sniggered. "Maisy, could you get me a glass of water?"

"Yes, Miss Ernestine."

Maisy left the room and Miss Ernestine listened for her footsteps to depart down the hall.

"I like her plenty," Miss Ernestine said. "She is different, I think."

"Maisy is a special woman," Mrs. Johnson said. "I find myself getting scared she will one day leave."

"Well . . . not before this one," Miss Ernestine said, playfully pinching Marlene's waist. "How is Henry?"

"He is doing well," Marlene answered shyly. "Ma, if I move from here, could Maisy come with me?" she asked Mrs. Johnson.

"Absolutely not," Mrs. Johnson said with a serious face.

Miss Ernestine laughed.

"Y'all think I am humoring you but that woman is not going anywhere," Mrs. Johnson added.

"But wait — you should not sound so eager with her," Miss Ernestine whispered.

"Oh, Ernestine, you sound so foolish sometimes," Mrs. Johnson said.

"I am very serious, Alice."

"Maisy is a hard worker, she is Christian, she does all her chores, she helps Marlene with her lessons; the least I can do is to be kind to her."

"That is fair," Miss Ernestine interrupted, "but just remember Geraldine."

"You society women and your gossip," Mrs. Johnson said, shaking her head.

"Aye, there is no proof of it, but I do remember Geraldine saying she had a fight with that woman before she died."

"Geraldine had fights with every woman. I may have even had a disagreement with her a little while before her death. You suspect I poisoned her also. Plus Maisy is so much more than your typical house girl. She is educated, and soon she will be able to afford a home of her own."

"Maisy would never hurt a fly," Marlene added.

"I would not suppose so either. But remember in the States there were masters who could probably say the same things of their slaves —"

"Yes, while treating them like animals. How can you make an argument with those people in mind? No comparison, Ernestine."

"There is a psychology to people who serve, Alice," Miss Ernestine said. "Look around. You people get vexed when I compare the two, but look around. Why are we so set on hiring help rather than doing things ourselves? Why are servants the qualifier for wealth for some of us? In fact, that is why I do not keep house girls and house boys in my home — because it reminds me too much of America."

"So I am wrong?" Mrs. Johnson asked, offended. She glanced over at Gbessa, whose childlike expression forced a smile from her.

"I did not say that," Miss Ernestine argued. "You are one of the kindest women I know."

"That is not fair, Ernestine. Don't ever compare us to Americans. Because your servants work the field, you are better?"

"Of course not. And I would argue that they are not servants. They are workers with homes of their own," Miss Ernestine continued. "They can leave at any time they want. I do not gather tribesmen. I hire them."

"See it as you will," Mrs. Johnson said.

Maisy walked into a thick and sudden silence that made her stop in her tracks. She looked as if she had walked into a secret she'd already been told, and feigned her normal air of contentment.

"I am your friend and your sister in Christ," Miss Ernestine continued stubbornly, and Maisy handed her the cold water. "I am just speaking my truth is all." Miss Ernestine walked to the table near the basin and set the glass down without drinking from it. Maisy stared at the full glass, and her smile dropped briefly, before again inching across her face. She hummed indifferently, in hopes that Miss Ernestine was finished.

That night, Gbessa stood up from the bed. She thought of the women and the brief conversation she'd had with Maisy before bed, when Maisy told her some of what the women had said, at moments seeming as if she was talking to herself, to which Gbessa carefully listened without speaking. She was unsure of what to think of the women beyond their wardrobe and their fascination with her, as if she were hiding something each of them desperately wanted. Other than with Khati, Gbessa had not had relationships or even conversations with other women and girls. She just watched. Knew them through their movements and all the conversations they never had with her. But the women in this house — not only had they looked her in the face for long periods, but they spoke to her directly, wanted to be close to her, to touch her. Confused by it all, Gbessa decided that she would escape from there that night.

After the crickets began singing, Gbessa crawled out of her bed and climbed over the windowsill until she fell to the ground below. The fall hurt her back, and she sat for a moment to regain her energy. The house faced the beach and Gbessa stood up quickly, ignoring the pain, to join it. "Fengbe, keh kamba beh," Gbessa sang. "Fengbe, kemu beh."

She walked across the beach and prepared to enter the ocean to swim underneath Ol' Ma Famatta's face when a gentle hand touched her shoulder. Gbessa turned around and it was Maisy.

"What you doing, Ma?" Maisy asked in Vai. "Come inside before they see you." Gbessa shook her head and turned around. Maisy grabbed Gbessa's hand, but Gbessa pulled it away. Maisy ran ahead of Gbessa, nearly stumbling in her nightgown, to block her from going farther. Gbessa tried to dodge her, but Maisy blocked her again.

"Please," Maisy said as she reached for Gbessa's shoulders, holding her gently. Gbessa saw the earnest look in Maisy's eyes, and it made her think of Safua, softening her by the moment.

"Come back inside. Please," Maisy said again, to which Gbessa finally nodded. Maisy led her to the side of the house, and they crawled back into the room through their window.

Inside, Gbessa lay on her back. She could hear Maisy struggle to catch her breath in the bed beside her.

"You well, why you'n tell me you were well? Enneh-so?" Maisy's whisper grew. "You will not be lazy here."

Gbessa lay still, unsure of how to respond to the young woman's interest in her actions.

"What your name?" Gbessa asked finally.

Maisy was startled by her voice. She was vexed with Gbessa for wandering away, but thrilled that she had finally spoken. "Maisy. What your name?"

Gbessa hesitated for fear that she would frighten Maisy by mentioning her cursed name.

"Gbessa," she said.

"Gbessa?" Maisy asked.

"Yeh. Gbessa."

"Okay, Gbessa. You can't be lazy," Maisy insisted.

"You Vai girl?" Gbessa asked. "You not Vai girl."

"But you think I not Vai girl, then why you ask?" Maisy said, giggling. "Go to sleep. We will talk in the morning."

"I leaving in the morning," Gbessa said.

"You not leaving, Gbessa. The people pay for you to be here to take care of the house and you will leave? They buy your medicine and you will leave?"

"Yeh. I going."

"And me too?" Maisy continued. "I take care of you, yeh? You will leave me too?"

Gbessa did not at first respond. "Thank you," Gbessa said finally.

Maisy turned on her side to face Gbessa's bed.

"You can come with me," Gbessa said.

"You not serious. You'n remember how the people found you?" Maisy asked.

"I'n remember," Gbessa lied.

"You'n want remember," Maisy continued. "It was bad. They found you nearly dead."

Gbessa dismissed the thought. "If you were Vai girl you will not talk to me so," Gbessa said. "You not Vai girl. How you know Vai?"

Maisy rested her head against her pillow. "I was a small girl when the people come take us." She began to tell her story in Vai. She was a small girl when her village was attacked by slavers and her family was placed in chains and led toward the ocean. On the way there a neighboring tribe waged a battle with the traders that left most of the captured and some of the traders dead. The rescuing tribe retreated, as did the traders, back to their ship without the captured Africans. When the battle died down and it became silent outside, Maisy crawled from underneath a bush to find both of her parents and all of the captured Africans slaughtered. She lay on her mother's chest crying and almost died from starvation, but traveling missionaries eventually found the battle site and carried her to safety. She traveled with them around the coastal region, where she learned many of the languages — Krahn, Kru, Gola, Mandingo, Bassa, and Vai — and even to London and America to study history and religion. As she traveled with the missionaries back to Africa to live in the new colony, her adoptive parents died of malaria along with a number of new settlers during the first decades. When she arrived she was hired as a tutor and maid for the Johnson family, who gave her a room to sleep in and meals in exchange for the care of their home and daughter.

"They give you room to sleep too," Maisy

said. "You go far from here and the slaving people will find you again and take you to America."

"America?" Gbessa asked.

"That where they take our people to suffer," Maisy said. "I saw it. They do bad to our people. Some of them good but it hard to find."

"America," Gbessa said again.

"Mrs. Johnson and all of them come from there. They want country for only our people, because of how they were treated there."

"They good?"

"Yes, most of them kind," Maisy said and became silent.

"Most of them," she repeated. "But . . . some of them don't think all of us the same. Some of them think . . . some of them think they smarter and better fit to lead than those who were already here."

"What is lead?" Gbessa asked, doing her best to pronounce the word: "leeee."

"To be king. Chief," Maisy said.

"Yeh," Gbessa said.

"You will be safe here," Maisy assured her. "You will like it here. Monrovia is a good place. I will teach you the language and you will work with me."

Gbessa could not return to Lai, and she

was not sure that if she returned inland she would find the company of the cursed men whom she had briefly traveled with.

"You'n got Ma?" Gbessa asked, recalling Maisy's story after a moment of silence.

"No, no Ma."

"My Ma die too," she said. "And my Pa. And the Ol' Ma and Pa I live with after. Everybody I know die. Except they curse like me. You will die too."

"Yeh. Everybody die," Maisy said in English first. "But we will all die," she said in Vai.

"No. I witch. Woman named Ol' Ma Nyanpoo kill her cat the night I was born and the people say I curse. I witch. I don't die."

"No," Maisy said, giggling nervously before her laughter drowned in the silence. "I'n believe in that thing. I Christian."

GOD OF CURSED PEOPLE

Gbessa followed Maisy around the beach mansion, her feet trailing the lines of the cool tile floors in the wide mansion hallways. Gbessa stood underneath the clock in the main room for ten minutes until Maisy realized that she was no longer being followed by Gbessa, and returned to the lavishly decorated room to retrieve her. As they worked, Gbessa stuck her head out of all the windows and looked onto the field at the men farming. She ran her fingers along the lining of the couches of the den and sitting rooms; she fell into the cushions of the chairs in the library; she opened the books and precociously flipped through the pages, turning them around and upside down to see if anything would fall out. When climbing up the stairs, Gbessa fell to her knees to crawl her way up.

"Stand," Maisy instructed her.

Gbessa looked up at Maisy, who ascended

the steps with ease. Maisy climbed a couple of steps in example, then extended a hand toward Gbessa. Gbessa imitated Maisy's steps, carefully lifting each foot one by one, until she reached Maisy's hand. She held it, was grateful for it.

She followed Maisy as she dusted and cleaned all twenty rooms of the second floor, quietly tiptoeing around the house since the sun was beginning to rise and she knew the family would be awake soon.

When they opened the door of the last room, Mrs. Johnson's daughter, Marlene, sat at a window-facing table. Upon hearing their entry, Marlene quickly covered a sheet of paper with her hands. When she turned to see that it was Maisy and Gbessa, she sighed in relief.

"Marlene, good morning," Maisy said. "You are up so early. I did not dust your room because I thought you were still asleep."

"Do not worry. I had something I had to do is all," Marlene answered, folding the sheet. She stood up and headed out of the room. Outside the door, Gbessa stood against the wall.

"Oh! She is out of the bed!" Marlene said with excitement.

"Yes, Marlene, I am going to begin giving

her chores today."

Marlene turned to face Gbessa, who instantly dropped her gaze toward the floor. She was sure by the way Marlene carried herself and the way Maisy responded to her that she was some sort of Sande. Marlene lifted Gbessa's chin to look at her face and Gbessa touched her hair. Marlene was beautiful, so beautiful that Gbessa smiled at the nuisance of it. What could one woman do with all that beauty? It was hard for her to look away.

"She is like a child," Marlene said, laughing.

"You are just different and new to her is all," Maisy suggested.

"She Sande?" Gbessa asked Maisy while still touching Marlene's hair.

Maisy laughed and replied: "No. No queens here."

"She speaks!" Marlene said with surprise. "What did she say?"

"She asked if you were a queen."

"How charming," Marlene said, smiling. "Maisy, you must do something with her hair before the ball." Marlene reached out and touched the long braid that ended at Gbessa's thighs.

In the mornings, Maisy dusted and swept

the entire house and prepared breakfast for the Johnsons before they awoke. The house was also connected to a barn, where Maisy gathered eggs every morning. After the family ate and she cleaned up after them, Maisy took a small portion of food to the field workers, who woke up the earliest to tend and pick the crop. They were mostly bought or commissioned tribesmen who lived close to the farm. Mr. Johnson, a tall and broad-shouldered, fair-skinned man, built a few small shacks on the corner of his property for the workers who had no family and needed a place to sleep. Mr. Johnson was one of the mayors of Monrovia, and spent his days at the grand mansion where other mayors and a white governor decided upon the laws and constitution of the free colony, tried criminals, and made plans on how they would expand and protect Monrovia. He usually remained in the house for breakfast, but left shortly after. Before feeding the farm workers outside, Maisy polished Mr. Johnson's shoes and prepared a small lunch for him to carry with him to the grand mansion. Gbessa followed her from sunrise to the moment Ol' Ma Famatta's light covered the farm, deeply fixed into night. At times Maisy seemed stressed by all that she had to do, frequently speaking to herself under her breath, reciting her long list of chores and items Mrs. Johnson had asked her to remember. But the chores, the movement, the inclusion, gave Gbessa joy. She had never been asked to help the other women on the farm in Lai, and all of her days in Khati's old house, with the exception of the few times she was visited by Safua, had seemed the same, all replaying, reminding her with each sunrise of her misfortune. In her first few weeks there, every day she told Maisy that she would leave the following day. At first, Maisy begged her to stay for her own sake. But eventually Maisy called her bluff.

"How can you leave me?" Maisy had said one night. "You are my sister now. My flesh. Flesh cannot leave you." At which Gbessa almost lost her breath. The kindness, the newness, stunned her.

When the morning meals were done and everyone and everything in the mansion were cleaned up, Maisy devoted two hours to giving Marlene lessons. Gbessa stayed close by the women during this time. She watched as they read together, conversed about topics in their way, sitting upright with their plenty clothes, long-sleeved blouses, voices as soft and words as soft as the bulbul. When Marlene was younger,

Maisy told Gbessa, she had tutored her in basic subjects like arithmetic and grammar. The lessons changed over time to French and some local languages (not Vai), and music, after Marlene mastered intermediate conversations. Now Marlene came to her only when she wondered about the meaning or spelling of a certain word. Since Marlene had grown too old for lessons, Maisy had used the idle hours between Marlene's infrequent inquiries to read her Bible. Since Maisy now had Gbessa to tend to, she used the time to teach her chores and English.

At first, Gbessa was clumsy. Instead of seasoning the cassava leaves with ground peppers, Gbessa dropped three whole ginger roots into the soup and ruined it. Instead of measuring the water in the rice to make sure it was not "puttehputteh" (too soft) or "raw" (too hard), she drew an entire bucket of water and poured it into the pot. Realizing how little the strange woman knew about the kitchen and how to keep a house, Maisy prayed to herself every time her patience grew thin, and explained to Gbessa what she should have done instead. She did so in Vai first, and then she repeated the same things in English.

"What can you cook?" Maisy asked.

"Rice," Gbessa answered.

"What else? That's all?"

"And fish," she added. "Roast fish. And bowled greens."

"That's all you learned to cook in your entire life?"

"That's all we had," Gbessa said. And perhaps she should have felt sad then, remembering that lasting, singing hunger from Lai. But instead she felt relieved, happy to be close to Maisy, whom, she believed, she was maybe beginning to love.

Maisy decided to speak only English to Gbessa one day, and after a morning of misunderstanding and frustration, Gbessa said, "Stop."

"What? What did you say?" Maisy asked with enthusiasm.

Gbessa did not understand her and grew more frustrated.

"Stop," she said again, remembering the word from the day she'd made the fufu so hard that it could not be swallowed.

"That is good, Gbessa!" Maisy said, clapping.

"Stop," Gbessa responded to her excitement with a straight face, this time holding her hand up in protest before she left the room. Maisy laughed behind her.

After lunchtime Maisy and Gbessa took a snack to the field and ate with the farmers.

Maisy usually carried a bundle of grapes that she shared with Gbessa and the men when they rested. When Gbessa laughed, the chewed grapes lay on her tongue.

"Do not open your mouth with food in it. It is impolite," Maisy warned.

Gbessa stuck out her tongue to Maisy and continued laughing. The grape peels hung loosely from her tongue and lips. She shook her head at Maisy and waved her hands in the air.

"Gbessa! And you must not laugh so loudly. You woman," Maisy said. Gbessa paid her little attention. Maisy, visibly happy to see Gbessa show such joy, shook her head and joined her, shrugging her shoulders and also eventually holding her stomach when the guffaws caught up to her. A few of the men shared in their joy for a moment, but afraid to be seen as lazy or disobedient, the rest of them stood up (some hissing through their teeth) and left the "foolish women" leaning on one another's shoulders.

Maisy kept a garden in the backyard of the mansion. There she grew fresh herbs and peppers, garlic and roses in the corner. Before dinner she tended the garden, picking a few herbs to cook with her meal or watering the plants that still waited to ripen and be plucked. As the wind rushed to meet Maisy's dark brown collarbone, Gbessa crawled into the garden, being careful — as she had watched Maisy do — not to step on any of the plants or flowers.

When Maisy turned to see that Gbessa was behind her, she smiled.

"Help me, Ma," Maisy said, and with a small garden knife made of tin, she cut a pepper from its root.

She turned around to face Gbessa, who instead of marveling at the tin knife, or the garden, or the roses on the side, or anything that Maisy would expect, waited for Maisy's eyes to catch hers.

"Help me," Gbessa repeated.

"Yes!" Maisy responded excitedly. "Help me," she said again slowly, her eyes nearly wet with pride at Gbessa's progress. She grabbed Gbessa's hand.

"Help me," Gbessa said again, wanting to say so much more than Maisy's repetition; wanting to know about so many unknown years and memories of the small woman in the garden.

After six months at the Johnson mansion, Gbessa eventually began to fear that Maisy would die or leave her, as so many before her had done; so during the week before the settlers' ball — as Maisy walked quickly around the house cleaning and cooking and finishing chores — Gbessa did just as she was told. While Gbessa was in their room folding clothes that had just been brought in from the line, Maisy joined her to inquire. Maisy closed the door and walked toward the bed with her hands swinging at her sides.

"Gbessa?"

Gbessa turned around, surprised that Maisy had sought her amid what she proclaimed was a "day of trials."

"Yes?" Gbessa's English was improving, and in her quest to please Maisy, she made it a point to say the words that she knew as frequently as possible.

"Did I do something wrong?"

"Wrong?" Gbessa asked.

"You vexed with me?" Maisy tried in Vai.

"Wrong?" Gbessa remained committed to the pursuit of the difficult language.

Maisy waited for her to respond.

"No. Not wrong," Gbessa said.

Maisy smiled and hugged her. She rested her small head on Gbessa's shoulder. Gbessa swallowed heavily to simmer the burning inside, but before she could return Maisy's hug, to touch her as she had been touched, Maisy pulled away.

At night before bed, Maisy opened the book that usually lay on the pillow of her bed during the day, and she read to Gbessa by candlelight.

"This passage is from the book of John in the New Testament," Maisy said.

As the light danced about the right side of Maisy's face and entered her mouth through the corner of her dark lips, Gbessa watched closely as her chest moved up and down and up and down and she exhaled the song of her book. She tried understanding the language when all she could hear was "Fengbe, keh kamba beh. Fengbe, kemu beh," calling her toward the dance floor of the flickering lights, beckoning her toward the dark lips; she touched her own lips to test the numbness caused by Maisy's voice. Ki fembuleh, ki fembuleh; and Gbessa glanced toward the window for her night flies and their humming. They were not there. It was her — it was Maisy.

Again, in her chest, Gbessa felt the load of all her years. The passion of Maisy's words made the feeling in Gbessa's chest so abysmal, so profound, that Gbessa coughed. Maisy looked up from the book.

"You all right?" she asked gently in English.

Gbessa nodded. Maisy smiled and continued reading. Gbessa walked across the room to Maisy's bed and rested her head on her lap. Maisy's voice now gently vibrated against Gbessa's head and she stroked the side of Gbessa's long braid as she read.

"See?" Maisy asked. "God is a good and faithful God. Nobody is cursed in his eyes."

No, Gbessa thought to herself but was unable to say. Perhaps none who learned to love, and love well, love like Maisy, could ever be cursed. After all, Maisy had also lost her family and her village. Maisy had also been alone with no home. She was cursed, too, Gbessa thought, and still she was so happy. She was not a Sande; she was more like a servant or war prisoner who cleaned up after her king and queen; still she was content. She was content with her garden and with her books — with Gbessa. Maisy said this book had made her pain go away. She was "at peace," she was "found," she was "new," she was "saved," she said.

"God," Gbessa repeated and looked at Maisy's face.

"Yes, Ma," Maisy said. "Everybody was once cursed but we were made perfect in God's eyes."

Gbessa was compelled by Maisy's teachings. She was moved by the possibility that Maisy understood what she felt or could identify with the memory of her exile. Maisy, too, had no home. Maisy, too, had no mother or father. And if what Maisy said about America was true, then Gbessa wondered if all the settlers in Monrovia had also had years in the forest, if she could really be considered one of them. Mrs. Johnson had also been made to leave her home in the world over the ocean — that place where they were also wicked to her people. Yes — perhaps everybody, in their own way, was either a witch or the king who loved her. And if Maisy was also an orphan and found joy in reading this book and talking to this "God" of hers, then could she? Maisy stroked Gbessa's hair.

"God," Gbessa said. "Want your God. God of curse people."

Gbessa now wore her blouse just as Maisy did — buttoned up to her neck and tucked in at the waist into a skirt. Gbessa now woke up on her own, sometimes even before Maisy, swearing to herself that in the distance she could hear a faint cock crow, and the old man Bondo lowering his forehead to the ground in prayer.

Gbessa could now cook, and Maisy let her prepare an entire meal on her own. Gbessa learned Bassa faster than she was learning English, and she would spend entire Saturday afternoons near the shack, speaking and

347

telling jokes to the field workers.

On Sundays, when she and Maisy accompanied the Johnsons to the settlers' church, Gbessa sat with her hands folded in her lap the entire time, trying to make out the words that the man behind the wooden podium was saying.

God: she understood this. She honored this God. Love: she had heard Maisy say this. Help: she understood this. Saved: she understood. She was now saved, according to Maisy. No longer cursed.

She knew how to drink from the tin cup so no one would hear her swallow. She knew how to eat with a spoon "like a lady." She had become friends with this new life; she knew all of it and remained only an arm's length away.

On the day before the ball, Mrs. Johnson told Maisy to rest since she'd expressed exhaustion from all the work she had done in the days before. Maisy did not remember the last day she had had with no assigned chores. She spent most of the day in the garden and she let Gbessa walk along the beach by herself. While Gbessa strolled, parallel to the bordering waves that splattered onto the coast, she wondered when last she had bathed in the ocean; when last she had let the water's banter swallow her as Ol' Ma Famatta sat and watched, hunchbacked against a crescent moon.

"Gbessa!" Maisy called from the house after Gbessa, as she strolled along the sand.

Gbessa turned from the ocean. I chased after her as she took quick steps back to the house to meet Maisy.

"Where did you go, my darling?" I whispered limply. "Where are you, my friend?"

Inside, Maisy waited in the room above a bucket with black residue that spilled over the side.

Maisy had mixed pine root in a bucket of black coals. She crushed the coal and the pine root together, and added olive oil and chicken's eggs.

"What there?" Gbessa asked in English.

"For your hair."

Gbessa touched the braid that hung down her back and pulled it over her shoulder.

"What?" she asked.

"Your hair."

Maisy touched her head.

"The color. I want to fix it for the ball," Maisy said.

"The ball?"

"Yes. Your hair for the ball."

While Gbessa was aware that there was something of a celebration that would happen soon, she never imagined that she would be a part of it. The Johnsons treated them fairly, but the life that Gbessa knew in their house barely included encounters with them. She did as Maisy told her, and otherwise communicated only minimally with the Johnsons. Gbessa went to the bucket and looked inside to find a black liquid substance so offensive to her nose that she used both of her hands to cover it.

"It will make your hair black," Maisy finally said in Vai. Gbessa held the red braid and was reluctant to let it go.

"What inside there?"

"Crush coal. Water. Pine root to make the color stay. Oil."

Gbessa glanced inside the bucket again.

"I will just wash it with this," Maisy explained. "Mrs. Johnson wants me to do it."

Gbessa, though still distracted and repelled by the smell, wanted only to obey what Maisy told her. She nodded.

"You all right, Ma?" Maisy asked.

"Yes."

■ ■ ■ ■

NIGHT

■ ■ ■ ■

It was in this way that Norman Aragon and June Dey continued through the inland kingdoms of the coast. The Sanwa. The Kanuri. The Fon. At times they stopped and rested, learning the land, living among the people who revered them either as powerful spirits come to defend them or as beggars to whom they had to show kindness in order for their villages to do well when the seasons transitioned. But usually, Norman Aragon and June Dey were fighting. The more they fought, the more the young men came to terms with their strengths. Sometimes Norman Aragon blended into the woods and forests, into the water and roads as they walked together. June Dey was used to it, and he knew his friend would always return to him by nightfall.

"Them men. They was more French, right?" June Dey asked Norman one night as they sat at the edge of a cave.

"Yes," Norman answered.

"Why you think they out here? More than others? In Africa and all?" June Dey asked.

"America not the only country with a colony on the coast," Norman Aragon answered. "The British and French got some land north of the colony. Callum, my Pa, mentioned it when I was young."

June Dey looked at Norman at the mention of Callum's name. June Dey freely spoke about the many ways he had used his gift while in America, including the first encounter that started it all, and realized he knew very little about Norman's past.

"Your Pa?" June Dey asked. Norman nodded. "What he was like?"

"Crazy man," Norman said, looking down at his hands, touching those old bruises caused by Callum's needles. "My Ma told him about her gift before I was born and he promised to take her to Freetown, but he got too greedy. Planned to take us to Britain all along. So we escape and he killed her while we was running."

"Damn," June Dey said.

"When he wasn't running one of his experiments he was kind to me," Norman said, his eyes locked on the blazing flame they'd made to roast their daily catch. "He told me stories and once when he went to town he brought me back wooden blocks. But he was no good to my Ma. He chain her up, beat her, make her sleep outside if she don't do exactly what he want."

June Dey sighed, a long, silent melody of a sigh reserved for when he thought of Darlene.

"We can . . . we should make our way to Freetown," June Dey said.

"No," Norman answered. "Not now. Maybe someday but this what we came here to do. This what Nanni would want."

"Sure of that," June Dey said. The coal fire crackled a few feet away from him and June Dey watched as the embers slowly died. Ashes floated and joined the lingering night flies, and the animals of the forest chattered in the shadows.

"I go with you," June Dey said finally. "You decide you want to turn around and go to Freetown. I go. You know Africa, like you say, and I be better off with you."

"I won't go," Norman said. "Not with everything we've seen. But . . . you should get to know Africa too."

"Yeh, I suppose. But maybe I don't feel close to it as you do. You say your Ma talked about it. Talked about coming back every day," June said. "But my Ma ain't. Fact is I come here by mistake."

"Can't be a mistake what we're doing," Norman responded.

"Not a mistake. But I ain't know nothing about no free colony until I woke up on that ship. My Ma, sometimes she talk about the North in secret and about how she dream of going up there with me and my Aunt Henrietta once in a while. But I knew she wasn't never going to try to go. And my Ma talked about Africa every now and again . . . about where we from . . . but it ain't seem like a real place."

"What do you mean?" Norman asked.

"It was like a Bible story or a fairy tale, seem like," June Dey said. "And you see folks get punishment for trying to go north. They make all of us go down to the field and the overseer make everybody watch and sometimes they nearly beat folks to death. That was after spending all they free time thinking about the North, dreaming it was someplace better, and the North was already almost too far to dream. But Africa. Couldn't afford to think about a place seem so far."

"Seem some folks were dreaming that far," Norman said. "Otherwise you wouldn't be here."

"Suppose you right."

"Besides, I think you owe it to your Ma then is what it sounds like," Norman said. "She was dreaming of the North and you come farther than she dreamed."

June Dey lay on his back and rested his head in his opened palms. A multitude of stars exploded in the distance.

"Where you think they coming from?" June asked after a brief silence. "The French. You 'spect the folks in the colony know?"

"Not too sure. But if they do not they will soon find out."

The two of them had gotten into many fights since their first encounter with the French, when Gbessa was still by their side. There were various groups of slavers, from Portugal and Britain and even the East, but most of their confrontations had been with the French. After that first day of fighting, Norman could not stop thinking about Gbessa. Every time he had wanted to use his gift to go find her, the cries of other villages had summoned them.

"The girl. What you think happened to the girl?" Norman asked June Dey.

"Can't know," June Dey said.

"You saw her wake up after that slaver made her faint," Norman said. "Think maybe she has a gift too."

June Dey had not considered this — that the woman who had traveled with them had also had an ability, had also been like him. "What you think she do?" June Dey asked. "Her gift?"

"It could be anything," Norman said. He had pondered this question himself as he wondered what had led him to Gbessa. Perhaps there were reasons for the color of her hair or skin. Perhaps she could even blend into the earth like he was able to, and had not been captured by the French as they had suspected, but instead had fled from them willingly. Then Norman remembered the state in which he found her — how the sand was dried to her skin, lips chapped, in the midst of her own waste. She had to have been lying there for months.

"I suppose it could be life," Norman Aragon said finally. "She should not have been alive when I found her, but she was."

When Norman Aragon said this, June Dey thought of Darlene. He remembered, quite vividly, the way she had looked against his chest after he realized that she had been shot and killed by a bullet that was meant for him.

"Maybe we see her again then," June Dey said.

Norman nodded. "Perhaps. We will enter

the Kong Empire in a day's time. I hope they as welcoming as others."

"They will be if we get there the same time as them French," June Dey said.

June Dey was right. Norman knew that an exploration of the coast by French settlers was something that was quite probably in full steam as they spoke. Protecting the inland kingdoms would be an unavoidable part of their journey.

There was a faint murmur coming from outside the cave.

"What you say?" June Dey asked, and heard the humming sound also.

"Not me," Norman said and he stood up, leaving the cave. Norman used stones that protruded from the sides of the cave to climb to the top. In the distance he noticed that smoke rose from a wooded area. He hurried back down and June Dey stood waiting.

"Let's go." Norman proceeded. He gathered his bag and headed toward the murmur with haste. After about an hour of alternating between running and walking with great urgency, they arrived at the wooded area.

"No!" June Dey said, clenching his fist.

They stood in the circle of what appeared to be a recently attacked village. Several of the houses were burned, and food was scattered and blood mingled with the dirt.

"Look around for survivors," Norman Aragon said, and went quickly to the remaining houses and pushed the doors open. No one was there. They had stolen everyone. Everything.

"Quiet," Norman Aragon said. "You hear that?"

The men listened closely to the wind, who carried with her the continued murmurs of the stolen Africans.

"You hear that?" June Dey asked.

"I hear it. It is not close," Norman answered.

June shook his head.

"Follow me, my darlings," I whispered. "Come with me, my son."

"Sh," Norman said. He proceeded farther into the village until he reached the road that led out of it on the other side. They knew they had arrived when the murmurs became quieter and quieter, eventually fading to more-urgent reverberations. The road they traveled was dense with forestry, with increasingly higher trees and less walking room between bushes and rocks, but Norman Aragon knew that clear land would be reached soon. There arose amid them both whimpers and what appeared to be conversing men. They journeyed farther toward the bothersome sounds until the forest began to thin again, with trees less abundant and invasive.

"Stay here," Norman Aragon told him.

"Why?" June Dey asked as his muscles tightened. "You hear that? Too many people for you alone. What if they hear you?"

"I need to see what is going on before you follow," Norman said. "It is no matter if they hear me." With that he left June Dey. He disappeared and June Dey's heart dropped, as it always did, when the man whom he understood so little of abandoned him with only a memory of his face.

This was the part that Norman Aragon loved. The moment his body became one again with the earth, when he understood all things too impossible for other men to fathom.

The sound of disappearance, from the sudden loudness of the earth's orbit to the dropping hearts of his bewildered audience to the shrieks of animals who witnessed what had happened: this had become his home, his family. The instant he disappeared, the weight of the world could be heard and deeply felt — the marriage of whimpers, howls, groans, chastising, French, broken English, bare bottoms against bloodstained dirt, ropes against wrists, guns against palms, everything, everything, all of their sounds pulled him in. Then. There was a silence just as potent, just as true. In the mountains, Norman had used his gift only to hide; since arriving in this colony, it was this gift that had exposed him, had found him. He moved at a quicker pace when he was unseen, with arms that felt extended minutes before him and legs that competed. Norman had no dreams then, no desires or thoughts. Only to stretch as far and as wide as he could into the undying silence, into all the beautiful things we cannot see.

Norman Aragon floated until he entered the space where the silence had led him. He floated between the final branches to uncover another village, very similar to the ones they had already encountered. Several houses stood in a cluster, surrounding a village circle. In the village circle were the survivors of two or three groups, which Norman identified by their facial markings, tied together in straight, parallel lines. There were mostly women — no children. It was the women who had been screaming; it was their voices that came to him in the wind. Some men in the circle were badly beaten; it seemed they had resisted the attacks that had resulted in their present circumstances.

Norman counted quickly. Thirty-two men in the first group of lines. Fifteen in the second group. Fifty-nine to sixty-three in the final. Frenchmen patrolled the lines and threatened the captured Africans with guns and spit. Others traveled in and out of the houses, which they had apparently made into temporary quarters and housing for their party of explorers.

A few of the men sat around a fire and devoured loaves of bread with roasted chicken. There were forty Frenchmen in total. He needed to know more. His goal was to make his way to the house from which it appeared the most men came in and out, but he was suddenly distracted by a company of a couple dozen more Frenchmen who came through the farthest woods and entered the village circle. The men were greeted by others and offered water and bread. A few entered one of the houses and Norman followed them. Once he was inside, Norman saw that eight or so men surrounded a table newly constructed of tree bark. They hovered over a map of what appeared to be the middle free colony and the territories that surrounded it.

"But we may attempt traveling along Monrovia's border," one said in French.

"Too dangerous," another said. He stood

with his hands pressed on his hips and shook his head while examining the map.

"So is continuing the unexplored territory. We have lost too many," the man continued.

"We will go farther inland until we reach French territory and travel around the American colony to the coast to ship these."

"That will take days!" another shouted.

"Yes, and half of us will ship back to Europe with these. The others visit the American colony and learn what you can of its governance," a man beside him said.

With this Norman Aragon exited the house, nearly breathless from the information he had just heard. He felt lightheaded and his heart pounded within him. It was then that he noticed the smell. It was a violent smell that nearly threw him to the floor with its aggression. He was instantly nauseated and swallowed the little that came back up into his stomach. His eyes filled. The smell, repugnant and unforgiving, circled him. Norman did not follow freely, but was instead pulled unwillingly toward it by my hand. Beyond the parallel lines and tiny houses, past the ruined village and into the woods he floated, floated toward the awful smell until he arrived at it.

"Come see," I whispered. "Come see."

It was the short holler that came from him, surprised and especially angry, that pulled him out of the Infinite. Before him, there was a hill of dead children with similar facial markings to those of the men and women in the circle. They had been killed, piled atop one another and abandoned to rot in the wooded country. A procession of earthworms surrounded the hill of children; in a tangled line they encircled the slaughter. The children's broken limbs poked out in the company of flies and an unrelenting stench of their former lives.

"My God," he said.

How could this place, this place that had managed to free their gifts, a refuge for so many, also manifest the darkest cavities of man? Of greed? Of his unrelenting wickedness?

Norman ran. He did not know if he traveled within the silence or outside of it. He did not care. He ran as hard and as fast as he could away from the dead bodies. He ran until he reached June Dey and collapsed before him.

"What happened?" June Dey asked when he saw him. He pulled Norman up from the ground and fetched water for him to drink. Norman sat up and drank from the coconut shell. June Dey waited for his words, his report. Norman just panted until he finally caught his breath. Caught his breath and finally broke down and sobbed. Cried until all that was hidden inside of him, the pain he had carried alone for so long, came out, came roaring out to June Dey until the wind captured it and took it with her to the later day.

Night.

When they arrived, the women were singing. They sang to numb what had been stolen and was now forever lost. Three different languages and they all sang together — words like Where they buried my baby and Come plead for us, God. Come for us.

Norman Aragon hid with June Dey in the woods at the entry to the village. There were a couple of French guards still awake and they sat together and nodded in and out of sleep to the women's soothing voices. Others lay asleep in pitched tents at the farthest edge of the village.

June Dey was thirsty for vengeance. The midnight moon burned in his eyes. Clouds stirred above them in the night. Norman glanced at June Dey quietly and nodded. He left him and went to the parallel lines where the rhythm and voices of the saints were lifted into the night air.

Norman Aragon traveled through the silence to the leader of the parallel line, whom he assumed was a chief or tribe elder. When he noticed that the Frenchmen who were guarding the prisoners had drifted off into a light slumber, he made himself briefly visible to the leader of the line. He made eye contact with the man and held his finger over his mouth. He disappeared again. The man was startled by Norman's whiteness, but Norman appeared close to his face and looked into his eyes.

"I am here to help you," Norman whispered desperately in English. He disappeared again. Norman looked for the one he knew was a tribal leader. He appeared only for a short moment, as soon as he saw that the watching guard had dozed off again, and pressed his finger to his lips. The moon beamed down onto the village circle. The wind gusted. Eventually the warrior leaders of each tribe sought one another's eyes. They were careful not to move abruptly, although they all understood that what they had seen was shared.

Their ancestors had arrived for their rescue. And their time for redemption had come.

One by one, Norman untied the leaders, who, instead of submitting to sudden movement, whispered to the women to keep singing.

And the women sang.

The men watched the guards and waited for them to drift to sleep again. It was then that they quickly untied one another. While they did this, Norman Aragon beckoned for June Dey to join him in the village circle. June Dey hurried to where the guards sat. For as long as June Dey could remember, being born in captivity had created a coldness within him, so cold that it burned. And it was this burning, this fire that he gathered when he called upon his gift. The brashness of those flames raged in his head, hardened his fists. June Dey snuck up behind them and pushed their heads together as forcefully as he could, and the men instantly collapsed, lifeless.

Norman Aragon retrieved their guns and threw them to June Dey. The women noticed this and escalated their singing, enlivened by the possibility. The captured Africans, all untied now, stood up. Many had little strength, but found their way to their feet and banded together in a mutual need for revenge. Norman Aragon went to one of the leaders and gave him the gun in his hand, but the man threw it down and yelled something loudly, his face furious, his eyes fighting back tears.

"Yes," June Dey murmured. He threw his gun down also. There was shifting within the tents where the Frenchmen slept. Whispers came then.

Outside, several dozen African men with broken hearts waited for them to approach. June Dey stood among them. Felt alive. Waited to see the faces of those who had killed the children Norman had spoken of.

One walked sleepily out of his tent and instantly, upon noticing the waiting warriors, ran back inside to gather others.

"*Les Africains!*" he shouted. "*Les Africains!*"

All at once men emerged with guns from their tents and the houses where they slept. However, the guns quickly flew from their hands and were pulled through the dust, collected by Norman as he ran invisibly between them. The guns passed the warriors and they spit on the ground at the traveling weapons.

"*Les Africains!*" the Frenchmen shouted. "*Regardez! Il est une chose des sorcièrs!*"

One by one they left their tents, trembling, lanterns shaking furiously in their loose grips, and they came face-to-face with the captured Africans.

"*Go!*" June Dey yelled and the men surged toward the tents, not with steel but with

370

fists, with tears, in rage, in thirst — wanting to break faces, shake the hatred out of these strange men who had stolen their civilization, disrupted their lives for no explained reason, wanting them to bleed until all of their children were reborn, revived, returned. No steel. Just heart.

No slavers lived under that moon. No more Africans died.

Restless, Norman stood up from the tree he sat against and retrieved a sheet of paper from a small linen bag that he and June Dey took turns carrying. He had been given paper by a scribe in a village they had recently visited — a gift in exchange for their protection. News was spreading among coastal groups via traveling griots and seers that men with fire sticks were stealing villagers. News was also spreading that in many recent cases, an ancestor arrived, one man in two bodies, one black, one white. The white half moved in and out of death, negotiating on their behalf, pleading for them to have more time on earth, while the black half sacrificed himself and took the pain of the fire sticks for them. Some thought June Dey and Norman Aragon were the deity Ibeji, divine twins Taiwo and Kehinde in the flesh. So when they arrived now, in some cases they were celebrated. In such a case, they were recently given gifts — clothes and silverware. Norman also received paper from a scribe, and clay on which to write using twigs.

Norman had heard many stories during his months on the coast, but how could the African heroes live when all of the griots were getting killed? He wanted to write them down. To write about June Dey's time in the forests of Virginia. To write of Nanni, the Moorestown Maroon.

"What you doing?" June Dey asked, sitting up.

"Looking for that clay," Norman said as he searched the bag. "I'm not seeing it."

"What you need clay for?"

"To . . . I want to write something down," Norman said.

"I see," June Dey said, nodding.

"I can't find the clay," Norman said.

"Sure we'll run into some before long. Clay ain't too hard to find."

"Or charcoal. Where is the last territory we passed that you saw coal?"

Before June Dey could answer, the two heard a rustling in the forest that made them both jump to their feet. Without explanation, Norman grabbed his bag and disappeared. He heard June Dey running closely behind him. Not far from where they had left, Norman Aragon uncovered a narrow creek that ran several feet below a hill. Three women dressed in torn lappas of extravagant colors took turns dipping their buckets from the top of the hill where they sat into the creek. As one lowered her bucket, the other two held each of her arms, securing her as she pulled up the full bucket of fresh water. One of the women had just finished retrieving a bucket when she spotted Norman. The woman pointed, and the others shrieked, quickly standing to their feet to retreat.

"Wait," Norman said, rushing to them.

June Dey emerged from the bushes, and the ladies dropped their buckets and ran. Norman caught up to them and blocked their path.

"Please, don't run. We're harmless," he begged.

The women huddled together.

"We won't hurt you," Norman said, and June Dey looked on, as if he didn't want to add to their fear.

The women whispered to one another in their language.

"We won't hurt you," Norman repeated in a lower, slower voice. June Dey went over to where the women were drawing water and gathered their buckets. With ease, he walked over to them with all three buckets. The women's eyes ran across Norman's and June Dey's faces and bodies, as if they were looking for traces of old friends, or, worse, old enemies.

"Go way!" one of them yelled finally. "Go!"

"You speak English? English?"

"Go!"

"Is your village close? We haven't seen a village for many weeks. We didn't know any were around."

The woman who had screamed attempted to retreat again. She dashed past Norman, who nearly lost his balance. She shouted something to her friends, who stood together, holding one another, their eyes swimming in terror at the sight of Norman's face.

"Where my son?" she asked as she began to cry.

"Your son. I don't know," Norman said, waving his hand again. "Look, we have nothing," he said, opening his bag to show the women the paper and other small items within it.

"We want to help," Norman said, closing the bag. "To help. Did someone hurt you? Like me?" he asked, extending his arms in example, and the words burned his tongue.

The looks on their faces, the looks the women gave, were familiar. That sort of fear had borne many children, and they lived now along that coast, and their faces all resembled their mothers' faces.

"He's right," June Dey added. "We want to help."

"No," one of the women answered finally. The women stood and eventually quieted when they sensed that Norman or June Dey did not have weapons to harm them. The men were going to do nothing more than stare until the women offered more words, so the two women, still holding each other, took a step in the direction their friend had just run. Their steps were slow, calculated. Norman did not stop them. He moved out of their way. So they took another step, and another, each one more urgent than the last, until they were running in the same direction their friend had. Norman nodded at June Dey, and the two followed the women, June Dey with their buckets of water still in his possession.

Less than a mile farther into the forest, they found a small village of no more than eight houses. The village smelled of peanuts, a soup, and a fire still burned at the edge of the circle of homes where a cook pot, steam rising, bubbled with the meal. A couple dozen women scrambled in and out of the homes, and a few Ol' Pas sat on a bamboo bench against the biggest house in the village. Through the open window of one of the homes, one of the women from the well, the one who had managed to escape, was wringing her hands as she illustrated her story. Women peeked their heads in and out of their homes to hear her, then rushed to their own designated homes and corners, some crying and shaking their heads at the bothersome news. Someone noticed the two other women from the well and shouted their names. The villagers rushed to their sides, a celebration that was no small beating of drums.

Norman and June Dey emerged from the forest, and as quickly as the jubilant shouts began, they waned, ended, and were reborn into cries more similar to what the men had heard throughout the villages they had encountered.

"Go! Go from here!" shouted the woman who was first to run, turning toward them, her slender arms flailing.

Two elder women entered the circle from a home with a tin roof. One was noticeably shorter than the other, barely reaching her companion's elbow. The two of them wore white lappas tied above their breasts and matching white head ties. One of the women held a rake, and the other a bamboo sharpened into an arrowed spear. Though they walked in stride, it looked as if they were racing each other toward Norman and June Dey.

Norman glanced over at June Dey, who lowered the buckets of water to the ground. The villagers shuffled into their homes, moving frantically to gather their things, as if a fire were swallowing the forest around them. Without hesitation, the two elder women pointed their tall weapons toward Norman's and June Dey's throats. Both of them raised their hands.

"Where them?" the shorter woman asked.

"Who?"

"Man them," she said, inching the rake closer to Norman's neck and pulling it back again several times. "You with Sam?"

"I don't, we were lost. We're wanderers here. Strangers, and we saw your women drawing water," Norman said.

"We want to help," June Dey added as the bigger of the two Ol' Mas eyed him.

"No help," the smaller woman yelled.

"We can help to protect you," Norman said.

Before Norman could say another word, the woman pressed the weapon into his neck, causing him to step back. He looked over at June Dey, who also appeared settled on the notion that they would not fight the women of the village. With their weapons, the two women pushed Norman Aragon and June Dey to a roofless ten-by-ten outhouse made of mud with a bamboo gate. The bigger Ol' Ma poked June Dey's back with the spear as he entered. She closed the gate, and members of the village ran to her and helped her seal it with an iron bar.

Norman and June Dey looked out the gate opening as the women returned to the village circle, where now-relieved villagers shouted recommendations of punishments and plans for their unwelcome guests.

■ ■ ■ ■

THE BALL

■ ■ ■ ■

On that night, Maisy and Gbessa placed all that they had cooked on two long banquet tables. The Johnsons' hall had two floor-to-ceiling windows so clear and welcoming that the sun spilled onto the oak floors. On the walls of this banquet hall there were several photographs, including one of Mrs. Johnson and Miss Ernestine with a dozen women wearing white hats and carrying umbrellas. There were also framed boarding tickets from the voyage to Monrovia.

At the end of the room there was a smaller table with three chairs that Maisy had designed with ribbons to seat the Johnsons before their guests. The other tables were draped with maroon suede and blue and white trimmings. At the head of the room, a small wooden platform hosted a band of violins and Kpelle drums. Maisy and Gbessa cleaned some one hundred wineglasses that waited in the kitchen near three barrels of imported wine that Mr. Johnson had recently collected from the port.

As the guests entered the banquet room — lovely women in bright-colored dresses escorted by handsome men in tailored suits — Maisy stood in the corner with Gbessa and pointed them all out for her.

"Those are the Yanceys," Maisy said in Gbessa's ear. "They were slaves in Mississippi. An abolitionist bought them and sent them here.

"Those are the Jacksons," Maisy said, pointing to a round woman who held the hand of a short, dark-skinned man whose head barely reached her shoulders. "Mrs. Jackson still writes home to her old master and his wife about how she is doing here. They send her packages twice a year.

"Those are the Johnsons, no relation to ours, the Coopers, the Dunlaps, and the Lowes; oh, be careful talking to Mrs. Dunlap. She has a lazy eye and is easily offended if you look away while she is talking to you."

Gbessa watched the guests mingle with one another before taking their places at the tables.

"That's Mr. Roberts. That's Mr. Augustine. He was a slave doctor in America."

Mr. Augustine waved at Maisy. She waved back with a smile.

"Those are the Palmers and the Fairmans. They are neighbors in Mesurado County and people say they treat their servants worse than they were treated in America."

The room became crowded quickly. As the band played violins and Kpelle drums, nine women entered the room wearing white and cream dresses.

"Sande," Gbessa whispered.

Maisy laughed.

"No. They are society women."

"Society?"

"Yes. I went to one of the meetings with Mrs. Johnson and all they do is gossip," Maisy whispered.

After the guests finished eating, Maisy and Gbessa gathered their plates.

"Who is the girl?" one of the women asked while still looking at Gbessa.

"Alice's new servant," another answered her.

"Oh. I thought she did not like keeping servants."

Gbessa did not look up at the women while they spoke. She continued to clean and even slightly trembled as she felt their curious eyes upon her.

When the other guests noticed how the society women were looking at Gbessa and whispering to one another, all eyes then traveled across the table and rested on the witch in their midst.

"What is your name?" one of the women eventually asked her.

Gbessa, unaware that she was being spoken to, kept her head down and tried to collect the woman's half-eaten plate of food. Offended that Gbessa had ignored her, the woman pulled back her plate.

"What is your name?" she asked Gbessa loudly.

The sound of chiming silverware ceased at the woman's raised voice. All eyes were on Gbessa.

"Name," Gbessa said, happy to remember the word, afraid to give the answer. "Gbessa," she answered.

The society woman waited a moment before handing Gbessa her plate, after which she began a conversation with another guest. The chiming of silverware resumed, and Gbessa hurried out of the hall and into the kitchen, carrying her pile of plates. She turned and saw that Maisy was behind her.

"I did something wrong?" Gbessa asked.

"No. What did she ask you?"

"Name."

"You told her?"

"Yes."

"Good. You did nothing wrong, Ma."

At the end of the night, Miss Ernestine went to the Johnsons' table with a young man who shared her eyes. He had orange-brown skin and long, woolly hair that he wore in a braid down his back. As they approached the head table, the Johnsons stood to greet them. After a brief conversation, Mr. Johnson stood up and raised his glass. The ballroom guests became silent.

"I thought we would never make it here," he began in a deep and melodic voice. "I thought I would never see a time when free black men and women could find fellowship without the harassment by or fear of those who deem themselves superior to us."

The crowd nodded. Some coaxed his words with short grunts and murmurs.

"A land like Monrovia was a fairy tale that would never be realized, and like Moses's people, we and our children and our children's children would remain wandering in the American desert that is slavery and inequality."

He was interrupted by momentary applause.

"But yes, brethren. Monrovia is real. Monrovia is real and we are home."

The crowd clapped. Some of the women patted the corners of their eyes with handkerchiefs.

"What he say?" Gbessa asked Maisy.

"He said he is happy to be here away from people who treated them badly," Maisy answered.

"Oh," Gbessa said, nodding. "Me too."

"We are where we were always meant to be — seasoned now by adversity, we can lead our fellow African brethren in a sound democracy under Christian principles. Thank God for the deliverance of Africa for Africans."

The crowd cheered again. Mr. Johnson waited for the end of their applause before continuing.

"Do not sleep, for Monrovia and her story have just begun. Yes, Monrovia will be the vanguard of Africa's resurrection. Her hairs will touch the lightning and she will protect and guide us all. We must — we *must* — build Monrovia!"

A few men stood up from their seats and raised their glasses toward Mr. Johnson. Others waved their hands.

"My passion for this land, though I love my neighbors and countrymen, is not solely because of you. It is for her," Mr. Johnson said, pointing to Marlene. He went to her and put his arm around her shoulders. "It is for her and her children and her neighbors."

With a handkerchief, Mrs. Johnson wiped her eyes. Miss Ernestine was now crying also.

"Which brings me to a very special toast," he said finally. "A toast that I have dreaded since the day she was born. Marlene will be married to Henry Hunter. They are engaged, and with our blessing, prayers, and support, they will continue building the next generation of Monrovia!"

The society women immediately rose to their feet in a rage of applause. Miss Ernestine could not contain her sobs as Henry left her side to join Marlene.

Gbessa saw them together and she thought of Safua. In her small corner she wondered what Lai was doing on that night, if the storyteller was to serenade the village children with tales of the mystical land. She ached for these stories. But that pain was not too different a feeling from relief that she no longer had to make friends with Lai's rejection. They went hand in hand, her thoughts of Lai and of Safua, followed by the memory of that long road that she was forced to travel alone after her exile. Gbessa wondered if Safua thought of her — or remembered the nights at Lake Piso when the wall between their stories crumbled to leave them standing face-to-face.

Henry and Marlene Hunter's first house was farther south and inland from Monrovia, in Sinou County. There, a new middle class had assembled, made up of returned slaves who could afford neither servants nor large fields to farm. This was true of smaller cities along the coast as well, where settlers farmed coffee which they traded along the St. Paul River. Unlike the owners of the mansions on the Monrovian beach, most of the residents of Sinou County tended their own farms. Henry Hunter decided that he would move there, since he'd always secretly despised the way the Monrovian society lived and how some treated their servants. He spoke to the men on his mother's farm as though they were his boyhood friends, made an attempt to learn their languages, and when he could, he made sure they had portions equal to his during mealtime. He wanted, as he told Marlene, to be as far from his mother and Monrovian society as he possibly could, planning secretly even to break free one day from the American Colonization Society's white governors and the Monrovian society's elitist mayors to form an independent country of his own. The only way he saw this happening was to move to Sinou's middle-class farming communities and to learn about the free colony for himself.

Henry's ambition is what attracted Marlene, who herself was from liberal and kind parents who never kept more servants than they needed. When they were only sixteen, she heard Henry speak to an isolated group at a society party for Monrovia's youth, where he voiced his frustration that though they were in a free colony, they were still governed by white Americans.

"Be reasonable, Henry. We need their help," another boy protested that night.

"We do not. We were taught that we needed their help. Which one of them farms your land?" Henry asked him.

The boy had no answer and in fact returned home that night and instigated a nightlong debate with his father about why the free colony still needed white governors. His father then shared the dangers of the tyrannical views of Henry Hunter with Miss

Ernestine, who dismissed them as pettiness. Several days later, while no one was looking, Marlene handed Henry a letter during a picnic. It read:

Dear Henry Hunter:
I share your ideology, however you are careless in your articulation of it. The crops from our farms are traded to vendors assigned by the "white governors" who you so adamantly contest. I doubt other countries would trade to a colony of Negroes. Look at what is happening to Haiti. They are the first black republic and already so poor from governments refusing to trade with them. The governors are a proper color. They remain the liaisons of most economic transactions of the colony. They are, however hard it is to admit it, responsible for society wealth. I am anxious for your rebuttal.

Sincerely,
Marlene Johnson

To this Henry Hunter responded:

Dear Marlene:
I am impressed that you are as intelligent as you are beautiful. I hope my

words did not offend you as they offended some others. To your point I argue only this: what is the color of money and who oppresses or is offended that it is not white? We must continue this face to face. I have to see you again.

Sincerely,
Henry Hunter

The two spent most of their spare time writing letters to each other. One day Miss Ernestine saw the brief exchange of letters from across a ballroom floor and insisted on making visits to the Johnson household to get to know the family (and Marlene) better, since Henry refused to disclose any details of his personal life to his mother.

It was the fear of offending the other society members that encouraged her to give Henry her blessing. Henry and Marlene were married only one month after the Johnson ball, and against Miss Ernestine's wishes, they decided to move to Sinou County with the inland farmers and free families. Sinou was southeast of Mesurado County, where Monrovia and newer, more American-influenced colonies were being born.

Gbessa moved in with Henry and Marlene

to help them care for their new home. Upon arriving at the house, Maisy led Gbessa to a small room at the back with a window overlooking a one-acre farm.

"This one is yours," Maisy said and placed Gbessa's bag on the floor near her bed. "I bought a gift for you," she said and handed Gbessa a brown box with a ribbon tied around it.

Gbessa opened the gift.

"It is a Bible. I know there will not be much for you to do until they start having children, so I thought you could work on the letters and words I taught you," she said.

"You visit?" Gbessa asked, as Maisy headed to the door.

"Sure. Yes, I will come whenever Mrs. Johnson makes a trip and maybe other times. You are not losing me, Gbessa," Maisy said. Gbessa wrapped her arms around her tightly. She thought that she would faint, or die, from the pressure in her heart, but instead Maisy held her up.

"Thank you, Maisy," Gbessa whispered. "Love you, Maisy."

Maisy pulled away and held Gbessa's face, lovely even through the red eyes and wetness.

"I love you, too, Ma."

"I not your Ma. You my Ma," Gbessa cried.

"No, I your sister," Maisy said in Vai.

"No, Maisy. You my Ma," Gbessa replied in English.

"Okay then, sister. I your Ma."

Gbessa hugged her again.

"I will visit you, you hear?" she said in Vai.

"Yes. Yes. Thank you, Maisy," Gbessa responded, nodding.

Maisy joined the Johnsons in the carriage outside. She wiped her face with a handkerchief that Mrs. Johnson handed her, and waved out of the carriage to Gbessa. Gbessa stood on the porch until Maisy and the carriage were swallowed by night.

Henry and Marlene Hunter called for Gbessa only when they needed help, and otherwise were self-sufficient in caring for their home and land. They encouraged Gbessa to practice her English, and to make friendships (where she could) with any house girls or nurses in the nearby households. But instead Gbessa preferred keeping to herself in her small room. There, she wrestled with thoughts of wanting to return to the village, any village, and wanting to be just like those on the other side of the door.

Sinou County was made up of returned American ex-slaves, Barbadian and Jamaican settlers, and a few indigenous people like Maisy, who had once worked as servants but could now afford settler-style homes and farms of their own.

Henry and Marlene Hunter were the first of the society people to move to Sinou County, and at first were looked at skeptically since they did not seem to carry themselves like most Monrovians. But after one year of living there, when the settlers saw that the Hunters worked just as hard as their servants to keep their home, they welcomed them and gave them tips on how to farm their land.

Before the rainy season, they taught them how to build drainage systems using palm leaves so their crop would not drown. Before the dry season, they taught them how to use the same system to make sure their plants remained hydrated.

Marlene's closest friend was a Trinidadian settler by the name of Anna. Anna was a stout woman with a short neck and a flat chest. Her words came out in a way Marlene called choppy and she rolled and cut her eyes after any bit of news, whether good or bad.

While Henry and Anna's husband, Zeke,

sat on the Hunters' porch in the evenings smoking tobacco and comparing their lives back in the States and the Caribbean Islands, Marlene and Anna sat at the kitchen table playing cards with Norma, another wife of a settler of Sinou County, who was pregnant with her seventh child. Norma hired a maid to help her with her children, so in the evenings if her husband, Joseph, decided to join Henry and Zeke on the porch, she could join their wives in a game of cards.

"It's a good thing Henry come here talking about all this independence," Anna said one night, looking over the fanned assortment of cards in her hands.

"Yeh, it sure is," Norma agreed, rubbing her protruding belly.

"I don't like them riding around my farm with their white faces. What you come here for, nobody invite you?" Anna laughed.

"All of them are not bad men," Marlene said in the governor's and sailors' defenses. She was more acclimated to life with whites in Monrovia and the States, and did not consider their presence as much of a nuisance as her friends did. "I just do not agree with them having their noses and opinions in all of colony politics and economy. It is as though they think we are incompetent."

"Well, in any case, I hope some sort of settlement on the colony is reached soon. I should not have a white governor in Africa or anywhere else," Norma said. "I should not have a white mayor voting on what should happen to my farm or children. We can vote for ourselves."

To avoid these conversations, though she was never invited to join in them to begin with, Gbessa remained in her room either reading the little she could of the Bible Maisy had given her or daydreaming of when she would see Maisy again. Once in a while she dreamed of Safua and wondered if he would recognize her if she ever returned to Lai. The thought equally excited and terrified her, but she convinced herself that staying in the free colony was her God's will. Maisy visited Gbessa, as she had promised to, making sure she carried with her the crushed coal paste to dye her hair. And when Gbessa was sent back to Monrovia on errands or to deliver letters to the Johnsons or Miss Ernestine, she slept beside Maisy in her old room, on her old bed, and they laughed and told stories into the night.

One night when Gbessa returned from running errands in Monrovia and visiting with Maisy, she entered the house to the sound of laughter as the smell of tobacco smoke charged toward her from the dining room. While accustomed now to answering questions about her ethnicity and hair, Gbessa was still very shy and avoided conversations with settlers whenever possible.

She quickly passed the entry to the dining room toward her room and hoped that she had not been seen.

"Gbessa!" Marlene called from the dining room. Gbessa shook her head, embarrassed to walk into the room where she knew they were hosting guests.

"Yes, Marlene?" she asked, still in the hallway.

"Come join us," Marlene said.

Gbessa walked quietly into the dining room. She placed the basket she carried on the floor near the entry. There in the dining room, Marlene and Henry Hunter, Zeke and Anna, and Joseph and Norma sat amid clouds of smoke in front of playing cards and an open bottle of whiskey.

"My God, girl. How your hair grow so long?" Anna asked, looking up at Gbessa. Gbessa sometimes forgot to braid her hair since leaving the Johnson house, and she let it scatter around her face and down her body.

"I do not know, Anna."

"It isn't voodoo, is it?" Norma joked, holding on to her stomach.

"Norma, that is rude," Marlene said.

"What?" Anna asked. "The girl is right to wonder. These country girls are up to many things."

"Island girls too," Marlene said, and both Norma and Anna quickly hushed. "I do not believe in that," Marlene said. "Besides, Gbessa is a Christian."

She pulled out a chair.

"Country people, free men, Islanders; we are all Negro people and likely to be unrecognizable from one another in this country in a few generations," Henry said.

Norma hissed through her teeth. "You can always tell a man from the bush," she said.

Country is what they called local tribesmen. The settlers in Sinou wanted to expand inland but the neighboring indigenous tribes fought to keep their territories and villages. This prevented settlers from growing the scale of farmland that most of them desired, and collectively accruing enough income to finally declare complete independence from America.

Gbessa had grown used to being teased by Norma for being "country," but never minded, since Maisy once told her it came only from a fear of losing her man.

"Women are naturally good," Maisy had said. "When a woman says or does a bad thing — a woman who does not know God — there is usually a man behind it."

"Did you need me, Marlene?" Gbessa asked.

"Oh yes, I want to introduce you to Henry's cousin Gerald. He finally arrived from New York."

Out of the darkness and smoke, a tall and wide-shouldered man with a boy's face emerged. The lamplight ran to his skin. He was a lighter-skinned man, almost pale, with full, pink lips, and hair that was braided neatly down his back. When he smiled the room was made better for it, and he carried himself as if he was altogether aware and fully convinced of his power. He wore a brown suit, the kind of suit that Henry Hunter used to wear before moving to Sinou, and held out his hand toward Gbessa.

"Hello. Gerald Tubman," he said, taking her hand. He kissed the back of it. Gbessa pulled it away and wiped the back of her hand against her dress.

"Gbessa," she said and wondered why the man had touched his mouth to her skin.

"Gbessa, it is a gesture of chivalry. He is only saying hello." Marlene grinned.

401

Gbessa nodded.

"Gbessa, you will wake up early to prepare us all breakfast, won't you? I would do it myself but I love your cooking and I want to show it off to Gerald."

Gbessa blushed. "Yes, Marlene," she said. "Thank you."

The next morning she made sure she braided her hair before leaving the room. Gbessa prepared eggs, cornbread, grits, and ham and placed them on the table. She waited for the Hunters and their guest, surprised that they did not come down while she was cooking, as they usually did.

When the grits on the table began to harden, Gbessa left the dining room and went toward the stairs to fetch them. As she turned the corner, Gerald jumped out of an unlit hallway, waving his hands.

Gbessa was startled and gasped while Gerald laughed.

"You all right?" he asked as she stood catching her breath.

"Why you do that?" Gbessa asked, annoyed. She passed him and headed toward the stairs.

"They left," Gerald said.

"What? Where they go?" Gbessa asked.

"A messenger came in the middle of the night on an emergency run for Henry. He was called back to Monrovia."

"When they come back?"

"Well — as of now, I do not know," he said. "You should come eat with me."

Gerald turned from her and entered the kitchen to eat. Gbessa followed him, unsure of what was expected of her in Henry's and Marlene's absence. She began to prepare Gerald's plate but he touched her hand while she served his eggs.

"I can do it," he offered. "Thank you."

He smiled once she took a seat and helped himself to the meal.

"I can dish your meal for you," Gbessa offered.

"No, please," Gerald said, holding his hand up. "I have not had a home-cooked meal in some time so I do not intend to eat with manners. Consider us even."

Gbessa nodded and watched him.

"You are not going to join me?" he asked her. "Eat."

Gbessa cut a slice of ham for herself and ate sparingly. Gerald laughed.

"That is all you will have? Is that what they taught you of culture and civilization?" he asked. Her response to his attempted humor was only silence. She continued to eat. "Of what tribe do you belong?"

Gbessa hesitated. "I was — I am Vai."

"Oh. Vai," he said and stared at her face. "You are very beautiful."

"Thank you," Gbessa said and gazed down at the table.

"I hope that does not offend you," Gerald said.

She shook her head. "Thank you," she said again softly.

"How long have you lived among the settlers?" Gerald asked. His movements, although fluid, were calculated. He ate and took great care to hide his nervousness. He turned his face and looked toward the window so he would not show how stunned he was by her striking and kind face. Her soft neck, her haunting eyes, her glorious hair, her gentle and spare words; he desired her and hid it with great difficulty.

"Two years now," Gbessa answered.

"Oh. Do you ever visit your people?"

"No," she answered.

"Hmm. I am sure that Marlene would allow it if you pleased."

Gbessa nodded.

"The Vai people live north, yes? From what I remember they are near the British colony border." He waited for her, and his breathing came at a nervous pace. "Are you going to ask me anything?" Gerald asked.

She would have said no but realized it

would be rude of her.

"You . . . an American?" she asked, hoping to change the subject.

"No. I am an African some generations removed." Gerald laughed. Gbessa was confused. "I just arrived from America, yes," he said.

"You were slave?" Gbessa asked him, hoped of him.

"No, but my parents were," Gerald answered and shifted in his chair. "Do you know the land well?" he asked, quickly changing the subject. "Do you consider yourself a suitable tour guide?"

Gbessa nodded.

"Are all African women as modest with words as you are?"

Gbessa shook her head. Gerald laughed again. She smiled.

"You will stay here?" Gbessa asked after a passing silence.

"Yes. Until I settle on a lot of land. I do not plan on using much of my money on land."

"Sinou County has good land," Gbessa said.

"Yes, so I hear."

"What you — What did you do in America?" Gbessa asked not long after.

"I was a shop owner."

"Shop?"

"I sold things," he said. "Clothes. Shoes. It was my father's business. He died and left it to me."

"You have Ma?"

"No. No — Ma. I never knew her."

Gerald resumed his meal. He lifted his cup and drank to soothe a still-parched throat.

"I never knew mine too," she said.

"Either," he corrected her and smiled affectionately. "You never knew yours either."

"I never knew mine either," she said.

Gerald was unsure of what words to give to offer her comfort.

"Excuse me," she said finally, and returned to her room.

She closed the door and stood with her back against it. She turned and knelt to peer through the narrow opening where her door met the wall. With an obstructed view, all she could see was Gerald's hand as it extended from his elbow and forearm, which rested on the table. He tapped his fingers rhythmically against the splintered wood. The dress, the room, that man, this feeling — all foreign. "Safua," she whispered, though even she could not hear it.

Later on that day Gbessa prepared lunch, which she and Gerald again ate together, entertained by few words and gestures of friendship and hospitality. She then prepared dinner and ate with Gerald under the same circumstances. By the next night, when Henry and Marlene had not yet returned, sleep ran from Gbessa. She left her room and went into the kitchen to pour herself a glass of water. She then entered the sitting room, where she knew she could get a view of the main road from the front window, and was startled by Gerald Tubman's presence. She shouted at the sight of him sitting in a corner chair directly in the moonlight.

"I did not know you were —"

"It is all right. Come and sit with me," he said, happy to see her.

"I could not sleep," Gbessa said.

"Neither could I. I plan to leave for Monrovia at dawn if they still have not returned," he said.

Gbessa nodded and drank. Gerald watched her lips as they brushed the rim of the cup.

"Tell me something about yourself," he said in that moment.

"Something?" Gbessa asked.

"Anything. What do you like to do?" he asked.

His question caught Gbessa by surprise

and her body grew warm with fear. She was not sure how to immediately answer, so they sat in the room in silence as the crickets sang outside.

"I like to sit near water. To swim," she said finally. It was the first thing that came to her mind and she grinned as soon as she said it. Gerald smiled as well.

"You swim?" he asked.

"Yes," she answered proudly, and was saddened that it had been so long since she had floated underneath the moon.

"When last did you swim?" Gerald asked.

"Some months ago. Maisy and I found a creek close to here," she said.

"Close to here?" Gerald asked.

"Yes," Gbessa said and blushed at the thought of swimming with the broad-shouldered man.

"Can you show me? Would you like to take a walk?" he asked.

"Now?" Gbessa was surprised by the proposition since she knew it was the sort of thing that Maisy would call improper.

"Neither of us can sleep," Gerald said. "Henry said it is a safe county. I will get a lantern."

"Not too long," Gbessa said before he left the room. After changing her clothes, Gbessa led Gerald out of the house and off the farm under a waiting moon. Neither of them spoke, and they remembered very little of the conversation that had inspired their odd adventure. The emptiness of the house made her uneasy and cold, so even side by side with his strangeness, she was happy to be with him and happier to be outside. When they stepped off the farm, Gbessa recognized the road that led to the creek and turned to take it. In the dark Gerald held her hand as they traveled the road. Her heart pounded in her ears. She heard it and it drowned out the other sounds of the night, even his breathing.

"There you are, my darling," I said, passing by. "There you are, my friend."

Gerald squeezed her hand toward the moonlight as twigs scratched her brown legs and night flies rested on her shoulders. Gbessa swatted the flies away and walked faster toward the narrow river.

"I hear it," Gerald said finally. The thought of sitting near water excited her.

They arrived at the creek and Gerald released her hand. He placed the lantern on the ground and brushed a space free of leaves for them to sit. When they had both settled, Gbessa sighed into the night at the moon's reflection on the creek's face.

"Wow," Gerald whispered. "This place

really is paradise."

The night flies returned and danced in front of Gbessa's face. Gerald caught one and held it in a closed fist.

"Let it go," Gbessa said with disapproval. "Make free." Gerald released the fly's electric glow and it floated away from them.

"Thank you," she said.

He watched her face in the gleaming light of the lantern. He followed religiously as her eyes exited his gaze to look upon the moving water.

"Thank you," she said again.

Overwhelmed with desire for her, Gerald turned her chin and kissed her. She pushed him away at first, and stared at his lips until he slowly came toward her again. She gently touched his face and he explored her tongue and lips with an opened mouth. Her body grew warm at the pure joy of his embrace. His fingers grazed her cheek and hair. Gerald's hands trailed down her body to her breasts.

"No," she said. "Stop." Once the words escaped her she bit her tongue.

"Okay," Gerald said and kissed her again. Night flies flickered in and out of view and the wind passed them to another morning.

When they returned to the house it was almost dawn and a man waited for them in the front yard.

Christopher, a Gola man who trained most of the horses in Monrovia, was the colony messenger.

"Christopher!" Gbessa called out to him as soon as she recognized his face in the morning dew.

Christopher approached them before they reached the porch step.

"Where are they? They all right?" Gbessa inquired.

"Sure, they fine. Sent me to come get you, Mr. Tubman. Henry says to tell you it is an emergency," Christopher said.

"Sure. I will head out now," Gerald said.

"There is a horse and buggy not far from here headed this way for you, sir."

"All right then. Gbessa, you will come too," Gerald said. "No need for you to stay here on your own." Before she could answer, Gerald left her side and entered the house for his things.

In the sitting room of the Johnson house in Monrovia, the society women, along with Marlene and other young women, sat, distressed and fanning themselves. Upon noticing Gerald, Miss Ernestine jumped to her feet.

"There you are!" she said and hugged

him. "I forgive you for not visiting me before going to see your cousin. Ladies, this is my nephew Gerald Tubman."

The society women nodded toward him, the younger women whispering to themselves behind their fans. Gerald greeted each of them individually.

"Gerald, welcome," Mrs. Johnson said, standing up to greet him. "The men are upstairs." She pointed toward the stairwell. Maisy, who had heard them arrive, entered the den and pulled Gbessa away. She took her to the kitchen, where she appeared to have been cutting peppers. Gbessa grabbed a knife to help her.

"I have to tell you something," they said simultaneously in Vai and laughed immediately after.

"What happened?" Gbessa asked.

"Something big, Gbessa," Maisy said, holding Gbessa by the shoulders. "The ACS is leaving Monrovia."

"What? When?" Gbessa asked.

"Soon. Some are even headed back on the ship that Mr. Tubman came on. But they are going and they are encouraging Mr. Johnson and other mayors to declare their independence from America."

"That is good then," Gbessa said. "That is what they want. Yes?"

"Not this way. When they go, Monrovia's army will be cut in half." Maisy looked over Gbessa's shoulder to see if anyone was coming. "They may not be able to protect it from being attacked."

"Attacked?" Gbessa asked and remembered the company of wanderers she traveled with: Norman Aragon and June Dey.

"Yes. Mr. Johnson and the rest are afraid that tribes will disrupt the peace. That means that most settlers in Sinou would have to move to Monrovia."

"Here?!"

"Yes."

"What are they going to do?" Gbessa asked.

Maisy sighed. "Mr. Johnson and the other mayors want the ACS to stay, but they will not."

"But Henry and Marlene, they want them to go. The people in Sinou do not like them."

"I know," Maisy whispered. "Henry has been arguing for two days for them to build an army of their own. He is the only one who thinks it is a good thing they are leaving now. That is why he called Mr. Tubman. He worked for an old army general in America." The remnants of Gerald's kiss tingled on Gbessa's lips. "How is he doing?" Maisy asked. "Is he a good man?"

"All right," Gbessa answered. Gbessa then suddenly pulled Maisy close to her and hugged her again.

"What did you have to tell me?" Maisy asked, pulling away.

"Nothing," Gbessa said. "I am happy to see you."

"Me too," Maisy whispered. Marlene entered the kitchen and the girls separated.

"Maisy, would you mind making us some lemonade?" she asked. Maisy nodded and she and Gbessa made glasses of lemonade to serve to the society women. They then made rounds carrying several trays up the stairs to a hot room where Mr. Johnson and other mayors stood around, some pacing.

Maisy immediately set down her tray and opened the window. Gbessa avoided the extended legs of those who sat and the pointing and waving arms of those who disagreed with the majority opinion. She went to Gerald, who stood with his back against a wall. She looked down at the tray as he took a glass of lemonade from it. He made sure to touch her hand while picking up his glass.

"Thank you," he said and Gbessa nodded.

She walked away from him as he watched,

414

letting the cold glass of citrus and ice cool his tongue and throat.

During the next several days the mayors called for one representative from each of the households of Monrovia, Sinou, Maryland County in the east, Careysburg and the Gribble and Island territories. I watched as horses sped down newly cleared roads that linked each county. Word had traveled quickly of the ACS's departure from the free colony, and as I wandered around Monrovia, it seemed the mayors all feared the worst for the safety of the small colony. While Mr. Johnson and the other mayors awaited news from America of how much of a monthly stipend they should expect, Henry, Gerald, and other young men rallied an assembly of the colony's settlers to meet on the lawn one July day to hear what Mr. Johnson had to say. On the field of the mansion, some hundreds of men and women gathered to listen to Mr. Johnson speak, banding together after rumors began to spread that the absence of the ACS would make them targets of attacks by local groups.

"Brethren!" Mr. Johnson yelled to the crowd. Seven other mayors stood behind him. Henry Hunter stood behind the mayors with Gerald Tubman. Below them, several men surrounded the stage with rifles. It was the rainy season but the rain had subsided that day, as if she knew of what was to come. I idled among the settlers. So far they were from prisons like Emerson.

"Brethren! We are alone now. We are alone in this wilderness — our home. It was a thing of impossibility to move, as they did so many of us, to a safe haven such as this colony; to see so many of us build and thrive on our own land; to see our children live the lives our forefathers prayed for." Before Mr. Johnson could proceed, the crowd erupted in applause.

"We are babes, still learning to walk this promised land and to learn its language. Dreamers — all of us — a country of dreamers, all of us, to have ever agreed to the journey across the ocean, futile and fatal for some of our loved ones and friends, and still a battleground for so many of you who stand before me.

"Yes, we are alone now!" Mr. Johnson continued. "We were not born free people in this world. No, we were not born free people. And those of us born without the shackles were told that we would fail — and look now. Look around you. Look what has been realized among us."

The crowd shifted, taking a moment to look around at themselves. Most of them were already crying.

"When I was a boy I asked my father what it meant to be a free Negro man. I had heard white men refer to my father as such, but I did not know what about this freedom made it so exceptional that it needed to be said. Why did my father not call them free white men? Why did they need to mention that he was free?

"That was when my father told me that my freedom as a Negro man was different. I was free, you see, he assured me, but there were some places where I could act free, and some places where I could not act free. There were things I could say —"

"Yes," the crowd agreed.

"And some things that I could not say! So as a boy I told my father, 'But then I am not free.' And my father looked at me, unknowing of how to reason, how to explain to his son that because he was a Negro man, freedom was something different for him — until now."

Mr. Johnson smiled widely and looked up at the sky. He waved toward heaven as the crowd clapped through his delivery.

"They said you would be lost forever,

yes?"

"*Yes!*"

"And yet — yet — it is not they who tended your farms or built your houses. I say — I say — if it is their protection that we fear losing; if it is an army of men who think us incompetent we fear losing, if it is the men who prefix your freedom, then I say *let them go!*"

The crowd roared with excitement.

"*Let them go!*"

The crowd celebrated together, some with tears running onto their necks. They slowly quieted and begged for more from him. Mr. Johnson wiped the sweat from his forehead with a handkerchief.

"We are free," he said, settling, his voice slightly hoarse. "And this freedom, this liberty is what caused you to risk your lives to journey here. This liberty is what will build this nation into the next century, and the century after, and the century after, and the century after! For our children and all of our grandchildren! For all of this land — let us remember this day! We will die reciting, and in the name of our new and honest freedom, in the name of our liberty, we shall call this land, our new and bold and free and honest country, *Liberia!*"

There was a series of meetings in the following weeks among the mayors of Monrovia and those who were perceived as leaders of each community. There it was decided that an army of local settlers would be formed to protect the new country. Henry Hunter convinced the mayors that a military base would have to be placed in Sinou County. All agreed that Gerald Tubman would lead the army, and a house was to be built for him immediately. He was also given two horses. During the meetings, Mesurado County was named, and in that county the new capital city of Monrovia would be established on the coast. The settlers began publishing a newspaper, circulated in Mesurado, Sinou, and other mainland counties, with updates and news on the political organization of the new country.

Toward the end of one of these meetings, two boys no older than sixteen years entered the room walking side by side. Their shirts were wrinkled and both looked to be missing buttons and neither of their frock coats fit well — both were too big for their thin frames.

"Is it over?" one of the boys said, and immediately examined the faces of each man in the room, as if looking for where his words had run off to.

The men in the room looked toward the pair, raising their brows.

"Nearly," Mr. Johnson said. His colleagues halted their exit to survey the young men.

"Excuse us for interrupting," one of the boys said, his accent thick with hints of the inland. "My name Ezekial. This my cousin Elijah."

"Very well then, my Old Testament young brothers," Mr. Johnson said, smiling. The others in the room were humored, chuckling underneath striped handkerchiefs and gray mustaches. "What can we do for you?"

"We were sent by my father, who stayed behind to watch the farm. We live in Maryland County," Ezekial said.

"Who is your father?" one of the mayors asked.

"Bennette Hill. From South Carolina."

"There is a small community out there," the mayor said to the others in the room, though it seemed as though he said it to remind himself, not his colleagues.

"I see," Mr. Johnson said. "What can we do for you? You folks in Maryland still having trouble negotiating with the native people?"

"No, not, no," Ezekial said, rapidly shaking his head. "It's just . . . my brother recently saw something. Some trouble. My father thought to come report it formally."

"He sent you alone?" another asked.

"He didn't want to leave my Ma and sisters on the farm after it happened," Ezekial said, his voice now shaking. "Tell him, Elijah."

"I was out coconut farming . . ."

"Can't hear you," someone yelled from the back of the room.

"I was coconut farming," Elijah, the younger boy, said, not much louder than the first time, aware that all eyes were on him. "And I saw white men lead some group of Grebo people. They look bad."

"They had been beaten," Ezekial said, speaking up for his cousin with exaggerated hand gestures. "He says they were in ropes, around two dozen of them. My father said they may be here trading."

"Slavers?" Mr. Johson asked skeptically.

The room erupted into disapproving chatter.

"There's no more slave trading going on along the coast anymore," one of the mayors said.

"Slavers. You're sure they were slavers?" Mr. Johnson asked. "Some Negroes have white skin." He looked around the room, as if apologizing for saying this. "Are you sure it wasn't a settler with prisoners?"

"Yes, sir," Ezekial said as Elijah nodded.

"They didn't speak English," Elijah said, barely audible.

"They didn't speak English," Ezekial repeated loudly. "They were not settlers, sir."

"I'm sorry, young man, but that's hard to believe," a mayor interrupted. "Trading has been outlawed for some time."

"Slavers. How would we manage that?" another stressed from the corner of the room. He rubbed his brow with a handkerchief. The conversation in the room resumed, some born of stress, some born of disbelief.

"No use worrying about nothing seem unlikely," a settler dissented.

"Trading has been outlawed for nearly four decades," another added.

"Still," Mr. Johnson said, holding up his

hand to quiet the room. "We can send a few soldiers to the area to look around."

"No harm in that," one of the men added.

"You all come to my home to sleep tonight, and we'll send some men with you in the morning," Mr. Johnson told the boys. "How does that sound?"

Disappointment cloaked both of their faces, but Elijah and Ezekial respectfully agreed. "And since your father's a churchgoing man, tell him to make sure he comes to Monrovia sometime to worship with us." Mr. Johnson feigned a smile, and because the others in the room barely laughed this time, he was certain the ugliness of their thoughts was related, their fears like uncomely identical brothers, and they were terrified to look each other in the face.

While Henry and Gerald stayed in Monrovia, Marlene and Gbessa returned to Sinou County. The excitement and anticipation of the settlers' rebirth traveled along the new republic's coast.

After one month, Mr. Johnson's messenger rode into Sinou County to take Marlene and Gbessa back to Monrovia. Upon their arrival, Gbessa joined Maisy in the kitchen, but Maisy did not know why they had been called. She gazed out the kitchen window onto the beach, and Gbessa's thoughts ran to her past. It came to her sometimes in dreams, and once a day while she was awake, reminding her of the curse of her witchery — a curse that she knew stayed with her, even underneath the black hair and buttoned blouses.

"What are you thinking about?" Maisy asked, startling Gbessa. Before she could speak, her stomach turned and she became dizzy. She held her stomach and leaned over the edge of the window, where she vomited everything she'd eaten that day.

"Gbessa," Maisy said, concerned. "You're not well."

"I'm well," Gbessa countered. "Just in my head too much, that all."

On the following morning when Gbessa and Maisy passed the Johnsons' sitting room, Miss Ernestine and two other women sat with Mrs. Johnson and knitted. Miss Ernestine was noticeably agitated when she recognized Gbessa. Maisy decided to enter the room to speak to the women before going about her chores.

"Good morning. How do you do?" she asked them. All of them spoke but Miss Ernestine, who stared at Gbessa peculiarly. The other women then also periodically gazed toward Gbessa with suspicion, though they tried to appear as if they were fixed on their knitting.

"What did you do to him?" Miss Ernestine asked Gbessa finally.

"What?" Gbessa asked, shaking her head. She looked at Maisy. Maisy was confused.

"To Tubman. Gerald Tubman. What did you do?" Miss Ernestine interrogated her.

"What?" Gbessa asked, pondering the worst. Had he died too? "Nothing, Miss —"

"You opened your legs to him?"

"No!" Gbessa blushed.

"You are lying. I know your type of woman — you have no sense of decency," she muttered under her breath.

Gbessa remembered the kiss and was immediately ashamed. She was afraid to tell Maisy.

"Ernestine, just calm down," another woman said. "We will pray over the girl and for the union and that will be it. Let the Lord work as he pleases."

"No decency," Miss Ernestine muttered.

"That is enough, Ernestine. Enough!" Mrs. Johnson finally said, dropping her knitting needle. Gbessa turned and ran from the room. "My God, Ernestine. You are corrupted," Mrs. Johnson said and followed Gbessa.

Inside their room, Maisy held Gbessa as

she wept. Gbessa quivered with fear that she would be banished again. Mrs. Johnson entered Maisy and Gbessa's room and closed the door.

Upon notice of Gbessa, Mrs. Johnson sighed and shook her head.

"He was waiting until tomorrow to ask you, but the wait, as you perhaps know now, would be in vain," Mrs. Johnson said.

Gbessa turned from Maisy's embrace and faced Mrs. Johnson.

"Gerald Tubman has decided to take you as his wife. He is going to ask you tomorrow." Maisy took Gbessa's hand. "I am sorry for Ernestine, but you should expect it, Gbessa. Gerald is going to become a very powerful man, and whatever the reason is that he chose you, your life will change. Do you understand that, Gbessa?"

Maisy stroked Gbessa's hair.

"What?" Gbessa asked, though her voice was barely audible. Her head pounded.

"You have to learn to defend yourself now. I cannot speak for you, Gbessa. Neither can Marlene. Neither can Maisy," Mrs. Johnson continued.

"You are marrying into society, Gbessa," Mrs. Johnson said finally, after a prolonged silence. "Do you understand that?" Gbessa pulled away from Maisy and stared into her face.

"Gbessa, do you understand?" Maisy asked with a proud grin.

He would be her husband. She would be his wife. This is what he had wanted, what he requested. Gbessa heard her heartbeat in her ears.

"Yes," she answered finally. "Sande."

As a child, when she leaned against the fissure of wood at Khati's house in Lai, or knelt by the door and peeked through the wooden fissures onto the village circle, there was usually a Poro man and a Sande touching each other so that she could see. They could show affection to each other in public — hold hands and even kiss each other's noses to an audience of all the wooden houses bordering Lake Piso. The Poro could touch her arms if he chose, or brush a resting fly or bird from her legs. The Sande could run to him and touch his chest; she could slap his arms playfully until he grabbed her and took her back to his wooden palace. It was ordinary for them, for royalty, to laugh and touch and kiss and whisper in this way. It was ordinary even for commoners to know one another in this way. But not for Gbessa, who found only

427

traces of that sweet and infinite thing through the peephole of her Ma's home. So she hunted it, haunted it through the tiny opening until it rode on my back and crashed into those neglected mud bricks, staining her with its residue.

What now? What happens after the thing? It never leaves, never comes off. It stays and stays, it transforms. It is a thief of time, of solace, of mind. And if the thing does return any of one's peace, after it is finished, the size of what remains is like a mustard seed. Some people manage to grow this remnant into something different — a version of happiness that tries, every waking moment, to resemble yesterday, to restore their battered spirit to its former self. A mustard seed. That is all she had left to give to Gerald. Not even enough to fill a bulbul. And where would she farm this seed? This was not her home.

She would be a Sande now, yes, but who was this king who asked for her hand? This was not for her, and inside there was a battle between the young witch and the woman who would walk down the aisle to be Gerald Tubman's wife. She sat on Henry and Marlene's porch on a rocking chair that whined as she rode it. The day was almost gone. The hanging leaves barely moved in the evening breeze. A bulbul cried in the distance and Gbessa closed her eyes. She thought of the suffering of her childhood, then of Gerald's kiss. She thought of the forest, but also his voice. Thinking of him frightened her, embarrassed her. They had spent so little time together, yet he had chosen her among the beautiful and well-born women of Monrovia. The possibility that the deceit of who she had become would be exposed shortened her breath. She was born a witch. And what king could love a witch? Who but Safua? Maisy was to sew her dress for a church ceremony to which only a handful of society families had been invited. But when she met Gerald at the end of the aisle, who would save her from her truth? He would die one day and she would not. All of society, Mrs. Johnson, Maisy — their eyes would close forever one day and hers would not. She would see this new Liberia born and maybe die, and maybe be born again. And maybe die again. And who would be brave enough to love a woman like that? Who but Safua? A hand gently grazed her shoulder. Risen out of her thoughts, she opened her eyes and saw Gerald smile down at her. Gbessa stood and the rocking chair continued to move behind her.

"No, please sit," Gerald said. "You look so peaceful. I don't want to interrupt you. Just to sit with you." Gbessa nodded and sat again, and Gerald pulled a chair from the corner of the porch to join her. She was afraid to think of Safua in front of him. Afraid to think of her curse or Gerald might hear it. So she hummed with the crying bulbul in the distance until the right words unsettled her tongue.

"You choose me," she said softly.

"Yes," Gerald said, enraptured by her beauty. He reached for her hand and held it. She smiled and continued humming, continued gazing out onto the outlying field, silencing herself.

"I not like them," she said.

"I am not like them," he corrected her.

Her skin grew warm. "I am not like them," she said quietly.

"We should go riding later," Gerald said. "I can teach you how to ride one of the horses. If you'd like."

He touched her hand, and when Gbessa looked at him and nodded, he smiled perfectly, in his way. He was tired after spending most of his time with Henry and others, justifying his choice of Gbessa as a bride. In an argument, Gerald admitted to Henry that even in Sinou, where the younger and more liberal settlers had chosen to live, there was a shared understanding of both superiority and responsibility when it came to the natives. Instead of seeking out tribesmen to work on farms as an indulgence of luxury or convenience, like many families in Monrovia did, the Sinou settlers felt it was their responsibility to provide economic opportunity and access to civilization to indigenous people. If local tribesmen ever denied their reaching out, Sinou settlers were just as surprised and offended as a Monrovian settler would be that "these poor, uncivilized" would deny their good graces.

Gerald warned Henry that the freed slaves who occupied Monrovia had rather quickly adapted to the new land as an American abolitionist would to a Southern state with a significant Negro population. If the abolitionist offered a Negro a job tending his farm and that Negro turned it down, the abolitionist would take offense, because how dare the Negro neglect the opportunity of his own life's advancement? Much as the settlers thought, this abolitionist did not consider that the opportunities presented to the Negro were still confined to hard labor and service, and thus there was no opportunity that a man of good education and social standing would take advantage of. There were settlers who taught their servants, as the Johnsons had educated Maisy — but Maisy, unless she married into society or married another servant who was able to save up enough to buy land and build a home of his own — would remain a house girl for a very long time. She would be an old woman before she was able to build a home. Gerald understood, after only a short time in the colony, that these settlers would somehow always have an upper hand in Liberia, even the settlers in Sinou and in the settlements like Arthington, farther north, who had developed a functioning middle class and chosen to live in neighboring territories with the natives of the land. He saw this as the first matter to confront when appointed head of the small army, but the mayors very promptly dismissed his claims as issues of minor importance in the grand scheme of Liberia's independence.

"We will have to visit all of the tribes within our borders and become allies with them," Gerald argued. "In order for us to remain safe, they have to believe that this is still their land — that nothing has changed."

"But it is not entirely," a mayor argued. "And much has changed. Everything has changed."

It was for this reason, the ongoing tensions over land between the settlers and indigenous groups, that he chose Gbessa to be his wife. He was aware of the commotion it would cause in society and was attracted to her enough that he found no ill in his sudden proposal.

"You are mad," Henry had argued when Gerald revealed his pending proposition.

"No, I am quite well. She is healthy, beautiful — why not?"

"She is uncivilized, uneducated," said Henry.

"And I do not require a wife who knows more than she will use," Gerald argued. "She can keep a household and hold a conversation. Her language and manners will improve with time."

Gerald argued that he wanted the settlers to consider the implications of their own prejudices, the irony and possible repercussions. And Gbessa was beautiful. Gbessa was perfect.

So two short weeks later, as she approached him from the entry to the church, he saw not only the promise of a new wife, but also the promise of a new Liberia.

And on that day, as Gbessa took Gerald's hand again, she thought of Safua and she

433

missed him, wanted him. She wanted in that moment to return to him and tell him about Maisy's God and the new country; she wanted to show him her hair and clothes; to look into his face near the lake until the sun rose. On her wedding day, when fate and all of her friends stood in attendance, the old woman in a daylight moon, the ocean waves, the rice fields, she whispered to them underneath her veil.

"Go find him, find him, find him," she chanted. "Find him and tell him to come."

I married Gbessa's whispers, her hopes that Safua would reach her before dark.

"Take care, my darling," I sang. "Take care, take care, take care."

■ ■ ■ ■

DISAPPEARED

■ ■ ■ ■

Her name was Sia. That is what June Dey noticed she answered to when the children in the village called her. Sia like a baby bulbul's first song. Sia, whose shoulders could be the resting place of those bulbuls during their first flight. There were slender hips underneath her lappa — June imagined it — and a button navel, and she moved as though she were dancing with each step. June Dey had touched her skin once — between the gate as she handed him a wooden pitcher of water on their second day in the village prison. She smelled like fresh coconut and mint, and June Dey inhaled deeply, wishing she would stay just a little while longer. This was the fifth day and he still felt her on his skin. After they'd touched she looked up at his face, at his eyes, through the gate, and back down at the pitcher as if answering the nagging questions of a young child. After that, after they touched, she did not return. Another girl, no older than ten, brought June Dey and Norman water and pawpaw once a day. Sia had handed the pawpaws to the girl from across the village, and when June Dey pulled it through the gate, he smelled their skins for traces of coconut and mint.

The men still hadn't returned to the village, so the Ol' Mas, the elders, kept their weapons close to them. Until the men returned, they said, Norman Aragon and June Dey would remain in the prison.

On the second morning, before Sia approached them with the water and something in June Dey changed, or rather settled, he suggested breaking the gate in the night so they could flee. Norman had scoffed at the suggestion.

"If we leave, how will we help them when the slavers come?" he asked, as if lecturing June Dey. June complied, but they hadn't spoken except to say "excuse me" while taking turns relieving themselves in a hole in the corner of the prison's dirt floor. June paid careful attention as Norman yelled questions to whoever was close to the cell.

"Why is the village so small?" "What's the name of it?" "Are you hiding?" "Who is Sam?" "Does everyone here know English?" Girls on their way to the well ran when they passed the prison, and Norman was in a spell of interrogations. When the girls were far enough into the forest, June Dey could hear them giggling. The women near the village stove, pounding fufu, boiling soup with conversing smells that visited each home and lured the villagers outside with their collective spell, gave Norman short answers: "Sam say he help" and "Every learn. All English." They rambled throughout the day, mostly talking to themselves in their language, leaving only a few openings for "Where the man them?," a question that seemed so heavy it would cause them either to sit down or walk to the edge of the village and look outward, as if, at just the right angle, a looking glass to the outside world could be seen through the dense network of trees. The few Ol' Pas who had been left behind also spoke among themselves, mostly in their language, laughing at Norman and his stream of questions. It was the children, the boys and girls too young to venture to the creek or to battle, who entertained him until their elders shouted for them to leave the prison. They spoke English best, sometimes choosing the language over their own as they dared one another in various games in the village circle. A young boy ran to the prison to retrieve a pebble, and Norman had asked: "When is Sam coming back?" The boy stared at Norman's hair before he picked up his pebble and returned to his friends. The next day, he returned to retrieve a pebble, and it seemed to June Dey as if the young boy was waiting for Norman to ask him the same question. He loitered, and scavenged for the pebble, though it was clearly in view. When Norman finally asked him again, "When is Sam coming back?," the boy answered quickly: "Sam no come back. Papa go kill him." Before Norman could respond, the boy asked, "You know Sam?"

"No," Norman answered. "We come to help."

At this, the boy ran away. Later he returned with friends, and returned the day after that, and the day after that. Each time they took turns answering Norman's questions, practicing their English, and giggling until they were called away. June Dey looked on as the children, with curiosity, took turns speaking to Norman Aragon. On one occasion, an Ol' Ma rushed to them waving a broom so they would leave the prison, at which they scattered like dried leaves in a newborn storm. Based on the children's conversations with Norman, June Dey gathered that the entire village, including

440

the missing men, comprised no more than seventy inhabitants, all somehow related. They learned English from a group of Anglican missionaries, or maybe only one who lived among them for some time before departing during the previous rainy season. Shortly after the missionary left, a man whom they called Sam had settled among them. He was an exile from another village, and he spoke many languages, but not English.

Sometime before this, when the dry season refused to give up its seat to rain, Sam convinced a crew of boys that they should travel with him to the coast to find work with traders. When some weeks passed and neither Sam nor the boys returned, all of the men in the small village went to the coast to get them, sensing there was something wrong. They had not yet returned.

June Dey gazed beyond Norman and the children to where Sia was sitting in the village circle, using an iron tool to cut greens before handing them to another woman to grind before throwing them into a steaming cookpot a few feet away from them. She took care of each leaf, cutting them as if they had feeling. She handed the bundle in her hand to the woman sitting next to her, then she looked up, straight past the children and Norman to June Dey. He coughed, surprised, and he was not sure if she caught his eyes because she could sense that he was staring, or if she did so on her own. The possibility of the latter made him stand up.

"Come!" Sia shouted at the children, breaking her gaze from June Dey's. The children ran away at once, and she continued what she was doing.

"Do what again?" Norman turned and asked June Dey. He hadn't said much the previous days, so his voice startled June Dey.

"What?"

"You just said 'do it again,' " Norman said. June Dey shook his head. Shrugged.

"You're hearing things," June Dey said, and waited until Norman turned around to seek her again.

On the following day, so early that the morning hadn't yet found her color, June Dey woke up to a rattling of the gate. When he opened his eyes, Sia stood before them, silent. June Dey and Norman rose to their feet, stretching from the discomfort of the tiny keep.

"Come," Sia said, opening the gate as the feet of the bamboo swept the dirt. Norman and June Dey followed her, passing the fire stove on the way to a house at the other

442

end of the village circle. Sia entered the home and waited at the door for Norman and June Dey, whose bodies moved slowly from the muscle aches and stiffness. Inside the house, the Ol' Mas who had interrogated them on the first day sat quietly in two wooden chairs, their lappas without wrinkles, their weapons still in their hands.

"Sit," Sia said, pointing to a space on the floor across from the Ol' Mas, in front of two warm bowls of fufu and fish stew. Sia remained near the door as Norman and June Dey sat, and without hesitation devoured the bowls of food.

"You know Sam?" Sia asked.

"No," June Dey said with a mouth full of food. Norman simply shook his head.

"Where you from?" Sia asked from the door. June Dey turned to face her, swallowing the ball of starch, but before he could speak she said: "Don't tell me. Tell the chief."

June Dey faced the Ol' Mas again, their faces like statues. The smaller Ol' Ma dug into June Dey's eyes as if something she had lost, something precious to her, had made a home there.

"America," June Dey answered, the pepper stew staining his mouth.

"Where America?" Sia asked June Dey's profile.

"Over the ocean. Far from here."

"And you?" Sia asked, though Norman did not turn to face her.

"Jamaica. An island. Also in the Americas."

"Why you come here?"

"I come to find Maroons in Freetown. Then I see everything and want to help," Norman said.

June Dey avoided eye contact with the Ol' Mas, who still hadn't broken their gazes. He looked to the dirt floor, the wooden legs of their chairs, the hems of their lappas, the mud wall beyond.

"What everything?"

"There are soldiers. Slavers roaming the coast," Norman said, breathing heavily, perhaps from the pepper, perhaps because he had been waiting all week to plead his case. "We suspect they are looking for slaves to take to the Americas."

"And how you will help? Only two men?" Sia asked.

June Dey glanced at Norman, who shook his head in response to what he knew June Dey was asking.

"We can help," Norman insisted. Sia watched them eat.

"Your English. It's very good," Norman said, treading lightly. "The children say a missionary lived here for many seasons. Taught you all about God and taught you English. Where did he go?"

Sia turned her back to them, to the question, to look out the window as the day crept into the circle, and the first woman rose and marched toward the creek with her buckets.

"We don't know. He just go."

"Did you . . . work with him closely?"

A rooster crowed many times, and his chicks could be heard scurrying behind him. Sia leaned her head against the window's edge until it seemed the rooster was bored of his ritual.

"I was his wife," she said finally.

June Dey's heart fluttered.

"The chief want you to go look for Sam and the boys," Sia said, turning again to face them.

"Why?" June Dey asked, unable to suppress his confusion, his sadness that she had been spoken for, and immediately regretted it.

"The ancestors told them you will help," she said.

"But you practice Christianity here, yes?" Norman asked.

A smile inched onto Sia's face. Her cheek-bones gave praise.

"My husband take four families from our old village when I was girl. We settle here and learn new God. Learn English. God come into our house and we welcome him and love him like he love us. But the house God come into still ancestor house. You leave your house when visitor come?"

Sia did not wait for them to reply.

"Sam say he take the boys for work. Chief listen to God and say yes," Sia said, pointing to the Ol' Ma with the rake. "Now she remember it ancestor house. Now she listen to ancestor," Sia said.

They were all that was left. A few dozen in that village. The women, the children, and three Ol' Pas rich with years.

June Dey stared as Sia's silhouette graced the window against the backdrop of what remained of the tiny village. She was beautiful. Her mouth, her spirit. He was sorry for her, but also envious that she could not imagine the horrors that would have awaited their fathers and brothers if they had indeed been caught or betrayed by Sam, a man they trusted, likely as quickly as they had dropped their guards for him and Norman. In the daylight the forest cooed and screeched around them.

"Chief want you go find Sam and the boys," she said again.

"We can try," Norman said.

"You leave to —"

The sound came first, disrupting the music of Sia's words. The sound like lightning had just struck the closest forest tree and sent it crashing into the shoulders of others around it. A dark red liquid slid from Sia's mouth and down her chin, as she collapsed onto the floor, and her body spilled over with blood. The Ol' Mas stood and rushed to the door, but Norman and June Dey hurried past them. June saw birds retreat from the branches of the neighboring trees.

Outside, a band of ten men blocked the entry to the forest. The sight of them caught June Dey by surprise. They were black. They looked similar to the warriors June Dey and Norman had fought beside in weeks past, except their eyes overflowed with unfamiliar hatred. Hunger. Three of them held guns, and smoke rose from the mouth of one of those guns. June Dey heaved at the sight of the smoke. He could still smell the coconut from Sia's lifeless body. One of the attackers held a knife to the throat of the woman who'd left that morning for water. She sobbed, her eyes closed, her hands against her heart. Before another moment passed, Norman disappeared, prompting the crowd of men to sounds of shock and despair. June Dey knew that Norman was making his way to them — to steal their weapons, to break their fingers. He readied himself for the bullets, for the fight. But he trembled. For the first time, he trembled. The men. These men. They were black. Their faces were as dark as his, their stories separated only by the water's mammoth body. How could he kill them? He thought of Sia's face, her eyes, and the moments they stole from him, the instant he touched her skin, then the pain that covered her face when that bullet sank into her back. June Dey ran toward the men. And the bullets came and fell from his skin. Norman had pulled a gun from one of their hands, and June Dey punched the man so hard that his body was thrust into a tree several feet away. The man shouted from the impact, then fell, lifeless, to the forest floor. June Dey saw his body there, limp, as if he had been freshly beaten for not meeting Emerson's tobacco quota that day, and something crumbled in him. Before, it seemed, he had been fighting a color. Always a color that was an enemy. But in that moment, he battled something else. He fought, startled that the flesh that covered the breaking bones at the end of his fists matched the twilight of his skin. Startled, but what could he do? It had not been a color that he fought, but a spirit. Greed. Perhaps the warriors he fought with in previous weeks had foresight enough to reject this spirit, which extinguishes as much as it enriches, never one without the other. It was greed — that soulless, bottomless thing that killed mothers. Killed would-be lovers. Would not let him *be.*

That night they sat in the village circle near a fire the women had made to burn the bodies of their attackers, of Sia's murderers. June Dey sat by the fire, silently mourning her. He had made a hill of their black bodies, dressed in trousers likely bought through trade with the slavers. Norman Aragon unrolled the map he'd finally retrieved from his bag, which the Ol' Mas had confiscated on the first day. The villagers had buried Sia earlier that evening, and the women still wailed her death in the chief's home, pounding their fists against their lappas strewn across the floor. They asked Norman and June Dey to stay until they were finished mourning, so they could pack and find somewhere else to hide. Norman agreed, though June Dey noticed his anx-

449

iousness as he finally opened the map.

"What's wrong?" June Dey asked.

"There was a note in French writing in the pocket of one of those hunters," Norman said.

June Dey nodded, still shaken. "And the trousers," he said.

"And the trousers," Norman repeated. "French may be paying local hunters to fight for them. Find prisoners."

"Sound about right," June Dey said as the fire glowed against his face, and his lungs filled with the smell of burning flesh. "Sad some of us can be bought."

"No, there is no *us* here. Not yet. No Negro. Only tribes. They don't know what we know. They haven't seen what we've seen. They've been fighting other tribes for centuries for free. Sure they do it for tools and money."

June Dey sighed, disillusion flowing in his breath. He could fight. He would win. Fight those he considered his enemies — those who captured and enslaved, those who tortured and killed. But what of when those enemies changed faces? How could they not know what was happening across the ocean? Or not imagine it? June Dey felt sick. Betrayed.

"I must return to the free colony and warn

them — warn them about the slavers," Norman said. "They're infiltrating local tribes now. I have to warn them."

"I'll come too," June Dey said.

"No, you must — if you will, continue without me. Your gift is enough to fight alone."

June Dey was alarmed. He had not imagined traveling the continent alone, and hated the thought of losing the man who had become the only friend, besides his mother and the other women in the kitchen where he worked, that he had ever had.

Reluctantly, June Dey agreed. "And after you warn them? Where you go then?"

"I suppose — I suppose I will be disappeared," answered Norman. "But I will come back. I will come look for you."

"How I'm gone find my way around?" June Dey asked him.

"Here, you can take this," Norman said, handing him the map. "And when that fails, follow your instincts."

June Dey nodded.

"But I will be back," Norman Aragon said.

June Dey could not hide his look of disappointment. However, he knew he needed to know Africa for himself, no matter how vast a battleground it was and whether or not he would travel alone. That week. Sia's face and smell. Those men. Those black men. This place was something he needed to know for himself.

June Dey agreed, and as the sun left the sky for Ol' Ma Famatta's resting face, the men found a place in the village, amid the howling for Sia's soul, to lay their heads.

That night, Norman fell into the wilderness, blended into night as June Dey slept. He had planned to bid him farewell on the following day, but he realized that he, too, would suffer from the departure.

■ ■ ■ ■

SAFUA

■ ■ ■ ■

Miss Ernestine did not visit Gbessa and Gerald's home in Sinou County. Once Gbessa invited her to have dinner with them, and Miss Ernestine accepted, only to send a messenger at the last minute with a letter that read:

Gerald,
I am not well. Another time. Give the servants my best.
— Aunty Ernestine

Miss Ernestine then whined to the society women that Gbessa made her feel uncomfortable during her visits, and that that was the reason she never sat with them for dinner.

"She does not invite me," Miss Ernestine said over a cup of tea.

The society women nodded in support of their impossible friend. Once, Marlene invited Gbessa to ride with her to Monrovia to a society meeting, where rather than assisting in the planning for a fund-raiser with the other women at the table, Miss Ernestine interrogated Gbessa about how she was keeping her home.

"And how do you cook? What do you make him?" Miss Ernestine had asked. "You make dinner?"

"I only prepare some," Gbessa had answered naively. "One man who works on the farm has daughter who comes and cooks sometimes," she said, and Miss Ernestine released a raucous laughter.

" 'Comes to cook,' not 'comes and cooks,' " she said, laughing. Some others joined in on the laughter and Gbessa pretended to smile. She faced the table and was afraid even to cough for the rest of the event.

On another occasion, at the end of one of the society meetings, a gray old woman named Frances Tucker (one of Miss Ernestine's strongest allies) opened up her Bible and blocked Gbessa's exit.

"Hello, Mrs. Tucker," Gbessa said.

The woman glanced down at her Bible and opened it to a marked page and began to read loudly, stopping the other women who were leaving the room with her obnoxious delivery.

"Here in Proverbs it says 'Favor is deceitful, and beauty is vain; but a woman who feareth the Lord, she shall be praised,' " Frances said, closing the book.

"Yes?" Gbessa asked. "Do you fear the Lord, Gbessa Tubman?" Frances interrogated her.

"Sure," Gbessa said earnestly.

"Do you?" Frances asked again.

Gbessa nodded.

"You do not think parading that long hair of yours around without tying it up is vain? You do not think it is vain to show off like that?"

Gbessa touched her hair. "Vain?" she asked.

"Yes, vain. Wearing your hair all wild and homely may tempt married men. Do you know it is a sin to tempt married men?"

A couple of the society women who had surrounded the confrontation offered their brief yeses and mm-hmm's as the women stood before them.

"I do not mean to do any such thing," Gbessa said, addressing all of them.

"Oh, Frances," Miss Ernestine interjected with a mischievous smile. "Leave my daughter alone."

"Yes, well. She should think about that, as

all our young, respectable women should," Mrs. Tucker said, making eye contact with the women surrounding them.

Gbessa avoided looking at them.

"We love you, Gbessa," Mrs. Tucker added. "We just want to make sure you're setting the right example."

"Yes, Mrs. Tucker," she said.

Once when Maisy visited Gbessa's house in Sinou County, some society women decided to accompany her and surprise Gbessa with a list of her duties for the fund-raiser. When Maisy sat down with them, one of the women promptly asked her for four glasses of water.

"I will get it," Gbessa offered, standing before Maisy had a chance to.

"Do not be absurd, Gbessa Tubman. That is why she is here. Why else? Right, Maisy?" the woman asked.

Maisy went into the kitchen. She poured the glasses of water and prayed silently for patience while waiting for Gbessa to join her. After a short while, when Gbessa did not, Maisy opened the kitchen door only slightly for a view of the sitting room. There, Gbessa sat contently with her guests, trying with utmost resolve to speak, smile, and host them as they pleased. That evening, after the other women left for Monrovia, Maisy stayed behind to help Gbessa clean. They were mostly silent in the kitchen, mutually alone with their thoughts.

"You didn't follow me for their water today," Maisy said finally.

"Water?" Gbessa asked. She had hoped Maisy wouldn't mention the awkwardness of their afternoon together.

"Today they asked me to collect water. Normally you follow. Even when they tell you not to." Maisy wiped a glass and set it on the counter.

"Maisy," Gbessa said, looking into her eyes. "This. All of this is hard for me."

"Me too," Maisy admitted, missing Saturdays on the Johnsons' field with Gbessa.

"If I make you happy I make them vexed," Gbessa said. "It is not easy for me when they are vexed." Her voice cracked. She looked down and Maisy was sorry that she had been so hurt by Gbessa's rejection, so jealous.

"I am sorry," Maisy said, touching Gbessa's shoulder. "I am being selfish. I just fear losing my sister."

Gbessa hugged Maisy tightly, leaning her head on her friend's shoulder. If only Maisy knew that her sister was already dead, had already died one hundred times before that

459

moment, each time she shunned the ever-present memory of Safua and Lai. She was a ghost of her former self, the loveliest kind, but still only the walking remains of a girl who once was.

When Miss Ernestine finally asked Gbessa to organize a ladies' breakfast, word came to her via post, only two days prior. One sentence read: *This Thursday's breakfast will be at your home, but I expect you will send word if you are not able.* After reading the note, Gbessa left the messenger on her porch and hurried inside to begin planning. She arranged a full and thorough cleaning of the house and porch, and carefully planned a meal of rice and potato greens with yams and baked bread. She asked one of her farmers to have his daughter come to the house at once to help her prepare.

Gbessa finally sat to make a list of the twelve or so women she would invite. After completing the list, she realized that she had forgotten Maisy's name, and she started to write it down, but stopped. She had never guessed during her time at the Johnsons' that she would ever desire the things that Mrs. Johnson and Marlene desired — a neat home, reliable workers, dresses that made her stare long and hard into the mirror when she wore them, and, most important, acceptance. But that wanting was like a forest weed — it would inevitably grow, as its circumstances encouraged it to, and one day it would be as hard to pull it from its roots as it is a tree.

Gbessa did not write Maisy's name down. And she hosted her ladies' breakfast, all the while being careful of how she sounded, and mindful of how she ate — in small bites and one spoonful at a time, just as Maisy had taught her.

Gerald was a dutiful husband. He treated Gbessa as he thought a husband should treat his wife. He was her provider and protector, he paid Maisy for Gbessa's English and reading lessons, he listened to her when all of the daily duties of his career were filled and he lusted after her greatly. Gerald formed the Liberian army quickly, with recruits from all counties and a few neighboring assimilated tribes. The mayors commissioned builders for a small military base and prison one mile north of Gerald and Gbessa's house. From her opened window, she heard the men training as Gerald led them through the woods and rain to defend their new country. Gerald complained to her that after Liberia had declared its independence, the American

461

Colonization Society had sent little help to the settlers. Over time, its letters revealed that America was waging a battle of its own, a possible civil war that would "change the country forever."

"What does that mean?" Gbessa asked Gerald one night as he repeated the words.

" 'Change the country forever.' Isn't everything always changing forever?" she asked, proud of her improving ability to express her complex thoughts in English.

Gerald smiled.

"You are clever," he said, though when she tried to engage others with the same ideas during dinner parties at the Johnsons' mansion or other social events in Monrovia, he gently tapped her shoulder or leg. "It's not time," he would whisper. "Stay committed to your lessons with Maisy for now. It is not worth giving them reasons to gossip."

When visiting Monrovia, Gbessa no longer slept in Maisy's room, and she greatly missed chatting with her friend. She slept in a guest room with her husband and sat silently beside him during dinner one night, trying earnestly to fulfill the routines of cutting her food neatly. Marlene sat beside her with an enlarged belly. She and Henry were expecting their firstborn, but rather than staying in Sinou to rest she had decided to join her husband and Gerald, to keep Gbessa company during the dinner. "We need the allies," Gerald had joked to them en route to Monrovia.

"Mrs. Tubman, when can we expect children from you and the general?" a woman named Mrs. Thomason, with pointy shoulders, asked from the end of the dinner table that night. There were three other couples at the Johnson mansion that night: Mr. and Mrs. Johnson, the Stackers, and the Hills. Miss Ernestine was also present; she dropped her utensils and cleared her throat when this was suggested. The conversations around the table ceased and all eyes turned to Gbessa.

"Yes, Mrs. Tubman," Mrs. Johnson chimed in playfully. She had always been fond of Gbessa since she'd worked at her house. "It's been about a year now. We would love to see your family grow." Gbessa looked down at Marlene's growing stomach. She was doubly embarrassed that she did not know how to answer their question, and thankful that Gerald had not yet made her pregnant. Although she fought to convince herself of the happiness and the privilege her new life and God afforded her, the thought of having a cursed child made her ill.

"Soon. I hope," she said in a low, bashful tone. Gerald put his arm around her shoulder. She welcomed his support by touching his leg with a trembling hand. She wanted to change the subject, as she had seen others do before, by asking Mrs. Thomason how her family was doing or how she had fared during the last rainy season. But her fear of saying the wrong thing caused a dry stillness around the table, broken only when Gerald brought up an issue with one of the barracks that were being built.

In Sinou the following morning, Gbessa opened the window that overlooked her field. The workers at Gerald and Gbessa's house were Kru men with singing voices who pulled Gbessa's spirit to the window during the day, in a rocking chair that Gerald had made her for their anniversary. She moved with their hummed harmonies; dreamed with their songs until her throat closed with heat and water sat at her eyes. She was a stranger to the woman who occupied her mind.

As she rocked, I brushed her face, raised the collar of her dress.

"There, there now, darling," I sang. "There now, my friend."

There were some things that did not change.

Although maids were present to help her cook and clean, and Kru men in the field to tend their farm, Gbessa did most of the household chores herself. When she positioned herself in front of her stove on nights she prepared dinner, the maids looked at her with surprise; Gbessa waved her hands at them to leave the room.

"But Ma Gbessa, you not want us clean?" they asked her as she swept, afraid that Mr. Tubman would fire them when he learned his wife was doing their work.

"No. I can sweep myself."

"But Ma Gbessa, you not want us cook?" they asked her as she stirred the rice in the large black pot.

"No. I can cook myself."

Her chores were the only thing that quieted her mind. When Gbessa was finished working in her house, she went to the field to help the men tend the farm. While she was shoveling dirt one day to plant eggplant seeds, Gerald Tubman saw her from the road. Gerald unmounted his horse and walked to the field where Gbessa stood. He turned her around and took the shovel from her hands.

"What are you doing?" he asked, his eyes chastising her.

"Making my garden," Gbessa answered.

"That is why you have these men. You needn't tend your own farm," he said and threw the shovel down. A Kru worker ran to him and picked up the shovel. Gbessa bent down with the man to take the handle.

"Go inside," Gerald told her sternly. Gbessa did not move. "Go!"

Gbessa went slowly into the house, looking back at the Kru workers as Gerald fussed with them for letting his wife ruin her hands. When he entered the house, she stood in the kitchen and he felt guilty for yelling at her. Gerald approached her and kissed her cheek.

"You are not angry with me," he said, pleading. Gbessa shook her head and he offered her kisses, first on her cheeks, then on her neck for forgiveness. The kisses persisted and the smell of a long and restless day emanated from his skin. Eventually she moaned for him and acquiesced to his stronghold on her buttocks. Gerald lay her down on the kitchen table and entered her as though they were not fussing, driven by his passion and growing desire for the woman. She folded her arms around his back, closing her eyes, and as always when pleasure moved her toes, her ends and edges, she thought of Safua.

From then on, as she farmed one of the

field workers kept a lookout for Gerald Tubman or anyone else from Monrovian society.

"Ma Gbessa," the workers would say, "you not want us help? Chief will be vexed."

"No," Gbessa answered. "I can tend my own garden."

One morning after Gerald left home, while getting dressed Gbessa heard commotion outside among her field workers. As she approached the field, the workers were talking to a tall, pale man whose wild head of hair could be seen in the distance. When she arrived where they stood, Gbessa was stupefied at the sight of the familiar face.

"Ma Gbessa," one of the men said. "The man traveling and want water."

"My God," Norman Aragon muttered and squinted. "It is you." He confronted her, a reserved woman with a stark difference in her posture and hair from what he remembered four years prior, confident eyes, and the clothes of an aristocrat's wife. "Do you — do you remember me?" he asked with an encouraging smile.

Gbessa glanced at her field workers and back at Norman.

"No, I am sorry, I do not," she lied.

"You speak," he whispered, stunned. The disappointment that then crept onto Norman's face stung her. His clothes were torn, unpresentable, and his face was unshaven. "But I have fresh water. You are welcome," she said. Norman nodded apologetically and followed her across the field.

"Ma Gbessa, we help you?" a worker shouted after her.

"No. Keep working."

In the kitchen, Gbessa led her visitor directly to the table.

"You may sit," she said, carefully pronouncing each word. He sat and eyed the impeccable design and cleanliness of the room. She had hung Gerald Tubman's pictures on her wall, as well as a newly taken photograph of herself sitting with other society women. She had the finest table linen and chairs and it was in a glass that she served his drink. Gbessa stood across the room as he drank. He lowered the glass and stared as she stood in visible discomfort.

"May I help you?" she asked finally.

"Yes," he said. "I was looking for one Mr. Gerald Tubman, the army general — and I was directed here."

Gbessa nodded. "He is my husband," she said. Her timidity and soft voice could not hide a thick accent, which Norman assessed carefully.

"Yes. I gathered that," he said.

"He will not return until evening but you

are welcome to stay," she said genuinely.

"I thank you," he said.

Gbessa poured herself a glass of water and quickly drank.

"And you do not — you do not remember me?" he asked again.

She remembered him clearly and recollected his gift and the people she had seen him save.

"You must stop saying that. It is impolite. I am a married woman," she said. Gbessa folded her arms across her body. The silence further provoked his suspicion.

"Pardon me," Norman said. He stood up from the table, and after a moment of contemplation, he vanished. Startled, Gbessa glanced around the room. She went into the den, then rushed into her bedroom and the sitting room to look for him. She ran back to the kitchen and Norman reappeared before her. Gbessa panted where she stood.

"And were you not frightened?" he asked calmly. "Do all Monrovian women respond to the supernatural with such grace?"

She was humbled. "You must never do that or I will ask you to leave," she demanded. "I am Christian. I do not like such things. It's witchcraft."

"*Witch*craft?" Norman asked, astonished,

offended. "My God, what have they done to you?"

"Nobody has done anything to me. I have been saved," she said. Fatigued by her denial of herself, of him, he sat down. He would have wept for her if there had been tears left, for nothing was so tragic as this.

"It was you. You are the girl," he said after a painful swallow. "And you would hide it."

"Hide my curse. Did I have choice?"

"Hide your gift," Norman said sternly. Gbessa thought of that afternoon with the French, the pain in her head, the sharp blade.

"Africa is dying," Norman added. "People — your neighboring tribesmen. Whole provinces are either being physically captured or mentally poisoned to capture others. You witnessed some of it — it continues and you have cause to hide."

Gbessa looked away from him.

"Do you not understand?" Norman persisted. "Your people need —"

"My people cursed me," she interrupted coldly, though the claim made her think of Safua. "Hid me in the forest and for what? Superstition. To think the children before me who died in that forest and none of those children were what they said."

"Perhaps not. But you were special. You

470

lived. You *have* a gift."

"What gift?"

"Life!"

"My life was taken for worldly superstition," she said and paced the room.

"Your life was saved by a gift from God."

"From God?!"

"Yes. Does not your doctrine preach that he created all things? A talent so miraculous, so powerful, and you dare hide it!"

"That is enough," she said with diminished patience.

"And to be drawn in such a way to others — like myself," Norman continued and stood up. "Do you not understand it is your responsibility to help? That you are a part of something bigger?"

"That is enough!" she shouted. Her back door opened and a field worker entered.

"Ma Gbessa, you all right?" he asked as strings of sweat descended his face. He wiped his head and looked around the room. "Where the man?"

Gbessa turned to where Norman was standing and saw only floating dust in the streaming light of the sun. "I'm all right," she said. "I gave him water and he went."

The worker nodded and peered into the room again before exiting the house. Just as soon as the door closed, Norman Aragon reappeared, leaning against an adjacent wall.

"You must leave," she said calmly. "I respect the manner in which you used your . . . your circumstance. But I leave the gifts to my God," she said.

"I see," Norman said dismally.

"You may tell me what you want to share and I will tell my husband for you. He is tired when he comes home and you would cause more stress."

"My cause was not to burden you, only to warn him."

"Warn him?" Gbessa asked.

"Yes. It is possible that the slavers we have encountered in our years on the continent may have interest in Monrovia." Worry coated his eyes and Gbessa felt sorry for him. That this man would disrupt his travels and risk his own safety, and even further sustain the nuisance of her denial, made her also ache inside.

"My husband's army does well to protect the colony," she said with a shaking voice. "I appreciate your journey to tell us, but we are protected," she said.

Despite her ignorance, Norman remained committed to his message.

"They are desperate. They are plenty and they grow with time —"

"Thank you," Gbessa said, interrupting

him. She looked into Norman's face and witnessed the collapse of his spirit through his eyes. "You must leave before the workers think you are still here," she said, heedless of his message. "May God bless you."

Norman followed Gbessa to the opposite end of her house where an open front door allowed the wind to rush in. The gust made his eyes water further as he slowly departed. When he was in her yard, Norman turned around to face Gbessa as she stood in her doorway.

"You must remember this. Remember what happened. Remember you have a gift." He stuttered the words just as Nanni had said them to him, just as he had recited them in time, and the memory of her made the waiting tears rush down his face. "Make your home in the forests. It will take care of you," Norman continued with trembling lips. "Find your way back —"

His body escaped and his words haunted Gbessa as I entered and hovered in the corners of her home. The door closed and with a wavering hand and heart Gbessa prayed. She hid her fear that Lai could be ruined. Or, worse, that an impatient past was forever waiting in the darkened hollows to be resurrected and a broken heart unveiled.

■ ■ ■ ■

She dreamed of Norman's visit for weeks after. He had changed so much since the few days she had traveled with him. So had she — the floor-length dresses in her reflection made her unrecognizable from the woman she had been only a short time before. Was time that powerful? That cruel?

Gbessa watched the field workers from her window, afraid that perhaps if she went outside she would summon Norman and his reckless warnings again. The workers were practical, and though Gbessa regularly heard their jokes and laughter from inside the house, they worked hard during the day with little trouble. One afternoon following Norman's visit, as she looked onto the field from her window, two of the men pushed each other while a few others dropped their shovels and hoes to break up the fight. Upon seeing this, Gbessa ran to the field.

"Stop!" she called out. "Stop it!"

The men stood up from where they were wrestling, and the others scrambled to get back to work.

"What happened here?" she demanded.

"Sorry, Ma," one of the men said, retrieving his shovel.

" 'Sorry, Ma' not answer," Gbessa said. "What happened?" she asked again. This time louder.

"He say Bassa people can tell lie," one of the perpetrators said, pointing to the other.

"That true?" Gbessa asked the other man. He nodded.

"You know all the Bassa men and women them?" Gbessa asked.

The man shook his head. He folded his hands over his chest, appearing more and more nervous as her voice rose.

"Then don't talk that foolishness here," she said. "No Bassa, no Kpelle, no Vai people on my farm." Vai filled her mouth. "We Liberian here. The only way this place here will last is if you people stop talking that foolishness. People dying for their own country and we got our own?"

She caught the stupor within each of their eyes.

"Enneh-so?!" she asked again, though it was clear they barely understood what had stirred her anger. It was Gerald she wished she were saying this to, not them.

"Sorry, Ma," one of the men said quickly, and the others followed with prolonged apologies and begging hands. Gbessa wanted them to answer her question — but they did not have it, could not know the terror beyond their Liberia.

At dawn one autumn day, as Gerald lay beside his wife, a horse rode onto the Tubman farm.

"Mr. Tubman!" Gbessa heard in the distance. "Mr. Tubman!" she heard again. Gerald quickly lifted his head from sleep and sat up in bed. Gbessa lit the lantern on the floor and put on her robe as Gerald got dressed. The two ran to their front door, and a messenger dashed up their porch steps, nearly breathless, and said: "We're being attacked! We're being attacked!"

Gerald ran back to his room for his rifle and shirt. Down the road, Henry Hunter's horse clopped along the dusty pathway of dawn.

"Come!" Henry called, passing the house and riding quickly toward the army base. Gerald ran out of the house.

"Lock the doors!" he yelled back to Gbessa. The messenger had a horse waiting for Gerald on the road and he darted after Henry toward the base. From a distance she could hear what sounded like the explosion of bullets and screaming men.

A panicked Gbessa locked the doors of her house and her windows, and she sat on her bed with her lantern, waiting. Shortly after, she heard a company of horses ride past the house. Gbessa ran to the front window, where she saw familiar faces, mostly society men from Monrovia, riding quickly down the road. Several moments later, another group of horses stampeded toward the base. Gbessa's mind retreated to Norman — his haunting presence and warning, and the anxious month that had followed. She walked throughout her house with her lantern, holding it up as she approached corners and pursued his face. The empty house stood still as horses moved in the distance.

"Show your face!" Gbessa said, circling her rooms. But no faces were there. None but hers.

A loud knock jolted her. Gbessa remained motionless at first, unsure if she was ready to reacquaint herself with Norman. The knock came again, this time accompanied by a whiny and recognizable voice from the other side. It was Maisy, she realized, and sighed in relief. Gbessa ran to the door and let Maisy inside. The two of them hugged as men on horses continued to pass in front of their house.

"What happened?" Gbessa asked.

"The Vai people attacked. Some from the North. A group of them came to Monrovia. Nobody got hurt, but some Vai men were killed."

"What?" Gbessa lost her balance and Maisy ran to her as she fell to the ground. Maisy leaned Gbessa's back against the wall and went to the kitchen to bring her water. Gbessa drank it immediately.

"Who did they come to?" Gbessa asked frantically.

"Some of the Yanceys' crops were burned. Before they got to the house, their servants shot some of them down and fought the others. They are walking them to the prison now."

"Any white men with them?" she asked.

"No, no. Not that I have heard."

Gbessa struggled to breathe normally.

"Gbessa, we have to go to Monrovia," Maisy said, interrupting her thoughts.

"What?"

"They want all the women to go to Monrovia. Christopher is collecting Marlene now."

Gbessa did not want to go. She did not want to leave her house, or the hard floor on which she sat.

"You are worried? You are concerned for your people?" Maisy asked naively. "I am sorry. I am sorry for you and for them."

Gbessa finished her glass of water, staring out into the void of morning, swallowing heavily as multiple uneven thoughts made her shiver with sweat.

When they arrived in Monrovia, the society women and others sat together in the parlor at Miss Ernestine's house.

"We cannot go to Mrs. Johnson's?" Gbessa asked before they entered the front door.

"No. Everybody is here," Maisy said.

When Gbessa entered the room, all eyes turned to meet her and the talking, crying, and whispering suddenly quieted. Gbessa went toward Mrs. Johnson and Marlene, who only slightly nodded their heads before looking away and commencing conversations with others beside them. Gbessa stood near the window, where the wind scratched and begged her attention, and Maisy stood beside her.

"They vexed with me," Gbessa said in Maisy's ear. Maisy shook her head.

"Gbessa Tubman!" Frances Tucker yelled

from across the room. Gbessa glanced at Mrs. Tucker and folded her hands nervously across her chest.

"Yes?" she asked and feigned confidence, even though she was well aware that all of the skepticism in the room was directed at her.

"What tribe did they say you were from? Before they bought you?" Mrs. Tucker asked loudly. Gbessa shifted against the wall. She opened her mouth to speak, but the words at first did not come. Her stutters pushed them out.

"Excuse me?" Gbessa asked, shaking.

"You heard her, Mrs. Tubman. Was it not your tribesmen who were running around ruining farms this morning?" Miss Ernestine said, interrupting Mrs. Tucker's response.

Gbessa pushed her back against the wall. Would she have been wrong to say she was not Vai? After all, had not the Vai people exiled her and called her cursed? Had not the Vai people disowned her? The thoughts rushed to her head as her heartbeat pressed against her blouse. The wind kept scratching on the window, and Maisy opened it slightly to let cool air in. The wind rushed to Gbessa and fluttered behind her ears and neck, danced in between her fingers as she fought for the courage to surrender.

"I am Vai," Gbessa said. "Yes."

Some of the women gasped. Others shook their heads at her behind their fans.

"Do you know them then? Do you know those people who ruined the Yanceys' farm? Are they your people?" Miss Ernestine grilled her.

"Miss Ernestine, I beg your pardon, but Gbessa has not been back to that village for nearly five years," Maisy interrupted, tired of watching her friend, her sister, take on the burden of their words.

"Maisy, please do not," Mrs. Johnson said, to stop her from participating in something that was not her place.

"So what?!" Miss Ernestine said, raising her voice.

"Now, Ernestine, we are all upset. But you do not have to be harsh," Mrs. Johnson said calmly.

Miss Ernestine hissed through her teeth.

"Maisy, go to Ernestine's kitchen and bring us all some water," Mrs. Johnson instructed her.

Maisy went to the kitchen and Gbessa followed her.

"Where do you think you are going?" Mrs. Tucker asked.

Gbessa stopped and turned around. She

dared not suggest that she would help Maisy get drinks.

"I need to get fresh air," Gbessa said.

In front of the window in the kitchen, there was a curtain sewed with blue fabric that stopped just below the shutters. Gbessa pushed the curtain out of her way and pushed the shutters open.

"You all right?" Maisy asked her as the running water drowned out her voice. "Do not make them vexed today, Gbessa. They are right. You are no longer a kitchen maid. You are the wife of a very important man. You are one of them."

"Do not say that," Gbessa snapped.

Maisy shook her head and continued to prepare the clear glasses of water for the society women to drink.

Gbessa stuck her upper body out the window and breathed in heavily, closing her eyes. When she opened them back up, she saw four men on horses from Gerald's army approaching on the road.

"Some are still headed to Sinou?" Maisy asked when she heard the horses' hooves.

"Yes," Gbessa said, still looking out the window.

The last rider held a rope that hung from his lap and stretched behind his horse. Gbessa leaned her body farther out the window to lengthen her view. The rope was tied to a procession of a dozen men. With one look, Gbessa knew they were Vai. Their shoulders and arms, the way their heads were slightly lifted to the sky as they walked; their clothes and skin.

Her heart dropped.

"What?" Maisy asked, as if she had heard it.

"Vai men," Gbessa said quickly.

Maisy ran to the window to look with Gbessa. Blood ran down the backs of the men who had been beaten during the invasion, and lingered on the dusty road that led to their imprisonment. It was a warriors' procession and Gbessa looked on, noticing the Poro initiation marks on some of their necks and shoulders.

"Oh, this is just awful." Maisy sighed, returning to her water glasses.

As it was too painful to keep her eyes on them, she finally gave up on her search for his face. It was then that the last warrior of the line caught her eye. Gbessa leaned out the window.

"What?" Maisy asked behind her. Gbessa did not respond.

The last of the men had heavy eyes that forged a frightful path before him; even from a distance the road in his view burned with fire, and ashes scattered on the road behind him. He was a Poro man with clenched fists and a head slightly raised to the sky as he walked, though he was wrapped in ropes and chains that tried to confine him.

And then quite suddenly Gbessa was lost, a child again in care of a labyrinth of trees and magic that canvassed his farewells. While she had imagined seeing him again would make her hide her face, she now wanted to run and fall into him, into his chest and mouth, into his fists and fury. When she hoped the wind would come to her rescue, even it ran toward the procession to check the face of the last man in line.

"Safua!" Gbessa yelled out. "Safua!" She could not help it. She waved her hands out the window. "Safua!"

The procession of men stopped and looked toward the window. Maisy dashed to it and pulled Gbessa away. Maisy pushed Gbessa against the wall and placed a hand over her heaving mouth.

"What is the matter with you?" Maisy asked, shaking.

Maisy quickly closed the shutters and settled the blue fabric back in its place. She picked up her tray of water from the table and reentered the sitting room, where the society women wondered what had taken her so long.

Gbessa's hand rested on the buttons of her blouse as she struggled to catch her breath from yelling. She wondered if he had heard her at all.

The Vai warriors in the Sinou County prison were talking to no one. Vai people had never attacked the colony before and many settlers grew nervous that their strike would set a precedent. There were no interpreters who could get a word from them, and the generals and mayors could not stomach any more beatings. It made more sense to Gerald Tubman to have them hanged as an example to other indigenous tribes than to keep them in the prison and risk the possible corruption of other convicts.

The warriors tried to hang themselves with the ropes around their ankles and wrists. It was the Poro man's way to die at his own hand before the adversary killed him. Since the prison was consistently guarded, the warriors' deaths were prevented, and they were chained to the walls of their cells. The warriors then refused to eat, and after one week they were so emaciated that Gerald Tubman ordered that they be force-fed one meal a day.

At home, Gbessa grew restless. She also found stomaching meals to be very difficult. Maisy kept her secret and did not disclose that Gbessa had recognized one of the prisoners. Liberia was tense with nervous energy, and nobody knew what actions would follow the surprise attack.

"Rescue me from these thoughts, O Lord," Gbessa prayed.

Gbessa was unable to concentrate on anything. She demanded that her workers perform the most menial tasks — closing her shutters, fanning her face as she forcefully rocked in her chair facing the window. Her servants sensed that something was wrong with her, but after hearing that it was her tribesmen who had attacked, they were more helpful around the house and farm.

"Rescue me from myself, O Lord," Gbessa pleaded in empty rooms.

After Gerald revealed to her that he was planning to hang the men, she waited until he left for the prison the next day to weep over a bucket of cold water. She then ordered one of the Kru men in her garden to go find tobacco for her.

"Tobacco?" the man asked, perplexed.

488

"Yes, you heard me!" Gbessa yelled at him. The man returned when it was almost evening, and Gbessa spent the following week in her rocking chair, chewing and spitting the tobacco into a small wooden bowl as she gazed out her window. She shook when she bathed, prayed: "Rescue me from these thoughts, O Lord. See that I remain a good wife. A good woman."

She neglected to fold her hair for days and it hung wildly from her head until one of her helpers braided it down her back while she rocked in her chair. It was no use. She had to see the prisoners. She had to see *him*.

One night Gerald came home to find that Gbessa had cooked him roasted chicken and collard greens over rice, corn, and fried plantain, all stretched over their table.

When Gerald sat to eat, Gbessa separated his portions, cutting the chicken breasts into slices. She was especially careful in the way she served him. He sensed her nervousness. He watched as she took her own seat, but rather than taking a bite of the food on her own plate, she stared into his eyes.

"They are Poro men," Gbessa said suddenly, finally.

"Who?" Gerald asked.

"The Vai prisoners," she answered and picked up her fork in an attempt at a casual exchange.

"What is Poro?" Gerald asked with a tinge of suspicion and jealousy.

"Poro men are a Vai society. The strongest boys are chosen to be warriors when they are very young, and the leader of them is the king of the village."

His silence implored her to continue. She held her silverware but, like him, had not eaten a bite.

"They protect the Vai people. Without them the villagers will die," Gbessa said and her voice trembled.

"So what?" Gerald asked, finally raising his silverware to commence his meal.

"I do not think you should hang them," she said finally. "Let me try to talk to them."

"What?"

"To talk to them," she pleaded and remembered her own exile.

"Surprising you want to defend them now — you have made no effort in all the time I have known you to even return to your village."

"Yes," she admitted humbly. "I am just curious why. The cause of the attack. Why they would now risk the safety of their village. Their village cannot live without them."

"And with them, Monrovia dies. Sinou

490

dies. Everything we have built — Liberia. They live and we risk attacks that can compromise everything. Is that what you want?" Gerald asked abruptly. Gbessa noticed both the anger and the hurt in his eyes from across the table. She should have gone to him and hugged him, held him, but the thought of Safua had all of her right mind — all of her energy.

Gbessa shook her head.

"No, Gerald," she answered and finished her meal in silence.

A few days after, Gerald headed to Monrovia early in the morning to meet with Mr. Johnson and other mayors about the prisoners' silence, and how to prepare for future attacks. Gbessa watched the dust rise behind him as his horse galloped from the house.

When Gerald left, Gbessa roasted chicken and prepared jute leaves over rice, corn, and eggplant wolloh. She placed the plate of food in a basket, and told her workers she was going on an errand.

She was unexpectedly enlivened by the fact that her past was now only a one-mile hike north. As the bottom of her dress swept the dust on the trail, Gbessa spoke Vai out loud, rehearsing what she would say to him, preparing herself for how he would look now after enduring the harsh conditions of the Sinou County prison.

When Gbessa arrived at the wooden structure of bars and chains, a rank smell met her nose and she coughed into her sweaty hands. The prison faced a massive field where Gerald had trained the new Liberian army. On the field, a group of men stood with rifles hanging from their shoulders. Other men and boys were scattered about, some sitting and talking, some standing and exploring the functions of their new weaponry.

At the gate, larger soldiers stood together laughing at something one of them had said. When they saw Gbessa approaching, the men stood straighter, and scattered from their small huddle to appear busier than they were.

"Mrs. Tubman," one of the soldiers greeted her. Gbessa smiled.

"Hello, Emric," Gbessa said. "I came to bring the prisoners food." She held up the basket. The men reconvened in a semicircle facing her.

"That is fine of you, Mrs. Tubman, but they do not eat."

"That is because they have never tasted my cooking," Gbessa said.

Emric laughed.

"If you insist. I will take it back for you," Emric said, reaching for the basket. Gbessa did not let go of the handle. Emric pulled it and Gbessa held the basket close to her.

"I would like to deliver it myself, thank you."

"That is kind, Mrs. Tubman," Emric began, "but I am sure the General would not approve."

"He would. Ask him," Gbessa said.

The men looked at each other.

"He is not here. He went to Monrovia today," Emric said.

"Then I imagine what a gentleman would do is give a lady the benefit of knowing what she prefers," Gbessa said.

Emric folded his arms across his chest.

"Why don't you come back tomorrow, then, with the General?" he asked.

"The food will be cold by then," Gbessa said.

The soldiers laughed. Emric considered his circumstances, unsure of the decision he should render to the General's stubborn wife. He lifted the lid of the basket to see what was inside.

"Sure then. Go with her, Duly," Emric said to one of the men.

"Thank you, Emric," Gbessa said and nodded. Her heart rose with excitement.

Duly led Gbessa to the wooden structure of bars and chains. Some of the cells were facing the field outside, but as Gbessa passed them she realized that the prisoners were other criminals. They were not Vai men.

Duly turned the corner into the jail and unlocked a door with chains bound securely to the handle. When he opened it, the smell inside rushed and filled Gbessa's mouth. She coughed.

There were no windows in the cells. When Duly opened the door, he retrieved an old lantern from the floor, which he lit and held out in front of him as they walked. The prison was quiet except for a constant dripping of water that leaked from the ceiling and into a blackened puddle below.

"Watch your step, Mrs. Tubman," Emric said.

Duly led Gbessa to the back of the prison, where a large cell held three dozen men. Gbessa went to the cell and touched the bars. She searched their faces quickly. She recognized Cholly, the fisherman's brother, Safua's uncle, sitting with his eyes facing the ground. She wanted to call out to him but did not. Ol' Pa Bondo Freeman's grandson was also there, though he was hardly recognizable since the conditions had reduced him to skin and bones. Gbessa expected the men to avoid her face, to look away since "de witch" stood before them. But no; they did not know her, did not recognize her.

Instead, the ones with their heads lifted toward the sky gave her the same glances and jeers that they gave Duly, some hissing at her as she stood. Gbessa searched their faces with the hope that he would meet her eyes. He did not. He was not there.

"You can drop the basket here. The feeders will make sure they eat it when they come in."

Gbessa continued to search the prison desperately for the Poro king. Where had he gone? Had they killed him already? Whom had she seen walking that day?

"You can drop the basket here," Duly said again.

Gbessa finally nodded, discouraged, and dropped the basket.

"How much food is in there? They will make sure the other one gets a portion also," Duly said, looking toward the prison's exit.

"The other one?" Gbessa asked, enlivened.

"Yes. He seems to be the leader of them. He is the hardest to deal with so they isolated him."

Duly held his pointer finger up to Gbessa, where the imprints of teeth lined his skin.

"While we tried to feed him," Duly explained.

"Where is he?" Gbessa asked, her heart jumping, voice shaking.

Duly shook his head and walked along the large cell to a corner cell, which was separated from the other chained prisoners by a cement wall.

"Here," Duly said.

Gbessa picked up the basket and she walked weakly to the cell. She clenched the handle in her grasp as she neared it. She had thought of him every day for most days of her life and now she would finally see him again. At first, Gbessa wanted to slap him for not coming sooner. She would then watch his eyes and hope he regretted sending her away, hope he still wanted her and wanted to protect her. Her knees shook as she walked. She had imagined this day at every moment she'd thought of his name or face. What would he think of her now? What if he did not recognize her? Gbessa straightened her hair as she approached. Safua had come. Safua was finally here. Duly raised the old lantern. Inside, chained to a wall near the bars of the entrapment, with dried blood hanging from his ears and his lips,

Safua looked back at her, his nose and lips, his skin and boyish shoulders, his ears and curiosity.

But his eyes were different.

The eyes were not his.

Safua was not here.

He looked like him, but the boy who sat chained before her was his son, the prince, the boy they had proclaimed dead, the boy whose death they had said was her fault. The boy whose death had caused her exile.

"My goodness," Gbessa whispered, holding her hand over her mouth. She dropped the basket and darted through the narrow prison hall and out the door. Gbessa ran to the side of the building outside and vomited onto the ground.

The men outside offered her water but she refused.

On the following day, Gerald Tubman awoke at dawn and headed back to Monrovia. He had returned home after dark, so he did not go to the prison and was not aware of where his wife had been that day.

It was Safua's son and not him. So where was Safua? Why had they come? She needed to know the whereabouts of the king. The urgency made her weak, delirious.

Gerald's absence encouraged her to return

to the prison, where Emric and Duly stood at the gate, amazed that she had ventured that way again.

"They did not take to the food," Emric told her. Gbessa carried another basket in her hand with more of the same dishes. In order to get the men to eat, Gbessa knew she would have to convince Safua's son to eat first.

"That is fine. I made it right today," Gbessa said.

"You certain, Mrs. Tubman?" Emric asked.

"Yes."

"I do not want you to get sick again," he warned. "At least let us bring them outside so you do not have to enter."

"No," Gbessa said.

Finally, Duly led Gbessa to the back of the prison, where the large cell held three dozen men. He turned and headed to the corner cell, where inside the boy sat as he had the day before, looking through the bars at Gbessa as she approached. She knelt down so their eyes leveled. The boy had to be sixteen, Gbessa thought to herself, the same age as Safua when he carried her to the forest for her dong-sakpa, so many years before.

"What your name?" Gbessa asked him in

the Vai language. The boy creased his face as he looked at her, struggling to find familiarity in her features.

"What your name?" Gbessa asked again. The boy did not respond. Gbessa waited for him, but she heard only dripping in the distance, water that fell into the cold and sullen puddles below.

"I know your Pa," Gbessa continued finally, after more of a silence than she could bear. "I Vai girl. I know your Pa."

She hesitated before his name left her lips, aware that its utterance would be either her redemption or her regression to a world of curses and abandonment.

"Safua," Gbessa said finally. Her heart dropped.

The boy turned quickly toward her and shouted. He wrestled within his chains and the friction scraped his skin.

"The Poro king — Safua. I know him. You his son, enneh-so?" Gbessa continued desperately, afraid that the prince's reaction would cause Emric and the guards to force her to leave. When he looked like he might be about to speak, when even his anger separated from his mind to spill out of his mouth, he stopped pulling at the chain and turned away from her again. Gbessa sighed in dismay. She reached for the plate inside of her basket and pushed it underneath his cell bars. Gbessa stood up to walk away, and the bottom of the plate scraped the dirt as the boy roughly pushed it back underneath the bars.

"Leave it there," Duly said. "They will feed him later."

Gbessa nodded and headed down the narrow hallway out of the prison.

"If you know my Pa, then you know he dead!" the prince yelled out at her suddenly. "If you Vai you know they come take him and put him on ship. Kano went to hunt and'n come back and my Pa went to look for him and they put him on ship. You'n Vai girl!" the boy shouted through the bars. Gbessa's legs stopped moving.

"What?" she whispered to herself.

"He spoke!" Duly exclaimed.

Duly hurried to the cell. The prisoners pleaded with the prince for orders of how they could protect him further, and asked who was this strange woman who knew their language? Gbessa returned to Duly's lantern light, as he knelt in front of the boy's cell, smiling.

"What did he say?" Duly asked. "Speak to him again."

Gbessa's legs moved, however numbly, to the boy's cell.

"What you say?" Gbessa asked him as she fought tears that formed in her stomach. Gbessa dropped her basket and gripped the prison bars. The boy looked down at the plate, which Duly pushed back underneath the bars. He tore the chicken breast and ate it as Gbessa watched eagerly and waited for the repetition of words that did not come again.

He had said: "If you know my Pa, then you know he dead."

When his mouth moved, what came out was: "If you know my Pa, then you know he dead."

"If you know my Pa, then you know he dead," it echoed.

Safua was gone now and so was a part of her. First Gbessa cried into her palms as she knelt alone in her bedroom. Then, after wiping her face with fingers stained with the lingering smell of tobacco, she grew angry and jealous of him. Mean and selfish ol' Safua, who had turned her away just as quickly as he had promised to follow her always. She wished it had been her instead. For who was she but the witch of the village? He was king. Perhaps just as he had protected her, he could also look after other cursed children who would come after her.

Something had left her and escaped out

an opened window; she recognized the empty space it had left. Safua was finally gone. Her king had been stolen.

From her room, Gbessa heard the front door of her house close resonantly. The footsteps that followed were just as invasive, and they came upon her as she stood looking out her window onto the road that led to the prison.

Gerald entered the room and slammed the door behind him. Gbessa turned to face him and he noticed that she had been crying. His eyes were red, his teeth clenched tightly together, and he glared at her so furiously that she thought she might turn to stone. Gbessa remained silent and waited for him to come to her. Gerald reached her and his left hand swung from his side and fought against the frenzy and objection of the wind until the palm of his hand met her jaw, sending her flying against the wall before she fell to the floor.

Gbessa did not touch her skin, where the stinging made the wetness in her eyes come forth. She was unsure what had happened, since her mind had been elsewhere until the moment she realized she was on the ground, looking up at the furious maniac who had met her at the end of the aisle.

He had changed for the worse since the

invasion, and in that moment Gbessa hated him, hated him for it with her whole heart. She did not speak and Gerald raised her to her feet, unable to say anything himself, unable to express his disappointment and jealousy.

His eyes burned into her and she frantically searched his face. But he was not Safua. He was the man whom she had been told she would spend her life with. His face and his bed and his rocking chair and his house and his God, these things she was trained to love and want, seeped out of her eyes and Gbessa screamed into his face. She held her jaw and rubbed the skin he had slapped. She hated him, wanted Safua, hated him — so she unbuttoned her blouse and slapped Gerald back as hard as she could. She slapped him again and he stared at her with great surprise. Gbessa breathed onto his face and screamed — scratched him and wanted to bite him, bite his cheeks and his lips, his neck and his chest. She scratched his face and Gerald hit her again, this time more softly, not wanting to hurt her, enlivened by her wildness and audacity. She slapped him hard on his nose and he raised his hand to hit her again but Gbessa bit it. Just as quickly, as ruthlessly as she had freed herself from her blouse to reveal her full and voluptuous breasts that flew madly while she attacked him, so did she release the skirt from her waist. It dropped to the ground and Gbessa thought of her years in the forest, remembered them only vaguely, and grew angry with herself for pushing so much of who she was away. Naked now before him, free now and equally unafraid, she continued to slap Gerald Tubman as hard as she could across his face and head. He tried defending himself but she tore at his shirt until it hung from his arms. Sweat rose from his muscles and his scent filled the room. Gerald picked her up, resisting the blows of her insanity, and threw her onto the bed. Gbessa, with her dress hanging from her shoulder due to their scuffle, sat up to continue attacking her husband, and, unable to restrain himself from the lovesickness this woman had cursed him with, he clutched one of her breasts and rapidly put it in his mouth. He sucked, nursed until she was so over-whelmed by the pleasure that she stopped fighting, panted, and cried profoundly until finally she wrapped her hands around his head.

The last of the sun's rays drifted from Sinou County to other lands and waters, and in the dark he breathed onto her, into her, entered her with a force so self-seeking but still so tender that she pushed her hips as far as they could go into him. Reciprocated his fury. Needed him, needed it, all of it. Mourning, she was, for the lost king and his apologue, with tears so plenty that they fell from her face onto Gerald's back as they pushed and pulled each other's bodies.

Gerald let her use him. He drowned in the woman he had never met. He bit and tugged at her, drilled into her — let Gbessa do with him all she wanted. Let Gbessa take what was rightfully hers.

The men were to be hanged in two weeks, Gerald explained to Gbessa at the kitchen table the following morning.

"It is the only way we can deter future attacks," he added.

Gbessa was unsure whether to speak up. When she finally opened her mouth, Gerald spoke first.

"What did the boy say to you?" he asked, overcoming his pride and resentfulness. Gerald remembered Emric's face when he revealed that Gbessa had been visiting the prisoners without his knowledge.

Gbessa did not know how much Emric or Duly had told Gerald. Her face and body still ached from their sleepless night. She imagined that he knew she had spent the entire day outside of the cell watching and waiting for the boy to say more to her. The prince had said nothing more; he had only finished the meal that she had provided and turned his head away from her toward the opposite wall.

"He told me that I was not Vai," Gbessa answered and remembered how the boy's words had hurt her, more than if he had called her a witch, because at least she was known as a Vai witch — cursed, but still one of them.

"If he did not think you were truly Vai, then why would he talk to you? You, and not the many interpreters before you? Not even Maisy, who can get anyone to speak." Gerald shook his head. His face tightened once again. They both became quiet.

"I know his father. I knew him," Gbessa said finally.

"What?"

"He looks identical to the Poro king, the king of the village when I left it," she said. "I knew who he was, and I told him that I know his father."

Gbessa stared at her interlocked fingers.

"And what did he say?" Gerald asked and moved to the edge of his chair.

Afraid that Gerald would sense her vulnerability, that her voice would crack if she opened her mouth, she waited.

"He told me that the king was dead," Gbessa said. "He suspects he is dead. He mentioned a ship. And he said if I was truly

508

Vai, then I would know that." If she stopped talking then, she knew she would fall over the table in grief, so she continued. "Something is wrong, Gerald. There is a reason they attacked, a reason for all of this — and I think, I think if you give me time then perhaps I could get him to tell me more. I could get him to tell me why they did it. Vai men do not attack unless they are defending themselves or if their land or people have been offended. They are farmers; they have been farmers for centuries — they have no need of Sinou or Monrovia."

Gerald leaned forward as she spoke, contemplating her proposal.

"How do you suppose you will get him to speak if he does not believe you are one of them?" he asked.

"I do not know. But I will try," Gbessa responded.

From across the table, Gerald's eyes traced her face. Gbessa wrestled with Norman Aragon's warning and suddenly wished he were there.

"Gerald, if we are attacked, can we defend ourselves?" she asked.

"Yes. Our technology far exceeds the indigenous," he said.

"Yes, but what if we are faced with —" Her words were stunted by fear of distracting Gerald from her main goal: to return to the prison.

"With what?" he asked. Gbessa timidly shook her head. He expected her to continue pleading with him, but instead Gbessa sat and waited for him to speak. Gerald waited for assurance, comfort in knowing that her past had not stolen her from him, but Gbessa remained reticent.

Gerald stood up from the table and walked out of the room, passing Gbessa, who grabbed his arm and pulled him back.

"Please," Gbessa said, looking up at him.

Gerald freed his arm from her grip and squeezed her hand gently before laying it back on the table.

"Two weeks," he said to her, and left the house through the back door.

Gerald moved Safua's son to one of the outside cells, so that his wife would not have to enter the denigrated prison. When they took the prince out of his cell, the other prisoners commenced a riotous protest by attempting to cut themselves with their chains.

Gbessa arrived at the prison every day at dawn, and she was the first person the prince saw when he woke up. Then she offered him food and other gifts — stories of her love for Lake Piso and Lai's outlying forest. On the days when Gerald was at the prison or working at the nearby military base, Gbessa went home with him in the evenings. On the days that he went to Monrovia to meet with the other mayors in preparation for the hanging, she stayed until it was almost night, beseeching the prince's words in exchange for his life. Gbessa pleaded with him to no avail. The thought of his death made her lie awake in the night. She could not be responsible for it — not again.

"I want to help you," Gbessa said to him. "They will kill you, you'n talk to me."

For seven days, Gbessa sat outside of the prince's cell waiting and watching. For seven days he said nothing. On the seventh night, Gbessa was tired and annoyed at the prince's stubbornness and callous neglect of her. As Gerald called for her to ride home with him, she stood and she hissed at him as he sat with his head tilted away from her.

"You stubborn like your father. Maybe you be better dead like him," she said before walking away.

Gbessa stayed at home the following day and she spent the afternoon sitting on the porch overlooking the Kru workers as they tended her farm. In the middle of the day,

Maisy went to Sinou to deliver something to Marlene. When she was finished with the errand, she visited Gbessa's house. Maisy updated Gbessa on what was going on in Monrovia, and Gbessa listened silently as she wondered what Safua would have tried in order to get the prince to speak. That night when Gerald arrived, the three of them ate together silently at the table.

Later on, Gbessa quietly left her bedroom while Gerald slept. Down the hallway Maisy rested in a guest room with no windows. Gbessa tiptoed into the room, walked to the bed, and lay beside Maisy, whose breathing was interrupted when she felt Gbessa sink into the bed.

"Is everything well with you and him?" Maisy whispered in the dark. "Is he kind to you?"

Gbessa nodded.

"He is not the same when he comes to Monrovia," Maisy continued. "There is worry in his eyes; grief even." Maisy waited for Gbessa's inquiry but Gbessa lay motionless beside her. "Miss Ernestine worries for him," Maisy continued. "She gossips to all of society about how, if Gerald is not careful, you will be Monrovia's downfall, and when she found out that Gerald was sparing their lives so that you could visit them,

512

she nearly rode here on her own to spoil your name.

"They have not said anything to you yet, have they?" Maisy asked. She felt Gbessa's head move on the bed. "I worry for you, Gbessa. Let the men hang. It saddens me as well, but the longer you plead for them, the more people will begin to point their fingers at you."

The women lay on their backs, facing the ceiling in the dark. Gbessa had suspected that there was a reason for Maisy staying, since she always hated to impose on Gerald and rarely remained with them overnight. She contemplated Maisy's words.

"I am sorry, Maisy," Gbessa said finally.

"Don't tell me. Go tell the others that."

"No, I am telling you. I am sorry," she said again. "Sorry I changed."

"Everybody changes, Gbessa. You are better than when you came."

"I am not."

"You are," Maisy insisted.

"I am not better. I am not worse. I am changed. I am a different woman. I forgot myself. And I am sorry."

Maisy did not continue arguing. She lay silent in the dark.

"He is dead," Gbessa said, breaking the silence.

"Who?" Maisy asked, frightened to hear Gbessa's answer. "Who is dead, Gbessa?"

"I knew the boy's father. The prince in the jail," said Gbessa. "I knew his father and now he is dead."

"Is that what the boy told you? Is that what he said?"

"Yes," Gbessa said, her voice cracking.

Maisy stretched her hand across the bed to find Gbessa's hand, which was trembling on her stomach.

"I am sorry, Maisy," Gbessa repeated.

"Okay, okay, Ma," Maisy said. She squeezed Gbessa's hand in hers, and turned to face her old friend as she wept.

Maisy visited the prison with Gbessa on the following day and sat beside her outside the prince's cell. She sat silently as Gbessa pleaded with the boy to speak to her. The boy said nothing; his head remained tilted away from her. At the end of the day, as she and Maisy stood to leave the cell, Maisy shook her head at how cumbersome the process seemed to Gbessa's emotions and will. As the two women walked away, Maisy turned around and revisited the cell. She held the bars and looked down onto the boy as he sat unaffected by her presence.

"You will die in four days, I hope you

know," Maisy said to him in Vai. "If you truly loved your village or your people then you would speak." Maisy then left him and rejoined Gbessa on the road back to the house in Sinou County.

The next few days brought Gbessa the same fate. She grew weaker as she left the small cell where the prince sat, with no more words, less hope than the day before.

Two days before the scheduled hanging of the Vai prisoners, Gbessa sat without energy outside the prince's cell. When the day was almost finished, and when again the prince stayed silent as Gbessa sat waiting outside his cell, she turned to him and said, "You'n Safua son. You got his face and shoulders and the Poro mark, but you not the Poro king son. Safua would speak to save the others."

The prince, outraged by her words, turned to her and shook the bars of his cell violently.

"Yeh," Gbessa said, concealing her excitement that he had responded to her. "That good for you. Good for you coming die for lying. You not a Vai man like you say."

The prince continued to shake the bars, snarling at her as she faced him fearlessly.

Duly and Emric ran to the cell from the field.

"You all right, Mrs. Tubman?" Duly asked behind her.

"Yes, Duly. I'm fine."

The prince opened his mouth to speak, but upon noticing the men approaching, and the smile of encouragement that snuck onto Gbessa's face, he stopped and settled. He sat back against the wall in his cell, and tilted his head away from Gbessa. She sighed, exhausted by the failed effort.

Gbessa's face was sunken in despair; her shoulders and head pulled toward the ground.

The wind came to them and floated along Gbessa's ears. She breathed her in.

Then —

"How you can say I'n Safua son? How you can say that?" the prince asked angrily. Gbessa knelt in front of his cell and held the bars. She turned around at first to call Emric or Duly back, as she had been instructed to do in the event that he spoke again, but she fought her duty and with silent excitement faced the prince.

He stared at her through the bars.

"How you can say I'n his son? Enneh-so?" he asked, seeming delusional and broken in the small hole.

"You'n Vai girl. If you Vai girl, you will never say that thing."

As Gbessa waited for more, the sky opened up and the wind flew back toward her.

Gbessa nodded her head. "I Vai girl," she pleaded.

"You Vai girl then where your Sande mark?" he asked.

Gbessa's heart was tortured by this. Fearfully, she continued. "I want Sande mark and they'n give it to me," she admitted as her voice broke. "They push me far from them. I beg for Sande mark and they say I will never be Sande."

"Hmm," the sound left the prince's nose.

"Still, they push you and you go to white man?" he asked.

"They'n white. They like us."

"No, no, they like you," the prince quickly disagreed. "I'n like them. I Vai man. I Poro man," he refuted.

"You Poro man who no see nothing but hisself? Enneh-so? I know Poro man once who tear out his heart for Lai. Who tear out his heart for his Sande and his son. He see everybody and you can't see nothing but yourself."

"That not true," the prince said loudly. "You'n know me."

"I know your Pa."

"You'n know my Pa. You know my Pa, you

know the white man take him. He dead. You know the white man take him in the water," the prince said.

Gbessa wanted to reach her hands through the bars and shake him. She wanted to shake him and then enter his mouth where the words sat, held captive by his pride and animosity.

"What?" she asked, suddenly out of breath.

"Ehn You see? You'n know nothing," he said.

"What white man?"

"You'n know nothing!"

"I know your Pa. Long, long time from here, I know your Pa. He was my friend," Gbessa stuttered and battled the emotion within her. "Your Pa. He was my only friend."

Gbessa waited for more but the prince sat silently.

"I want help you but you will die, all of Lai will die if you'n tell me why you come hummock the people farm and county."

"The people know why," the prince said stubbornly.

"No-oh. They'n know. They'n know." Gbessa was patient for a rebuttal. "Please," she continued. "Not for me. Not for yourself. For your Pa. That what he would want.

I know it."

And then, as easily as the wind came down from the sky that day to rush past them, he set the words free.

When the prince was done, Gbessa did not call for Emric to take her home. She ran along the dusty road from the prison. Gbessa ran through her field and up onto her porch and through her hallways and into her room, breathlessly, in search of Gerald, so that she could pass along the words that the prince had given her.

"Gerald!" Gbessa yelled, swinging her bedroom door open. He was not there. "Gerald!" she called.

Gbessa then ran to Henry and Marlene's home, where she thought maybe he had gone to speak with Henry. By the time Gbessa reached their home, it was dark outside. Marlene opened the front door, surprised that Gbessa was visiting.

"Gbessa," she said, unflattered by her former maid's presence.

"Hello, Marlene," Gbessa said, catching her breath.

"What's wrong?" Marlene asked as Gbessa stood panting on the porch. Inside, Gbessa heard the laughter or Marlene's usual guests, Anna and Norma. She did not want to go inside.

"Is Gerald here?" Gbessa asked.

"No. He and Henry were called to Monrovia. They should be back tonight," Marlene said. "Come in."

"No, that's fine. Have a good evening," Gbessa said, walking dizzily down the steps of Marlene's porch. She headed quickly back down the road to her house. Inside her room, Gbessa looked out the window as she waited for Gerald to return. Running had exhausted her, and she felt her eyes grow heavy in the moonlight. Gbessa went to her bed, where she sat anxiously with her legs crossed in front of her. After looking out the window from the bed, then out the door as she rested her back, then, expecting Gerald's horse to pull up at every minute, she drifted in and out of sleep.

As the bulbuls chatted outside of her window at dawn, Gbessa rose quickly to find that the other half of her bed was empty and Gerald had not come home. She stood and looked out of her window toward Monrovia, then toward the prison.

After bathing, Gbessa dressed and went to the prison in hopes that she would find her husband. When she arrived there, Duly was riding on a horse in the field. Gbessa walked past him toward the cells.

"Where are you going, Mrs. Tubman?" Duly asked, stopping.

"To the prison. I need to talk to Gerald."

"Nobody's there, Mrs. Tubman. They came and got the prisoners this morning and they are all heading back to Monrovia," Duly said.

"What? Why?"

"They decided to change the date of the hanging," Duly told her. "The mayors want to do it today. To get it over with. The prisoners have not spoken —"

Before Duly finished speaking, Gbessa darted back down the road toward her house. She ran, fighting tears and a piercing pain in her thighs as her feet begged her to stop. She could not. She would not.

Gbessa reached her house, where the workers had risen to tend her field. She hurried to her barn, where Gerald's horses were caged. Gbessa grabbed the reins of one of the horses and freed him from his stable. She quickly mounted the horse and rode through the open barn doors as sunlight met the horse's hooves. The workers looked up from the field, bewildered, as Gbessa rode away, continuing down the road toward Monrovia.

In Monrovia a crowd gathered in front of the Johnsons' mansion. None of the society members were present, and Gbessa knew they were inside the mansion. Gbessa ran into the house, breathless from her journey there. She heard voices coming from the banquet room, and she hurried to where she knew they all were gathered. As Gbessa passed the kitchen, Maisy recognized her and ran to her.

"Gbessa! What are you doing here?! Where are you going?" She pulled Gbessa's arm in the hallway.

"To talk to them!"

"No! Gbessa. Do not! It is not your place. You will make them more vexed with you," Maisy pleaded.

Gbessa lifted Maisy's hand and thrust it down.

"It *is* my place," Gbessa said.

"Gbessa! Please!"

But Gbessa sped down the hallway and into the banquet room, where all of society, the mayors and their wives, the Johnsons and Miss Ernestine, Henry Hunter and Marlene, Gerald Tubman, congregated as

Mr. Johnson addressed them all. The door swung opened, slamming into the adjacent wall.

"They must not die!" Gbessa shouted. The crowd turned to face her. Gerald went to Gbessa and grabbed her arm, attempting to pull her out of the room. Gbessa resisted and pushed his arm. He grabbed it again, embarrassed at her insubordination, and again Gbessa wrestled with him to release her.

"Stop it!" she said.

Gerald squeezed her arm. "Control yourself," he said in her ear as she fought him. When Gerald realized that she would not submit, after a heavy push of his chest, he backed away from her.

Gbessa faced the crowd again.

"They must not die!" she pleaded.

"The girl has gone mad," Ernestine shouted.

"Mrs. Tubman, none of us want to bestow death upon any one of our countrymen," Mr. Johnson said calmly from the end of the room. The crowd turned their heads to face him again. "But they are criminals and they must be punished."

"Mr. Johnson, Mrs. Johnson," she said, resting her eyes on Marlene, who quickly looked away as Gbessa faced her. "The boy, the leader, spoke to me yesterday. I wanted to tell you, Gerald, but you did not come home."

"What is she talking about?" Henry asked.

"Lai, their village, was attacked by Frenchmen. I know they were Frenchmen because I encountered them before, a long time ago. The boy said they attacked them and stole some of their people to sell. They took his father — he is likely on his way to America now." Gbessa's voice shattered at the thought of Safua as a captive slave, suffocating in the bowels of a foreign ship.

"He was only protecting his village and his people."

"Impossible!" Mr. Yancey shouted from the crowd. He stood up from his chair, outraged. "We scout the borders and there are no more traders."

"What happened to that scouting trip with the two brothers that visited here some years ago?" someone asked.

"Nothing. Nothing was found," another answered.

"It has been made illegal in the States and the islands and all of Europe." The society people nodded their heads, and Gbessa regretted not warning them after Norman Aragon's visit.

"Yes, Mr. Yancey. But they are coming

from the inland to attack the nearby villages. They are still trading. They have settled north of us," she said.

"That's true, in fact," Mr. Palmer said. "There are settlements north and east of here."

"But it does not make sense," Mr. Yancey protested. "Why would Frenchmen want to attack Liberia? And why not Freetown? It is a British colony; they could get more from the British by kidnapping their people."

"I suppose it is because they know Liberia is free now, Mr. Yancey. They know we are not protected — as protected as we once were," Gbessa said in deference to Gerald as she turned to face him. "They are still trading. They are still selling our people."

"So why didn't your Vai people go pick a fight with them, then? Why us?" someone shouted.

"Anyone who is not native to Liberia, to them, is foreign and is to blame," Gbessa said. "Please, spare their lives. They can help us," she said.

"Help us?! Please, the girl has gone mad! Look at her! Do not tell me you people are listening," Miss Ernestine said in disbelief.

Gbessa realized how she must look to them. She had hardly gotten any sleep the night before, had run all about Sinou that morning, and her hair hung loosely from her head.

"Ernestine, please," Mr. Johnson said, holding up his hand. Miss Ernestine continued fanning herself. "Continue," Mr. Johnson said to Gbessa. Maisy poked her head through the doorway to listen.

"I suppose that without protection from the States, the French — or British — may try to take Liberia for themselves. After all, free or not, we are all black people. We could speak to the tribal leaders," Gbessa petitioned. "The Poro royalty. We could ally with them. It is what my husband wanted in the first place. They know the land and where the country has been offended already. They can help the army," Gbessa pleaded.

"This is absurd!" Mrs. Tucker said. "Excuse me, Mr. Johnson, men and women. How do we know she has not already allied with them and is plotting against the colony? How do we know she was not sent here to destroy us all?"

"Mrs. Tucker, if death were my mission, you would not be here to object to me," Gbessa said boldly. The society women sounded their disapproval.

"You see?!" Mrs. Tucker said loudly. "I told you she hated me. I told you the girl had hatred in her heart." The society women agreed and made it known by cutting eyes and hissing teeth toward Gbessa. Gbessa walked to the middle of their meeting and spoke to them freely.

"I beg you," she pleaded. "Their death will be the first in a long line of deaths. The attacks will continue. The killing. We will all be sent back to the States."

"We will not. We are free," one of the older society men said.

"And how will they know if you go in chains?" Gbessa added. "Back to slavery? Who will know that you were free?"

The society people stood to their feet in protest of Gbessa.

"Be still!" Mr. Johnson said. "Everyone. Be still." The crowd quieted and sat down.

"Gbessa Tubman," Mr. Johnson said, "I suggest you do not mention the States or slavery or freedom. You know nothing about it and it is offensive to those of us who do."

Gbessa nodded.

"Forgive me," she said. "I do not mean to offend you, or anyone." She was exhausted from speaking, from running, from pleading. Gbessa looked back through the doorway where Maisy stood resting her head.

"I speak not only for the freedom of the prisoners, but for our freedom — for Liberia. The Poro are strong men. They are the strongest of all of the armies in the West," she continued. "They can even rally other tribes. Something is wrong and we can fix it by sparing their lives and talking to them.

"It is not my duty to object to your laws. I did not come here to disagree with you," she said, moving about the room and searching for their eyes. "I live a humble life in Sinou. I help my servants. I care for my husband. I knew no home until I was found and brought here to the colony."

Her voice broke, yet it was then that she finally found it.

"I did not have a home of my own. But my life was saved and it is my duty to save in return. People who even once, who even cast me away from them," she said. "People who turned me away and, even now, do not recognize me or care to know me. My people, who now think I am white. Who think me cursed. They are still my people."

They walked across fields and over hills. Some rode on horses, some troubled their feet to take them through the green country-side. They walked through creeks and swamps, holding their guns above their heads as the animals gave audience to the mixed caravan. They did not rest until they arrived at Lai — the society men, all of them, and the women who were brave enough to follow, Gbessa, the prince — Safua's son — and the other Poro men who had survived the imprisonment. They walked during the day and night. They were free now and led the way through Junde, a small village of tribesmen whom the prince called to follow them. After Junde, a narrow footpath was covered by a brush of trees. The prince moved the trees out of his way. In the far distance, a village stood dancing in the heat rays of the sun.

It was just as she had remembered it, the same open space that she had traveled to after surviving the forest. "Gbessa the witch, Gbessa the witch, Gbessa the witch," she murmured to herself and did not cry, but rather called Safua's spirit unto her, into her. She knew she would not see him; however, the memory of how he had looked when she returned so long ago was fresh to her. He had been playing with his son in the circle when the villagers announced her return, and in the distance he had stopped and caught her eyes. She remembered his furious lips. There were tiny houses made of wood and straw that formed a circle, woods surrounding them, and Lake Piso behind them. Lai. At the same moment that she recognized everything in the forgotten village clearly, so did the sun recognize her, and it kissed her hard, like a mother's embrace of a child assumed lost or killed. The sun shone on her until the strands of her hair color were revived and the red veil of her cursed childhood returned to her head.

"Gbessa the witch, Gbessa the witch," she murmured to herself and anticipated the chaos that would follow once her identity was revealed to the prince. But none came. As they approached, surviving men and women ran out of their houses to meet the prince and the other surviving Poro men. They rejoiced together in the circle. The mayors watched them as they danced briefly. The villagers ceased their rejoicing upon noticing the suited men and shortly after wept when they realized that some men had not returned.

"That the witch there!" an old man yelled suddenly from his porch, unable to believe his eyes, not noticing that he had disrupted the short celebration of the Poro prince's return. The sun shone directly onto where she stood until the redness of her hair was exposed. "That Gbessa the witch there!" The people of the village shrieked as they finally recognized her face and distinguished her from the crowd by her hair. The prince was alarmed, but he held his hands up to silence the frantic members of his village. The mayors and other members of the colony who had journeyed to Lai stepped away from Gbessa in amazement as the sun streamed onto her. Gerald stepped away from her also and gaped at her head and mismatched face, her foreign eyes. She was surrounded again, but this time by both her new and old worlds. The Vai people, blinded and unbelieving, did not know whether they should praise her for her proven tenacity and immortality or cast her away again. There was something suddenly joyous about her, glowing and unafraid. There was something alive in her — her childhood, her curse, her king.

Elder exited the praying lodge and slowly approached the commotion in the village circle. Gbessa bowed her head toward Elder, and he also nearly fainted with disbelief. The witch who had once killed Safua's son, the prince whom he and the other elders had revived after his seizures ceased, had now returned to him in the company of Poro men.

"Gbessa," he said, amazed.

"Yes," she answered in Vai and raised her head. "It is me."

■ ■ ■ ■

KILIMANJARO

■ ■ ■ ■

In his fifth year in Africa many things had changed, but he remained the same. Whereas once he swore that he could hear Norman Aragon's footsteps beside him, the sound of his friend had now weakened to a memory.

June Dey appeared much older than his years — darker, with a full beard that hung to the end of his neck, and usually he was naked and too beaten by the sun to mind it. He had reverted to the emotions of his original exile in the Virginia woods — anger, depression, confusion. He wondered what his life would have eventually turned into if he'd had no gift. He thought of Darlene's face, her full cheeks and soft, unopened eyes as she floated down the river. Some days he closed his eyes under the sun and sought her spirit and her scent. June Dey fought both on his own and alongside warriors. He slept and ate among them; he hunted with them. It was June Dey's desire to defend the men and women he met, but he equally wanted to belong to them and soon realized that he could not have that. Many tribes revered him as a spirit or a gift from the ancestors. Others saw him as a god. Few suspected he was a devil sent by a warring tribe. No matter where he traveled, no matter how hard he fought, the possibility of a harmonious life with Africans remained elusive.

One day June Dey found himself in a wilderness of baobab trees. The crowns of the trees mingled in the clouds; their smooth, grayish-brown trunks were capacious, solid as rocks. The path seemed endless, lined by the mighty baobabs on either side.

June Dey met me there, through the spirit of an old woman who sat between two trees, crying. He approached me, and as I knew he would, men like him who had never fallen in love since their mothers and could not bear to see any woman cry, he stopped to see what could be done.

"Old woman," June Dey said with the little Swahili that he had learned.

"What you say?" I answered in English. I lifted my head and showed my face to June

Dey, a face just like Charlotte's, that story I once was.

"I am Kilimanjaro," I said. "Here to help you."

June Dey smiled and his cheeks and eyes reminded me of Dey.

"Okay, Kilimanjaro," June Dey said. "How is it that you know English this far east?"

"I know everything," I said, and could not help but continue crying. "All the languages, all the people, all the land."

"Nobody knows everything, old woman."

"I know everything," I said again. June Dey laughed.

"If you know everything then tell me my name," June Dey said.

"What is your name?" I asked, wiping his face.

"You know it already, then why do you ask me?" June Dey asked.

"I ask you because you do not know your name either," I said. I chuckled, briefly relieved of my sorrow.

"My name is Moses," June Dey said.

"No, no, no. Your name is not Moses," I insisted.

June Dey was silent.

"You need me to tell you so you can go save her. Save them."

"Save them?" June Dey asked. He listened

to the wind for cries or prescience of another battle. "Who?"

"That place. That people. Your people," I said. "But you will not be alone. The wanderer Norman will appear again to help you. And I will be there too."

"What did you say?" June Dey asked, kneeling before me. "How do you know . . ."

"You need me so you can save them."

"Save who?" June Dey asked, desperately.

"The girl who will save you. Who will save us all."

"What girl? Who are you?"

"The girl with the biggest gift of us all. Life. If she was not a girl or if she was not a woman; if she was not a woman or if she was not a witch, she would be king," I said.

June Dey stood up, convinced that he was entertaining a fool.

"Why do you riddle me? You sick?" June Dey asked.

"I am not sick and she is not king. She is a witch. She has a gift like you and you do not know your own name."

"My name is Moses," June argued again.

"No."

"What is my name then?"

"Ask your mother. Have you not asked her?"

"I have not seen my mother in a long

time," June Dey said and looked genuinely saddened by it. I laughed again.

"Yes, you have," I said. "She is right there," I said, pointing toward the sun.

June Dey looked up and saw nothing. "Right there," I said, pointing to my left. June Dey looked quickly to his left, and looked as though Darlene's or Henrietta Emerson's ghosts would haunt him on his journey. But they were not there. I then pointed to my chest.

"You tease me," June Dey said. "She is not there."

"She is here. She is all around you," I said, my hand steady against my heart.

"I do not see her."

"Okay then. Ask your father," I said.

"I have no father," June Dey said.

"Yes, you do." I laughed. "He is right there," I said, pointing to the ground. June Dey looked quickly at the ground. But no footprints were there. He had searched all over Africa for traces of a mother or a father. None were there.

"You tease me," he said and turned to leave, certain that I was a medicine woman who had lost my mind to sorcery and had been rightfully abandoned in the mountains.

"Wait!" I called. "June Dey is your name," I said finally. "June Dey, whose mother lives in the wind, once named Charlotte, and whose father lives in the hurricanes, a man once as strong as you."

"What did you say?" he demanded.

"June. June Dey."

"June," June Dey repeated, and it felt real.

"The girl needs you. Go back."

"I am too far from her," June Dey contested.

"Why do you object? You are more powerful than you could imagine as a boy. You were born free. But until you found your gift, you did not know your freedom. But now that you know your power, what will you do with it?"

In his silence, I held his face between my hands. I saw Dey underneath his skin.

"I am here, my son," I said, finally, into those beautiful cheeks and eyes. "We are all here. We have all come to fight.

They arrived in Monrovia: the caravan of settlers and farm workers, the prince and the mayors and other men of society, Gbessa and her elders, Gio men and Bassa men and Krahn men and Kpelle warriors, the new Liberian army and Henry Hunter and Gerald Tubman.

All the impressions that life had made on Gbessa, principally on those nights beside the lake with Safua, that still remained as much a part of her existence as her hands and feet, all shrank in the presence of what now filled her — love — that beautiful other mask of God. She found it again in the confrontation with her past and her communion with Safua's lost spirit and his truth — that he remained in Lai that day, not to reject her, but to protect others like her, to protect those who could not beat death, a vow that had now cost him his life.

Countless ships prevailed over the waves

and came forth, all full of armies, guns, cannons, and metal articles, one hundred thousand times what was in Monrovia's wooden stables. All of them now who marched on the soil, Liberians, looked toward the ocean at the ships that sailed toward them.

"They are French!" a settler said, pointing toward the flags that sailed high above the ships.

"God help us," Mr. Johnson said, shaking. "We are too late."

"No!" Gerald shouted. "Everybody is here. Everybody will fight!"

The settlers numbered a few hundred with all of their men — the army and all the home owners, the mayors old, the servants, and any boys who were willing to defend their country. They approached the shore trembling, but it was the fear that fueled them, the final chance to defend their black mothers and names, their tortured histories and all who were left behind, all who would never see freedom. They squeezed their guns, their shirts unbuttoned. A few older settlers who had taken their shirts off for the ensuing battle revealed scarred backs, bodies that still showed the memory of their past afflictions. There were tears that worried some of their faces, but the anger only made them come alive.

The indigenous also numbered several hundred. They were men and boys, some with weapons carved of the minerals of their land, some with borrowed guns, all thirsty to protect what was rightfully theirs, land they refused to forfeit. There were small huddles among them, divisions established by language and rank. Poro warriors instructed the others on what would be done. They pointed willfully at the looming ships and shouted, grunted with anger, burned with hunger.

Gerald looked out onto the shore at the defense, hopeful though equally distressed by what could possibly wage death on all of them. The Poro men scattered about the hill that overlooked the ocean, shouting back and forth about how they would attack. How no more of their people would be stolen. How they would not lose again.

While the groups gathered and planned, waited for the ships to land or a word from their generals and kings for when to strike, all the women were instructed to go to the Johnson mansion to hide for safety. The women went there to hide and pray — all of them except for Gbessa.

Gbessa the witch who had orchestrated the defense — who knew in her heart and felt through the passage of Safua's spirit that not even the glorious fleet that assailed the small country would rightly confront her curse — left the men where they stood and headed to the beach.

"Fengbe, keh kamba beh. Fengbe, kemu beh," she murmured as her bare feet sank into the sand. "Fengbe, keh kamba beh. Fengbe, kemu beh."

Love swallowed her fear and Gbessa continued toward the ships. Let them come. For what had death ever succeeded at but mocking her? She was enough.

"Fengbe, keh kamba beh." The words drifted from her lips as she walked in a state of near delirium and joy, and a set of footprints suddenly emerged in the sand alongside her. Gbessa moved slower when she noticed the steps and the compelling presence of another.

Norman Aragon appeared. His bare feet dug into the sand. His trousers were torn and he had aged greatly since she last saw him. His sunken eyes were recovered, his hope restored by her bravery. He looked out onto the ocean as the ships forged ahead.

"You come," she said.

His arms hung by his side and his lips were compressed, but his forgiveness and the softness of his presence drew Gbessa

546

toward him. He was happy again not only to assist in the rescue of a kindred soul, but to be cast in a grand collision, to arrive when his past and future needed him as much as the girl did. Yes, he was there. He had come back to wage war.

She went forth.

The wind blew in a calamitous frenzy around them, thick with anticipation. I carried with me the sound of their heartbeat, men and women once separated across continents. They named her Liberia. I called for the dust and sand below to join me in the air. I awakened the hurricanes and danced. Dared the captors to challenge me. Dared them to confront what they could not see, deemed invisible. Yes, I am here. I am all around you.

The ocean wrestled within itself, resurrecting ghosts underneath the chaffing bellies of the ships. The mothers of those who fought, those forever lost and downcast in bottomless ocean graves, arose and stirred. Dared those ships to repeat the million agonies of their people. The ocean and the lasting cadavers of stolen mothers tussled with the waters.

"Roll away," I cried, and waves crashed against their sterns, rocked and swayed in the ocean as thunder sounded above them.

Gbessa was not alone, and walking alongside her protectors, she understood that she never had been. "Fengbe, keh kamba beh. Fengbe, kemu beh." She remembered Safua's voice, and imagined him singing to calm those others in the drumming hollows of some foreign ship. "Fengbe, keh kamba beh. Fengbe, kemu beh." *We have nothing but we have God. We have nothing but we have each other.*

She went forth.

She went forth and the wind moved Gbessa's face toward a hill on the far shore, where a man arrived and looked down at where she stood. It was June Dey. June Dey, barely recognizable now from years of distance and a bearded face, landed onshore with the wind's assistance. Norman Aragon and Gbessa saw him and were sure that their redemption would be complete. Now, in the final moments before this glorious fleet of ships, his spirit rejoiced at the sight of Gbessa and Norman, and the reckoning that he had come to fight with them. He had come in the name of Darlene and so many others blended into the wind. He was there. They were all there. All come to fight. All ready.

Gbessa stumbled in the direction of the ocean. Norman Aragon and June Dey followed. And the freed men of Monrovia, the settlers, the Poro warriors, the Africans, the earth, and the gifted dashed furiously toward shore to meet the armies of the approaching ships.

One boat arrived first and a dozen or so men filed out, forming a line on the shore, their backs facing the ocean, their rifles pointed outward and ready to shoot. Norman vanished, and in a matter of seconds the Frenchmen's rifles were thrust out of their hands and strewn out onto the shore. June Dey sprinted down to aid his friend, arriving just as other frontline boats landed and shot at the hundreds on the beach, waiting. The bullets crashed into him, falling off his body, which he used as a shield to cover as many Monrovians as he could.

"Don't shoot!" Mr. Johnson yelled out, with his hands raised in the air. "We can discuss. This land is legally ours!"

"Don't shoot!" the settlers shouted in unison.

But another round of bullets flew toward those on the shore. Norman Aragon pushed those guns out of the hands of the adversaries, and June Dey rushed to block the bullets from penetrating the skin of those waiting to fight. Unable to hold back any longer, the men charged toward the Frenchmen at the mouth of the ocean. Some used their fists, others cutlasses from Monrovian farms, clashing against the shining blades of those who challenged their freedom. June Dey picked up a fighter and hurled him into the ocean, into the distance, toward the other ships as they approached. As each boat arrived at the port, Norman Aragon fought with the Frenchmen for their weapons, his invisibility confusing them, scaring some to retreat. June Dey grabbed them by their heads, by their legs and waists, throwing the bodies into one another, enlivened by the company of those formerly enslaved, by the memory of Darlene and the many before her. Gbessa picked up a cutlass, fallen in the sand, and as the blade struck the sharpest end of a Frenchman's battle knife, it echoed on the beach. She moved quickly through the sand, fighting for Safua, calling to him through their song, "Fengbe, keh kamba beh. Fengbe, kemu beh." *We have nothing but we have God. We have nothing but we have each other.*

Gbessa was the only woman on the shore, weaving through the warriors and fighting settlers, dodging their clanging weapons and the mouths of their guns, the carnage, the ringing in her ears. Another round of bullets came again, the eruption proving more than Norman Aragon could handle. The men fought to protect their land by resisting the influx of slavers. Not too far from where she stood, a Frenchman retrieved a cutlass from a fallen settler, near the bruised heels of those fighting, and ran toward Gbessa. She raised her cutlass in the air, resisting the weighted thrust of the Frenchman's advance. Each time he swung his weapon, Gbessa reacted quickly with hers, the melody of the clashing blades overpowering the waves. Her shoulders ached, her arms trembled, and she was unable to hold off his advance. The bullets increased in number, and as Gbessa fought, a knifelike pain numbed her waist. The Frenchman, seeing that a bullet had wounded her, ran to fight another. Gbessa fell to her knees, squeezing the linen of her dress between her fingers as blood quickly soaked it. On the beach, as far as she could see, Liberians battled together, outnumbered now, but not without passion; nearly ruined, but not without a fight. The bullet had maimed her, and she looked out toward the ocean to where Safua had been stolen, and her voice was too stunned for their song. The sound of the battle grew louder; she dropped the cutlass and touched the hole in her stomach where the bullet had penetrated.

But I will not die, she thought, "We will not die," she said aloud, blinded by the tears amid those hundreds of dueling men, and she fell onto the sand, awaiting her resurrection.

ACKNOWLEDGMENTS

I'm thankful to my agent, Susan Golomb, whose early belief in me and this book have greatly impacted my artistry and life. Huge thanks to the dynamic and incomparable Fiona McCrae; your guidance made Gbessa shine, and this opportunity is my very first dream realized. Thanks to Steve Woodward and Yana Makuwa for your insights, and Katie Dublinski and the entire team at Graywolf for living up to your reputation of being a rockstar house. Thanks to Janet Steen for your eyes on an earlier version of this book, as well as Lauren Martinez, Kimberly Wang, Rita Williams, Donald Gray II, Vamba Sherif, Kona Khasu, and other dear friends who have read excerpts, or third and fourth versions, or rambling emails and given constructive and valuable feedback. Huge thanks to the library at Skidmore College and my Skidmore crew (ZUKI!), the Community of Writers at

Squaw Valley, and Robtel Pailey and Stephanie Horton for challenging me through the years. To the Freemans and Moores. I'm eternally grateful for the faith and humility of my parents, Augustus and Mamawa; my brothers, David and Augustus Jr. for sending me that *Family Guy* clip of Stewie on Brian's novel; for my big brothers, Pete and Kevin; for my nieces; for my sister Wiande, whose love is perfect; for my sister Kula, for your honesty and collaboration. And finally, to my husband, Eric. Thank you for holding my hand through it all.

FOR FURTHER READING

While loosely based on a short chapter in Liberian history, *She Would Be King* is a fictional retelling of the country's founding. If these pages inspired your interest in Liberia, I recommend the following works:

Clarence E. Zamba Liberty, *Growth of the Liberian State: An Analysis of Its Historiography*

C. Patrick Burrowes, *Black Christian Republicanism: The Writings of Hilary Teage (1805–1853), Founder of Liberia*

D. Elwood Dunn, editor, *Liberian Studies Journal* (Volume XIV, Number 2)

Stephanie C. Horton, editor, *Sea Breeze Journal of Contemporary Liberian Writings* (2004–2011)

C. Patrick Burrowes, *Between the Kola Forest and the Salty Sea: A History of the Liberian People Before 1800*

William Henry Heard, *The Bright Side of African Life*

Robtel Neajai Pailey (scholarly works)

Patricia Jabbeh Wesley (poetry)

Vamba Sherif (novels)

ABOUT THE AUTHOR

Wayétu Moore was born in Liberia and raised in Spring, Texas. She holds a master's degree in creative writing from the University of Southern California, and a master's degree in anthropology and education from Columbia University, where she held a Margaret Mead Fellowship. She's a graduate of Howard University and the New York State Summer Writers Institute, and her writing can be found in the *Atlantic, Guernica,* and the *Rumpus,* among other publications. She is an Africana studies lecturer at the City University of New York's John Jay College of Criminal Justice. She lives in Brooklyn, New York.

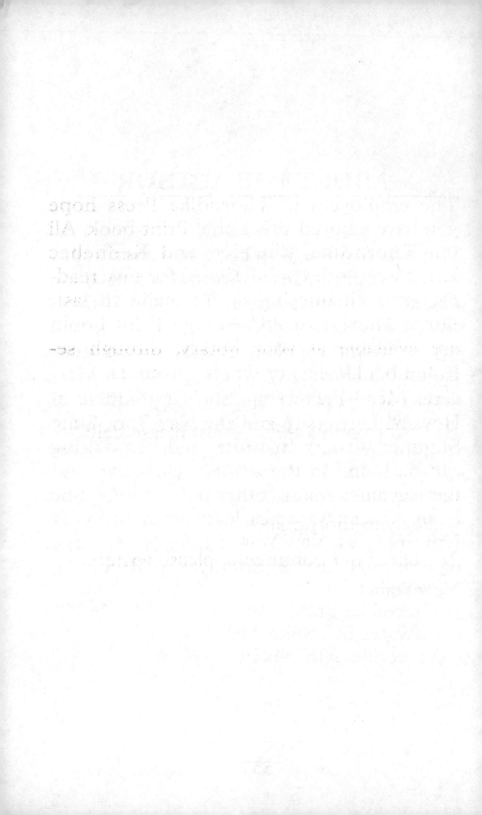